## THEIR FULFILLMENT
## WAS CRUELLY SUSPENDED...

"Oh, Geoff!" The ecstatic cry was torn from Lindsay's throat. But something was very wrong. Her eyes flew open to meet the ferocity in Carey's.

"Who in the hell is Geoff?" he enunciated coldly.

"He—he's not important. Please, Carey—don't!"

But he had already drawn back to the edge of the bed, and she drank in with a sense of loss the smooth sheen of muscle across his torso, his lean thighs.

"Damn you, Lindsay. You were using me as a substitute!"

His scathing words dropped into sudden late-night stillness. He was wrong, but Lindsay didn't speak—only thought, Geoff and Carey.... She couldn't win with men.

Her ex-lover had tainted her past with his lies, and she had wounded Carey in a moment of overwhelming passion that would never come again....

**MAURA MACKENZIE**
is also the author of
**SUPER?OMANCE #6**
**SWEET SEDUCTION**

Denise's new job was ideal—to a marine
biologist, the research project in the
Bahamas would be fascinating. And it
would allow her no time to dwell on
past traumas.

Besides, the opportunity to work with a
famous oceanographer like Jake Barstow
was a dream come true!

But the dream turned into a nightmare as
Denise became involved in a subversive
scheme that threatened both the project's
success and her relationship with Jake.

She had no choice but to tell Jake the truth,
but it would cost her plenty, his respect, and
his love....

MAURA MACKENZIE

# MIRROR OF THE HEART

A SUPERROMANCE FROM
WORLDWIDE

TORONTO · NEW YORK · LONDON

For Donna,
whose dancer's dreams inspired my own.

———————————◆———————————

Published August 1983

First printing June 1983

ISBN 0-373-70076-8

Printed in Canada

# PROLOGUE

THE GLASS SWING DOORS were pushed inward by a forceful hand. The receptionist looked up from her desk, her eyes flickering as they ran over a tall man in a charcoal tailored suit and crisp white shirt that emphasized both the tan of his lean face and his expertly trimmed dark brown hair. His eyes, too, were mid-brown, she noted when his impatient stride brought him to her desk.

Her expression clearly indicated that he was far from the average run of male visitor to pass her utilitarian government-issue desk, and she inquired huskily, "May I help you, sir?"

"I have an appointment with Mr. Corben," he informed her in a brusque New York clip. "Carey Hudson."

"I'll get his secretary for you." Despite the fact that she was well past the awkward-teenager stage, her finger trembled on the intercom button as she spoke to the disembodied voice of the secretary. Moments later, a woman dressed quietly in a heather-toned skirt suit stepped off the elevator, introduced herself as Marion Keyes, then bore him away to an upper floor. The receptionist followed them with her eyes and gave a faint sigh when the elevator doors closed behind them.

"Go right in, Mr. Hudson," the secretary invited at her boss's door, a faint flicker of her eyelids as he brushed past, betraying an interest her outward demeanor denied.

A stocky overweight man came from behind his uncluttered desk with outstretched hand, which was shaken in perfunctory fashion by his visitor. "Good of you to come, Mr. Hudson."

Dark brows rose dryly in an arc. "Does a citizen have a choice when he's officially summoned to Washington?" Hudson dropped into the steel-and-imitation-leather chair his host indicated. The older man returned to his own swivel seat behind the desk, a desk that was strategically placed so that light flooding in from the square windows behind it fell on his visitor and left his own expression obscured.

"It would have helped if I'd been given some reason for being called away from some very important work," Hudson went on, his eyes going disparagingly around the plainly furnished office. "What are you—the I.R.S? I'd have thought my tax dollars alone would provide you with a lot more luxury than this."

Corben allowed himself an acid smile. "No, I'm not the I.R.S., but my office wouldn't be any grander if I were." He picked up a yellow pencil from the neat stack beside his hand and twirled it between his fingers as he adroitly changed the subject. "What was the important business I took you away from, Mr. Hudson?"

His visitor shrugged. "Nothing that would interest the government. I troubleshoot for various enterprises my father's involved in, a wide range of companies.

Commercial spies exist in most corporate ventures, it seems. My job is to flush them out and put a stop to their activities. As I say," he ended casually, "nothing to interest the government."

"Mmm." Corben leaned his elbows on the black-topped desk and continued his play with the pencil while he looked assessingly at the other man. His silent stare from neutral gray eyes might have made anyone else uncomfortable, but Carey Hudson outstared him until Corben gave a satisfied grunt and leaned back in his chair.

"How would you like to do some investigative work for the government, Mr. Hudson?"

Brown eyes clashed with gray for a moment. Then Hudson said bluntly, "I wouldn't. I haven't felt the urge to be a G-man since I was ten years old, and I'm not in need of a job—unless you know something I don't."

"I know quite a lot about you, Mr. Hudson," Corben conceded casually. "To name a few things: your mother died when you were a child, and you haven't got along too well with your father since he started marrying women half his age when you were twelve. You turned down the executive suite in favor of the more mobile life of tracking down company spies, which any reasonably competent security company could handle just as well. You like women, but you've never tied yourself down to any one in particular. Should I go on?"

"No, dammit!" Hudson's eyes were brown marble as they stared across the desk. His voice edged with contempt, he went on, "You've convinced me, as I've long suspected, that nothing is private as far as the government is concerned. My God—'' his well-marked brows lifted in irony ''—the paperwork must be sky-high if you have a dossier like this on everybody's personal life! But if you think—''

''What I'm asking you to do has no connection with individual privacy or personal sensitivity,'' Corben cut in, pointedly harsh and businesslike as he leaned forward in his chair. ''You may not be aware of it, Mr. Hudson, but there's a war going on in the world today—a little-known, unconventional war, but it *is* going on and the United States is part of it.''

The brown eyes looked momentarily startled, then began to glint with caustic mockery. ''Very dramatic! And I suppose *you're* the C.I.A!'' He pushed his hands against the upholstered arms of the chair as he unwound his long body from its Spartan contours. ''You're wasting my time and yours, Mr. Corben. I've no interest whatsoever in becoming involved in your cops-and-robbers operation, so—''

''Not if it concerns the security of your country, of the free world?'' Corben rapped out as he, too, rose, his skin tinged a rosier red. ''We don't play cops and robbers, Mr. Hudson. We leave that to people like you, who dabble in trapping clerks who fall for a bribe from a rival company. My business is serious. It involves the security of thousands—millions—of people it's our job to protect.''

The younger man checked his rapid stride toward the door and looked back at the rotund yet energetic figure behind the desk, his eyes narrowed thoughtfully. He voiced his suspicion. ''Why me? If what I'm doing is so unimportant, why the hell should you pick me for the task of saving the free world?''

"Your connection and your relevant experience make you the only candidate,'' Corben said quietly. "If you'll sit down again, I'll tell you more.''

# CHAPTER ONE

LONDON'S MORNING SKY was still an obscure gray mass when Lindsay Tabor let herself quietly out of the black-painted door of the Georgian town house and stepped briskly down the short flight of wide steps to the lamp-lit sidewalk. Hitching up the collar of her raincoat to ward off the dampness that was London in October, she adjusted the weight of her shoulder travel bag more evenly and continued with a long swinging stride around the half-arc of the square toward the wider main road beyond it.

Lindsay's walk, her English friends told her, would betray her anywhere as an American. No European woman was brought up to display such deeply rooted confidence in her walk. She smiled wryly to herself now as she heard the sharp clicking sound her heels made as she passed the once elegant town houses, transformed from Georgian opulence into present-day offices and apartments.

Her own abode was just such an apartment, and something of that bygone age still lingered in its lofty ceilings and balconies overlooking the central park area. It was large, consisting of a spacious living room and separate dining room, four bedrooms and a fully modernized kitchen carved out of a fifth.

Even though it housed four women of widely divergent tastes and occupation, they were never cramped, mostly because three of them were absent much of the time. Penny and Davina traveled far and often in their jobs as flight attendants, as Lindsay did as a tour director. Helen was the only one to enjoy the regularity of a nine-to-five job, as secretary to the president of a property company.

Lindsay cursed the cobblestones paving the alley leading to the street; tourists in this part of London might find them quaintly picturesque, but they were exceedingly hard on the feet. Her thoughts went back to Helen as she came at last to the wide thoroughfare with its pedestrian island in the middle. A steady routine suited the older woman, and Helen had become a bulwark of security for the younger members of the apartment quartet, always ready to listen to a heart's outpourings or throw together a hasty meal at any odd hour of the night.

Vainly Lindsay looked to right and left, but the street was empty of normal traffic, let alone a taxi. Hitching the bag, which had become heavy, up onto her shoulder again, she set off at a fast pace for the hotel four blocks away. Hadn't it been her wish to be independent of public transport that had made her choose to live in this pricey neighborhood?

Eurospan, the company she worked for, always began its luxury coach tours to Europe at this ungodly hour, and usually on Sunday mornings like this one, when the rest of the world seemed dead. Still, she consoled herself as she crossed the first intersection, she wouldn't change places with Helen and her regular hours. Always, at the start of every tour, there was this sense of excitement, a going forward into the unknown where anything could—and usually did—happen.

Her mind flipped briefly back to the elderly couple lost in Venice's winding alleyways despite the clearly marked signs; to the possessive matron of a precocious teenage daughter who elicited screaming wails from her mother's ample bosom when she was discovered in a compromising position with one of the better-looking hotel waiters; to the ten-year-old boy who had a similar tendency to disappear but whose tastes ran to the religious rather than the erotic. He would be found kneeling solemnly and prayerfully before the more realistic of the religious statuary in the churches and monasteries on the tour.

*Praise be.* She heaved a thankful inner sigh. *No kids this time.* Fall tours were smaller, more intimate groups of mainly elderly Americans, this branch of Eurospan catering exclusively, unashamedly, to the affluent who could afford to indulge their taste for luxury.

And luxury they got, from suites in some of Europe's best hotels to flowers greeting the women passengers each morning on the sumptuously equipped bus that took them on their pampered way across civilizations already old when America was born. Perhaps that was why, Lindsay reflected, her own countrymen plunged into their sampling of European history with so much enthusiasm; at the same time, with Eurospan, they could enjoy the amenities of their younger culture.

She directed her steps around the last corner and saw the imposing front entrance of the hotel. Her muscles tensed with a familiar thrill that was part excitement, part anxiety. Once in a while an exceptionally demanding passenger would show up and destroy the harmony of the tour. Would there be one like that this time? She went mentally through the list of passengers whose names were already engraved on her mind. The Harbens, Strangeways, Dakers, Timms and Ferruccis made up the couples contingent. Three singles completed the group, two women and a man: Charlene Warner, Lila Beaumont and Joel Carter.

Bypassing the hotel's main entrance, Lindsay went farther down the street and turned into the less elaborate entry to the world of Eurospan. Luggage was piled in the red-carpeted hall, and as she stepped by the expensive-looking suitcases she glanced into the open lounge area, where some of her passengers were already congregating. A small dark man was introducing himself volubly to a couple opposite. Ferrucci, she guessed, playing a game of matching up names to faces that she often indulged in before actually meeting her charges. More often than not, alas, she was wrong.

"Hi, Sally," she addressed the blond woman leafing through some documents behind the short counter on her left. "Everything okay?"

Sally grimaced, her fair-skinned, usually pretty face now contorted. "Is it ever, on departure morning?" she despaired. "There are still five more to come—including, I hate to tell you, a late booker."

"No problem," Lindsay said easily, dropping her shoulder bag behind the counter. "We're not exactly crowded this trip, are we?"

"No, but somehow I have a feeling about this one. He could be the sleeper."

The sleeper.... The one sent by the company on occasional trips to check up on the competence of the tour director and driver. "He?" was all Lindsay asked as she came up beside Sally and glanced down at the passenger list. It was a replica of her own, with the exception of one handwritten name at the bottom. Hudson...Carey Hudson.

"He," Sally confirmed. "He's coming in from New York on the night flight, so he may be a little late."

"How late?" Lindsay queried, frowning. "We have to get down to Dover in good time to catch that hovercraft to France. Snoop or not, he'll be left behind if he doesn't arrive for the scheduled departure."

"Careful," Sally cautioned, unusually serious. "He could be a staff member of the company that's just bought Eurospan, not just an ordinary sleeper."

"So? He should appreciate the fact that I keep the tour on schedule."

Stemming her angry eruption, Lindsay turned abruptly away when a tense-looking couple came into the hall and glanced, bewildered, around them. Sally's confidence-inspiring honeyed voice inquiring, "May I help you?" followed her into the inner office, where coffee was warming on a hot plate. Rinsing a cup at the minute sink in the corner, she poured herself a generous portion of the strong black liquid and stared unseeingly at the cramped row of filing cabinets as she drank it.

Having a sleeper aboard worried her not at all. Her record with the company was excellent, and very little disturbed the normal sunny balance of her nature. But having aboard a representative of the conglomerate that had recently swallowed Eurospan in its giant maw did! She would have nothing in common with a man dedicated to the commercial aspects of the business; her job consisted of relating to people on a human level. Oh, there had been hundreds of top-flight businessmen on her tours, but even they had relaxed as Eurospan's bus wheels carried them at a leisurely pace through Europe. A corporation man on business wouldn't relax in that way. She would feel uncomfortable under his company-oriented scrutiny.

Sighing, she replaced the cup and turned back to where Sally was processing another couple. Good. That meant there was only one to go—the darned Hudson man, who threatened to make this trip a disaster. But perhaps her assistant was mistaken, and this Carey Hudson would prove to be an obscure accountant with an even more obscure company.

"Let's get started," she said tersely to Sally as she strode through the office to the hall. Meek or belligerent, Hudson would have to survive without her introductory talk to the passengers, her orientation lecture.

"May I have your attention, please?" Sally's English accent sounded with bell-like clarity from the far side of the lounge, and an expectant hush fell over the group. "I'd like to thank you all for being so prompt in arriving. It makes things so much easier for us and enables us to keep to our schedule. You'll find that this is very important as your tour progresses. But now I'll hand you over to your tour director, Lindsay Tabor, who will no doubt have more to add on the subject of timeliness and other more interesting topics. Lindsay?"

Sally stepped aside, leaving the field clear for Lindsay, who felt every eye in the room assessing her. The looks were guarded now, but such was the nature of tours that within days the passengers would regard her as a cross between a benevolent schoolteacher and a helpless girl who needed parenting. She let their eyes become familiar with her dark hair, loosely curling to her shoulders, her heart-shaped face dominated by deep brown eyes, her generously curved mouth that hinted at an easy smile. When the scrutiny descended to the chocolate brown skirt and blazer, the cheerful yellow blouse, she began to speak.

"Welcome to Europe." The startled murmurs when she was recognized as an American, like themselves, was familiar to her. Smiling, she went on. "Right now I know your names but not your faces. However, that won't take too long to remedy once we're on our way, and I can assure you that we'll know one another very well by the time we return from our month's trip. But for now, there are a few things I'd like to make clear to my passengers before we start off, so here goes."

Her eyes as busily assessing as theirs, she went into her routine of preparing them for the trip, touching on currency exchange, customs of the countries they would visit, her own availability at all times to assist them.

"I should warn you," she stated with a touch of dryness, "that the bus—or coach, as it's called in England—that we'll be taking to Dover for the hovercraft trip to France is not the same one that will be waiting for us at Boulogne. Our tour proper won't really begin until we reach—"

A flurry of movement in the main hall drew her eyes up and stopped the words in her throat. A man, striding rapidly toward them, turned back with an impatient gesture to thrust money into the hand of a taxi driver who had just deposited a large brown suitcase beside the rest of the luggage. Then the stranger turned his attention to the assembled company in the lounge, his eyes remote until they came to rest on Lindsay. They seemed to widen in surprise as they took in the dark cloud of her hair, the neat conformation of breast, waist and hip, the slender lines of her legs under the knee-length skirt.

For her part, Lindsay felt the potency of his male assessment and tightened her lips as she pulled her own gaze back to the expectant group, retaining a blurred impression of tallness, of broad shoulders filling a well-tailored gray suit, of a chin darkened by a recent growth of beard.

"One thing I'd like to stress before we begin," she addressed the company at large, "is that punctuality is of prime importance at all times. So however enchanted you may be by a small French village we've stopped at for lunch, or how fascinating you find the wonders of ancient Rome, the cardinal rule is that you return to the bus at the appointed time. This not only helps us keep to our schedule but adds to the comfort of your fellow passengers.''

Sally slipped away from Lindsay's side and went to greet the latecomer, her eagerness obvious long before she reached him. Drawing her attention back to her passengers with inner misgivings about Sally's vulnerability, Lindsay completed her orientation talk and went forward to meet the passengers who would be under her care for the next four weeks. Smiling, mentally joining names to faces, she was conscious of the tall figure bent over Sally's counter, signing papers with what Lindsay was sure would be a confident flourish. He was that kind of man.

''There *will* be time to take in some of Europe's historical sites?'' Paul Strangeways, a university professor from Chicago, queried anxiously. Lindsay's smile encompassed both his ascetic stooped figure and that of his younger, well-dressed wife, Mary.

''We spend several days in each of the major centers,'' she assured him brightly. ''Paris, Florence, Rome, Venice and of course Vienna, which is our last stop. Naturally it would take longer than the few days at our disposal to study these areas in depth, but you should be able to sense the atmosphere and learn something of the history in the time we'll be spending in each city.''

Atmosphere was obviously what Carl and Betty

Timms were seeking, too. Artists, they had every intention of making full use of the backgrounds they would discover along the way. They were almost like twins, their garb identical—well-worn blue jeans and matching jackets, thick, high-necked sweaters. The look-alike appearance extended even to their fair hair and pink-tinged skin, the latter obscured somewhat on Carl by his prolific growth of beard.

Frank and Irene Harben were what Lindsay mentally termed a "corporate couple." Slightly overbearing and more than a little self-satisfied, Frank Harben would never be overshadowed by his plump docile wife, who smiled a lot and said nothing.

Moving on to the Ferruccis, Lindsay reflected that silence like Irene Harben's was unknown to the likes of Tony Ferrucci, who noisily explained that he ran a fast-food outlet in Columbus, Ohio, and that he had won this trip to Europe via roof-lifting sales.

"I really didn't want to take the time away," he confided to Lindsay, "but Gina here wanted to see the places the old folks talked about. So here we are."

Lindsay smiled, ignoring his loud pink-and-black-checked jacket. "I'm sure you'll really enjoy the tour. We spend quite a while in Italy as well as Switzerland, France and Austria."

She moved on determinedly and made a quick assessment of the three singles taking the tour. From past experience, she knew they could sometimes cause havoc in an otherwise balanced party. Hope sank when she shook hands with Charlene Warner, an unnatural blonde of indeterminate age who possessed all the signs of a ripe woman anxious to make the tour a holiday in the broadest sense. However, the other two singles made her less apprehensive. Joel Carter seemed an innocuous young man, his smile shy under a shock of soft disorderly brown hair. An introvert, she guessed, too shy of women to make waves among the female passengers.

The only problem with Lila Beaumont, she decided with a resigned inner smile, would be to keep the middle-aged woman's confused state in some kind of order. Already she was darting, birdlike, between the numerous pieces of baggage at her feet.

The presence of the Dakers, Brad and Debora, boded well for the even tenor of the tour. Lindsay took to the relaxed, pipe-smoking Brad and his attractive, bright-eyed wife immediately. If only every trip could be composed of couples as undemanding as she suspected the Dakers would be, her job would be pleasant and easy.

Escaping into the hall, she found Carey Hudson watching her sporadic progress with intent eyes— eyes that were, she discovered on closer inspection, a lighter brown than her own and flecked with pinpoints of gold.

"This is Mr. Hudson," Sally belatedly divulged, evidently still mesmerized. "He's an executive with—" She turned innocently perplexed eyes on the man who towered above her five-foot-four frame. "I'm afraid I can't remember which company you're with, Mr. Hudson."

"That's not surprising," he returned in the abrupt tones of a New Yorker. "And I've no intention of getting into that now." The flick of his eyes as he turned them on Lindsay was like an abrasive caress. "I'm here to leave the corporate world behind and enjoy all this European tour has to offer, Miss. . .?"

Lindsay had the inexplicable feeling of being impaled on the hard shaft of his gaze and she was gauchely tongue-tied until Sally hastened to her rescue.

"This is Lindsay Tabor, one of our most popular tour directors," she stressed in a voice that sounded gushy to Lindsay's ear. Yet how could she blame Sally when her own speech seemed to have frozen into a solid block? It was ridiculous, unheard of, for Lindsay to let herself become vulnerable to one of her passengers. And she wouldn't, she told herself fiercely, her dark eyes flashing to life as they met the amber of his. She was as aware as the next woman of the sexual aura some men exuded. Carey Hudson was one of them. It didn't mean she had to act like a smitten teenager.

"How are you?" She allowed her slender fingers to be crushed momentarily in his powerful grasp. "I hope you heard the last part of my orientation talk, Mr. Hudson. Punctuality is of supreme importance on a tour like this."

His jaw tightened in unison with his grip on her hand as he shot back grittily, "Maybe you'd like to rearrange the airline's schedule to fit in with your itinerary, Miss. . .Tabor?"

Lindsay bit back the several retorts that sprang to mind as she pulled her hand from his. As a passenger, he threatened to be an obnoxious complainer.

As the company spy, his brusque manner could be designed to try her. Deciding that discretion was the better part of a tour manager's job, she turned to Sally.

"Is Jack loading the baggage?" she asked crisply, ignoring the Hudson man, although she noted from the corner of her eye that he moved restlessly toward the corridor leading into the main lobby of the hotel.

"He's seeing to it now." Sally sighed dreamily, her eyes soft and wide as they followed the rangy figure. "He's the answer to a frustrated maiden's prayer, but I'd watch out for our Mr. Hudson, Lindsay. He wouldn't tell me which company he's connected with, and that can only mean one thing."

"I can cope with his kind." Lindsay shrugged, less sure than she sounded. Sally's warning, given as a result of the casual friendship that existed between tour and office staff, struck an answering chord in her, but she had no intention of playing a game of "Is he—is he not?" where Carey Hudson was concerned. There was more than enough to occupy her in other areas, and having a sleeper aboard gave her no qualms. He would be treated in the same way as any other passenger.

She turned to watch the elderly porter as he diminished the stack of luggage, carrying it out to the capacious storage area under the bus, which was parked at the curb outside the entrance. When the last piece had been picked up and borne through the glass doors, she went to the lounge and beckoned to the passengers to follow old Jack out to the vehicle.

Wincing inwardly as Tony Ferrucci passed by in

his sport coat of many colors, she counted heads as her wards ambled past her, an exercise that would become second nature to her in the weeks to follow.

One was still missing when Jack, his iron-gray hair sticking up spikily from his head, came back into the empty hallway and told her perkily, ''That's the lot, ducks. I put your cases in last, as usual—last in, first out, eh?''

''Thanks, Jack.'' Lindsay pressed a note into his expectant palm and looked back at Sally behind the counter. ''You'll send Mr. Hudson out when he gets back?''

''Sure you want me to?'' A smile broke over Sally's fair features as she added with another sigh, ''I'd be more than happy to entertain him until you get back.''

''You'd be welcome to him,'' Lindsay retorted sourly, lifting her travel bag and briefcase, hoisting the bag onto her shoulder, ''if he weren't on *my* passenger list and therefore my responsibility.''

''Lucky you.'' Sally returned Lindsay's farewell salute and stared after her enviously. ''If only I had your command of languages, I'd be the one to make that man's trip a time to remember!''

Lindsay's thoughts were far more down-to-earth than the awestruck Sally's as she shepherded the last of her charges onto the utilitarian bus that would take them to Dover and the hovercraft service to France. Numbers would mean more to her than names for the first few days of the tour, until she automatically associated a name with a face. Carey Hudson, a newly purchased newspaper under his arm, was the last to board the vehicle.

"Hardly a deluxe conveyance," he commented sourly, one heavily marked brow uplifted as he scanned the battered outlines of the bus.

"As I've already explained to those who turned up promptly—" Lindsay lost her calmness in a flashing spurt of temper "—this isn't the bus that will take us across Europe. We'll be met at Boulogne by a—"

"Don't bother to repeat it all for my benefit," he drawled, seeming bored as he swung athletically onto the lower step, looking back at her from there. "That way, you'll be able to surprise me as we go along."

Lindsay's mouth firmed as she followed him, relaxing as she smiled at Bob Pelham, the shuttle driver between London and Dover. She busied herself stowing away her hand baggage. Surprise him, indeed! The woman capable of doing that probably hadn't been born yet.

Straightening, she scanned the seated passengers, making an automatic count of heads. Everyone on her list was present, and she nodded to the driver and took up the hand microphone as she pulled down the foldaway seat beside him.

"Hello again, everybody," she said brightly. "Our journey to Dover will probably take a little longer than usual this morning, because a very special event is taking place in London today. It's the start of a race—not a horse race, for which the British are famous, but an antique-car competition to Brighton on the south coast. If you'll watch as we edge our way past these vintage cars, you'll see that their owners are dressed in their idea of roaring-twenties style—leather jackets and helmets and the goggles that were necessary in those days for eye protection.''

Turning her head, she let her eyes run lightly over the passengers, seeing the rekindling of animation that had been somewhat dampened by the necessarily crisp orientation lecture coming after the jet lag of a transcontinental plane journey. One pair of eyes stared back blandly into hers.

Carey Hudson was obviously unimpressed by the twenties vehicles belching acrid smoke from their exhausts. For a moment, Lindsay's dark gaze held his steadily. Then she shifted her attention to the side window closest to where she sat. However much her charges would enjoy this unusual start to their vacation, the slow-moving race vehicles could hold them up for half an hour or more. There was no trace of tension in her voice, however, when she lifted the speaker to her mouth again.

''Hyde Park, on our left, is a vast area of green parkland that is much appreciated by Londoners, who come here on their lunch hours if their workplace is nearby. It's also well used on summer weekends. The section we're passing now is known as Speaker's Corner. This is where anyone, however radical his or her views, can come and voice them on Sunday mornings.''

Feeling her way into the personalities of her passengers, Lindsay pointed out various historical landmarks as the bus made its way with painful slowness through central London. Days would pass before she would be able to gauge with any accuracy the tourists' level of humor, the depth of their interest in historical anecdotes meted out on a regular basis.

When the stirring panoply of age-old buildings had been left behind and the less attractive environs of London encroached on either side, Lindsay put down the microphone and went forward to distribute the cards she'd mentioned in her orientation lecture. The information contained on the cards would smooth border and hotel entry and make passports solely the passengers' responsibility.

"Don't you collect the passports and keep them all together?" the man at her first port of call queried officiously.

Lindsay glanced down at her clipboard list. "It's Mr. Harben, isn't it?" A corporate head, used to having details taken off his hands. When he nodded, she explained, "We find it much simpler to have all the information needed on the cards, Mr. Harben. Security measures for your passport and other valuables are available at all the hotels we'll be staying at."

"Hmm," he acknowledged sourly, and his faded wife gave Lindsay a placating smile. "I certainly hope the vehicle in France is an improvement over this one." As he spoke, the rickety bus jumped and shuddered over a rise in the road, causing him to tighten his narrow mouth even further.

"As I mentioned in the lounge—" Lindsay schooled her voice to evenness "—the tour proper starts as soon as we reach Boulogne, and I'm sure you'll have no complaints about the transportation from then on."

She passed to the seat directly behind, sighing inwardly as she guessed that the Harben man would likely come up with any number of complaints before the trip was over; he was just one of those people overly impressed by his own importance.

Some twenty minutes later, after chatting with the remainder of the passengers apart from Carey Hudson—who was unashamedly asleep in his seat toward the back of the bus—Lindsay walked forward and resumed her seat beside the driver. Bob Pelham was one of the more mature drivers, well used to the vagaries of each passenger load, and his sideways glance with slightly raised brows spoke volumes. Lindsay's faint nod and smile answered him in similar vein—there was no one aboard that she couldn't cope with.

Except.... She frowned and glanced down at the clipboard on her lap. Carey Hudson wasn't the usual kind of passenger. For one thing, he was far younger than the norm for this type of tour. True, the other male single, Joel Carter, was even younger, but Lindsay sensed he was the artistic type lured by Europe's fabulous art treasures. His personality was in marked contrast to Hudson's. Where Joel Carter was gently effacing, the Hudson man was abrasively sure of himself. Whether he was awake or asleep, those mid-brown eyes with their curious flecking remained with her, sending a premonitory shiver down her back.

Shrugging almost imperceptibly, she glanced around before picking up the microphone again. If he was the sleeper, as Sally had surmised, he was going about his job in a very lax way.

"We're passing through Kent, known as the Garden of England, on our way to Dover and the hover-

craft that's going to take us to France for the start of
our European tour. Soon we'll come to the hop
fields, which...."

Lindsay unwound her spool of information, which
by now she could recite almost without thinking.
And why not? She'd worked for Eurospan for two
years now, and other, lesser tour companies for a
year before that. At twenty-five, she was well
qualified for the job. Always fascinated by languages, she'd mastered three—French, German, Italian—and knew enough Dutch and Spanish to get her
by.

That she'd been able to indulge her penchant for
languages had been mainly due to the unselfishness
of her parents, who'd sponsored her three years of
study in Europe, a year each in Paris, Heidelberg and
Rome. Studying in Europe had been an unrealized
dream for her father, David Tabor, professor of
economic history at the University of Pennsylvania,
and he'd been adamant that his daughter should have
the chance that had been denied him, more particularly because she was specializing in languages. And
looking at her daughter's shining eyes, Deirdre Tabor
had given her reluctant blessing, too.

They hadn't, of course, expected Lindsay to make
use of her linguistic talents in the tourism field. Snob-
bishness wasn't a word in their vocabulary, but
they'd expected their only child to return to the States
after her European studies and take a highly paid
job, preferably in Philadelphia, where her home had
always been.

Lindsay often had to remind herself that, while she

was her father's only child, she was Deirdre's second. At eighteen, her mother had married a man in her own country, a well-to-do Englishman, and had had a son by him ten years before her husband's death in a hunting accident. That was the kind of life the Raines family had indulgently lived—stables, polo, hunting—and Deirdre had given in to the blandishments of her dead husband's family to leave his heir in England when she'd married what they regarded as an obscure American teacher. That same disapproval had kept Philip in Europe throughout his youth, so that Lindsay had never met the half brother whose background was so different from her own.

That is, not until she'd come to Europe to begin her studies. She could still remember the excitement, the dryness in her throat as her plane descended at Heathrow Airport. She had fantasized a lot about her half brother in distant England, almost making a god of him out of the lonely depths of her only-child existence. Deirdre had fed the fires of her imagination when she returned from her infrequent visits to see her son, unaware that her daughter soaked up like a sponge the tales of Philip's brilliance, his good looks, his impeccable manners. Jealousy didn't enter into it. Philip was too remote geographically to pose a threat to her own close relationship with her mother.

All the talk, all the pictures hadn't really prepared Lindsay for the reality of the devastatingly handsome brother who met her in the airport reception hall. She had been overawed by the tall, athletic-looking Englishman, with hair as black as her own, whose bearish hug told her without words that he had longed for the family contact as much as she had. He'd swept her off to his comfortably rambling house in Surrey, close to London, which he shared with his wife, Elena, and their two children.

The autumn haze of the English countryside passed by without her noticing as she recalled how much she'd wanted to have Philip to herself, even just for that day of their meeting, resenting his wife and the children she hadn't yet met. But that feeling lasted only until Elena came shyly to greet her in the hall, giving her a hug almost as welcoming as Philip's had been. There was a lingering sadness in Elena's eyes that brought out Lindsay's strong protective streak, and the two quickly became friends.

It was a sadness, she gradually learned, that stemmed from Elena's Polish background. She had met Philip at a scientific conference in Berlin, where she had acted as interpreter for the Polish members, and they had fallen in love—impetuously so, considering Philip's reserved English nature. But his powers of persuasion must have been mighty, because Elena had never gone back to her homeland, despite the fact that her elderly parents still lived there under a restrictive regime. They had been married as soon as the formalities were completed, and Elena hadn't seen her parents since.

Even yesterday, Lindsay recalled, there had been a wistfulness about Elena's wishing her well on the tour, which would end in Vienna, so close to her homeland.

"I envy you so much sometimes," she had said in her accented English.

"Envy me?" Lindsay had laughed disbelievingly. Elena seemed to have everything she wanted—a husband who adored her, two children who hardly ever spoke a sentence without "mummy" in it, a gorgeous house in the best English-country tradition, as well as a distinct lack of financial worries. Philip's brilliance at Oxford had led to a high-salaried position with the nuclear-research establishment not far from where they lived. Elena had been blessed, and blessed again, with some of the best that life had to offer.

"I'll trade with you any day," Lindsay added half-seriously, smiling up at Philip when he came and slid an arm around her waist. "I think it's time you took your wife away on vacation, Philip. The danger signals are up when she begins to want all the hassles of my job, coping with the cranks, the weirdos, the hotels who insist they've never heard of us until we arrive hungry and tired at 11:00 P.M."

A wail sounded from upstairs, and Elena gave Lindsay another quick hug. "That's David. He's probably filled the bathroom with soap bubbles. Goodbye, darling. Have a good journey, and we will look forward to seeing you when you return."

Lindsay watched her sister-in-law run lightly up the curving staircase, then turned with a sigh to Philip.

"Well, I really do have to get back to town and pack for tomorrow, so—"

"Lindsay..." he began hesitantly, a frown etched between his black brows. "Can I ask you to do me a favor?"

She smiled up into his face but sounded puzzled when she said, "Of course. You know I—"

"Just come into the study for a minute, will you?" he interrupted again, and she followed him across the hall to the book-lined den that was his private domain. She felt more than a little bewildered when he went behind the desk positioned to one side of the deeply mullioned windows and unlocked a drawer, extracting a weighty buff-colored envelope. He held it out to her as he came back to the center of the room.

"Will you deliver this to an address in Vienna for me? I can't go into detail, but the Hilda Keller this is addressed to is helping us get Elena's parents out of Poland, which as you know is difficult, because when she married me she virtually defected. The Keller woman has contacts in Poland, but it's imperative she receive these documents to facilitate the old people's departure." His eyes darkened with a pain Lindsay could sympathize with. "Elena doesn't know anything about this, and I don't want her to know until her parents are reunited with her, or...." He left the sentence dangling, but Lindsay could well imagine the consequences for the old couple if the attempt to free them failed.

"Of course I'll do anything I can to help Elena," she offered impulsively. This was her newfound family, and her words were sincere.

"Bless you, darling. All you have to do is to keep this envelope in a safe place and deliver it by hand to Hilda Keller as soon as you get to Vienna. Remember this address: 216 Friedrich Schmidt Platz. The rest will be taken care of by others. You do realize that this is a hush-hush kind of thing?" he went on, worried. "There's no danger to you, but it wouldn't do for this envelope to fall into the hands of—"

"Darling?" Elena's voice floated down from above. "Will you bring Amanda's teddy bear from the sitting room? She will not go to sleep without it."

"Lindsay?" Philip questioned hoarsely, adding to her mounting sense of unreality. It was all so cloak-and-dagger, so James Bondish, but Philip's concern communicated itself unmistakably.

"Yes, yes, I'll do it," she said hurriedly, stuffing the buff envelope into her shoulder bag. Philip had gone when she raised her head again.

The heavy envelope was in her travel bag now and would be placed in the safety box at each hotel, along with Eurospan cash and records.

"Going to tell them about Dover Castle, dear?" Bob broke dryly into her meditation, and Lindsay stared dazedly around, realizing that the ancient castle was indeed looming up on the horizon.

"Oh. Sure. Thanks, Bob."

Her sensibly manicured nail pressed down on the microphone button, and she began a quick sketchy history of the castle that had housed many of Britain's historic personages, not the least of whom was the bride of the fated Charles I, Henrietta Maria, who had rested there for several days, recovering from her tumultuous voyage from France after her marriage by proxy to England's reigning monarch.

Disposing rapidly of the unfortunate queen, who had been destined to lose her husband under the sword of an executioner, Lindsay went right into the instructions for the hovercraft ride to Boulogne.

"We've found from past experience that boarding is simplified if we travel independently after reaching the terminal, so you'll be on your own until we meet again at the other side. Coffee, tea and very simple meals are available at the terminal for those of you who feel the need of sustenance. And I should remind you that we won't be reaching Paris until early evening, so please plan your meal with that in mind. Currency exchange is available. . . ."

A gray and sullen English Channel awaited them as the bus pulled up in front of the glassed-in terminal building. What else, in October? Lindsay stood up and made one further stipulation.

"Please keep your seats until I've purchased our tickets for the Channel crossing. I'll hand these out to you as you leave the bus."

Hopping down the steps, she went with her free stride to the ticket counter, where a laconic clerk doled out fifteen tickets. She was back at the bus entrance in time to hand them out to the group, who had ignored her instructions to stay aboard.

"Be there at eleven-fifty," she intoned again and again, handing out the tickets.

"Oh, my," Lila Beaumont, one of the singles, said distractedly as her tiny clawlike hand clutched at the scrap of paper. "Where do I go? I suppose I should eat something—don't we really get to Paris until nighttime?"

"I'm afraid not. You go right through there and to your left," Lindsay directed kindly, adding as an afterthought when the older woman peered uncertainly at the blank glass of the doors, "If you'd like to wait, I'll show you where to go."

"Oh.... Oh, thank you, honey. Where should I wait?"

"Right where you are is fine." Lindsay's smile was still elastically brilliant when the last passenger made his descent from the bus and looked at her quizzically, his tigerish brown eyes flicking from her to the fussy older woman at her side, who was checking and rechecking her numerous pieces of hand luggage.

"Did I heard you say I can get some French money here?" he asked with a tetchiness she would have associated with Frank Harben, the company executive.

"You did, Mr. Hudson," she returned evenly, pointing to her left. "Over there—although you'd have got a much better rate of exchange in London, you know."

"I didn't exactly have time to go into the niceties of foreign exchange at Heathrow Airport at five-thirty this morning," he retorted dryly before swinging off in the direction she'd indicated.

Lindsay watched him go, noting his athletic stride that was unimpeded by the heavy weekend bag slung over his shoulder. If he was, indeed, the sleeper, he was now playing his part to the hilt. He could be a novice recruited by the company to report on overall performance, but somehow he didn't seem to fit the type—more like a hard-hitting businessman far removed from the petty level of company spying.

But who knew with this new company—conglomerate—that had taken over the Eurospan operation? This would be its first involvement with a tour, and it wasn't beyond the realm of possibility that it had chosen a company executive to make firsthand appraisals of the individual tours.

"Can we go now?" a plaintive voice sounded at her elbow, and she turned to look down into perplexed and anxious blue eyes.

"Of course, Miss—Mrs. Beaumont," she corrected herself. "Right in here. What would you like to have?" She seated the older woman at a steel table designed for four.

"Well, I really don't know. What would you suggest?"

Lindsay reeled off the familiar menu, her eyes abstracted as they went over the large dining area, pinpointing all but one of her group. Like homing pigeons, the easygoing Dakers had settled together with the Strangeways—Paul Strangeways, the university professor who had been anxious to know about the time allotted to Europe's art treasures, and his wife Mary, an alert lady a couple of years younger than her husband. Lindsay breathed a sigh of relief. It helped considerably when the various tour members hit it off. They usually did, like gravitating toward like.

At another table in the crowded buffet, the other two singles were sharing with Carl and Betty Timms, the artists. Joel Carter was talking with shy animation to the couple, but Charlene Warner, the well-built blonde, looked bored as her eyes went restlessly around the close-set tables. A woman in search of a man, Lindsay couldn't help thinking, but destined to be out of luck on this trip. Joel Carter was obviously not the type she was looking for—although Carey Hudson, she suddenly realized, was apparently unattached.

She frowned, only half-hearing Lila Beaumont's order for meat pie and chips. Giving the other woman a fleeting smile, she went to join the self-service line, her thoughts running rampant beneath her serenely uncreased brow.

Maybe he would fill the bill for the voluptuous Charlene. Such unlikely matings had happened before on her tours. Neither of them, she imagined, was looking for a permanent relationship—just someone to share the unforgettable sights of Europe with. If they did pair off, it would solve two of her problems. She wouldn't have Charlene to worry about, and Carey Hudson would be too engrossed to nitpick about the operation of the tour.

So why did the thought of the two of them cozily pairing off send a sharp twinge of irritation through her?

THE HOVERCRAFT SKIMMED noisily toward France, spray obscuring whatever view there might have been on this dismally overcast day. Cushioned on a layer of air, the craft accomplished its journey in record time, but Lindsay secretly preferred the more leisurely Channel ferry crossing, where there was time to stroll the decks and slowly prepare for the advent of Europe.

"Would you like something from the bar?" A uniformed attendant, looking remarkably like Britain's

Princess Anne with her fair hair swept under an azure blue bowler-type hat, paused at the end of the row of seats.

"Nothing for me, thanks." Lindsay glanced questioningly at the diminutive figure by her side, reflecting wryly that Lila Beaumont was already sticking closer than a limpet to the nearest pillar of authority—her. "Would you care for a drink, Mrs. Beaumont?"

"Oh." The blue eyes blinked rapidly, darting up to the statuesque blonde in the aisle and back again to Lindsay. "What kind of drinks do they have?"

"Scotch, vodka, gin," the attendant recited patiently. "Or you can have tea, coffee or a soft drink."

"Oh, my." Lila Beaumont fluttered helplessly like a bewildered hen, then looked to Lindsay for guidance. "What do you think?"

"It's up to you, Mrs. Beaumont. Perhaps you'd like some tea?"

"Yes. Yes, I'll have tea," the older woman agreed, relieved to have the decision taken from her. But as the attendant took orders from the other passengers in their row, she dithered again. "Well, maybe I should have—I'm very nervous, you know—I think maybe I'll have—did you say you have Scotch?"

"Yes, madam." The attendant was noticeably cooler.

"Well, then, I think I'll— Oh, yes, why not? I'll have a Scotch and soda."

Lindsay stemmed the tide of impatience that flowed through her. She'd had difficult customers before, and she would surely cope with this one. None, however, had been quite as indecisive as Mrs. Beaumont, and she could foresee innumerable embarrassing incidents occurring in the days ahead. On the other hand, the older woman appealed to her maternal instinct.

Conversation lagged in deference to the penetrating roar of the hovercraft's engines, and Lila Beaumont busied herself, when her drink arrived, with balancing it on the precarious heap of hand baggage she juggled on her lap.

Resting her head against the high seat back, Lindsay closed her eyes. Was she destined to play mother to passengers like Lila Beaumont for the rest of her life? She had pushed any other form of motherhood out of her consciousness after Geoff. Geoff Boler.... She let the name seep into her mind. Dear God, how she had loved him, wanted to be his wife, the mother of his children. It had all seemed such a viable dream in the drenching heat of a Roman summer....

She had met Geoff almost at the beginning of her sojourn in Rome, at a party given by her two roommates, who, like herself, were American expatriates. A hazy kind of magic had seemed to envelop her senses from the very first time she'd laid eyes on the loose-limbed American who yelled "Texas" from every pore of his lanky body. An aura of glamour surrounded him, a reflection of his status as Rome correspondent for a highly regarded American newspaper.

He had taken her out to the narrow balcony overlooking Rome's less prepossessing rooftops and made verbal love to her. The physical aspect had come later, when each brush of skin against skin evoked all the hidden longings Lindsay had suppressed against the day when, she mused romantically, the right man would come along.

Geoff had seemed so superbly that right one. He had been the first to set the flame to her slumbering senses, the first to reach down into the heart of her and draw forth the deeply sensual part of her nature. Until Geoff, she had never known that madness of the senses, that longing for a male touch on her shivering skin, that overwhelming need for the final fulfillment.

A fulfillment that had taken place so naturally, so rightly, that she had known it couldn't be wrong. Her lids quivered over her closed eyes as the memory of that first time seared her mind.

They had wandered back hand in hand to his apartment, the evocative strains of soft Italian music lingering around them long after they'd left her apartment. There seemed no need for words as they entered his second-floor apartment and reached hungrily for each other, her mouth softly trembling against the hard demand of his. It had been a soft night altogether. The shimmer of moonlight through the uncurtained windows was softly romantic. The bed he lowered her to after slowly undressing her was soft, too. Most of all, her skin had never felt so soft as his hands ran sensually over the full curve of her naked breasts, the flat tautness of her stomach, the spun silk of her thighs. His skill had made an old wives' tale of pain, and she had hardly paused in her enjoyment of the moment she had waited for all her life, it seemed.

That single night had sparked a craving in her that made her throw caution to the winds. She began cutting language classes to be with him, not only at night but in the drowsy siesta time after lunch. Her parents wouldn't approve, she knew, but how could they help liking Geoff when she introduced him as her husband?

She wasn't foolish enough to dream of the traditional rose-covered cottage, but her knowledge of languages could help him tremendously in his work. If he were transferred to the Paris office she could translate for him, and the same for West Berlin, Madrid—although her Spanish was a little shaky. Nothing would matter once they were truly together. They would be a team in every aspect of their lives. If Geoff wasn't as enthusiastic as she was about their rosy future, what did it matter? He was a roving newspaperman, used to his freedom. But that would change once they were married. She would prove to him that one woman was all he needed. . . .

She had been happily, deliriously in love—until that afternoon when the phone call had come. . . two phone calls, the first a disturbing jangle to their aftermath of love.

"You'd better answer it," she had murmured, her lips tender as they traced the bearded outline of his chin, exulting when he seemed reluctant to pull himself from the bed and leave her. "It sounds important."

"Ringing telephones always sound important," he muttered irately before rising in slow motion to take up the receiver on the night table by the bed. "Jesus, Mort, it's not the most convenient moment in the world.... All right, all right, I'll cover it!" Slamming the receiver back in its cradle, he looked down at Lindsay, his eyes devoid of any emotion but anger. "The Pope's giving an audience to some American bishops, and I'm supposed to cover it." His voice grew gentle as his fingers traced the warm contours of her mouth. "Don't go away, sugar. I'll be back as soon as I can, and we'll take up where we left off, hmm?"

Incapable of doing otherwise, Lindsay nodded mutely, squashing the resentment that flooded over her. As Geoff's wife, there would be many such calls away from their life, their bed. She would just have to get used to it.

She stretched under the covers when he'd gone, visualizing again the bright future that waited to be unwound. Geoff Boler's wife...Mrs. Geoffrey Boler...Mrs. Lindsay Boler. Any version sounded golden to her ears. She turned onto her stomach, her slender arms hugging the pillow that still held the scent of Geoff's hair, the cologne he used. Children would be born to them, perhaps a dark-haired, dark-eyed boy and a blond girl with eyes as blue as Geoff's....

She was still stretched out, dreamily forecasting the future, when the phone began to ring again. Turning quickly, she drew herself up to a sitting position and reached for the receiver.

What followed then would always be shrouded in a haze of unreality. The operator, speaking the precise English of a foreigner, informed her that there was a call from a Mrs. Boler in the United States.

So immersed was she in her dream that Lindsay began, "But I'm—" before catching herself up. How foolish of her! It must be Geoff's mother on the line.

"Is this Signor Boler's residence?" the operator demanded impatiently.

"*Sì,*" Lindsay responded automatically, adding in English, "but he's—"

"Go ahead, caller," the inexorable voice interrupted. "You are connected."

A woman's lighter tone came distinctly on the line. "Is that you, Geoff?"

Static fluctuated on the international line, or perhaps it was in her own head. "Hello?" Lindsay said loudly into the receiver. "I'm sorry, Geoff isn't here right now. Can I take a message?"

There was a sudden clearing in the airwaves, making the ensuing words echo with crystal clarity in her ear.

"This is his wife speaking. . . . Who are you?"

Lindsay stared blankly at the cream-colored wall behind the night table, seconds slipping by as her mind tried without success to grapple with the other woman's statement.

"Are you still there?"

"I— Yes, I'm here. I'm. . . nobody important," she said starkly, only later realizing the significance of those words. "I. . . work with Geoff and just stopped by to deliver some papers. He—he had to leave a few minutes ago.... I was just leaving myself when the phone rang.'' She was babbling stupidly, guiltily, as if the other woman had witnessed that recent love scene with her—oh, God—her husband!

"Well, would you mind leaving a note for him before you go—'' Was there a note of sarcasm ''—asking him to call me the minute he gets in? David, our younger son, is sick, and I think Geoff should come home.''

Lindsay's throat was parched, her lips cracked with dryness. Younger son? There must be two. Geoff's children....

"Yes, I—I'll see that he gets the message.''

Her hand groped for the telephone cradle. Then she leaned back on the indented pillow, disembodied sounds roaring in her ears. Geoff was married... *married!* He had children, two of them, with his wife. Oh, God, he hadn't said a word. No wonder he'd seemed evasive when she mentioned marriage, had steered her clear of the people he worked with.

She had stirred enough to get dressed by the time Geoff breezed back into the apartment and found her sitting, miserable and silent, on the old-fashioned chair pulled out from under the kitchen table. Once glance at her frozen face told him that something was drastically wrong.

"Lindy?'' He used his pet name for her, concerned but not alarmed as he knelt beside her and put comforting arms around her waist. "What's wrong, honey? You look as if you've had some really bad news. Is something wrong at home?''

She stirred then and looked without feeling into

the eyes that had filled her dreams for months past. He looked the same, she thought dully. Strange. For her, nothing would ever be the same again.

"Your wife called from the States," she said woodenly, her eyes fixed on the vivid blue of his, observing the sudden blink of surprise that was immediately followed by a shady guilt, making the existence of his wife an established fact. "Your son— David, I think she said—is ill, and she thinks you should go home. She wants you to phone her right back."

Geoff's large hands tightened around her waist, but the leap of concern in his eyes was for his son, not her. "Oh, God. Did she say what was wrong with him?"

Without waiting for Lindsay's head shake, he was on his feet and bounding into the living room, where he reached for the extension. He seemed not to notice when Lindsay slid painfully off the chair and went to get dressed in her outdoor clothes. As she closed the entrance door, she heard him say, "Janey? What's wrong with David?"

She hurried down the steps, not wanting to hear his explanation for her own presence in the apartment, if he made any at all. Maybe his wife—Janey—was used to his passing liaisons with other women and condoned them as long as he was available, as he obviously was, for family crises....

A sudden quietness, apart from the excited chatter of passengers, alerted Lindsay that the hovercraft had berthed at Boulogne. Getting to her feet, she automatically put out her arm to assist Lila Beaumont to the aisle.

"My, that's quite an art you have," her tiny companion murmured with admiration. "One moment you were fast asleep, and the next you were wide awake!"

"I've learned to catnap," Lindsay answered briefly. "It helps clear my mind for what's ahead."

Had she really cleared her mind, she wondered as she shuffled with the others toward the exit. Geoff was still in her mind, if not in her heart, and she had dozens of abortive relationships to prove it. He had left his mark on her, as surely as if he had branded his identity in blazing letters. Other men had been attracted to her since, as she had been to them, but none of them had ever come close to unfreezing the numb inner core Geoff had left her with.

# CHAPTER TWO

LINDSAY HUNG THE MOST CRUSHABLE of her dresses behind the white louvered doors of her bedroom closet at the discreetly elegant hotel close to the Place Charles de Gaulle in Paris. Although Eurospan provided her with accommodation only slightly less luxurious than that allotted to paying passengers, she occasionally felt a twinge of nostalgia for her days as tour director for a lesser company.

For one thing, there had never been this void at the prospect of an evening in Paris. On the less exclusive tours, there had always been a sense of camaraderie between her and the passengers, even on the evenings when dinner wasn't provided by the company. But Eurospan discouraged too intimate mingling with clients, and there were few communal dinners on their tours, so Lindsay ate alone most of the time. There had been exceptions when she'd joined a party requesting her company, or the table of a solitary traveler ill at ease in a strange city. But generally she was expected to eat on her own.

Not that she had to in Paris. She still had good friends from her student days here, but she always felt happier being close to the hotel for the inevitable calls on her attention. Passengers always wanted to know the best places to eat, the best floor show to see, the best historical sights. There was, too, the umbilical cord of her nightly phone calls to London.

Emptying the shoulder bag of the necessities she always carried with her, she used the top drawer of a delicately carved walnut dresser to store first-aid supplies, scissors, sewing repair kit. Her fingers reached automatically into the outer pocket of the bag for forgotten items and encountered the bulky envelope Philip had given her to deliver to Hilda Keller in Vienna.

She should have stowed it in the hotel's safety-deposit box along with the Eurospan items, but she'd forgotten. She could do it later tonight or in the morning.

A frown marked her brow as she rezipped the compartment and pushed the bag to the rear of the closet. She was still frowning when she stepped under the shower and let the warm water erase the ravages of the first day's travel. The slight uneasiness she'd felt the day before when Philip had given her the package was magnified tenfold now that she had leisure to think about it.

What was inside it? Money to secure the old couple's freedom? Or something more important on the international scale? It didn't take a genius to know that Philip's job, involving as it did nuclear research, was a sensitive one as far as East-West relations were concerned. He'd never talked much to her about what he actually did, but she hadn't asked him, either, knowing her own limitations in the field of science. For all she knew, she mused as she used the hotel's hard-milled soap to lather herself, Philip could be bartering nuclear secrets in return for Elena's parents. Vienna, where she was to deliver the envelope to this Hilda Keller, was a hotbed of intrigue and double-dealing. . . .

Grinning at her own soaring imagination, Lindsay rinsed off and stepped out of the tub, reaching for the biggest of the fluffy white towels hanging on the rail. Philip was too much of a proud loyal Englishman to sell out to foreign powers, for whatever reason. Besides, he'd assured her that there was no danger to her in delivering the missive, and she trusted him completely.

The door bell buzzed discreetly as she walked back into the elegantly furnished bedroom, and she frowned as she went toward it, tightening the belt of her white terry robe. A passenger, she guessed, presenting her with one of the minor crises that inevitably cropped up on the first night out. Why couldn't they have telephoned, she wondered irritably, though she made a conscious effort to erase the scowl from her face.

Unlocking the door, she pulled it wide, her fingers tightening on the V of her robe when she saw Carey Hudson framed squarely in front of her—a completely transformed Carey Hudson. His thick dark hair was brushed neatly back from his tanned forehead, a plain white shirt made a stark contrast to the black of his evening suit—no frills or colors for the hard-nosed company snoop—and his mid-brown eyes made her feel at a distinct disadvantage as they roved assessingly over her skimpy attire.

"Mr. Hudson. Can I help you?" She injected helpful but cool inquiry into her voice.

"I certainly hope so." The predatory gleam in his eyes made her feel naked, as indeed she was under the robe. Her tone changed perceptibly from cool to frigid.

"It wasn't necessary to come in person, Mr. Hudson. You could have reached me by telephone."

He shook his head, and even that gesture was annoyingly self-assured. "Not so. I've been calling you from my suite for the past fifteen minutes, and nothing happened. I was on my way out and thought I'd take a chance on catching you in person."

"I assume it's not an emergency, then." Lindsay tried, and failed, to keep the tartness out of her voice.

"It depends on what you mean by an emergency." He shrugged and came closer, leaning against the door frame as he eyed her quizzically. "Would you describe a male passenger desperate for company at dinner in romantic Paris as being an emergency situation?"

Something of Lindsay's skepticism was reflected in her near black eyes. The biggest misconception in the world would be to believe that a man like Carey Hudson was unable to find a suitable female companion for an evening in Paris.

"I'm afraid my duties don't include finding dates for single male passengers," she pronounced crisply, beginning to close the door.

"Just a minute." His lean, hard-boned hand pressed the door open again. "How do you know I'm not married?"

"I was referring to your ticket basis, not your marital status, which doesn't interest me in the least."

His black-lashed lids drooped over his yellow brown eyes. "Well, I'm not married. Have you any idea how refreshing it is to meet a woman who's not interested in changing that state of affairs?"

"You have all my sympathy," Lindsay retorted dryly, "but don't count on me to help you out. Fraternizing too much with passengers is definitely frowned on by the company." Which he should know, if he was in fact the sleeper—or was he testing her?

"Oh? What's the company's interpretation of too much?" He insinuated himself a little farther into the room. "I hadn't planned on ravaging your personal or company morals...unless, of course, you make that choice for yourself. Come on," he coaxed ingratiatingly. "What the company doesn't see it won't worry about."

Oh, really, how obvious could he get! "You're very new at this job, aren't you?" she asked with a trace of indulgence. He gave her a blank stare.

"How did you know—"

"That you're the sleeper?" She smiled with sudden freeness into his startled eyes. He seemed naively surprised, and she liked him better for it. "It's not surprising that the new owners of Eurospan should want to check up on our performance. I'm just surprised that they didn't find someone more...." She hesitated delicately, for some reason not wanting to hurt his feelings. "Well, usually they're not so obvious."

"I *am* new at this job," he admitted a trifle sheepishly, "and— Look, do you mind if I come in for a minute?" Inbred caution made Lindsay hold her ground, and he shrugged in exasperation. "You know I work for the company, so what are the odds now? I didn't ask for the job. I was stuck with it."

Hearing the murmur of approaching voices along the corridor, Lindsay relented and opened the door wider, closing it as he came into the room. She leaned back on it and faced him thoughtfully.

"So why did you take it?" she asked reasonably, again running her eyes over the male perfection of his confidently set shoulders, narrow waistline, tapered hips. Every attractive line of him proclaimed that he was executive caliber.

"It was that or—" He stopped abruptly and stared at her, his eyes shrewd under his heavily marked brows. "How much do you know about the Endor Corporation?"

"The what?"

He sighed, then went on with exaggerated patience, "The company that just bought out Euro-span."

"Oh. I know nothing at all about it." She shrugged, the movement parting the terry robe to expose the clear valley between her breasts. Her hand went quickly to adjust the slackness, but not before his gold brown eyes dropped to the suggestive rise of honey-toned flesh. "It doesn't really matter to me who sits in the high seat. I do my job in the same way, whoever's there."

It was obvious her reply hadn't pleased him when

he frowned and said tensely, "You should take an interest in the company that employs you. It's a vast one, and there are lots of opportunities for bright young people."

"Like yourself?"

He nodded seriously. "You could say that. My—the president, J.C.—believes in his top people knowing how the bottom layers function—which is mainly why I'm along on this trip."

So he *was* an executive, putting in mandatory time as a spy for Endor's new acquisition.

"I'm not overly ambitious at this point," she stated coolly. "I'm happy in what I'm doing, and I do it well, I think."

"From what I've seen so far—" he nodded "—I'm inclined to agree. But I'd prefer to discuss the whole setup over dinner. I understand that your time is taken up during the day by your duties, but your nights are pretty well your own, aren't they?"

His words conjured up the sensual indulgence of Arabian nights, and Lindsay felt a distinct pang of disappointment. Somehow she had expected more of him than the usual heavy groping after a dinner date.

"I don't work nine-to-five hours, Mr. Hudson," she said sharply. "But I have a duty to the pa—"

"So you'll have dinner with me," he said, more as a statement than a question as he moved past her.

She gave him a burning look. "Do I have a choice?"

"None at all," he came back blandly, giving her a tight smile as he turned back to face her. "Shall we say thirty minutes? I'll be waiting in the bar downstairs, the one just off the lobby."

Lindsay almost slammed the door behind those confidently set shoulders. Then she turned back into the single room that nevertheless sported a capacious double bed. God, how she hated his type! Confident, too sure of his own business acumen and his attraction for women, careless about the tender feelings of those less hardy than he.

*Well, Mr. Hudson,* she mocked silently as she went toward the closet, *I'll have dinner with you, but you can forget the romantic night hours.* She'd like to keep her job with Eurospan, but not in return for the favors of her bed. She'd met too many of his foot-loose type, who expected sex in payment for a dinner his company was paying for—in this case, the Endor Corporation. Endor—eagle—bird of prey. Appropriate.

Impelled by the promptness that was now second nature to her, she entered the elevator thirty minutes later and pressed the button for the lobby. Even without the openly admiring glance of a man in evening dress who got off at the second floor, she knew she looked her best. The sleek fit of the white silk dress she had bought on a whim in Rome last summer, its folds softly draping over the fullness of her rounded breasts, contrasted dramatically with the warm tan of her shoulders. Topped by a matching stole in heavy silk, the dress imbued her with a confidence that would more than match Carey Hudson's worldly attractions.

A flurry of fur, mosaic-patterned dress and perfume applied with a lavish hand greeted her when she stepped off the elevator.

"Ah, there you are, Miss, er—" Lila Beaumont gasped breathlessly. "I've been waiting for you to ask if you— Well, I know you recommended the hotel dining room, but it looks so...unfriendly. I'm all alone, you see," she explained as if Lindsay didn't know, "and nobody seems to care about elderly ladies traveling on their own."

Elderly ladies indeed, Lindsay scoffed silently. Lila Beaumont was easily several years younger than her mother, and Deirdre would have strongly objected to being labeled as "elderly." Still.... Her heart warmed to the hint of tears in the older woman's voice, and at the same time she thought of a marvelous way to spike Carey Hudson's guns. He could hardly object, as a high-ranking officer of the Endor Corporation, to taking along a lonely passenger to dinner.

Smiling, she put a hand on the other woman's arm. "Why don't you come with us? I'm having dinner with Mr. Hudson at his request, for the same reason that you find yourself alone. Come along. He's waiting in the bar." She walked confidently off, trailing the breathlessly protesting Lila Beaumont behind her.

"Oh...well, really, do you think he'd want me to? I'm sure he won't want me along if he's planned on having dinner alone with you, Miss, er—"

"Nonsense. He'll be delighted." Lindsay plowed through the standing drinkers at the entrance to the bar and pulled Lila Beaumont after her when she spied Carey Hudson sitting moodily alone at the far end of the counter, nursing a drink in the shelter of his hand.

His head swiveled as if sensing her arrival, and she could do nothing to prevent the sudden rush of blood to her cheeks when his brownish gold eyes went appreciatively over the cunning cut of her dress, meant to emphasize all that was female about her.

"I brought along Mrs. Beaumont." She dragged the older woman into his view. "She foolishly thought she'd be intruding, but I assured her that you'd be delighted to have her join us for dinner."

His eyes bored calculatingly into hers for a moment before flickering to the palpitating woman beside her. "Of course," he confirmed brusquely. "Can I get you ladies something to drink?"

"Oh, I'd love—"

"No, I don't think so," Lindsay overruled the other woman's eager acceptance. "I don't know about you two, but I'm absolutely famished."

"So...." Their escort detached himself from his perch and stood up, towering over Lila Beaumont by a foot or more, over Lindsay by several inches. "There's a cab waiting for us," he informed them in a voice that could have displayed more enthusiasm. "I'll go ahead and make sure it's there."

"Oh, dear," Lila Beaumont fretted as his tautly held shoulders cleared a way through the busy bar. "Do you think he really wants me along? I really shouldn't come with you...."

Lindsay put a reassuring hand on her arm as they emerged into the foyer. "Don't be silly. Of course it's all right for you to come. Mr. Hudson isn't the kind of man to say yes when he means no."

She urged the older woman on, and they passed

through the massive glass doors to the canopied, red-carpeted entrance, at the end of which stood a remote and somewhat irritated Carey Hudson by the open back door of a taxi. Of course, Lindsay thought dryly, he *would* be organized about transportation in this busiest of cities during the dinner hour.

She stepped in ahead of Lila Beaumont and slid across to the center, instinct telling her that Hudson wouldn't appreciate the older woman's fluttery nearness in the cab. What she wasn't prepared for was her own breathless awareness of his body close to hers as he catapulted into the seat beside her and passed an irritated arm along the seat back behind her shoulders, making room for himself in the narrow confines of the rear seat.

His instructions to the driver were terse, precise, and Lindsay could almost feel his anger radiating from the hard thigh pressed to hers. Should she be thrilled that a man of his attractiveness was displaying what amounted to a jealous tantrum because their dinner for two had turned out to be a trio? Hardly. He just happened to be one of those men who didn't suffer older women gladly. Younger ones, yes. They probably flocked around him, feeding his colossal ego.

"Oh, my, isn't that the Arc de Triomphe?" Lila Beaumont gleefully massacred the French language as they rounded the flood-lit edifice, edging their way through several lanes of dinner-hour traffic. "Do you think we could stop for a minute and take a look?"

The startled driver, who evidently understood

English, turned his head, the movement coinciding with the pained hiss of Hudson's indrawn breath.

Lindsay leaped soothingly into the breach. "You'll see it tomorrow on the guided city tour. You're going on that, aren't you?"

"Oh, yes, of course." The older woman, distracted, sat back. "Silly to be in Paris and not see everything, don't you think? In fact, I've put my name down for all the extra tours. I can't wait to visit the palace at Monaco. I always thought they made such a nice couple, didn't you? Of course, she hadn't made any movies in years— Well, she couldn't with all her royal duties to perform, could she? Such a shame... that tragic accident. Perhaps the prince will be greeting visitors, though...."

Lindsay leaned back—against Carey Hudson's muscled biceps, she realized in that instant before their arrival at the restaurant—and let the spate of nervous chatter flow over her. Time enough when they reached Nice to tell the other woman that a royal audience was not included in the tour. A sigh escaped her. Her original assessment of Lila Beaumont was proving to be correct. She promised to be the most exacting, and exasperating, of her passengers to date.

Although there was nothing remotely funny in that thought, something about Carey Hudson's long-suffering expression as he helped her from the taxi highlighted the ludicrous situation that the fluff-headed older woman had imposed on them, and her smile was replaced by a throaty chuckle when he drew her up beside him.

"Something's funny?" he growled, tightening his grip on her fingers.

"She's really quite sweet, you know," she comforted him in a low tone, and thought she heard him swear under his breath as he turned to help the befurred matron, who followed her from the cab. While he dealt with the driver, Lila looked anxiously around the deserted side street, where the only sign of habitation was the restaurant in front of them.

"Do you think it's safe?" she stage-whispered, shivering and drawing her mink more closely around her. "I've heard so much about Europe and how careful you have to be."

"I'm sure Mr. Hudson wouldn't bring us to a place that isn't completely safe, Mrs. Beaumont."

"Thanks for the vote of confidence," the man himself inserted dryly from behind. Taking an arm of each, he urged them toward the dimly lit restaurant.

It was small, dark, the atmosphere calling to mind the late last century, even to the flicker of gas lamps attached to the wall beside each booth. Although the area was familiar to Lindsay, the restaurant was not. This kind of ambience had been far beyond her reach in her Paris days.

"Would you care for a drink before dinner?" Hudson, sitting opposite, addressed the question to Lindsay.

She asked for white wine, and then her eyes went in unison with his to the fluttering Lila Beaumont, who, faced with a decision, typically dithered.

"Oh, my," she breathed, "what should I have?

Maybe I should have white wine, too—although that doesn't agree with me."

"There are other drinks besides that," Carey reminded her, his effort to remain patient straining his voice. "You could have Scotch, a martini, vodka, gin—"

"Gin and orange," she decided triumphantly. "That's what they like in England, isn't it? I'll have that." The happy beam on her face was immediately replaced by an indecisive frown, one that was becoming increasingly, and painfully, familiar to Lindsay. "Or maybe I should stick to what I know— I think I'll have Scotch and soda."

"Fine," he said tightly, lifting his hand, and when the waiter approached gave the order in swift perfect French before she had time to change her mind yet again.

Lindsay looked speculatively at him across the red-checkered cloth. He hadn't acquired that flawless accent from taking a crash course at some American language school. She recognized that the idiomatic diction could only have come from living for some time in France, as she had herself.

"How long did you live in France, Mr. Hudson?"

Apart from a faint flicker in his eyes, the question seemed not to surprise him. "I spent a couple of years here in our Paris office." He shrugged. "My— the company I work for has extensive European holdings and feels it's important that company people have on-the-spot experience. Since most of the staff here speaks only French, I had to pick up the language in a hurry."

"You speak it very well, Mr. Hudson," she approved, lifting the glass the waiter placed at her elbow and giving him a silent toast.

"Why don't we drop the formality?" he suggested with a trace of irritation. "We can't spend an entire month together as Mr. and Miss—or—" he remembered the unwelcome third "—Mrs."

"What a good idea," the older woman responded brightly. "We're all Americans, and I think we should stick together when we're in foreign countries. Please, both of you call me Lila."

There was a stilted little ceremony, whereby each of them raised glasses and murmured the others' names. Lindsay was surprised at how acutely aware she was of the way her name sounded on Carey Hudson's—Carey's—lips. His voice seemed to have taken on a more husky, sensual note.

She caught herself up wryly. The wine, innocuous though it was, must be going to her head. What could it possibly matter that the company spy spoke her name in a voice that was almost a caress? Recognizing his physical attraction was one thing; allowing it to go further was out of the question. How many times since Geoff had she felt the stir of desire for a man she was with, and how many times had she backed off at the last minute, earning herself some well-deserved appellations? Besides that, he was a company man, and she could live without that complication.

When the menus arrived, Carey adroitly avoided a repetition of Lila's indecision over the drinks by saying charmingly, "Would you ladies allow me the

pleasure of choosing dinner? I'm very familiar with
this place and—''

"That would be lovely," Lila cried, her eyes bright
from the whiskey as she turned them on Lindsay.
"It's so wonderful to have a man take charge, don't
you think? I certainly miss. . . ."

Lindsay would have preferred to choose her own
meal but nodded agreeably to Carey while the older
woman chattered on about her late husband's protective chivalry. A minor compromising of her independence was a small price to pay for a peaceful
dinner.

The appetizer, tiny shrimp and mussels in vinaig-
rette dressing, was followed by beef bourguignon,
the rich stew originating in the Burgundy region. It
was a dish Lindsay had tried to duplicate when all her
London flat mates had been home—a rare
occasion—but even with the addition of a full-bodied
French wine and the incomparable Dijon mustard,
the flavor had never quite equaled the dishes she'd
sampled firsthand in France.

The Burgundy wine that accompanied the meal
sent the blood circling warmly in her veins, and she
found herself humorously describing her own efforts
to duplicate the dish for the enjoyment of her unap-
preciative roommates. Lila, for once, was silent apart
from an occasional giggle, and Carey was warmly
relaxed and smiling as she recounted the tale with
added comical embellishments, making her feel
bright and witty.

He really was attractive, she mused as the conversation became more general. If only his hair had been

blond and not dark brown, his eyes an electric blue and not a soft goldish brown, his shoulders less confidently wide, she could have opened up to the unmistakable admiration in the eyes that met hers often across the table.

A twinge of irritation shot through her at her own persistent dwelling on Geoff. He had treated her abominably, returning her loving trust with deceit and blithe unconcern. For him, she had been a pleasant interlude in his Rome assignment. For her, at the time, he had been her life, his betrayal spoiling her for any other man.

"Would you prefer cheese or pastries for dessert?" Carey penetrated her introspection.

"Mmm? Oh. I think I'll have cheese. What about you, Mrs., er, Lila?"

"Well, I'm not a lover of cheese," the older woman began doubtfully, and Carey stepped in once more with a suggestion.

"I can guarantee the excellence of the crepes," he said persuasively.

"Crepes? That's pancakes, isn't it? Oh, yes, I love them."

"I think you'll enjoy them. They're very light and sweet." He turned to Lindsay. "Which cheeses would you prefer?"

"I guess some Camembert and a little Roquefort."

"Nothing more adventurous than that?"

"I'm not a particularly adventurous person, Mr.— Carey."

"Strange," he mused softly, his eyes meaningly quizzical. "I'd have said you were."

Another conversation was going on under the surface, one whose meaning was familiar to her. So many men traveling on their own were looking for quickie romances, no strings attached, as Europe's wonders unfolded around them. Why should he be any different?

"What I've asked for will be fine," she said crisply, turning her attention to what Lila was saying. Why should she feel this disappointed because Carey had turned out to be just another hopeful candidate for her bed?

While he indulged himself with the more exotic cheeses she had refused, she watched him surreptitiously. No other company spy, in her experience, had his savoir faire, his total familiarity with his surroundings. Physically, he was a woman's dream come true. Single, with rugged looks that passed for handsome, he was obviously a man stamped for great things in the corporate world. So why wasn't he married? Men like him were pounced on by altar-minded women almost as soon as they stepped through college graduation doors.

The coffee he'd ordered came as she finished the last of her wine and cheese. Sipping the strong sweet brew, she joined lightly in the conversation. Carey, as he now was in her mind, was really quite nice in his handling of the older woman. Lila tended to defer without question to anyone forceful enough to make decisions for her.

"Come to my suite for a nightcap," Lila invited gaily when they were once more in the quiet hotel foyer.

"Thank you, but it's late and I have an early call in the morning." Lindsay looked around at Carey. "But don't let me stop you, Carey. You're not scheduled for the morning city tour, are you?"

"No," he returned evenly, turning to Lila and dazzling her with his smile. "But Lila is, and I wouldn't dream of keeping her from her beauty sleep—not that you need it," he added with skilled flattery, "but I know from experience that trekking around the Louvre and Notre Dame takes a lot of stamina. I could never get enough sleep on my first trip to Paris."

But not because of the rigors of sight-seeing, Lindsay told herself tartly. It took little effort to imagine that the younger Carey Hudson would have been no less attractive to women than he was now.

"Perhaps you're right," Lila conceded as they entered the elevator and sped upward, adding as they reached her floor, "Well, thank you for a lovely evening. Maybe you'll both be my guests for dinner later on in the tour."

"I'll look forward to it," Carey replied with grave gallantry, and as the doors closed he leaned forward to press the sixth-floor button.

"You don't have to come up with me," Lindsay said hurriedly, uncertain of her own emotions.

"I always see my date home," he retorted with the innocence of a high-school senior.

"I'm not exactly a date, Mr. Hudson." She forebore from using his first name, as if that would keep him in his place—he the company executive, she an employee low on the totem pole.

"Thanks for a delicious meal," she went on when the elevator slowed and stopped. "And good night."

She was halfway down the carpeted corridor when she realized he had followed her from the elevator. Was he going to be one of those casual escorts who suddenly pushed for something far less casual? It seemed so, she thought resignedly as they reached her door and he paused there with her.

"Well," she said firmly, "I guess this is finally good night. Thank you again."

She knew he wasn't to be put off that easily when his arms came around her as she sought the doorknob with her key, which stupidly didn't want to find its matching niche.

"Isn't it usual to thank your escort more concretely than that?"

Before she had time to think, let alone form a reply, he had spun her around and into his arms, so that the supple folds of her dress were pressed against the firm outline of his thighs. Her hands automatically splayed in rejection across the front of his dinner jacket, her mind registering its thick smooth lines, her hair falling back from her face. She looked coldly up at him.

"If you want concrete, Mr. Hudson, you'd better go to the nearest building-supply house. You won't get it from me."

The chipped ice in her voice, she thought, would have frozen an iceberg, but it had no such effect on Carey Hudson. Instead, he tilted his head to one side, his faint smile reaching his yellow brown eyes.

"You have a quick tongue, Lindsay," he mused

softly, his eyes crossing her face in a reading gesture, "and I'm wondering what's made you that way. I doubt that you're naturally cold—in fact, I'm pretty sure you're not—so there must have been a man in your life who treated you badly. Or is it that there's a man in your life right now? Is that why you're flashing the hands-off signal?"

Acutely conscious of his warm hands spanning her rib cage, Lindsay stiffened between them. "My private life is just that, Mr. Hudson—private. Now will you please let me go?"

A cold shiver—was it of relief or disappointment—trembled briefly through her when he immediately did as she asked. She caught the soft lower part of her lip tightly between her teeth as she dully watched him bend supply to pick up the room key, which had fallen from her fingers. The traitorous key slid like a hot knife through butter into the lock under his competent hand. Then she was in the room and Carey was closing the door behind them as if he had every right to be there.

"Would you please leave?" The tone she had intended to be assertive came out as a half-strangled plea, and her heart began to beat in her breast like a newly captured bird. What was wrong with her? She had fended off far worse threats than Carey Hudson in the past few years, men made amorous—or worse, violent—because of alcohol.

Carey wasn't drunk. But he was dangerous... dangerous in a way that wasn't too clear to her at that moment.

"I'll leave when I've satisfied myself about something.'' Standing close to her, he reached out a long-fingered hand and again drew her unresisting body to his.

Bewildered by her own compliance, Lindsay stared up into the face that was suddenly so near. He looked different from this angle, his jawline blurred yet predominant, his mouth full and gentle yet forceful, his eyes. . . . She seemed drawn into their yellow brown warmth, her will paralyzed as he bent his head to kiss her. Her thoughts scattered and snatched at brief openings to awareness. His mouth, instead of ravishing hers as she might have expected, was warm, soft, probing. . . unbearably sensual. After an instinctive rearing back of her head, she relaxed against the insistent hand guiding her lips to his, helpless against the languid tide of desire that ebbed and flowed through her.

''No, please,'' she breathed when his lips left hers and traced an erratic pattern of kisses down the warm column of her throat to the pulse that had begun to beat in wild response. Negating her own plea, her body molded willingly to the long lines of his, suppressed needs surfacing as her thighs felt the taut readiness in his. Her hands fluttered up to mesh in the dark thick hair at his nape, and her mouth parted when his lips reached for hers again. She was drowning in a sea of sensation she hadn't know since. . . Geoff!

Her body immediately went limp, her hands falling uselessly on his shoulders, and Carey straightened, his breath coming in heavy rasps as he held her way from him.

"At least I've proved one point," he mocked tersely.

"What?"

"You're not really frigid—and the man you're holding yourself for isn't as important as you think." His hands dropped from her and he stood back, a revealing pulse beating at his temple. "But I have a month to prove my point."

Lindsay stared wordlessly at his well-knit figure as he went to the door and passed through it. She stood immobile for long moments after he'd gone. She felt used...but not really that. That would have meant he'd kissed her against her will.

She turned back into the room, trembling, and removed the dress she'd bought on a whim in Rome. Rome, where she had first discovered love; Rome, where she had stilled her memories with frenzied shopping sprees; Rome, where Geoff had initiated her into the wonders of erotic love.

Dear God, could she really have wanted a smooth operator like Carey Hudson to extend that experience?

# CHAPTER THREE

"SOMEONE'S MISSING."

Lindsay ran the point of her pen rapidly down the list of participants in the morning tour of Paris. Frank and Irene Harben, Paul and Mary Strangeways, Brad and Debora Dakers, the Ferruccis, the Timms, as well as the reserved Joel Carter were all assembled in the red-carpeted foyer the next morning.

"Mrs. Beaumont?" Lindsay's eyes ran quickly from one face to another. "Has anyone seen Mrs. Beaumont this morning?" Drat the woman. She was going to hold them up and throw the whole day out of kilter.

"We met her going back to her room as we came down," Brad Dakers volunteered, turning to his wife, who according to the information card was a writer like himself. "Didn't she say she'd forgotten something, hon?"

"Yes. Yes she did." Debora turned her beautiful but myopic eyes in Lindsay's direction. "I'm sure she'll be down any moment now, Miss Tabor."

"Fine. And please—" Lindsay held up an attention-seeking hand "—I'd like all of you to call me Lindsay. Miss Tabor is much too formal for the kind of relaxed tour we're going to have. Yes, Mr. Harben? Did you have something to say?"

"Yes, I do." The irascible man cleared his throat officiously. "I think you should make it clearer that everybody should be on time. It's now—" he flicked back the cuff of his smoothly tailored sport coat "—ten minutes after nine. We were supposed to move out at nine, and I don't see why we should—"

"Oh, good morning, everybody!" a breathless coo came from the rear of the group. "I thought I was going to be late, but I see I'm not. Isn't it clever of Lindsay to get us all here well in advance of leaving time?" Mrs. Beaumont beamed, meeting Frank Harben's frosty stare without a flicker before going on to confide, "I couldn't remember where I'd put my passport. I searched everywhere in my suite before I recalled that I'd handed it into the desk, as Lindsay suggested."

"Shall we go?" Lindsay, seething inside and smiling outside—the perfect setup, she had often been told, for the creation of peptic ulcers—led her charges to the waiting bus.

*"Bonjour,"* she greeted the tall, practically emaciated city guide who awaited them there. *"Comment ça va?"*

He shrugged his bony shoulders expressively. *"Comme ci, comme ça. Et vous?"*

Her "Don't ask me" in his own language stamped a faint smile on his lugubrious features as he watched the embarking passengers.

"Not many," he commented, still using French and giving her what amounted to a reproachful look.

Mindful that this student of the Sorbonne hoped to carry himself through the winter from the bounty of Eurospan passengers, Lindsay answered with what she hoped was soothing reassurance.

"They are few, but generous, I think."

It would have helped considerably if the weather had been more generous, she reflected morosely as she took a seat toward the back of the bus, leaving the microphone at the front in the capable hands of the Parisian guide. Rain was misting down in thin undulating sheets, blurring the outlines of the historic buildings they passed, filming the wide-spanned windows with a sheen of condensation. But not surprisingly, the guide's romantically accented English held the passengers enthralled, as did the sprays of long-stemmed red roses at each woman's place.

"Good morning," the guide began. "My name is Jean-Paul, and it is my honor to display to you some of the wonders of historic Paris. If you have a question, please ask me and I will be happy to answer it as well as I can." He made an awkward bow, then took his seat beside the driver, looking to right and left as they entered a massive open square.

"You have heard about the French queen Marie Antoinette?" he queried haltingly as the bus edged its way into the Place de la Concorde. "She lost her head in this square a short time after her husband, Louis XVI, was parted from his in this very same place. The people of Paris went in revolt in 1789, you know? They rose up against the nobles, who had everything but left them with nothing. Marie Antoinette is rumored to have said before that time that if the people had no bread, they must eat cake. A stupid remark from one who had everything to those who had nothing, was it not?''

Lindsay, temporarily relieved of her responsibility, settled more comfortably into her seat and gazed unseeingly through the foggy window. Had the fated French queen really said that? Or had her enemies among the nobles spread that and other vicious rumors to bring about her downfall and that of her weak but gentle husband? Lindsay had always been particularly interested in this portion of French history, and she had always found it hard to believe that Marie Antoinette would display such crass ignorance of the people she ruled at her husband's side. How different the fate of France might have been if Louis XVI had displayed less gentleness and more of the flamboyance and vigor of his ancestor, the Sun King, Louis XIV.

"Later—I think tomorrow—you will be visiting the Louvre and its art treasures.'' The guide's microphoned voice broke into her historical pondering. Lindsay blinked to attention, although she could almost recite his spiel herself—without, of course, his charmingly broken English, which always seemed to enthrall many female passengers. "There you will see the renowned sculpture of the *Venus de Milo* and the *Winged Victory*, which is a *magnifique* statue from the second century B.C.''

His eyes flicked to Lindsay's with this last, flamboyantly delivered statement, and she looked away, hiding a smile. Every city guide wanted to enlarge his area of operation, and Jean-Paul was no exception.

Who could blame him? Supporting oneself while attending the Sorbonne was no easy matter these days, and the added separate tour of the Louvre would supplement his meager income. But, she sighed inwardly, the exclusive Louvre guides no doubt needed their share of the tourist pie also.

Lifting her hand, she cleared a space in the condensation misting the windows. The ancient outlines of the Louvre, housing some of the world's greatest art treasures, never failed to impress her. She had tagged along with the passengers on her first trips as tour director, but now she preferred to leave them to the expert ministrations of the designated Louvre guide and find her own way into the lesser-known but no less fascinating sections of the museum. Alone, a product of the twentieth century, she would enter the realm of Louis XVI and his wildly extravagant wife and the times of the earlier Louises of France, even pausing reflectively at the mementos of Napoleon's regime.

Perhaps she would do that this time, too. Unaccountably, a vision of Carey Hudson visiting the museum at her side floated into her mind's eye, a vision she dismissed immediately. How ridiculous to connect him with an interest in prominent people of a bygone age! To him, no age would be more important than his own. For him, the fortunes of one long-dead emperor would be no more engrossing than what was happening to one Carey Hudson right now.

"We are now approaching Notre Dame." The guide's reverential voice entered her consciousness. "This Gothic cathedral was begun to be built in the twelfth century, and it took another full century before it was completed. As we descend from the bus, you will note the two bell towers—twins, no?'' His heavy attempt at humor was greeted with silence. ''When we go inside, you will notice the famous rose windows, which, I am afraid—'' he scowled darkly through the bus windows ''—will not be at their best today. You will have to believe me when I say that no sight is more beautiful than when the setting sun glows through the one which is called Northern Rose. Today we shall see very little of their true beauty,'' he repeated with a Gallic shrug of displeasure that indicated, Lindsay knew, scant concern, according to the mercurial Parisian's view of things. Tomorrow the sun would shine—if not then, it would surely make an appearance the next day.

She opted to stay inside the bus while the group toured the ancient cathedral. She appreciated the opportunity to elevate her legs on the entrance passenger seat, a habit she had acquired early on in her career. Those relaxing minutes would mean more as the tour progressed, enabling her to face the inevitable long days when rest was impossible. Slipping just the heels of her wedge shoes off, she reached down, massaging her ankles.

''You are tired already?'' Pierre Vallon, the driver, swiveled in his seat and raised his dark eyebrows in a penetrating survey.

''No,'' she replied, speaking his language with the fluency she had acquired over the past few years. ''But there is such a thing as being prepared, *n'est-ce pas?*'' The words were accompanied by a wry grin as

Lindsay leaned back against the interior wall of the bus. Pierre knew as well as she that long days lay ahead, days that started at this time of year in darkness and sometimes ended the same way. Days when long hours of travel between stopping points were hard on a tour manager's nervous system, entailing alertness when her real inclination might be to doze, as many of the passengers did.

"There will be few problems this time, I think."

Pierre's statement was half question, half satisfied observation at the prospect of conveying a manageably light load around Europe. By the same token, tips at the end of the tour would also be lighter, but there was the added compensation of fewer demands, fewer complaints.

"Perhaps not." Lindsay closed her eyes and bent her head back to the blue gray suede upholstery. Lila Beaumont could prove more bothersome than the majority of the passengers, but Lindsay's qualms were centered on Carey Hudson.

Physically, he had affected her as no other man had since Geoff. Even now, when her group was being carefully shepherded around the hallowed precincts of Notre Dame by an experienced guide, small fingers of remembered sensation trailed up through the taut curve of her abdomen to her throat, titillating her with visions of what might have happened last night. She drew in her breath in a throat-catching sigh. The long-drawn-out kisses of would-be lovers never inspired more than a faint flicker of interest in her. Carey, in his dangerous way, had been different. Why?

Men with broad, sinuously muscled shoulders and narrowly tapered hips were nothing out of the ordinary. Even men with Carey's rugged forceful features weren't all that scarce. So why did her fingertips still tingle with the remembrance of their touch on the smooth thickness of his jacket, the straining outline of his neck when he bent to kiss her? Honesty, the touchstone of her existence, rose up to plague her.

She had been thinking about Geoff too much, resurrecting the emotions that had led her to his apartment in Rome so long ago. Whether or not her thoughts had meandered purposefully away from Lila Beaumont's inane chatter on the hovercraft wasn't the question. The fact was her mind had been left free to wander in memory passages far better kept closed. Would she have responded to Carey in quite that way if she hadn't already exposed the chinks in her emotional armor?

Anyway—she roused herself to alertness when the subdued murmurs of the Eurospan group reached her unwilling ears—Carey wasn't likely to repeat the previous night's episode. Her sudden lack of interest must have dented his male pride. A vagrant twinge of curiosity rippled through her as she rose to greet the returning passengers. What would it have been like to be made love to by a man like him?

SHE WAITED AT THE HOTEL DESK behind a line of her charges, who were, for the most part, bedraggled and not a little put out by the vagaries of the weather. But then, she reflected, they must have made allowances at the time of their booking for the possibility of bad weather at this time of year.

Paris at any time of year, she reminded herself firmly, was Paris—however sodden the autumn-tinted boulevard trees appeared. At least the bulk of the tourist influx had ebbed by October, leaving the city's historic streets and sights relatively free for the discriminating few. One of the few approached her as she edged closer to the dark-jawed reception clerk.

"Miss Tabor—Lindsay," Betty Timms began hesitantly, "is it possible for you to arrange for Carl and me to stay on here for a while? We're really inspired, and Carl wants to take advantage of the unusual light effects we noticed at Notre Dame and elsewhere."

Carl and how many others, Lindsay thought with dispassionate clarity, but her smile was tinged with understanding when she looked into the earnest pale blue eyes of Betty Timms. So many artists had approached her with the same request, only to find greater challenges in the snatched glimpses of fishing villages on France's southern shores or of Italy's misty grandeur.

"Normally the company would arrange for you to pick up a later tour," she said regretfully, "but this is the last of the season. And I'm afraid the policy is that there are no refunds for a canceled tour unless—"

"What are you talking about?" Carl Timms came up beside them, giving his wife a disapproving frown.

Lindsay repeated what she had told Betty, although she was sure Carl had heard, and his brows lowered farther as he took his wife's arm.

"Of course we're going to carry on with the tour," he said gruffly. "Paris is Paris is Paris," he stated so insensitively that Lindsay winced. "It's still going to be here if we decide to come back."

"But you said...." Something in Betty's softly distressed eyes sent a sympathetic, though faintly irritated, quiver through Lindsay.

"I said I'd like to paint Paris sometime," Carl dismissed her rudely, then forced a smile for Lindsay's benefit as he pulled Betty away. "For God's sake, we've paid for the whole tour...."

Lindsay turned away with a mental shrug, only vaguely surprised that a seeming free thinker like Carl Timms should sacrifice his art for the money aspect of the tour. It was strange how often the ones who looked most like artists were the farthest removed temperamentally. It seemed, too, a rather unhappy marriage of opposites, she mused, smiling abstractedly at the Dakers as they passed, triumphantly waving their key. Betty seemed so very subservient to her stronger-willed husband. However, marital discord among her passengers was none of her business. Her job was to see that they were cushioned in worry-free luxury for the four weeks of the tour.

Still waiting in line at the desk, albeit a little closer to the key-issuing clerk, she let her eyes wander blankly around the deep-carpeted foyer, drawing in her breath when the unmistakable figure of Carey Hudson came thrusting through the glass entrance doors. Her heart jumped so sickeningly in her breast that she turned her back, trembling, hoping he wouldn't notice her and come across. Her own reaction puzzled her, but she couldn't speak to him now, not in front of half a dozen other passengers.

How easy it had been, not seeing him all day, to dismiss last night's scene, or at least reduce it to manageable proportions. Now, with her heart thumping wildly from just one glimpse of his athletic physique, she found herself reduced to adolescent embarrassment. Her shoulders contracted defensively when she heard his pleasantly pitched voice behind her.

"So what did you think of Paris?" he asked.

"Wonderful," Mary Strangeways replied. "You should have come with us."

"I wish I could have. Business isn't too appealing in a city like Paris, but I'm hoping someone will take pity on me and liven up my day by having dinner with me."

"Why not join us, Mr. Hudson?" Irene Harben gave her husband an approval-seeking look. "There's just Paul and Mary and us. We thought we'd try somewhere authentically French tonight."

"I'm sure Mr. Hudson had different company in mind," Frank Harben put in stiffly, giving his name to the clerk and grasping the proffered key with an irritable nod of his head. Favoring Lindsay with a pale gray wintry stare, he asked sourly, "Are we to line up like this to get our suite key at every hotel in Europe?"

*Yes,* Lindsay wanted to reply wildly, *and it's even worse in Florence, Rome, Venice.* Instead she summoned up her best tour-director manner and said courteously, "No, today is the exception, Mr. Harben. The hotel is quite full, and most people return at this hour. I'm afraid waiting a little for your key is one of the drawbacks of staying at one of Paris's top hotels."

"Hmm. Come along, Irene. There's not much time if we're to leave for dinner at six-thirty."

The Strangeways trailed along behind them, and Lindsay glanced up to meet Carey's thoughtful eyes.

"Why didn't you tell the old ba—bat to go to hell? But you wouldn't do that, would you? You're too good at your job to risk offending your clients."

Confused by the seemingly sincere compliment, Lindsay made a flip reply. "Thank you kindly, sir, and I hope you'll put that in your report at the end of the tour." She took her key from the clerk, who knew her and had it ready. Turning back, she said brightly, "Good luck for tonight, Mr. Hudson! I hope you'll find...congenial company." She was unprepared for the fierce grip of his hand fastening on her arm and swinging her around to face him.

"I will if you'll agree to have dinner with me," he said tersely. Catching the surprised lift of her brows, he added, "There won't be a repeat of last night. I realized as soon as I got back to my room that I'd come on far too strong. I'd...like to make it up to you, if you'll let me."

"There's no need for that," Lindsay said with less certainty than she had intended. Damn him! Why did he make her so aware of his attractiveness that she found it hard to meet his too direct eyes? "The company prefers that we don't become too involved with passengers—''

"I'm hardly that, am I?"

"What?"

"A passenger," he answered with an impatience she was beginning to recognize. "There are certain aspects of a tour operation that you could clarify for me, inside problems only you can talk about intelligently."

Lindsay hesitated, not because the flattery pleased her, but she had been a little less than fair last night, dragging Lila along with them so that business talk was impossible. And it seemed feasible that a man like him would delve very thoroughly into every aspect of any operation his company was involved in. About to open her mouth to reply, she was distracted by the sight of Charlene Warner bearing down on them, her arms filled with packages, her eyes lighting up avidly when they caught sight of Carey's well-built frame.

"Well, hello, there." She ignored Lindsay completely. "I've had the most fabulous day visiting the fashion houses—even got squeezed into a Dior show this afternoon, and now I'm whacked out. I think I'll have to have a drink in that little bar over there." She smiled archly in obvious invitation for Carey to join her, deigning to notice Lindsay now, but only to thrust the assorted packages toward her. "Take these to my room, will you, Miss...er...."

A quick flash of temper turned Lindsay's eyes into frosty daggers. "I'm sure the desk will be able to fix you up with a bellboy, Mrs. Warner," she said levelly, feeling a twinge of satisfaction when the other woman's mouth tightened into an unattractive line, which, as she remembered Carey's presence, disappeared instantly.

"I thought it was your job to take care of details like that for the paying passengers," she observed haughtily, dismissing Lindsay as she again turned to Carey with an ingratiating smile. "Will you join me, Mr. Hudson? Perhaps we could take in dinner a little later, too."

His eyes met hers with a quizzically amused look. "Unfortunately I have another engagement, so I'll have to pass it up for this time."

Charlene's eyes narrowed. "Two dates in one day with that beautiful dark woman I saw you having lunch with at the Ritz? It must be serious!"

"It is." He nodded, openly smiling now. "She's the Paris agent for one of our European companies—and very much in love with her husband, sad to say."

"Oh. Well, then, maybe another time?"

"I'll look forward to it."

Traces of the smile still lingered in his yellow-flecked eyes when he turned back to Lindsay. "Eight o'clock all right for you?"

"Do you think you can take two business meals in one day?" she inquired with veiled irony.

"That's why I came along on the tour, isn't it?" He glanced at his watch and frowned. "I have to make a call to the States—so eight it is?"

Lindsay nodded, and he strode off toward the elevator, every inch the forceful business executive. Hard to imagine him making passionate love to her less than twenty-four hours ago! But this evening was to be devoted strictly to business. There would be no more of that. Following him slowly to the elevator, she wondered whether the thought pleased her, or the reverse.

The telephone was ringing in her room when she entered, and she threw her purse and clipboard onto the gold silk of the bed cover as she hurried to answer it.

"Oh, Lindsay, I'm glad I caught you." Sally's English accent floated across the wire from London. "I want to leave early tonight, and you're the only one I hadn't heard from."

"Heavy date?" Lindsay hazarded, kicking off her shoes and sinking into the gold satin tub chair beside the night table, raising her aching feet to rest on the bed.

"Mmm, a real dream of a man—but I mustn't use up company telephone time telling you about him now. He's something like your passenger, Hudson, only not quite so dishy. How is he, by the way?"

Lindsay's heart unexpectedly began a crazy beat as she stared at the wall behind the elaborately scrolled headboard. "He's...fine. He's asked me to have dinner with him tonight, as a matter of fact," she confided recklessly for the pleasure of hearing Sally's appreciative whistle.

"Watch it, dear—remember, he may not be what he seems."

"I'll watch it." For some reason she didn't want to tell Sally that he was, indeed, the company spy.

"Lucky you," Sally said enviously. "The man of

your dreams and Paris, too. It's a fatal combination, you know.'' Her voice suddenly became brisk. ''Anyway, how are things going so far? Any complaints?''

''No, but there seldom are in Paris. There's still a long way to go, and some of the hotels aren't as grand as this one. I'd much rather end the tour in Paris and leave everybody content and happy.''

''They'll be just as happy after the Imperial in Vienna,'' Sally dismissed matter-of-factly. ''Have you telephoned Lucerne yet?''

''Not yet.''

''There shouldn't be any problem, but you might get in touch with them if you think you might be late arriving or anything like that.''

''Don't I always?'' A thread of irritation sharpened Lindsay's voice. At times Sally treated the tour directors as inexperienced children, however many tours they'd undertaken. Sighing, she let it go for this time, and after a few more words they ended the call.

Deciding to have a leisurely bath before getting ready for her dinner date with Carey, she took off her skirt suit and hung it in the closet, smiling faintly as she recalled the three-cornered dinner last night. Carey had been furious to begin with, but on the whole he had handled Lila beautifully.

As he probably did most of the women who came into his orbit, she reflected, allowing her curiosity about the ''beautiful dark woman'' he had lunched with to surface as she lay blissfully in a warm bath. The fact that the woman was married meant little in the circles he moved in. Had he known her when he'd worked at the company's Paris office? Had an affair with her then?

Her eyes drifted down to contemplate her body, looking at it as a man like Carey would see it. He would like the long slender lines of her legs with their permanent dark gold color, the taut yet softly curving rise of her stomach, the full swell of her dark-tipped breasts emerging like islands from the surrounding water. The thought shocked her—that she had wanted him to make love to her last night, wanted to wipe out once and for all the memory of Geoff and the havoc he had caused in her life.

Sitting up abruptly, she reached for the soap and lathered herself determinedly. One day she would test the waters of a new love, but not with a man who simply had to raise a finger to have women come running. . . nor with a man whose first loyalty was to the company they both worked for.

SHE GAZED AROUND in surprise when she realized that the restaurant Carey had brought her to was one she had frequented while studying in Paris. Puzzled, she glanced up at him as he led her up the angled staircase to an upper dining room and to a small red-clothed table that afforded a view, through latticed windows, of a small square in the Latin Quarter.

"How did you find out about this place?" she asked as he settled her in one of the ladder-back chairs and went to take his own place opposite. Even without the formality of evening wear, he looked superbly turned out in a dark lounge suit and a crisp white shirt, the blood red of his tie a perfect match for the red-shaded candle that flickered between them.

"I lived in Paris for two years, remember?" His eyes glowed in the soft candlelight as they went over her simply designed dress of white wool, his dark pupils seeming to contract when they came up to the raven cloud of her hair brushed loosely around her face and lingered on the moist outline of her mouth. Embarrassed suddenly, Lindsay looked down and fiddled with the cutlery at her right hand.

"Oh, yes, so you did." She looked up to glance around at the diners at the adjoining tables. "But I wouldn't have expected an American executive to find his way this far into the Latin Quarter."

"Maybe I didn't have executive tastes then," he responded dryly, acknowledging with a nod the waiter who laid menus at both their places.

"If I may make the suggestions, *monsieur*?" he deferred to Carey, and at the latter's agreement in well-accented French, he delightedly reeled off a complicated list of house dishes that were the restaurant's specialties.

*"Merci, monsieur, madame."* He gave a polite bow before withdrawing to let them make their choice.

Carey frowned down the length of the menu, then looked over inquiringly at Lindsay, who was scanning her own. "Any ideas as to what you'd like? I can recommend the pâté if it's anything like as good as it used to be."

"And I can recommend the bouillabaisse," she retorted, scanning the menu again, "but I can't seem to find it."

"You know this place?" he asked, surprised.

"I studied in Paris for a year," she explained, smiling faintly in reminiscence. "We'd come here whenever we could, which was usually when one or the other of us got our allowance check from the States. But not," she emphasized wryly, glancing around again at the well-dressed fellow diners, "in the rare atmosphere of this dining room. It's a lot cheaper downstairs. A single serving of bouillabaisse could keep a person going for quite a while." Behind her smile, her eyes grew thoughtful as she remembered Helen, Jacob, Paul—all Americans studying in Paris; Michel, Jean-Paul, Catherine—the French members of their group.

"You studied at the Sorbonne?" Carey's eyes took on an intent look across the table before he glanced down at the menu and suggested, "Let's leave that for now and concentrate on what we'll have. What would you like to start with—pâté, escargots, mussels?"

"I'll have the pâté," she selected crisply, never having developed a taste for snails or mussels, despite her years in Europe. She made no comment when Carey, ordering the meal, decided on mussels for himself. A strange kind of tension, spring-coiled inside her, seemed to have robbed her of her appetite, so she asked for a simple sole *meunière* to follow, while Carey ordered a hearty casserole. Out of the blue she wondered what he had eaten for lunch in company of the, according to Charlene Warner, beautiful dark woman. His business acquaintance....

Wine list in hand, Carey ordered white for her, red to accompany his own meal. He was so supremely at home in these surroundings that Lindsay wondered how many women he had entertained in just such a fashion, how strange it was that he had never married.

If indeed he hadn't, she thought, surprised by her own naiveté in believing him without question. It didn't seem credible that such a dynamically attractive man hadn't at least one marriage in his background. Of course he could have; all he'd said was that he wasn't married right now.

"So tell me about yourself," he interrupted her speculation. "What brought you to Paris to study?"

She shrugged. "Oh, I had a flair for languages, and my father arranged for me to stay here with the family of an old colleague of his, the Dumonts. I spent a year here, another in Germany at Heidelberg and one in... Rome."

If he noticed her pained hesitation, he gave no indication of it. "So that accounts for your facility with languages." He leaned back when the wine arrived at the table, waiting for Lindsay to sample hers before tasting his own. At their mutual nod, the waiter filled their glasses and glided away. "Couldn't you have put that ability to better use than in the job you're doing?"

"You sound like my parents." She grimaced, lifting her glass to sip the excellent wine. "I'm happy in what I'm doing for now. It's an interesting life, you know—" she leaned her elbows on the table and directed sparkling eyes at him "—being a tour director. How many women of my age know Europe as well as I do? And I meet lots of interesting people.''

"Lots of pains in the neck, too," he rejoined dryly, the strong fingers of his right hand with their immaculately cared-for nails curling casually around his glass as he lifted it to his lips. "You have a lot more patience than I could ever have. The Beaumont woman, for instance...!''

Words seemed to fail him, and Lindsay smiled tolerantly. "I've met worse—I think!" The smile was transformed into a laugh, and she saw his eyes drop to her mouth. "She told me today that she's been married three times.''

"Don't tell me." He held up a shielding hand. "They all died from aggravation.''

"I've no idea what they died of or if they're dead at all. All I know is that she's pathetically dependent and that she's my responsibility for the next four weeks.''

Lindsay found herself relaxing in a way she wouldn't have thought possible as the meal progressed. This wasn't entirely due to the wine. Carey drew her out about herself and her family, showing a flattering interest in them and even questioning her about her half brother.

"What does your brother do in England?" he asked casually.

Lindsay felt the glow of pride that was never far under the surface where Philip was concerned. "He's into nuclear physics—much more brilliant than I am, in fact.'' she deprecated in a teasing tone, her eyes shining. "He's with the British government's research team, and it's just as well he never talks about his work, because science was never one of my strong subjects.''

"Does he travel a lot in his profession?''

The question might have puzzled her at another time, but for the moment she was too anxious to boast of Philip's importance in the scientific world. "Oh, yes. He goes to international conferences every year. In fact, it was on one of them that he met Elena, his wife. She was an interpreter for the Polish delegation, and they just—'' she shrugged happily "—fell in love. There was a lot of red tape to go through before they could marry, of course, because of Elena's being a Polish citizen, but they battled it through and they've been supremely happy ever since.''

He seemed thoughtful as he ordered filtered coffee, neither of them wanting a dessert from the wheeled cart that was whisked up to their table at length after the main course had been cleared.

"I've told you a lot about myself,'' Lindsay challenged, emboldened by the effects of the wine. "But you haven't said a word about yourself—for instance, why you chose the Endor Corporation for your career.''

"It wasn't so much a matter of choice as of doing what was expected of me,'' he said moodily, a shutter falling over his eyes, making their gold brown warmth cool.

"Your parents expected you to become a corporate giant?''

He smiled remotely. "That's my father's dearest

wish. I've no idea what my mother would have wanted for me; she died when I was six.''

Lindsay let out a faint sigh. ''I'm sorry. It must have been awful for you to grow up without a mother.''

''I didn't,'' he retorted dryly. ''From the time I was twelve, my father presented me with stepmothers who were only a few years older than I was. The only one who had any maternal feelings was his third wife, and I lost interest when she was discarded and numbers four and five came on the scene.''

''Oh.'' Impossible to pretend that she could understand the comings and goings of temporary mothers. Deirdre had always been the mainstay of her own young life, always there, always staunchly loving and supportive.

''But don't let's dwell on my unusual childhood.'' Carey drew her briskly back to the present. ''What I'd like to talk about is your life with Eurospan. Where do you think the operation could be improved?''

IT *HAD* BEEN a businesslike dinner, Lindsay reflected when she closed the door to her room and leaned back against it, hearing Carey's soft footfalls retreating along the corridor. So what else had she expected—a wildly passionate overruling of her tightly controlled sexual feelings? Carey Hudson was competent to do that, she realized, but he had made no effort to do so when they arrived at last at her door. His good-night kiss had been perfunctory, remote, his lips dry.

"Sleep well, Lindsay," he had said. "Will I see you tomorrow? What's on the agenda?"

"The Louvre in the morning, Versailles in the afternoon. I guess you've been to both many times."

"As a matter of fact, I haven't been to Versailles at all. Maybe I should remedy that tomorrow."

She had resorted to flippancy. "Glad to have you aboard. It's an afternoon trip, so we won't be leaving the hotel until one."

"I'll do my best to be there. Good night, Lindsay."

Damn the man, she thought now, crossing to the dresser, finding little to fault in the image reflected back at her from the triple mirrors. Her black hair framed a face that was both animated and wistful, her eyes seeming to form two dark pools. All evening she had felt his admiration, maybe something deeper, as they talked.

Her hand pulled viciously at the zipper of her dress, and she stepped out of it as it fell in gentle folds at her feet. She hadn't wanted any greater commitment, had she?

# CHAPTER FOUR

WITH THE TYPICAL UNPREDICTABILITY of Paris weather, the next day dawned bright and clear. Cloudless blue skies met Lindsay's sleep-hazed eyes when she pulled back the heavy draperies from her windows, and she sent up a prayer of thanks. Not for the Louvre visit—weather didn't really matter for the viewing of art treasures within the overwhelming massive structure. But Versailles was something else again. Only a few miles south of Paris, the exquisite palace of kings was impressive even in wet weather but superb on a day like this.

All of Paris seemed to rejoice in the autumn sunshine. Sidewalk cafés were doing a brisk business as the streamlined Eurospan bus passed along the Champs-Elysées, the air soft and warm and faintly hazy, conducive to locals and visitors alike making the most of whatever balmy days were left before winter set in. Strollers meandered by the Seine's calm flow, Lindsay noted as the bus disgorged its passengers at the Louvre, and she decided to join them instead of wandering, as she had originally planned, in the lesser-known sections of the museum. No city in the world could beat Paris on a day like this, and she had no intention of wasting one moment of it.

As soon as she handed her group over to the museum's English-speaking guide, Lila Beaumont rushed up to her, trailing her inevitable wool scarves.

"Oh, Lindsay, you'll make sure we see the *Mona Lisa* and the *Venus de Milo*, won't you?"

Lindsay smiled. "I won't be coming in with you, but the guide will see that you view the most famous artworks. I'll be waiting here when you come out."

"Oh, dear. I thought you'd be coming in with us," the older woman fretted, and Lindsay was relieved when Joel Carter came back from the main body of the group and offered to stay with Lila.

"I've toured the Louvre quite a few times," he said shyly, "and I'd be happy to explain things to you as we go along."

"How very kind of you," Lila fluttered, her eyes contrastingly sharp as they fastened on Lindsay's. "Why aren't you coming in with us? There surely is nothing for you to do out here."

"I'll be wandering along the Seine," Lindsay explained evenly, "preparing for this afternoon's visit to Versailles."

"Oh, well...."

Lindsay gave Joel Carter a sunny grateful smile when he put a hand under Lila's elbow to lead her toward the retreating group, and she was surprised when color rushed pinkly into his long thin face. Shyness in a man of his age, early twenties, she guessed, was unusual—and welcome in an age of cynicism, she decided, turning back to Pierre Vallon, their driver, who was lighting a cigarette as he leaned against the distinctively marked bus.

"You have made a *formidable* impression on him, that one," he remarked, nodding his jet black head in the direction of the hurrying pair.

"Impression? I doubt if I've spoken more than ten words to him so far."

"A man needs no words to admire a beautiful woman," the Frenchman said in his own language, his liquid black eyes going eloquently, boldly, down over her lilac suit that did nothing to minimize the enticing lines of her figure. "I have told you many times that I would gladly leave my family for you."

Laughing, Lindsay delivered a playful blow to his arm. "What? And have a good woman and four children on my conscience forevermore?"

Still smiling, she turned on her heel and headed for the Seine, intent on joining the strollers. Pierre was harmless enough once he accepted the fact that a woman had no intention of engaging his affections and breaking up a long-standing relationship with his wife. Lindsay suspected that the driver, with the looks of Adonis and the physique of Hercules, had broken his marriage vows time and again, but she had never entertained any real desire to become his light of love. He had often implied that other tour directors were more approachable than she, but that was their business.

Paris was at its enchanting best in the warm autumn sunshine as she walked slowly beside the river, pausing occasionally to browse idly among the prints and etchings offered for sale at stalls along the way. The subdued voices of the traders were in stark contrast to the constant rush of traffic over the innumerable bridges spanning the Seine.

Breathing in the air and atmosphere equally, Lindsay decided that if she ever had a choice of which European city she would live in, it would surely be Paris. History breathed from every cobble of its ancient streets, yet the French were at least as au courant—the world of fashion was a prime example— as any other Western country.

Turning back at last into the Tuileries Gardens, Lindsay felt the familiar excitement of knowing that the magnificent layout of trees and boulevards, with their totally French obeisance to regulated beauty, were the inspiration of the Medici Queen Catherine. The gardens had been perfected a hundred years later by the famous Le Nôtre—the man, she reminded herself for her spiel to the passengers that afternoon, who had been the architect of Versailles.

Glancing at her watch, she saw that it would be at least an hour until the Louvre tour ended, and she sank gratefully onto one of the park benches surrounding the pool where, in summer, children sailed their miniature liners and sailboats. Now there was almost no one to disturb the peace, apart from a few elderly men basking in the last of the hot sunshine.

It *was* hot, and she slid off the jacket of her suit, baring her arms to the sun. Who knew how much sunshine the rest of the tour would hold? Switzerland, yes, perhaps; Nice, almost certainly. But Rome? October could be weather for tanning or miserably cold. The same applied to Venice, where the rains of fall could chill to the bone. Vienna would have the brisk air of prewinter, but somehow weather didn't seem to matter in a city like Vienna, with its opera and music.

Thinking of Vienna brought to mind the envelope

Philip had given her to deliver to Frau Hilda Keller. What kind of woman was she, to take the risk of negotiating the freedom of Polish citizens? Imagination conjured up a black-clad and blond-haired heroine from the Second World War, boldly endangering her life in the cause of freedom. But Hilda Keller was probably entirely different. What would make a woman turn to underground dealings to help an elderly couple reunite with their daughter? Perhaps she'd had—or still had—close relatives of her own in one of the iron-curtain countries. . . .

Too restless to sit still for long, Lindsay got to her feet and began to walk again, her jacket slung over her arm. She smiled and warmly returned greetings to the elderly folk who meandered past on their morning strolls through the gardens, their eyes dwelling with pleasure on her fresh and darkly attractive appearance.

She paused to let the rush of traffic pass before crossing to the Louvre, her eyes reflecting her self-absorption, until a taxi passed in the lane closest to her and she opened her eyes in shocked awareness.

Carey Hudson sat in the back, his dark-suited arm around the slender shoulders of the woman sharing the seat, a woman who turned her head into his shoulder as if seeking the hand that gently stroked the wavy fall of her long black hair.

Lindsay took an involuntary step backward, but Carey was so absorbed in the other woman that he missed Lindsay completely. The taxi spurted ahead, and she watched dazedly until its black outline merged with the other traffic turning the corner. Then she crossed numbly to the other side of the street, her inner vision still filled with that revealing glimpse. His expression had been quite different from any she had seen so far on his roughly handsome features—concerned, caring, even a little helpless.

Helpless? Carey Hudson? She gave an audible grunt of derision, drawing curious glances from a party of German tourists. Blushing, she quickened her steps and headed for the Eurospan bus, noting as she neared it that it was deserted, with not even Pierre's knowing eyes to distract her.

Leaning against the bus as the driver had earlier, she pondered over why she had been so shocked to see Carey in an intimate position with another woman. It wasn't as if he'd pursued her in a romantic way since that first night of the tour. In fact, she recalled again how disappointed she'd been last night when he'd placed that noncommittally cool kiss on her lips by way of saying good-night. So why was she feeling as if he'd placed a well-aimed blow to her midriff?

"WEREN'T WE SUPPOSED to leave at one?" Frank Harben queried irascibly from his seat three rows back.

Again Lindsay glanced at her watch, frowning at the dial that read one-ten. Carey hadn't shown up, despite the delay in departure. Had she really expected him to? Probably by now he was consoling the Frenchwoman in the way he knew best, she thought with unexpected sourness, pulling down her foldaway seat after signaling to Pierre that he should close the doors, her hand reaching for the microphone. But it was several moments before she could compose her voice for speech, her mind filled with glaring visions of a shaded bedroom somewhere on the Left Bank and silken sheets tumbled from lovemaking.

Drawing a deep breath, she said lightly, "Good afternoon, everybody. I'm sorry about the delay in starting, but we had expected one more passenger to join us on our trip to Versailles." She paused. "As we'll be traveling mainly through city streets for a while, this might be a good opportunity to refresh your memory about the royal palace we're going to see.

"In the beginning, Versailles was a simple hunting lodge, built for that purpose by Louis XIII, who gradually bought up most of the surrounding land. The central core of the magnificent Palace of Versailles today is that same hunting lodge, although it was of necessity enlarged to accommodate the courts of Louis XIV, the Sun King, and his descendants. The palace was occupied right up to the revolution, when Louis XVI and his wife, Marie Antoinette, lost their lives.

"I'm not going into detail about the structure itself, because your specially chosen guide will do that much more effectively than I could. However, you may be interested to know that in order to accommodate the Sun King's overflowing court, the city of Versailles was built and to this day is regarded as a masterpiece of town planning—as is, of course, the Champs-Elysées, which was constructed at about the same time."

Into her familiar spiel now, Lindsay heard her own

voice flowing evenly on, pausing only occasionally to point out the more important historical residences along the way. She was prepared, from long experience, for the unified gasp of her passengers as the massive sand-colored palace with its long and narrow blank-faced windows came into view. It was a sight that never failed to move Lindsay herself, and she sat with her charges for long moments after Pierre had parked the bus, drinking in the symbol of bygone grandeur. Finally she clicked the microphone on again.

"I'll introduce you to the guide who'll be taking you around the palace," she explained, glancing at the clock prominently displayed on the front wall above her. "Then I'll meet you back here at four sharp. For those of you who decide not to see at least some of the gardens—which would be a great pity on a day like this; they'll be magnificent—there are cafés to our left, where you'll find any kind of refreshment you require. Please do remember that we must leave right at four to avoid rush-hour traffic, so don't get too carried away with either the gardens or the refreshments!"

Pierre, gallant as always, handed each female passenger from the bus as if she were the most important woman in his life, a great romantic touch for young and old alike. Lindsay led the group toward the palace entrance, pointing out the former barracks and the kitchens where the royal food had been prepared in lavish abundance.

"The serving men had to rush across this cobbled courtyard," she expounded, "up a long flight of stairs and endless corridors in order to keep the dishes warm, but it was seldom that anyone, including the king himself, ever ate a really hot meal. Being a servant in those days was no picnic!''

Murmurs of revolutionary sympathy for the long-dead servants filtered through to her from behind, and she smiled inwardly. Few of the moneyed Americans taking the tour had any real conception of what it must have been like to live in the days when life was cheap and a servant had no significance at all in the scheme of things. That fact seemed surprising, when the complement of servants numbered around fourteen hundred or more in the heyday of Versailles. None of her passengers, she guessed, would have expressed an atom of sympathy, let alone taken measures to improve the conditions of lower class people, had they themselves lived as nobles in that age of splendor and appalling poverty. Would she, had fate designated her to live as Marie Antoinette?

''How could they eat anything, knowing there was such hardship in producing the food?'' Debora Dakers wondered aloud, and Lindsay warmed to her sincere distress. But her husband, Brad, inserted a cool note of realism.

''Oh, come on, hon. Things were different back then. The peasants expected to be treated that way, and they were probably damn glad to have a job in the royal household. It's not like expecting Maggie to cook dinner for us in primitive conditions and then run a mile to lay it on the table.''

Presumably Maggie was the Dakers's family cook back in the States, and Lindsay agreed with the level-headed Brad that conditions of three centuries ago had no application to today's situation. Still, she was ambivalent about the gross luxury enjoyed by a minute portion of the population while the rest scratched for a meager living, although another part of her thrilled to the sight of an opulence that would never be seen again.

After handing her group over to the expert guidance of a vivacious Frenchwoman, Lindsay wandered alone into the gardens through a side gate, deciding that sunshine was more important than gilded grandeur. Passing the Orangerie, which in the days of the Sun King had sheltered more than a thousand orange, palm and pomegranate trees, she walked over to the outdoor ballroom. It was situated in a grove of trees that secluded it from the rest of the overwhelmingly splendid gardens. Louis XIV had held balls here from time to time, his guests dancing on a central marble floor that no longer existed.

Instead, the gold and yellow of autumn leaves made a crisp colorful carpet for the floor of the arena. Lindsay's imagination took flight as she sat on the top tier of the rock-and-shell stonework and leaned forward, her elbows resting on her knees, her hands supporting her chin as she gazed pensively around.

The creative side of her vivid imagination had always been a natural gift for her, and within moments the isolation of her surroundings faded and the Romanlike arena became peopled with the shadowy mortals of long ago. She heard the music of the king's musicians, saw the elegant figures of both sexes in imported brocades, satins, lace, taking measured steps across the small dance floor. She felt a distant summer evening's warmth on her skin. Her own dress of white satin interspersed with the dull gleam of gold thread was tight at the waist and rib cage and pushed her rounded breasts up to semiexposure under the low bodice.

But magnificent though her gown was, she was outdone in splendor by the man who approached her and asked her to dance with him. Her eyes were dazzled by the yards and yards of varicolored ribbons adorning the man's fashionable suit, the heeled shoes and the elaborately dressed white wig that added inches to his height.

In French he murmured, "Will you dance with me, *madame*?"

*"Oui,"* she responded in a flattered whisper, and half rose to go into his arms. At the same time, the chattering voices of twentieth-century children touring the gardens brought her crashingly back to reality. Straightening completely, she whirled around to face the all too real man who had asked her to dance. "Whwhat are you doing here?" she stammered, her cheeks reddening furiously with embarrassment.

"Seems I came just in time to be part of that dream you were having," Carey remarked lightly, taking a seat on the narrow-tiered ledge where she had been daydreaming and pulling her down beside him. The lightweight, beige-colored suit he was wearing made him look like an aristocratic Frenchman, but the dusty stone seat would do nothing for its immaculate appearance. "You seem surprised to see me," he went on, an odd kind of glow in his eyes as he turned his head to look at her. It was almost as if he were happy to be there with her—but, she reminded herself dryly, that was probably the aftermath of his assignation with the dark Frenchwoman. "I said I'd try to make it."

"I presumed you meant on the bus." She sounded prim, and he gave her another sidelong glance.

"That was my intention," he said evenly, "but something else came up."

"Yes, I know."

His brows shot up as his expression sharpened, and Lindsay wished she could bite her tongue out.

"How could you possibly know that?"

"I—I happened to see you as I was crossing from the Tuileries to the Louvre. You seemed...occupied."

"Oh." After the one softly spoken word he said nothing for several moments, and Lindsay squirmed in agonized self-reproach. What in the world had prompted her to let him know she'd seen him in that distracted intimate moment? She'd sounded more like a suspicious wife than a relatively insignificant employee of the Endor Corporation. "And what conclusions did you draw when you saw me with Mariette?" he added then, almost casually.

"It's not my business to draw any conclusions about my passengers' activities." Again she sounded prim.

"But you're bound to have thought something when you saw us in what must have been a compromising situation at that point."

Lindsay waved a dismissing hand and tried to control the flash of pink into her cheeks. "As I've said, it's not my business."

"Did you think we were lovers?"

"Oh, really!" She started to get up, only to be pulled back to his side, this time much closer, so that the hard line of his thigh pressed implacably against hers.

"At one time we were lovers," he said deliberately, as if trying to shock her. Her involuntary gasp proved he'd hit home. "But that was a long time ago, and it only lasted until she met the man she's now married to. We're no more than friends now, and it's a friendship that includes her husband. She happened to need a shoulder to lean on today, because Philippe met with an accident this morning and I was taking her to the hospital. We didn't know his condition until we got there and found it was just a minor traffic accident."

Acutely uncomfortable, Lindsay muttered, "You don't have to tell me all this. It's—"

"I know. It's none of your business," he finished dryly, then reached out with his hand, sliding it down over the sleeve of her jacket until it touched hers. She stared down stupidly, noticing the way his dark tan contrasted with the lighter olive of her skin. "I'd like to make it your business, Lindsay. Last night, I— When I got back to my room I realized how much I'd wanted to stay with you, to make love to you. I sensed that you wouldn't have been altogether unwelcoming. Am I right?"

Sweeping anger made her voice quaver. "You sensed too much, Mr. Hudson!" she exclaimed brittlely. "My job doesn't include quickie affairs with passengers, even if they are executives of the company.'' She jumped to her feet, so humiliated that she could have screamed and stomped on the dried leaves underfoot. It was too soon to recognize that her anger was spurred by his accurate gauging of her feelings. ''Now if you'll excuse me, I have to get back to the bus and do the job I'm paid for.'' Oh, God, now he would think she wanted extra for sexual services!

But that thought was apparently far down on his list of considerations. Standing, he easily topped her by several inches in height. He seemed unflurried, almost pleased. That annoyed her, too.

''I had no intention of treating you like a one-month stand, if that's what you mean—or of using my position with the company as a persuader. Nor have I ever paid for what can be a mutually satisfying relationship. All I'm saying is that I'd like to get to know you better, and if in the process we both feel we want to take it farther, then. . . .'' He shrugged, drawing her reluctant attention to the broad lift of his superb shoulders.

Had he been this cut-and-dried in his affair with the beautiful Mariette? Or had he grown cynical about the man-woman relationship later, when she had rejected him for the man who was now her husband? Either way, Lindsay wasn't about to fall at his feet in maidenly swoons.

''You'll get to know me quite well as the tour progresses, Mr. Hudson,'' she deflated him crisply. Glancing once more at her watch, she said, ''Meanwhile, I have a job to do.''

''I'll walk you back to the bus.'' He accepted her

decision so readily that her emotions did another flip. Her rejection seemed not to have affected him at all.

"How did you get out here?" she asked coolly as he followed her from the gold-leaved ballroom, matching his long stride to her shorter steps.

"I got back to the hotel too late for the bus, so I rented a car—it's a beauty." Suddenly he changed into another personality, this time a boy eager to impress her with the intrinsic qualities of the car he had rented. "It's a Mercedes 450SL and it goes like the wind. I should really get one of those for back in the States."

He said it so nonchalantly that Lindsay could only conclude that Endor must pay its executives extremely well. A twinge of curiosity had her wondering what Carey's life-style was like back in the States. A Park Avenue penthouse would go with the quality of the suits she'd seen him wear so far, and an elegant attractive woman to drape on his arm when he attended social functions. No permanent attachments, of course—just a series of bedmates for "mutually satisfying relationships." Huh!

He touched her only once as they walked back toward the parking area, and that was only to draw her back to a standstill as he drank in the grandeur that was Versailles.

"It's a fantastic pile of stones," he commented with quiet admiration, "but I wonder if they felt it was worth it when the ax fell on their necks."

"Unfortunately," Lindsay retorted, never able to resist an appeal to her historic sense, "Louis XVI and Marie Antoinette paid for the accumulated sins of their predecessors."

"Wasn't it always that way then?" he suggested as they resumed walking. "Charles I in England was beheaded because he'd been following the precepts of divine rule handed down by his royal ancestors. Czar Nicholas of Russia and his family were executed because he favored the autocratic rule *his* forebears had established."

"That's very true—" she entered into discussion eagerly "—but can you blame them for sticking to the only principles they knew? In hindsight, it's easy to see what they should have done to save themselves and the monarchy they felt was a God-given trust, but—" She stopped, not only because they had skirted the palace and were now approaching the parking area, but because his knowledgeable interest betrayed a fairly extensive study of her own passion, European history. It was the last area in which she would have expected them to find common ground, and the realization intrigued her so much that when he asked if she had time for a drink before taking up her duties, she accepted without hesitation.

Miraculously, he found a reasonably secluded table at the rear of the crowded café. Lindsay ordered café au lait in prosaic contrast to his request for coffee and cognac. Their knees touched of necessity under the tiny table for two, and Lindsay was unbearably aware of the intimate pressure of his hard kneebone and sharp male shins against her own. She began to chatter in a way totally alien to her nature.

"Of course, if you go farther back in history, to Roman times, say, you'll find the same kind of slavish obedience to customs handed down from previous emperors. Have you studied Roman history at all?"

she asked brightly, stirring too enthusiastically at the coffee the waiter had placed at her elbow.

"Not a lot," he returned laconically, appearing almost bored. "Not after I realized that they threw away so many golden chances to make lasting changes in the world because of their foolish decadence and self-seeking."

"I suppose they did," she acknowledged, "but they laid the foundations of much of our civilization today. Just think of—"

"Will you have dinner with me tonight?" he asked tersely, interrupting her nervous flow, so that she stared at him, stricken.

"I—no. I already have a date for tonight," she improvised hastily, for the moment not questioning her automatic defensive response.

Carey frowned. "Oh? One of your friends from Paris days?"

"Well, yes, as a matter of fact." She seized on the excuse. "Michel has been— Er, he's been tied up in legal matters so far this trip, but he's free tonight." Would Michel forgive her for the lie that was less than white? Of course he would. What he didn't know would never hurt him.

"He's a lawyer?"

"Yes, he is. He—he's with the justice department." That was no lie. Michel had risen brightly and very rapidly on the French legal scene. He also had a superbly chic wife and three charming children.

"Is he the man in your life?"

She stared at him uncomprehendingly. "The... what?"

"The man you're holding yourself for. Oh, come on, Lindsay," he said impatiently. "I'm not a complete idiot. That first night in Paris, you were soft and warm and, yes, even passionate—until you thought of him."

And he was entirely too astute for her good, she told herself sharply. Summoning a cool clipped tone, she retorted, "I'm not saving myself for anyone, Mr. Hudson. Michel happens to be a very special person in my life—" that was no lie "—and I see him whenever I'm in Paris. He's—"

"Well, I do declare!" a delighted voice sounded beside them, and Lindsay looked up to meet Lila Beaumont's beaming smile. The other woman held up a waggish finger, waving it back and forth in an irritatingly coy arc. "No wonder you didn't join us on the tour of the palace!" She sank uninvited into the chair her long-suffering companion, Joel, purloined from a recently vacated table. He drew up another from the same source to sit close to Lindsay.

"Goodness! That guide must have taken her manners from those awful women who carried out Hitler's orders! Would you believe that she screamed at me just because I laid the point of my little finger on one of her precious tapestries? Confidentially, Lindsay—" Mrs. Beaumont leaned closer, "—I'm sure you could find someone less...aggressive than that woman to conduct the tours. Why, she even—"

"Madame Rivien is one of our best guides," Lindsay said coolly. "If she's a little enthusiastic about preserving the relics of Versailles, she has every reason to be. Her ancestors were advisers to the French kings in matters of taste.''

"Really?" Lila's supreme indifference showed. "Well, I think you should find someone more...congenial to tourists. I mean, it's all very well—'' her Southern accent deepened ''—but after all, we *are* paying passengers, and I think the least she could do would be to show a little respect for our...status.'' She turned an arch smile on Carey. "Don't you think so, Carey?''

"If she's what Lindsay says she is," he responded dryly, "then I'd say no. I imagine that if my ancestors were responsible for so much grandeur, I'd be inclined to watch every tourist finger mark on priceless tapestries, too.''

Lila seemed offended. "Well, I hadn't been swishing my hands around in hog swill, as she seemed to think! What's wrong with trying to put yourself in Marie Antoinette's shoes by touching the wall hangings she'd touched?''

"Multiply your fingers by a thousand," Carey retorted, "and you have a tapestry smudged by skin oil...."

Losing interest in a battle she had seen fought many times before, Lindsay turned with a strained smile to Joel. "How did you enjoy Versailles?''

"M-me?" he stammered, his shallow skin flooding with pink from her attention. "Well, I—a lot of people thought, you know, how decadent it was, but—I really enjoyed all that gilt and elegance. I wouldn't have liked being a court flunky in those days,'' he admitted shyly, "but I sure would have liked being the Sun King for a while!''

Lindsay suppressed a smile. The mind boggled at imagining the diffident Joel in the role of absolute monarch. The retiring Louis XV, maybe, or easygoing Louis XVI, but the flamboyance of the Sun King? It didn't seem likely. Still, he was nice in his shyness—a direct contrast to the man sitting directly across from her.

"I know what you mean," she agreed, able to better understand a man who wove such fantasies. "I keep reliving Marie Antoinette's life and doing my darnedest to alter the course of history."

"Really?" Joel grinned with incredulous eagerness and followed her like a puppy dog when she made her excuses to an animated Lila and a bored-looking Carey, threading her way outside. There were still twenty minutes until departure time, and Pierre was nowhere to be seen, having locked the bus and gone off to join the other drivers in a small café tucked away at one end of the street.

"I really envy you, you know," Joel confided bashfully, leaning with her against the bus that was warmed from the sun. "You know so much about it all, and you speak French so well, too." His long sensitive fingers brushed the brown lick of hair from his forehead. "Where do you eat dinner?" he blurted out, boldly for him.

"Dinner?" The roar of a powerful sports car drew her attention to a roofless, blood-colored blur shooting past them. Behind the windshield, Carey concentrated frowningly on the dark cobbles ahead of his spinning wheels, his lean features immediately recognizable. She and Joel must have been clearly visible to him, but he spared them not one glance. For a moment Lindsay experienced a surprisingly strong vision of herself sitting there beside Carey, her black hair flying in the wind, laughing with him. . . .

"Oh, I . . . don't eat anywhere in particular." She recalled Joel's burningly spoken question as the flashy car disappeared, emitting a blue gray puff of diesel fumes.

"Would you— I mean, could you have dinner with me tonight?"

Lindsay looked at him in surprise and felt a sudden pang of pity for the gently anxious Joel, realizing for the first time that maybe it hurt him to see Carey Hudson so apparently successful, with many of the things in life that Joel might like for himself.

"Yes, all right," she agreed, silencing his subdued effusiveness by placing a finger on her lips, seeing from the corner of her eye that the first of her charges were drifting back. "Meet me outside the hotel at eight—and please, keep it to yourself. I'm not supposed to have dates with passengers."

Obviously thrilled at being singled out for her exception to that rule, Joel nonetheless contained himself as the other passengers began to collect around the entrance, waiting for Pierre to unlock their vehicle. Even when the bus swung out of the parking area and headed for Paris and the holidaymakers claimed Lindsay's attention with their excited impressions of Versailles, he sat with a quiet smile and said nothing.

# CHAPTER FIVE

THE ORANGE GLOW of the hotel lights seemed warmly familiar when she and Joel returned from a run-of-the-mill meal and, if she were honest, the most awkward she'd experienced in a long time. It wasn't the ambience of the tourist-type restaurant he'd taken her to that was responsible—at least, not entirely. The stark truth was that Joel just wasn't Carey. He didn't have the other man's savoir faire, nor that certain chemistry....

She had gone with Joel for just that reason. But unrelieved adoration, she decided halfway through dinner, could be a trial, too. Joel was so obviously smitten by her that his hands trembled as he poured the wine he'd selected. His nervousness impeded the easy flow of conversation and filled her with such ambivalent feelings that she was relieved when he at last asked for the check. For Lindsay found his efforts to please endearing, as she did his flattery, to a certain extent. She also sensed his innate integrity and sensitivity, and guilt mingled with her pleasure as they ended the evening.

"Thanks again for dinner," she murmured as they walked up the steps to the hotel. Lindsay paused outside the entrance, indicating diplomatically that he shouldn't accompany her in.

"The pleasure was all mine," he returned with fervent sincerity. "Can we do this again sometime?"

She hesitated, then plunged in, knowing she had to nip this particular passion in the bud. "No, Joel," she said gently. "I think we'd better stop here before things get out of control. You see...the man I'm going to marry wouldn't like me to see too much of any one passenger."

Had she come on too strong with the flattery, suggesting that she couldn't trust herself to control her emotions with Joel? Evidently not, for his eyes took on a mournfully understanding look.

"I'd hate to come between you and your fiancé," he gulped nervously, but something in the straightening of his narrow shoulders told Lindsay he wasn't entirely crushed by her rejection. Still smiling, she stepped through the glass entrance doors and halted abruptly. A formidable-looking Carey was pacing the floor, his face thunderous.

"Where in hell have you been?" he demanded savagely when he caught sight of her. She might have been wearing Cinderella's castoffs instead of the figure-defining multicolored brocade, judging from his imperious tone.

"Out to dinner," she retorted calmly, although her sixth sense was alerting her to the possibility of passenger disaster. *Please don't let it be a death,* she prayed silently. Nothing so serious had ever happened on one of her tours, though other tours hadn't been so fortunate. She saw Carey's eyes flick over her shoulder to Joel, who had followed her in too soon. "What's wrong?" she asked tersely.

"The hotel's plumbing system went haywire, that's what's wrong!" he stated with icy reproof.

"*All* of it?"

"Fortunately, no. They've had to move the Harbens to a room on the lower floor, and he's screaming blue murder!"

Lindsay almost gave in to her hysterical urge to laugh or to scream her relief. None of her charges had suffered bodily harm, so how important could the failure of the plumbing system in one room be? Unluckily, it had happened in the Harbens' suite, and she could well believe Carey's description of Frank Harben's apoplectic reaction.

Joel stepped forward. "Can I do anything to help, Lindsay?"

"No, thanks, Joel. I'll go up and talk to them." What surprised her most was Carey's disintegration when faced with what was virtually a domestic problem, though it involved public relations. "Which room are they in now?"

"Two-o-one," he grated, grasping her arm as she went to pass him. "You should have been here to cope with something like this—not renewing past pleasures with an old college boyfriend or—" he glanced scathingly at the still-hovering Joel "—with a passenger."

"Now see here—" Joel spoke up with surprising ferocity "—you've no right to talk to Lindsay like that! She's—"

"I'll talk to her any damn way I please," Carey grunted, turning his blazing eyes back to Lindsay when she pulled free of his grasp.

"This is neither the time nor the place to discuss

that, Mr. Hudson. Right now I have to go up and see the Harbens.''

Without making an even more embarrassing scene, Carey had no choice but to let her go, but the furious glint in his narrowed eyes burned holes in her back all the way to the elevator. Riding up, she sourly pondered his officious attitude. What gave him the right to criticize her evening activities, even if they did involve a passenger? Hadn't she spent two nights having dinner with him? Executive of the company or not, she had been just as unavailable for emergencies then, but that fact hadn't bothered him.

Dismissing him from her mind, she took several deep calming breaths as she walked along the wide corridor to the Harbens' door and pressed the room buzzer.

Frank Harben was still, as Carey had aptly put it, screaming blue murder when he let her into the room, which was admittedly much less comfortable than the bedroom suite the couple had occupied.

"I'll be sending a telex to London first thing in the morning," he threatened, a ruffled turkey cock strutting in his wine red robe past the closely arranged twin beds. His wife, Irene, gave Lindsay a nervous smile from where she sat in a blue floral wrap on the far bed, there being no other seating in the cramped quarters. Their ire was understandable.

"We paid for a first-class tour," Frank raved on, "and this is what we get! I want a refund on my money."

"The company will gladly reimburse you for the inconvenience," Lindsay assured him sympathetically, taking the wind out of his sails. "This room has a tab considerably below the suite you had. But there's no need for you to contact London yourself. I'll see to it first thing in the morning.'' She forced a placating smile. ''I'm really sorry this had to happen, but things do go wrong occasionally even in the best of hotels.''

''It wouldn't have in the States,'' he grumbled, but his temper had cooled considerably.

''Perhaps not—'' Lindsay gave way to a spark of irritation ''—but then American hotels don't have traditions going back hundreds of years, as many do in Europe.'' Taking a deep breath, she summoned another smile, mainly for Irene Harben's benefit. ''Anyway, I think you'll find that the beds are very comfortable, and we'll be leaving for Lucerne first thing in the morning.''

''That's another thing,'' Frank pounced as she went to the door. ''Why do we have to leave at such an ungodly hour? If it's such a long drive, shouldn't it have been arranged that we make an overnight stop halfway?''

''We leave early because we like to arrive in daylight, if possible.'' Lindsay reached for the door handle behind her back and squeezed it until she felt the blood drain from her fingers. ''In any case, Mr. Harben, I doubt if any small halfway hotel would meet with your approval. That's why we stick mainly to the larger centers.'' Opening the door, she stepped back. ''Have a good night, and I'll see you at the bus at seven-thirty.''

Retracing her steps along the corridor, she wondered exhaustedly if the job was worth the Frank Harbens of this world. As soon as the question formed, she knew the answer. Despite the complainers, the nuisances like Lila Beaumont, the sweet but awkward Joel Carters, the long hauls between stopovers, this was the life she loved best. What other job would allow her to indulge all her pleasures simultaneously: her love of history, her interest in people, accommodations in world-famous hotels that would normally be far beyond her price range? The good parts far outweighed the bad.

Opening the door to her room moments later, she reached a hand out to the light switch—and a million stars seemed to explode in her head before she slumped, unconscious, to the floor.

SHE CAME TO with the sound of an agonized moan echoing around her; it took several seconds to realize that the sound came from her. More time elapsed as she slowly recognized the softness of a bed under her, a damp coolness at her forehead.

"Lindsay?"

She struggled to open her eyes, but the lamp to her right glared yellowly into them, hurting so much that her lids dropped again. She had to be dreaming.... That sounded like Carey's voice calling to her. But it couldn't be. He was mad at her, wasn't he? No way would he sound that concerned about the monumental ache in her head. She tried moving it on the pillow and moaned once more.

"Lindsay!" Ah, that sounded more like Carey— clipped, short, abruptly impatient. "Open your eyes, Lindsay. Come on."

She tried to shake her head, but the pain that shot

through it stilled her again. "The—the sun's too bright," she whispered.

She heard him give an irritated exclamation, before there was a decisive click and he said, "It's all right now. I've turned it off."

She wanted to giggle. Was he really that powerful that he could turn off the sun just like that? Yes, he probably was.

"Lindsay, open your eyes and talk to me," he said in a low urgent voice that commanded obedience. Slowly, painfully, she forced her lids upward against a tremendous force of gravity. Dimly she saw his face leaning anxiously over her, and she put up a feeble hand to touch the hard rasp of his chin.

"I'm...all right," she whispered, then frowned. "What happened?"

"That's what I hope you're going to tell me," he said grimly, stroking gently at her temple when she winced, then drawing his hand away.

Clarity was returning through the curling wisps of low cloud that fogged her vision like the enveloping mists that occasionally shrouded the high Alps. She remembered talking with the Harbens, entering the elevator, walking to her room...and that was it. But no; she remembered reaching out for the light switch, and—

"There must have...been a power failure as well as...plumbing," she joked weakly. "I went to put the lights on and...they flashed in my head instead of...in the room." Suddenly she catapulted upright, ignoring the heavy pain in her head. "The passengers?"

"They're all right," Carey soothed, his hands firm but warm as they pressed her shoulders back to the pillow. Wearily she subsided. "Try to remember, Lindsay. Was anyone in the room when you came back?"

"No, I—I don't think so," she faltered. "It was the light...."

"All right," he said, sounding resigned. "Try to sleep now. I'll stay here with you."

"I'd...like that."

Had she really said those words that still lingered with her when she awakened hours later, a sun that was no longer blinding filling her room with a soft warm glow? Apart from a dull ache at the right side of her head, she felt rested, tranquil. Her eyes went around the dimly lit room, and she stiffened under the covers when they fell on the hunched figure deep in sleep in the tub chair beside the bed. Carey! What was he doing here in her room at—she glanced at the clock on the night table—at six-thirty in the morning? Had she—had they...?

Despite the numbness in her brain, a faint smile touched her lips. If he had shared her bed, he wouldn't now be sleeping uncomfortably on a chair inadequate for his frame. He would have been here in the bed with her.... Her eyes swiveled around the room and fastened with difficulty on the dress thrown casually over a high-backed chair near the dresser. A multicolored brocade, the one she had worn for dinner with—whom—yes, Joel Carter, the night before.

As remembrance rushed back in an overwhelming torrent, her hands explored under the covers and came up with the information that, apart from the soft fabric of her nightdress, she was naked, undressed by hands other than her own. The obvious inference was that Carey had removed not only her dress but her undergarments before sliding the nightdress over her head. Hot embarrassment flooded over her when she looked again at his sleeping form. Embarrassment and a slow burning anger. Who did he think he was to take advantage of a freak failure of the electric system?

"Mr. Hudson?" she called clearly, coldly. "Wake up, Mr. Hudson."

She thought he was too far gone in sleep to stir, but then his body tensed visibly and his head lifted. Lindsay's voice was stilled in her throat as she watched his lids flutter open, the leap of alertness in the gold brown eyes when he realized that she was fully awake and watching him.

"Lindsay!" His long body unwound from the chair. He came toward her. "How do you feel?"

"I'd feel a lot better if you removed yourself from my room," she snapped, lifting her chin when he paused abruptly and stared down at her. It gave her a perverse kind of pleasure to note that he looked less than his immaculate self. His hair was ruffled and fell haphazardly over his eyes, his chin was dark with a new growth of beard and his clothes definitely looked as if they'd been slept in—which they had. "I have to get ready for the day's trip to Lucerne," she pointed out dryly, holding the covers up to her chin, although it was probably too late for modesty now where he was concerned.

"You're sure you feel all right?"

"Of course I do," she stated loftily. "I got a shock from a faulty electric system, but I'm all right now. So if you wouldn't mind . . . ?"

"You don't remember hearing someone in your room last night before you blacked out?" he persisted, inspiring her to higher levels of irritation.

"No, I don't remember any such thing. It was a simple short circuit, not an international intrigue to get rid of me," she ended sarcastically, itching to throw the covers back and get into action but prohibited from doing so by his overly solemn presence. "Look, I'm all right," she insisted. "Why would anyone want to harm me? I—" she belatedly remembered her manners "—I'm very grateful for your concern, but truly there was no need for it. I'm fine."

It was only when he'd gone, tight-lipped, from her room and she was shrugging off her nightdress before getting under the shower that her own words came back to haunt her.

Of course there was no danger, no sinister-looking men out to get her. But.... Turning off the shower, she padded naked into the bedroom and pulled open the doors of the closet. Her travel bag seemed undisturbed, even the section where Philip's letter to the Austrian woman had been secreted. She had recently deposited the buff envelope safely in the hotel's security box. What else had she expected? Razor-blade slashes delivered by pock-faced agents of a foreign nation? It was too ludicrous to think that two elderly people, Elena's parents, could stir up an international intrigue.

IN THE FOYER later that morning, Pierre was supervising the collection of luggage destined for the stowage area of the bus.

"We are two rooms short," he grumbled, not at his suave best at this early hour.

"I'll hurry them up," Lindsay promised. Several cups of strong black coffee had helped to restore her to her old efficient self, and she now ran a practiced eye over the mound of luggage. "Who's missing?"

"Four-two-one," Pierre supplied grouchily. "And I think three-six-two."

A swift rundown of the clipboard lodged at her bent elbow told Lindsay that one of the delinquents was Lila Beaumont, the others, Frank and Irene Harben.

"Three-six-two was the Harbens' suite," she explained, "but they had plumbing problems and they're now in room two-o-one. You see to them while I rouse Mrs. Beaumont."

The travel morning thus started badly, and Lindsay sensed a distinct lack of interest in her patrons as she delivered her informative lecture over the intercom on the areas of importance they were passing through. Signposts to Fontainebleau, Villeneuve and the wine regions of Chablis and Beaune elicited little response. The headache that had left her that morning again began to send hammer points of pain into her skull on the right side. Her eyes happened to meet Carey's in the large rearview mirror, and something of her agony must have communicated itself to him, because he rose from his seat in the back of the bus and came down the aisle to grab the microphone from her hand.

"Why don't we liven this scene up a bit and let the tour director sleep off her heavy night?" he said with a leer that brought reluctant smiles to the bored faces of the passengers. He seemed not to hear Lindsay's indignant gasp as he went on, "Vineyards are all very well, but speaking for myself, I'm only interested in them if I see their products filling up the glasses on a dinner table!"

Encouraged by Carl Timms's whoop of "Right on!" he spent the next two hours cajoling passengers up to the front to display their artistic talents in song, speech and lewd limericks. Lindsay, her hands folded tightly in her lap, cringed at first but gradually relaxed as she realized that responsibility had been lifted from her shoulders for a while. But at the same time she felt a slow-fired resentment growing as Carey stepped out of character and became the jocular master of ceremonies.

The resentment simmered until Tony Ferrucci called plaintively into a momentary pause, "When are we stopping for lunch?" Standing, she took the microphone decisively from Carey's hand and said with cool efficiency, "In about ten minutes. There's a highway restaurant near Dijon, one of the few open at this time of year." She scarcely noticed as Carey passed back along the aisle to his seat. He swung into it and stared at her with attentive eyes as she prepared the group for the lunch stop.

"The restaurant is a self-serve place," she said brightly, "but the food is quite good." More to the point, she added silently, it was the only restaurant open within miles, so it was a question of take it or leave it. All of the passengers took it.

"Washrooms are to your left as we go in," she stated crisply as she led the straggling group across the covered ramp spanning the highway. "Tables straight ahead, or there's a snack bar with counter seating for anyone wanting a lighter lunch. There's also a sizable store area where you can buy anything from wicker ware to imported English cookies. But please remember that what you buy now, you'll have to carry around Europe with you, and space is limited on the bus.''

They would buy anyway, she knew, but perhaps they would settle for the small picnic hamper rather than the family-sized rattan chests designed for a dozen. Smiling, she stood in a central spot and watched her charges go their separate ways, the women and several of the men making a beeline for the goodies displayed in the vast store area, the remainder more intent on filling the gap between breakfast and now.

"When do you have your lunch?" Carey asked from behind, and she swung around. Idiot, she told herself, to have so little self-control that no matter how severe she tried to look, nothing could conceal the effect he had on her.

Her cheeks pink, she said, "Oh, I—I'll pick up a sandwich in a while." Her attention was caught then by an altercation at the snack bar. Lila Beaumont seemed to be at the center of it, so with a murmured apology to Carey, Lindsay hurried over with sinking heart to where a white-clad woman behind the counter was erupting into explosive French, wildly flailing her arms.

"What's wrong?" Lindsay asked the woman in her own language, and an almost comical expression of relief crossed the plump face.

"*Madame* asked me for this." She gestured to what was evidently the bone of contention, a dish of a jello-like substance planted squarely on the counter. The woman's thumb then jerked toward a neat stack of ham rolls in a glassed enclosure. "Now she says she has asked for that. I am very busy, *madame*. I have no time to—"

"There's obviously been a mistake." Carey stepped with suave assurance between Lindsay and the palpitating Lila, addressing the woman in impeccably accented French. "The lady has no French, so the mistake was evidently hers." He shrugged regretfully. "Perhaps you would be kind enough to overlook it and allow her to have what she wants?" His smile, if not the flowery speech, was enough to reduce the woman to a state of ingratiating cooperation.

"The woman is not quite...?" She pointed significantly to her head, and Carey unblushingly nodded sadly.

"She is your mother?" The woman's eyes were dark with sympathy, her pressing chores evidently forgotten for the moment.

"Not my mother, but... a responsibility, you understand?"

*"Ah, oui."* She understood, admiration for his sense of duty evident in the tender way she removed the wrong dish and substituted the choicest of the ham rolls. Smiling benignly at them long after Carey had murmured his too grateful *"Merci, madame,"* she sighed as she turned reluctantly back to her duties.

"Thank you so much, Carey," Lila gushed, blinking coyly as she stared up at him. "I don't know what I'd have done without you; she really was quite a frightening person. I *knew* I hadn't asked for that revolting concoction, but I just couldn't convince her."

"Think nothing of it," he said with a smile that set Lindsay's teeth on edge. Pulling away from him as they left Lila to enjoy her well-earned roll, she turned on him furiously.

"Why did you have to interfere?" she blazed. "I could have coped very well without you. Don't you realize that it undermines my authority when one of the passengers steps in and takes over?"

"Aren't you forgetting that I'm not just a passenger?" he reminded her stiffly.

"And aren't you forgetting that you're not the director of this tour?" she countered fiercely, suddenly aware that the Harbens and the Strangeways were looking curiously over at them from where they were browsing among a stack of children's toys. Lowering her voice, she added grittily, "If you want to take over my job and send me back to London, that's fine with me."

"Don't be ridiculous. I saw that you were in trouble and thought I could help, that's all. If you'd rather go it alone—"

"That's exactly what I'd rather do." She added with forced sweetness, "What happens if I get used to a big strong man doing battle for me on this trip? What will I do next time, and the time after that, when I have to cope all by myself?"

"I imagine you'll always find a man to take care of you," he retorted with level insolence, and Lindsay drew in her breath on an indignant hiss. He really was too much.

"I'm perfectly capable of taking care of myself. Watch me—I can even order lunch for myself!" Head flung back, her nostrils twitching with indignation, she marched off to the snack-bar counter and took a newly vacated seat, telling herself she didn't really care if Carey Hudson watched her or not. She'd had enough of his arrogance, his taking over when he imagined she was incapable of doing so. Like this morning.... It would have taken more than a small electric shock from her lamp to render her unable to conduct that or any segment of the tour. And just now with Lila. Nothing could have been simpler than to smooth over that minor incident. Damn him!

Her eyes ran around the noisy bustling highway stop, and she didn't know whether she was disappointed or relieved to find that Carey had melted into the background.

"IF YOU'LL BEAR WITH ME for a few more minutes," Lindsay addressed her weary group when at last the bus pulled up in the forecourt of a famous hotel overlooking Lake Lucerne, "I'll check in at reception and get your suite numbers."

A clerk at the extensive reception desk supplied her with the list of reserved accommodations, and she glanced down at it, making sure every suite had a view of the now darkened lake. With such glorious scenery visible from the front of the building, there would be hell to pay if one of her clients was given a suite with an exclusive view of the working entrails of the hotel.

"That seems fine," she told the indifferent clerk, who obviously disdained coach tours, however exclusive. "My passengers need a hot meal," she stated with a briskness that made his indolence disappear immediately. "It's been arranged, but I'd like you to check and see that everything is all right."

"It is all arranged," he confirmed with more interest, and Lindsay gave him a short nod before hurrying back to the bus. She couldn't really blame the hotel staff. It had been a busy summer for them, and they understandably looked forward to this break between sun and snow visitors.

"Sorry to have kept you waiting," she apologized briefly, "but now I have your suite numbers. Mrs. Beaumont, you're in suite two-three-one. Mr. Carter, you have four-three-four. Mr. and Mrs. Dakers in...." She read off the alphabetical list, only a slight tremor disturbing her tone when she came to Carey's suite, one-o-three. Her own room was on the same floor but situated in a far less favorable position than his double-balconied suite overlooking the wide expanse of the lake.

"Can we get something to eat here?" Tony Ferrucci put forward his perennial question as he filed from the bus behind his wife, Gina.

Lindsay smiled. "Yes indeed, Mr. Ferrucci. The dining room is ready for our arrival, and I'm sure you'll enjoy the cuisine. The hotel's famous for it."

Prodded by his plump pretty wife, he moved on toward the lighted entrance but turned back to say plaintively, "I never thought I'd say it in Europe, but what I wouldn't give for a good old hamburger and fries—even my own." With mournful surprise, he added, "Especially my own!"

"You never know your luck," she joked, hiding the weariness that was now beginning to make itself felt deep in her bones. "I won't guarantee they'll be as good as yours, but I'm sure the chef will do his best."

As usual, Carey was the last to descend from the bus. His immaculate appearance, the neat gray worsted trousers and blue gray loose-fitting sweater, irritated her unduly. It wasn't surprising that he should look spruce and alert, considering the fact that he'd spent most of the time since the lunch stop at Dijon in deep sleep, only rousing when they reached the outskirts of Lucerne. She had timed her historical anecdotes to the sensed mood of her passengers, walking the aisle between times to stretch her legs and take surreptitious advantage of the general lassitude aboard to note that, asleep, Carey lost the harsh lines edging his mouth and resembled the youth he must once have been. For the space of a few minutes, she had taken the empty seat across the aisle and contemplated his sleeping figure.

He had lost his mother at a vulnerable young age, and his father, from what she'd gathered, had been more interested in supplying himself with a succession of beautiful young wives than in providing his son with a mature understanding woman. Was that really the reason why he'd shied away from permanent commitment? Certainly it hadn't prevented him from developing into a man that women found attractive, even those possessed of solid husbands. That much had been evident from the interested glances sent his way when she'd dined with him in Paris. Even the overblown Charlene had been prepared to impale him on her predatory claws.

"You're on the first floor, Mr. Hudson," she said

crisply now. "Suite one-o-three. Dinner at eight-thirty in the Crystal Room."

"I heard your directions earlier," he remarked laconically, following her when she swung around and set a rapid pace into the hotel. He was behind her when she conducted her business with the desk, opening the safety deposit box to insert the Eurospan funds. Then, recalling Philip's letter to Hilda Keller, she withdrew it from her shoulder bag, stuffing it behind the envelopes bearing the company's distinctive logo.

"You would like your room key now, Miss Tabor?" the clerk asked, obviously anxious to relinquish his duties and have his own meal.

"Yes, thanks. One-o-six?"

"Is that satisfactory?"

"It's fine." Turning, she was surprised to find Carey still waiting for her. Barely concealing her sigh, she said tightly, "Is there something else you need, Mr. Hudson?"

"Only to talk to you about what happened last night." He followed her to the staircase, and they mounted the blue-carpeted steps side by side.

Lindsay halted on the landing, her expression annoyed. "Look, Mr.—Carey," she said with forced patience, "I appreciate your concern—I really do—but I think you've been seeing too many spy movies! What happened last night was a simple disruption in the electric system. I got a shock, and it's left me with the world's biggest headache. That's all that happened," she stressed, resuming her climb to the first floor. "I appreciate your sitting up with me all night, too, though I don't believe it was necessary." That must be why he'd slept so soundly for most of the afternoon, she thought belatedly, but she was too tired to indulge in pangs of conscience at that moment. "Your suite is along there." She pointed to the left, hitching up her shoulder bag and heading in the opposite direction without waiting for his reply, if he had any.

She hadn't lied about the headache. Her temples were throbbing heavily, making her feel sick. But that could be from hunger, she told herself as she let herself into the familiar room with its twin beds, twin windows overlooking the noisier, less salubrious part of the hotel. She had eaten little of her lunch, thanks to Carey's interference, but now her mouth watered at the thought of the wild duck in wine sauce for which the hotel was justly famous. There was no time for more than a quick rinse in the adjoining bathroom and a light application of makeup to her eyes and mouth. She would take a bath later before getting into the supremely comfortable bed. . . .

SHE MIGHT HAVE KNOWN the wild duck wouldn't be available, Lindsay thought wryly as she walked back into her room after dinner, but the quickly prepared cheese omelet had been more than a passing substitute. A bigger meal wouldn't have sat well with her anyway, she decided as she started the bath water running and discarded the travel suit she'd worn all day. The pain in her head had abated to a dull ache, and a couple of aspirin would solve the remaining problem.

The bath made her languid, relaxed, the soap she lathered on her body drifting up to penetrate and envelop her senses. Unbidden memories of Geoff's lean hands caressing her breasts, her hips, her thighs, rose to torment her.

*Oh, God.* Alert now, she snapped up the water release and reached for a towel as she stepped from the bath. Why did she still yearn for him like a lovesick teenager? He had used her in the worst way a man could use a woman, had abused her affections, her sexuality, her trust.

She rubbed vigorously at her body, chafing the skin until it glowed rosily. Her teeth bit down on the softness of her underlip as she looked despairingly up into the steam-hazed mirror above the vanity and longed hopelessly for Geoff. He was the one who had made her aware of her body, of the pleasure it could provide. Love had been something for their future, a precious gem to be treasured by that one special man. . . .

A knock she could barely hear sounded from the outer door, and she stared wide-eyed into the mirror for long seconds before reaching for her white terry robe and pulling it clumsily on as she crossed the carpet barefoot. Damn Carey and his imagined attackers! If his intention had been to make a nervous wreck of her, he was certainly succeeding!

"Who is it?" She conjured up a firm voice, her hand poised on the elaborately scrolled handle.

"It's me, Carey." The low voice barely penetrated the panels.

"Oh, for heaven's sake!" she muttered as her fingers grappled with the lock. Then he was inside, closing the thick door behind him. He was still dressed in the black blazer and gray trousers he had changed into for dinner, but it was the seriousness of his expression that held her attention. "Now what?"

"You didn't notice him?" he asked tersely.

"Who?" she countered tiredly.

"The man who followed us from Paris. For God's sake, Lindsay, he was hanging around the hotel in Paris, and now he's turned up here. He was in the dining room. Didn't you notice him?"

She looked neutrally into the goldish brown of his concerned eyes. "No, I didn't notice him, but so what? Some man is following our route. Is that supposed to bother me?"

"You're damn right it should! Look, Lindsay—" he gripped her shoulders with determination "—somebody's following you for a reason. Have you any idea what it is?"

"This really is too much! What in the world would I—" She stopped abruptly, wonder coming into her eyes. "There's no danger for you," Philip had said, but was that because he thought no one would suspect an innocuous tour director? A shiver rippled through her, and Carey looked intently into her eyes.

"You thought of something, didn't you? What?"

Her brain raced into high gear. If there *was* a man following her, and if he *was* after whatever Philip had given her, then Carey was the last one in the world she could tell. The Endor Corporation would look with a jaundiced eye, to say the least, on one of its employees even suspected of dabbling in espionage. Even the word sounded ridiculous to her ears, and her laugh was only slightly forced.

"Only that I carry quite a sum of Eurospan money around with me."

"What do you call quite a sum?"

She shrugged. "About five hundred dollars' worth of each currency—and then there's the money from the organized tours that are paid when the tour's underway."

Carey gave a disgusted snort and dropped his hands from her shoulders, and strangely she was aware of her nakedness more when his touch no longer warmed her through the layer of terry cloth.

"No one's going to chase you halfway across Europe for that kind of money," he said harshly, his eyes still narrowed intently on hers. "You're positive you can think of no other reason?"

"What other reason could there possibly be?" she said lightly, turning from him and walking toward the night table between the two beds. The aspirins rattled in the bottle she picked up, betraying her nervousness. "I think you're making gigantic mountains out of very small molehills. There's no international conspiracy to stalk me across Europe and bop me on the head at regular intervals. I'm not remotely concerned with state secrets—theirs or ours." Why had she said that? It would only prove to him that her mind was running on those lines.

"You may not be, but your brother may be involved in a nuclear program that could be vital to either side," he countered tersely.

Lindsay gave him a frosty stare. "My brother is as patriotically English as George Washington was American. There is no way he would dream of betraying his country, and especially not of using me as a means to do it." The aspirins rattled again, this time deliberately as she held the bottle up. "Now do you mind leaving while I cope with my headache and get some sleep?''

He seemed about to say something else. Then he nodded. "All right, but don't forget I'm just across the corridor if you need me—and be sure to lock your door after me."

"That, my dear Mr. Hudson, will be a pleasure!"

But the room seemed terribly lonely once she'd refastened the lock behind him, a feeling she seldom experienced on her trips. Feeling foolish, she checked the inner recesses of the closet and every other place that might secrete a sinister foreign agent. Then, in disgust, she swallowed two aspirins and crawled under the covers. He was making her as paranoid as he was himself!

Another thought struck her as she lay looking at the dark ceiling. Was he extending his role of company spy, insidiously playing on her nerves to see how much pressure she could stand? It seemed far-fetched, but what other explanation could there be?

# CHAPTER SIX

For Lindsay the night was filled with dreams of a demonic Philip leeringly handing her documents slashed across the top with a wide bank of red, on which stark white letters proclaiming Top Secret were superimposed. She was thankful to make her way downstairs for an early breakfast.

And surprised to see that Carey was already in the dining room at one of the tables overlooking the mistily calm lake. It would have been churlish to sit elsewhere, so she carried her self-serve plate of croissants and pats of butter and jam to join him. They were the only patrons of the dining room at that hour, and her voice held a tinge of irony when she asked, "May I?"

"Of course." He made a polite half-standing gesture as she settled herself opposite him. "How did you sleep?"

"Very well, and you?" She glanced at him as she broke a croissant and proceeded to add butter and jam to the flaky surface, only to find him white and tense under the surface layer of tan, as if he'd hardly slept at all.

"I had enough," he clipped, signaling to one of the sleepy waiters, who drifted over, coffeepot in hand.

Lindsay gave the waiter a sunny smile, and he blinked into appreciative alertness before refilling Carey's cup for what was evidently the umpteenth time.

"I've been thinking about what you said last night," she said brightly when the waiter had gone, "and all I come up with is that you're taking your job a little too seriously. It's one thing to report on the level of competence of the driver and me—quite another to create problems where none exist. I told you that my brother is involved with nuclear research, so you jump to the conclusion that I have state secrets stitched to my underwear and that some—" she shrugged irritably "—some thug is out to grab them from me. You really have been—"

"Oh, yes? Then what's he doing down here?" Carey interrupted in savage triumph. "He's right over there—just came in."

Lindsay automatically turned her head and looked at the man who was helping himself from the central buffet. Dapperly dressed in cream-colored trousers with a knife-edge pleat perfectly centered down each leg, what looked like a yachting blazer and a lemon yellow scarf knotted loosely at his neck, he looked more like a decadent playboy than a sinister agent.

About to smile and turn back, she did a quick double take. Something about that thirties-style pencil mustache and the carefully controlled shock of black hair struck a familiar note. Yes, she had seen him in Paris and written him off as yet another would-be panter after her charms. There were many such men hanging around the tours, seemingly fascinated by

directors who were easy on the eye but, more important, who were borne away the next day in a cloud of
diesel fumes. Short and sweet.

She turned back, a smile twitching at her lips.
"You mean *he's* your sinister prowler? Really! Yes, I
do remember him, but I'd sooner not. He's a kind of
camp follower," she explained to his bewildered expression. "Some men find itinerant female tour
managers fascinating because there's no time for
promises of eternal fidelity. It's a very transient relationship."

"I see," he said tightly.

"I doubt if you do," she countered lightly, turning
her head again to where the other man was settling
himself at a table immediately adjacent to the buffet.
Musingly she went on, "I think I should be flattered
that he's not running true to form. After all, he's
made the effort to follow me here. My charms must
be greater than I thought!"

"I wouldn't have taken you for a vain person," he
remarked sourly, yet something in his eyes sent a
strange thrill of awareness through her. Instinctively
she knew that he wasn't indifferent to her "charms"
himself, and the thought somehow pleased her. But he
just wasn't the kind to simmer jealously over another
admirer. Why would he, when his own attractions
made him fair game for any woman worth her salt?
No, he was probably still believing his own fantasy
that the man was a foreign agent and it was his duty as
an officer of the company to protect her. So she was
doubly pleased when the Frenchman, as she soon discovered he was, approached their table a little later.

"Miss Tabor?" he began, bowing charmingly. "They have told me at the desk that I must see you to accomplish my purpose. My name is Louis Perrault," he added.

Ignoring Carey's scowl, she smiled and said, "Won't you join us, Monsieur Perrault?"

"Ah, yes. It is very kind of you." Although he was attractively slim, he presented the image of a fussily overweight papa as he settled into a chair. He seemed as intent on ignoring Carey as the latter was on negating his existence. "Well, Miss Tabor, I have a request to make of you. Is it possible for me to join your tour here in Lucerne? I know—" he held up a hand to stem her automatic objection "—that it is mostly Americans you carry, but—" he shrugged with Gallic charm "—I have waited a long time to make a visit such as your tour encompasses, and I was desolated to find that this one is the last of the season. Unfortunately, because of business reasons, this is the only time available to me. Will it be in order for you to add me to your passenger list?"

"Well, I...." Lindsay paused and looked doubtfully at Carey, who surprisingly supported the idea.

"Why not? There's plenty of room on the bus," he said smoothly, though his smile was tight and never reached his eyes.

"All right, Monsieur Perrault." She pushed back her chair and stood up. "If you'll excuse us, Mr. Hudson, I'll see to the details."

She fumed inwardly all the way to the front desk, the Frenchman following closely at her heels. First Carey condemned the dandyish Frenchman as an agent of a foreign government, and now he was welcoming him to the tour with open arms. Men!

CAREY WAS ABSENT for the morning tour of Lucerne's old town, which, despite the fact that it was Sunday, was flourishing commercially with sales of Swiss watches and other tourist-attracting souvenirs.

Mary Strangeways, the professor's wife, dived happily into the display of precision watches, while Irene Harben added to her spoon collection with a solid-silver memento of their Swiss visit. Apart from Paul Strangeways and Joel Carter, no one showed much interest in her discourse on Lucerne's past, except when she talked about the covered bridge, which was one of the few remaining in Europe. The sprightly Louis Perrault threatened to be an embarrassing bore on the tour. He paid little attention to her spiel, concentrating instead on watching her with bright dark little eyes.

"We'll have a coffee break now," she announced with a raised voice halfway through the morning tour. "And I'll meet you back at the bus at—" she consulted her watch "—let's say eleven-thirty."

She and Pierre went, as usual, to a small café-cum-restaurant that few tourists ever found. They were greeted with a beaming smile from the plump Swiss proprietress, who ushered them up a few steps to the quaintly small coffee room. Down a few more steps to their right was the equally intimate dining room, and Lindsay glanced into it as they passed. It was the kind of place Carey would like, she thought unexpectedly, with its off-the-beaten-track atmosphere.

"Ach, why do always come with this one?" The café owner jerked her thumb derisively toward Pierre as they seated themselves at a cramped table for two. "You are too pretty to waste your time on such as him. You need a man of your own and children to take care of instead of all those tourists."

Fortunately Pierre didn't understand the woman's German, so he continued to smile happily while Lindsay replied, "The right man hasn't come along yet, but as soon as he does you'll be the first to know."

"Then let it be soon." Over her shoulder as she went off to get their coffee, she added severely, "You're not getting any younger, you know!"

Lindsay wrinkled her nose and smiled, then explained the last part to Pierre.

"She is right," he said with unaccustomed seriousness. To him, a twenty-five-year-old woman without visible attachment was cause for concern. "It is not, ah, *naturel* for a beautiful woman to be without *l'amour*. Why do you not like men, Lindsay?"

"Oh, I like them, all right," she said brightly, "but I'm happy the way I am until the right one comes along."

His brow lifted in disgust. "Ah, you are too *romantique*! Would it not be better to be prepared for this perfect man when he comes?"

With imperfect timing, a suave voice sounded from behind them. "Ah, Miss Tabor," Louis Perrault said with satisfaction, "I have found you at last. May I join you?"

"I—yes, of course," Lindsay returned weakly,

cursing her own foolishness in allowing him to join the tour. Was he going to dog her footsteps like this all through Rome, Venice and Vienna?

The café owner lifted her blond brows significantly when she returned with the coffee and a plate of pastries. Intercepting the questioning glance, Lindsay shook her head, and the proprietress nodded hers sagely in return. This was not the one. Her pale blue eyes raked over the unfortunate Frenchman and obviously found him wanting.

Lindsay felt an acute sense of relief when, after enduring a conversation dominated by the new passenger, she and Pierre escaped to the bus, leaving him with the almost untouched plate of pastries.

"He is no good for you, that one," Pierre commented as they relaxed and waited for the passengers to drift back. "The other one is a better choice."

"Other one?"

"The tall one." He shrugged. "The one who always sits away at the back. He watches you all the time when he thinks you don't see him."

A vagrant thrill of pleasure tremored through Lindsay. There was only one tall passenger who kept to the back of the bus. Yet she feigned ignorance.

"I don't know who you mean."

"The big one, the one who comes out last," Pierre enlarged impatiently. "I see him in the rearview mirror watching you...and perhaps wishing for an evening with you?"

"Then he'll just have to go on wishing!" Lindsay snapped, standing up as the passengers began to straggle back, irritated by Pierre's salacious expression, yet unable to suppress the involuntary picture that filled her mind.

CAREY DID COME on the afternoon trip up the mountainside, which impressed more with its scenery than with the slow crawl of the minitrain that took them to the plateau just below the summit.

Although she was the last to take her seat, Louis Perrault slid onto the same slatted wood bench after her, pinning her with his body to the pine frame surrounding the window. She could feel the muscular tenseness of his thigh against hers, fleetingly surprised at the apparent strength of his body. He didn't seem like the type to be interested in physical fitness. Opposite, Carey's eyes assessed her, and she looked away quickly to the slow-moving scenery outside the train. Was he really as bored as he looked, with Charlene's thigh pressed to his in the confined space?

The Dakers and several of the other passengers darted back and forth between the windows, snapping pictures of the unfolding landscape. Her heartfelt wish was to see Louis Perrault similarly involved in photography, but he had no camera slung over his shoulder—no other interest, evidently, than pressing her to have dinner with him that night.

"I would very much like to take you to a place I know of," he enticed her with melting admiring eyes.

"I thought you didn't know Lucerne?" Lindsay prevaricated coolly.

"I assure you I do not, but a friend has told me of a wonderful place to have dinner. It is quiet and very, very discreet, Lindsay."

Quiet and discreet enough to facilitate his major play? Oh, no. She hadn't the least intention of making his European trip a sexual odyssey to remember! "I'm sorry. I already have an engagement for dinner."

She sprang up when the train ground to a halt at restaurant level, smiling right and left to her group as she made her way to the exit door. "Yes, you can get lunch here. It's self-service but very good. Please be back at three-fifty to catch the gondola lift down."

Carey passed with a determined Charlene clinging to his arm, and Lindsay felt a sudden twinge of pity for the older woman. She seemed to be making a real play for Carey, the only male passenger who showed any interest in her at all. A shiver ran through her despite the heat of the day. Was that what the café owner, what Pierre had envisaged for her: past her best but still hoping for a knight-errant to rescue her from a life that had become merely routine?

After telling Louis Perrault, who was trotting faithfully along beside her, that she had duties to perform, she was relieved when he went to join the majority of passengers lining up at the self-serve counter. Satisfying herself that they could cope very well on their own, she then slipped hastily back into the sunshine and made her way toward the steep path that led to the mountain's peak.

She drew deep rejuvenating breaths when she at last stood at the summit and surveyed the craggy peaks around her, enclosing yet opening up into further ranges, on and on to infinity. Crag after crag soared and took its place in a magnificent panorama that had never failed to enchant her. Up here, nothing mattered except the awesome scope of nature in all her raw glory. It was a primitive revelation of the world's beginning, these mountains that had been thrust up as a result of some primeval heave of the earth. This view always made her thoughts and hopes soar, while reducing her problems to trivialities.

"It must have been quite a sight when these monsters rose up out of the earth." Carey not only had predicted her destination but had tuned in to her thoughts. He came up behind her, leaning his elbows as she did on the rock-wall barrier, his beige waterproof jacket barely touching the white wool of hers. "Can you imagine nothing but flatness and then... this?"

A turn of his head encompassed the sharply rising peaks, and in her state of euphoria—due to the altitude, no doubt—Lindsay allowed him to enter the world that she'd considered, until now, her private domain.

"I often wonder when I come up here what it must have been like for the first people who inhabited these valleys," she confided dreamily, her eyes going down to the valleys, then up the sometimes gradual, sometimes steep rise to magnificence. "What did they think? How did they make a living? How did they see the possibilities of all this?" She waved a hand, and Carey caught it on its downward sweep, his eyes seeming to have lost the tense wariness that normally shadowed them.

"I imagine they thought," he said with a half-amused, unaccustomed softness, "the men, anyway, that here they could make a home for the women they had their eyes on and the children who would follow. They could run sheep on the lower slopes and cows on the flatlands and pass on the valley richness to their sons, who would in turn make an even better living for their progeny.''

Lindsay twisted around to stare at his profile, seeing a wistful dreaminess in his eyes that made him look altogether different.

''Carey, that's... that's really beautiful,'' she said in hushed surprise, and saw the immediate withdrawal of his temporary tenderness.

His laugh was an affront to what she felt was sincere feeling. ''I thought that might appeal to you.'' His voice was tinged with brittle irony, and his hand tightened on hers. ''You really are a romantic, aren't you? I bet that right now your mind is filled with pretty pictures of his homecoming after a hard day's toil in the fields to find a dewy-eyed wife, her face flushed from her exertions over the stove, welcoming him to a hot meal and a warm bed.'' He slanted her a mocking glance. ''Like most true romantics, you haven't given a thought to the possibility that she greeted him with a scowl rather than a smile because he'd let the winter's wood supply run low and that she'd had to scrabble in the snow to find enough kindling to fire his hot meal. And in the corner there's a child huddled under a sheepskin about to die because there's no medical—''

''All right, all right,'' she interrupted furiously. ''I get the picture! Thanks for bringing your realism to bear on the subject. Now every time I come up here

I'll be sure to worry about the real facts of their lives! Now if you'll let me go, I'll get back to the facts of *my* life.''

Instead of releasing her hand, he used it to draw her suddenly toward him, the mockery completely gone from his eyes when they came close to hers, though his voice was clipped in that familiar way when he said, "I'm sorry. I didn't mean to spoil this place for you. Maybe I was just jealous of that man who had a wife like that to come home to.''

Lindsay searched his gold brown eyes for further evidence of mockery and found none. There was something unbearably poignant in the way he was looking at her, revealing a glimpse of whatever lay behind his conventional facade.

"So why don't you get married?" she asked unsteadily, making no effort to detach herself from his all too intimate hold that made her aware, even through their clothing, of the strong tensing of his body. Ridiculously, she felt an overwhelming urge to press her own softer flesh to his flat outlines, wanted the feel of his well-shaped mouth on hers. . . .

Huskily he said, "Maybe I will when I find a woman willing to scrabble in the snow to find enough wood to heat my dinner.''

One hand slid under the white wool of her jacket, radiating its coldness to her spine as his head bent and he kissed her. Lindsay was powerless to move, even if the mountains had decided at that moment to rearrange their contours. It wasn't a fierce kiss, or even a sensually potent one, as on that first night of the tour. But its deference, its caring quality inexplicably sent ever widening arcs of warmth radiating through her.

It lasted only seconds, but it felt like an infinity by the time he raised his head again and looked intently into her eyes. "You'll have dinner with me tonight?"

Her head seemed to nod of its own volition, although her instincts told her he wasn't really talking about eating.

"Ah, Miss Tabor—" Louis Perrault's voice intruded gratingly from behind "—here you are. No wonder you declined the unappetizing food below for this." He waved a hand to encompass the craggy peaks. "This view is *magnifique*, is it not?"

Lindsay, who had drawn quickly away from Carey, was sure the suave Frenchman had witnessed their intimacy and for reasons of his own was choosing to ignore it.

"It is, Monsieur Perrault," she said briskly, stepping aside and glancing one last time at the view before starting out on the downward trek. Over her shoulder she said crisply, "You can enjoy it for ten more minutes, *monsieur,* and then we must leave on the gondola lift." Her eyes met Carey's briefly before she resumed her long swinging stride.

For the first time, the sense of euphoria the mountains always inspired stayed with her as she descended to the restaurant level, but she knew the fact that her heart was racing had nothing to do with the altitude. She had committed herself to Carey, body and soul, for that night at least, and she had no regrets. Even the thought of last night's pining for Geoff had no power to dampen her anticipation. Perhaps she could finally exorcise him from her mind, her body. . . .

Her reverie was abruptly cut off by the return of the tourists spilling from the spacious restaurant that was set into a paved courtyard. On one of the benches she found Lila Beaumont in a rare moment of contemplation, her eyes drawn to the promontory jutting out over the stupendous valley. She brightened considerably when Lindsay came to sit next to her.

They chatted until it was time to go down in the lift that would return them to the base of the mountain. After rounding up her group, Lindsay soothed Lila's nervousness at entering the massive car that held eighty people at capacity. She was never happy herself with bodies packed so tightly around that it was difficult to breathe, but the descent was uncomplicated, and Pierre was waiting faithfully with the Eurospan bus to take them back along the lakeside drive to the hotel situated at the far side.

Breaking her long-held rule of waiting until every passenger had made an exit from the vehicle before she did, Lindsay preceded several others, including Carey, off the bus and strolled down to the waterfront, which glittered smoothly in the late-afternoon sun. She needed space to breathe, to think, but in one of the tree-sheltered bays of the extensive gardens she found Betty Timms on a park bench, a sketch pad on her knee. She and Carl hadn't gone on the afternoon tour, so Lindsay wasn't surprised to see that the sketch Betty was working on was almost complete.

"May I see it?" she asked, smiling as she sat down

beside the suddenly flustered artist. "I really envy anyone who can draw or paint. I'm not at all creative that way."

"Oh, this is nothing," Betty denigrated herself, though she hesitantly held out the pad for Lindsay's scrutiny. "I took up sketching and painting after I married Carl so I'd have something to do when we're in out-of-the-way places. But Carl's the one who has real talent."

"It must be great to have that kind of interest in common with your husband," Lindsay commented, her eyes on the sketch but her mind occupied with the question of which talents she and Carey shared. None that she could think of. Why did that thought give her a pang of misgiving? He wasn't the marrying kind; he had made that abundantly clear. Nevertheless, Betty's next words lifted her spirits a little.

"I don't think so at all," she said bitterly, surprising Lindsay with her vehemence. "Oh, I thought it might at the beginning, but most great men want to be one of a kind and free of—I don't know—competition from their wives."

Lindsay knew enough to steer clear of matrimonial bones of contention, and her eyes returned to the pencil strokes, interested to see that although the outlines conformed so well to the view opposite, what she was looking at was a cleverly executed artist's impression.

"This is very good—in fact, I'd say excellent, although I'm no proper judge. Is Carl doing the same view?"

"Oh, no, he wouldn't bother with this." Betty

waved a deprecatory hand. "He says it's too commercially pretty for him."

"Well, I'm certainly glad you don't feel the same way," Lindsay said with admiration, handing back the sketch pad. "This is really beautiful. As the saying goes, I don't know much about it but I know what I like."

"Thanks." Embarrassed by the praise, Betty's cheeks were pink as she closed the pad. She seemed relieved when, after a few more minutes, Lindsay got up and wandered back to the hotel.

Her relief might have turned to chagrin had she been able to read Lindsay's mind. She certainly came across some oddly matched couples on these trips, the tour director mused. Sometimes they seemed to have nothing in common whatsoever, yet some intangible bond kept them together for ten, twenty, thirty years or more.

Was it love?

Carey would have laughed at that romantic idea.

THE CALL CAME when she lay on her bed late that afternoon, hoping to nap before getting ready for her evening with Carey.

"Philip?" she identified the caller hazily.

"How are things with you?"

"Just fine," she said slowly. "Is something wrong there?" she added, anxiety sharpening her voice.

"No, no. Elena and the children are fine. I just wondered how your tour is going."

Lindsay stared stupidly at the black telephone rest

on the night table. Philip had never called her before on one of her trips.

"You're sure there's nothing wrong?" she asked suspiciously.

"Absolutely," he assured her heartily. "I just wanted to say that if you have too much baggage, you should dump some of it before getting to Vienna. You don't want to be overweight on the plane back to London."

If she had been bewildered before, she was stupefied now. Had Philip been drinking? No, he wasn't the type. But something was wrong; she knew it from his overly jocular voice.

"Philip, does this have something to do with—"

"I just don't want you to have trouble with the customs people again," he broke in, his voice amused. "They can be pretty rough, you know, and come up on you when you least expect it. My advice is to use your common sense and get rid of anything you think might think interest them."

His voice faded on the last words and finally petered out altogether. Long after the line went dead, Lindsay gripped the receiver with white knuckles, only relinquishing it when the hotel operator came through and briskly asked if her call was completed.

She lay back on her bed, but with a rigidity that precluded sleep. Her brain was working too busily to permit relaxation. What had Philip meant? Despite the teasing note in his voice, as of older brother to brainless younger sister, she sensed a deeper, more serious message.

Of course. It had to do with the envelope he'd

given her for Hilda Keller in Vienna. He was telling her to ditch it, the "excess baggage" he'd mentioned. But only if customs people were likely to prove troublesome. Oh, God, that must mean if foreign agents were on the bus and were aware of what she was carrying, she was to dispose of the envelope and so safeguard herself.

Lifting her hand, she bit down hard on her tensed knuckles. Had Carey been right to suspect that she'd been knocked out in Paris by someone intent on retrieving the information she was carrying? Her scalp crawled. Why had Philip exposed her to this kind of danger? He had assured her—

Even as the question crossed her mind, she knew the answer. Philip loved Elena to distraction and would do anything to complete her happiness, even to the point of exposing his sister to unknown danger.

Damn him! He could have at least given her the opportunity to accept or refuse her role in the drama of rescuing Elena's elderly parents from Poland! He must have known that she would refuse to place her job, maybe even her life, on the line for an old couple she didn't even know.

Then the unbidden memory of a framed picture in the drawing room of Philip's home washed over her: a gentle patient smile on the face of the gray-haired woman, whose eyes looked trustingly out from the frame; the proudly erect shock-haired man at her side, spirited defiance in his expression and stance. Then she knew why Philip had exposed her to the unfamiliar dangers of international intrigue. Those eyes, that stance must have haunted him even as they now rose up to firm her own resolve to play her part in securing their freedom.

SHE WAS STILL DISTRACTED when she went down to meet Carey at two minutes after eight. His telephone call so shortly after Philip's, confessing that he was at a loss to choose the best place to dine in Lucerne, had brought an automatic response from her.

The problem of what to wear had solved itself when she took from the closet the first dress her hand touched. Fortunately the brilliant mosaic of the thin paisley wool shirtwaist gave her dark coloring an animation she was far from feeling. But she was glad she'd worn that particular dress when Carey's eyes went appreciatively over her and his voice told her huskily as he held her jacket, "You look even more beautiful than usual."

So did he, she noted silently, in a well-tailored charcoal suit and the inevitable pristine white shirt. He must keep the launderers of Europe very busy, she thought with amusement as he put a hand under her elbow and escorted her to the portico. A taxi waited at the bottom of the steps.

Carey had obviously given the driver previous instructions, for he moved off immediately and went smoothly down the hotel drive to the public road.

Lindsay was acutely conscious of Carey and his effect on her as he drew her close to his side and slid an arm around her. She stiffened momentarily, then relaxed. This was the night of exorcism, the end of old longings, the beginning of...what? New ones?

But at least this time she was prepared. Carey's views on lasting relationships, marriage, were entirely up front. And she was no longer the starry-eyed girl who had dreamed of marriage, children, helping Geoff in his work. She had been so ridiculously naive.

The scent of her own perfume rose to mingle headily in the confined space with his provocative bay-rum after-shave. She made no effort to turn her head away when his fingers cupped her chin lightly and moved her mouth closer to his. She felt his breath briefly brush across her skin, and then he kissed her. Slowly, meaningfully, teasingly, he let his lips press until hers parted. Then he withdrew and laughed huskily.

"I think we'd better save this until later, don't you? I don't want you to arrive at the restaurant in such a state that you'll be too embarrassed to show your face there again. I gather you're quite well known there?"

Lindsay drew slightly away from him and smoothed the side of her hair that had been pressed into his shoulder. "I— Yes, I know Frau Schuller very well." Remembering the café owner's chiding remarks of that morning, she added, "She's a very motherly person. It bothers her that I'm not married and a mother of four myself, instead of shepherding tourists around Europe. So don't pay any attention if she tries to pair us off."

"I'll try not to," he returned, sounding amused.

At that moment, the cab drew up outside the small restaurant, and she studied Carey as he bent over to the driver and paid the fare, knowing he would be

Frau Schuller's vision of the man suitable for Lindsay's life partner. He was obviously well-heeled, impeccably dressed, exuding an air of command. Perhaps she could head off the fiercely maternal café owner and explain that Carey was no more than a.... A what? A casual dinner date? He was hardly that, when she was calmly preparing to spend the night with him!

"It's certainly small," Carey commented when, his hand under Lindsay's elbow, they entered the upper level of the café.

"That's one reason why I come here so much," Lindsay quickly explained. "It's not often that a tourist scents it out, but the food is excellent," she hastened to reassure him just as Frau Schuller appeared from the back and smiled delightedly when she saw who the latest arrivals were. Her shrewd blue eyes ran over Carey in approving appraisal.

"Ach, my dear, why did you not say this morning that you were coming for dinner tonight? I could have reserved a table for you, but as it is...." She shrugged, distressed.

"I called earlier to make a reservation," Carey interjected. "The name is Hudson."

"Ach—" the older woman struck her head with the heel of her hand "—of course. Mr. Hudson. Will you come this way, please?" To Lindsay, in an aside as they descended the stairs, she said with an approving roll of her eyes, "He is beautiful for you. You must marry him, *liebchen*."

Lindsay had time for no more than a warning shake of her head before the proprietress seated them at one of the three booths that, together with three tables already filled with patrons, comprised the dining room. To Lindsay's embarrassment, Frau Schuller began a blatant selling campaign of her virtues.

"You are fortunate, Mr. Hudson, to have so beautiful and yet so modest a girl as Lindsay on your arm tonight. She works very hard, and for what?" She waved her hand in a derogatory gesture. "Tourists! They have no appreciation for what she does for them. She would be a fine wife for a man such as yourself, a—" she looked with brilliant eyes at Lindsay's furiously flushed face "—a jewel in your crown. She is not like the girls you see today around you—now with this man, now with that. She is . . . *particular*!" she ended with a triumphant swell of her sizable bosom.

"All right, you've sold me. I'll take her," Carey inserted into the space, for who knew if he'd get another opportunity. Frau Schuller looked down at him, nonplussed, while Lindsay wished she could sink into the floor and disappear.

"Frau Schuller," she said instead, "could we have a menu?"

The bosom inflated still further. "You have no need of a menu. I myself will order your meal." As she stalked away, her large body tremulously intent on her mission, Lindsay dared to look at Carey's face, expecting to find frowning disapproval but seeing that his eyes had a dancing laughter in them.

"Is your real mother anything like that?"

"No," she confessed thankfully. "Mom believes in live and let live. No matter how much she might want me to get things together with someone she thinks would be good husband material, she'd never come right out and say it.''

"Good. I like her already."

Already? It sounded as if, in the future, he intended meeting her—but of course he was only being polite. There was no possibility after the tour was over that he would come to the warm Colonial-style house in Philadelphia and meet her parents. Unable to stop herself, she projected further and knew that her father, at least, would like Carey Hudson. Despite his still-water, university-professor demeanor, she suspected that he cherished dreams of being a man of action, a captain of industry, as Carey was.

To her relief, Frau Schuller remained in the background and sent a shyly buxom waitress in local costume to serve them cheese fondue, a dish that necessitated the intimacy of sharing cubed bread dipped into a communal center bowl of rich creamy melted Swiss cheese.

Carey's only comment as he hungrily speared the cheese-covered cubes into his mouth was, "This is good, although I'd have preferred a steak."

"You're too American in your tastes," she gibed, smiling as she pronged another square and dipped it into the creamy mass, bringing it dripping to her parted lips.

"Aren't you?"

The question came with such unexpected fierceness that she let the forklike prong hang, the cheese stretching elastically back to her plate.

"For some things, yes. But I enjoy European food, too." She put down her fork and sipped at the white wine that had come with the fondue. "You sound very chauvinistic, and I wouldn't have thought you were that—not unduly."

Why did she feel that his smile was forced as he, too, lifted his glass?"

"I'm not really. It's just that cheese doesn't satisfy my American taste for protein—lots of it."

"Then let's order some steak for you," she said contritely, feeling responsible for his hunger and lifting a hand to summon the waitress.

He caught her hand in mid wave. "It's not necessary," he stated quickly, a smile lighting the brown gold of his eyes. "I just want to get out of here," he added tersely, bringing into focus the unsaid purpose of their togetherness.

The wine that had seemed innocuous suddenly wove a dizzy spell around her senses. Pulses she had never before been aware of now made their turgid presence felt at her wrists, her temples, her throat. Without a word she rose and felt only peripherally the placing of her jacket around her shoulders, saw only dimly Frau Schuller's satisfied smile, smelled abstractedly the leather and stale smoke of the cab Carey handed her into.

"Lindsay?" he asked as the taxi moved smoothly away from the curb. "Are you feeling all right?"

"Yes, of course."

It was no lie. She really did feel more "all right" than she had at any time since Geoff. The soft warm feeling at the base of her stomach told her that she wasn't immune to Carey's male attractions, as she had been to the blandishments of Geoff's successors, men who had pursued, tried, and been repelled by her nonresponse. But there was none of that as she snuggled under the safety of Carey's arm, her face lifted invitingly to his as the taxi sped through the street-lit night to the hotel.

Like a dream she felt the softly sensuous brush of his lips on the fullness of her mouth, and her arm curled naturally around his neck as she strained her body to the muscled hardness of his.

"Carey?" she breathed as his mouth left hers and traveled down the smooth column of her throat, covering the strong beat of her pulse at the shallow indentation at its base.

"Wait," he counseled, his lips touching hers again briefly as the cab, amazingly, drew up with a flourish at the hotel entrance. Surely they hadn't arrived already? "Go in first and get your key," his husky voice whispered in her ear, "and I'll come to you later."

The dream continued as she left him to pay off the driver, her steps firm and confident when she passed up the red-carpeted stairway and gained the entrance hall. The night clerk seemed bored as he handed her key over and returned to the magazine he was reading. She crossed to the stairs and went up, her fingers touching lightly on the scrolled banister. Her room, when she let herself into it, was intimately cozy with its twin beds set close together, the heavy draperies with their green-leaf design drawn across the windows.

Like a somnambulist, she carefully hung up her jacket and unzipped her dress, catching it as it fell to her feet and arranging it, too, on a hanger in the closet. Her underclothes went into the beige canvas bag she used for laundry, and it was the work of a moment to slide the silky peach of her semitransparent nightdress over her head.

It was as she surveyed herself in the triple mirrors of her dresser that true feeling began to seep back into her. Her eyes took in the hazy cream of the flesh covering her figure, the rounded fullness of her breasts with their dark tips, the even darker outline that denoted her woman's center. Dear God, what was she doing here in the predictable comfort of a modern hotel room waiting for a man who, by his own admission, spurned commitment and meaningful relationships?

His knock, although it was discreetly soft, sent tremors of apprehension through her. She had to get rid of him, tell him—what? That she had changed her mind?

The door opened instantly, and Carey gave her a disapproving look.

"You should lock and bolt your door," he admonished severely, his eyes wrathful until they fell to the hurried rise and fall of her breast under the flimsy covering of her nightdress. His features underwent a metamorphosis then, crystallizing into a look of male awareness that frightened yet excited her. The click as his fingers shot home the protective bolt on the door echoed through Lindsay like a pistol shot.

"Carey, I...." She paused and ran her moist

tongue over lips that seemed too dry. The act seemed to incite his next move, which was to pull her slowly and inexorably toward him as he stared deeply into her eyes.

"I—I'm sorry, I just can't do this. No, don't!" The cry was jerked from her when he pulled her with a sudden movement hard against him, his arms cradling her from ribs to hips. "There's someone else." Her voice rose as she grew more agitated. "I know you wouldn't want to—"

"How the hell do you know what I do or don't want?" he demanded angrily, his fingers coming up to mesh in her hair, drawing her face up to the scowling darkness in his and to the hurt she thought she saw lurking there before he masked it. He sucked his breath in noisily in an effort at control, and at last he said quietly, "There's a word for you, Lindsay—one I'm sure you've heard many times before. But this is one time you're not going to get away with it."

His mouth fastened with determination on the startled parting of hers, his arms resuming their deadlock hold and intensifying it, so that every hardening muscle of his lean body imprinted itself with fiery warmth on her resistant flesh. The thrusting probe of his tongue into the soft inner planes of her mouth excited her, flicking at urges she had thought long dead, or at least controlled. Lindsay struggled for a moment, knowing this wasn't the way it should be between them. Then she relaxed against him, instinct telling her that he would back off when he found her unresponsive.

The strategy seemed to work temporarily. Sensing

her sudden yielding, he began a campaign to bring her to life again. His mouth, which had been so fiercely demanding, softened to warm persuasion as it left hers and wandered erratically across her cheekbone to the shivering sensitivity of her ear, his tongue now moistly provocative as it delved delicately and sent shattering crescendos of awareness through her.

"Please...don't."

Had that agonized moan come from her? Whatever, her plea went unanswered, and she swiftly plunged into a battle with her own joyous pleasure when his hands slid to her waist and shifted her away, but only far enough to give him access to the flimsy straps of her nightdress. Pushing them aside, he lifted his head from her upturned throat and paused to stare at the creamy-skinned fullness of her breasts, a rough sigh escaping from his throat as his hands came up to enhance the sexually abrasive touch of his eyes. Her breath was caught and held chokingly inside her when first his palms, then his fingers teased the nipples that rose and contracted so subtly in response to his caresses.

His eyes seemed as gleamingly alive as the lion's they resembled. Her own misted over when his head dipped to the swollen peaks and she felt the warmth of his tongue tightening the coil of tension that was building within her. A familiar feeling...yet so very, very different.

She was aware only of her arms tightly twined around his body when he gently disengaged them and bent to lift her, one arm under her knees, the other spanning her shoulders, and carried her to the nearer of the twin beds.

"Carey?" she whispered, her hands touching lightly at either side of his jaw, her palms feeling the male roughness there... a roughness that served only to intensify the molten torrent gathering speed and flowing like lava to every far-flung point in her body.

"You don't need this, do you?" was his answer, and she raised her hips to facilitate the sliding removal of her nightdress, her arm falling across her eyes as his hands left her. She heard the soft rustle as his clothing fell to the floor, and then he was standing over the bed, the awesome male beauty of his tanned body cast in the rosey glow of the night-table lamp. His frame was solid but without superfluous flesh; she judged that from the smooth sheen of muscle on his shoulders, his arms, his leanly contoured thighs. The evidence of his manhood was as perfectly created, it seemed to her, as the mass of dark hair fuzzing his muscular chest and tapering to a point above his navel.

Then he was with her on the narrow confines of the bed, his mouth seeking hers, then hotly caressing her jaw, her throat, the breasts that were greedy for his touch. Her hands, propelled by the irresistible force of her desire, ran slickly, familiarly, over the ridged nodes of his spine, the sweat-filmed flesh of his shoulders and down to the taut bind of his stomach muscles, reaching lower in a frenzied longing to impart the same tingling pleasure his mouth, tongue, hands were giving to her.

His deep groan told her that she had succeeded,

and she exulted in his quickened breathing, in his tongue tasting the light dew of sweat covering her breasts, her faintly indented navel.

Words seemed superfluous when he eased quickly over her, his hard thighs enclosed in her softness. Did she groan or did he when they merged in the timeless movements of love? Perhaps they both did...but Lindsay was conscious only of her own eager seeking for fulfillment and her own desire to please. Of their own volition, her hips rose to meet him, her arms meeting to cling around the sleek slippery surface of his back as tension coiled inside her and fought desperately for release.

"Oh, *Geoff*!" was torn from her throat at the moment when her mind, body and soul seemed to leave her, forging into a new form she didn't recognize. The tensely agonized moment was transformed into one of frightening suspension, and her eyes flew open to meet the ferocity in Carey's.

"Who in Christ's name is *Geoff*?" he enunciated clearly, coldly.

"He—he's not important." Lindsay tried to placate him, their growing sense of oneness more important at that moment than any false loyalty to her past. "Please...Carey, don't!"

She might have been talking to the wood he resembled as he drew back to the edge of the bed and stood up, staring down at her in frightening condemnation.

"Goddamn you, Lindsay, you were using me as a substitute for another man!" He bent quickly to pick up his clothes with even more speed than he'd discarded them, mocking her nakedness when he drew on his trousers and tucked his shirt forcefully into the waistband.

"No—please believe me, I wasn't!"

He strode to the door and looked back scathingly. "Do me a favor and tell that to Geoff, will you?"

Her eyes stared fixedly at him as he threw back the confining bolts and wrenched the door open.

"Carey?" she pleaded, but he had already gone, slamming the door behind him.

Damn, damn, damn! Lindsay rolled off the bed and picked up her nightdress, crumpled at the foot of the bed. Sliding it over her head, in vain she strove to avoid the image the triple mirror threw back: a woman whose heavily lidded eyes and moistly parted lips told their own irrefutable story.

*Oh, God,* she thought, anguished as she paced to the window and pulled aside the curtains obscuring the late-night stillness that hung over the hotel. Leaning against the window frame, she stared blankly at the impersonal string of lights illuminating the rough service courtyard.

What had possessed her to call out Geoff's name at that crucial moment? It wasn't as if she was still in love with him. The comparison between Carey's lovemaking and his was ludicrous. Indeed, the desire to compare had died as soon as Carey had truly begun to make love to her. Geoff had never been interested in her pleasure, she realized with a sense of surprise. He had never sublimated his own desires to the slow arousal of hers, as Carey had. He had relied on the novelty, for her, of a passionate relationship that had no future, only the overwhelming demands of the moment. And she had fallen for it, dreaming her own dreams that Geoff would have scoffed at if he'd been honest.

But was Carey any better? Perhaps, but only insofar as he'd promised nothing more than a fleeting romance that would end as soon as the tour did. So where did that leave her?

Marooned on a raft of unrequited passion, she told herself as she paced back to the bed, choosing the unruffled right-hand one to lie back on and stare at the ceiling. How lucky Elena was to have the undying and adoring love of her husband, she thought wistfully. Would there ever be such a man for her?

# CHAPTER SEVEN

Geneva, a one-night stop, came and went without noticeable incident. Only Paul and Mary Strangeways, the academics on the tour, and Irene Harben found abiding interest in the wintry Botanical Gardens they paid a perfunctory visit to before pressing on toward Nice.

"He's the man who made life pretty miserable for Mary, Queen of Scots, isn't he?" Paul asked halffacetiously as he indicated the austere statue of John Knox, who was among Europe's early Reformers.

"Yes, he did," Lindsay replied seriously, "and I must say I think he had a point. The royal courts in those days left much to be desired in the way of morality, and a lot of people rebelled against what they regarded as flagrant violations of God's laws as personified in the Bible. Knowing the wholesale corruption that went on in those days, I'm not sure I don't agree with them." Too late, she realized Carey had stepped rapidly over the crisp fall of leaves lining the walk and was well within earshot.

"It seems to me," he inserted enigmatically, "that each age finds its own level of morality. At that time it was important to Knox and other religious leaders that the letter of the Bible be observed whatever the circumstances. In the case of marriage, for instance, there was no room for alternative life-styles. Thank God, in our age, we're becoming a little more enlightened. People come together and stay together because that's the rational decision they've arrived at between themselves." His eyes flickered coolly in Lindsay's direction.

"You've obviously given the subject some thought," Paul allowed with a mildly ironic smile, "but I'm not sure you're right. It's all very fine to say that commitment isn't important, but I think it is." The silver-haired educator had obviously mounted one of his pet hobbyhorses, and Lindsay shifted her feet restlessly, for once anxious to reboard the bus and press on with their journey.

"There are all kinds of commitment," Carey retorted, ignoring her agitated movement, "not necessarily the church and state kind. But sure," he allowed magnanimously, "if marriage is the way two people want to go, then I'm all for it. The point I'm trying to make is that it's up to the two people concerned to make whatever decision is right for them, not the one that's expected of them in a traditional sense."

"Sorry to interrupt your philosophical discussion," Lindsay interjected at that point, studiously avoiding Carey's eyes, "but it's time for us to be on our way."

She relaxed when they were on the road again, leaving her charges free to doze or chat among themselves, her thoughts drifting involuntarily back to Carey's stance on commitment. What he had said was, on the surface, totally logical. But what would happen if one day he fell in love with someone who wanted the final commitment of marriage and he didn't? Would it change his way of thinking?

Hardly, she answered her own question as Pierre set out on the long journey to Nice. Women fell into his lap too easily for him to bother about lasting commitment to one. Wasn't she a salutary example of that truism?

It was late afternoon when the bus picked its way down through the Alps toward Nice. Clicking on the speaker, she said, "For those of you who'll be touring the perfume factory tomorrow morning, we'll be retracing our steps in this general direction to visit the Fragonard perfumery. I should warn the men on board that pure flower essence can be very heady stuff."

"I don't mind that," Carl Timms called suggestively from his seat, "as long as they provide the dancing girls to go with it."

Lindsay ignored the scattering of laughter, having had a clear view of Betty's embarrassed face. "Meanwhile," she went on brightly, "we'll be in Nice in about thirty minutes, and I'll ask you to stay in the bus as usual until I've checked things in the hotel. As you leave the bus, I'll hand you a list of good restaurants in Nice that you can choose from or not, as you like."

The sun that had plagued the passengers on the left side of the vehicle all afternoon was well down in the sky when the checking-in was completed at the glittering Mediterranean-style hotel facing the seafront.

When the last of her group had descended stiffly from the bus, she took her life in her hands and crossed the busy road to catch a fuller glimpse of a sunset she knew would be glorious. She walked a little way along the promenade, then stood in awed stillness as the panorama of colors began to fill the sky.

The whole world seemed filled with an orange red, gold and yellow artist's palette of vivid color. She was only vaguely aware of the amused glances of passersby who noted her rapt attention.

"Mind if I stay with you for a while?" An all too familiar voice sounded behind her, and she turned to face Carey, whose lean face reflected the muted bronze of the dying sun.

Not trusting her voice, she shook her head mutely and turned back to the sunset, finding her pleasure in it diminished because of his presence. It was the first time they'd been alone together since that abortive night in Lucerne and the emotions she had thought under control erupted tremblingly inside her. Over and over she had relived the love play between them, growing heated with embarrassment before a kind of fatalistic acceptance took over, the realization that he must have been right, that she had used him as a substitute for Geoff. She hadn't consciously been thinking of Geoff, but he'd been there in her mind just the same.

She was glad Carey felt no need to offer trite remarks about the sunset, which most people would have made in viewing the stupendous bursts of color that exploded on the horizon. He seemed to sense her mood and respect it, and it was only when a dull red glow was all that remained that he spoke.

"I'm beginning to see why you like your job so much," he said quietly. "Maybe I should transfer permanently to the tour side of the business."

Lindsay turned and gave him a brief surprised look before stepping across to the curb. "You wouldn't like it," she said crisply. "You'd hate having to deal tactfully with passengers after sitting for hours on a bus."

He joined her at the edge of the sidewalk, looking where she did at the streaming traffic bearing down on them. "You may be right," he admitted ruefully. "Public relations isn't my strong point, as you may have gathered."

Again Lindsay was surprised. What did he mean by that? That he hadn't been particularly understanding in Lucerne? No, he couldn't mean that. A man with an ego as powerful as his must have been grossly insulted by what he regarded as her using of him. He'd proved that by his coolness toward her ever since.

Dodging the issue, she said quickly, "I really must get back to the hotel. The Dakers will be screaming blue murder because their suite doesn't face the sea."

"They can have mine if they like," he offered casually, darting out a hand to pull her back when a fresh spate of headlights rushed toward them. "I prefer the back of the hotel anyway. It's a lot quieter."

"You're sure?"

"Absolutely." He glanced over her head, then

urged her forward across the momentarily empty street, keeping his hand under her elbow until they entered the hotel. His touch was like a fiery brand piercing the cloth of her jacket, but there was no time to speculate on that as she realized that her surmise had been correct.

Brad Dakers, puffing furiously on the pipe he had been denied on the bus all day long, lunged away from the reception desk and came across to them.

"Look, Lindsay, we're not at all happy about the accommodation we've been given. All we can see is laundry hanging on balconies, and all we can hear is the rattle of garbage cans."

Lindsay opened her mouth, but Carey beat her to it. "It seems there's been a mix-up, because I've just been complaining to Lindsay that I prefer a back suite. How about doing a swap?"

The contretemps was over almost before it had begun, and as Brad walked away satisfied, Lindsay turned with a tight smile to Carey. "I'll have to take back what I said about your way with passengers. Thanks a lot."

He pulled her back when she would have walked on to the desk. "If you really want to thank me, you'll have dinner with me tonight at a place of my choice." Feeling the stiffening of her arm under his hand, he urged quietly, "I think we ought to talk, don't you?"

"About what?" she asked, her eyes frosty.

"Several things," he returned steadily, his eyes unreadable as they rested on hers. "It's important."

"I really don't see what purpose—"

She saw his eyes go over her head, the flash of annoyance in them as a playful arm circled her shoulders.

"Ah, Lindsay, at last I find you!" Louis Perrault cried in his heavy accent. "You were not in your room or anywhere I looked in the hotel."

Lindsay's spine sagged with fatigue. "Did you need something, Monsieur Perrault?"

"Only that you will have dinner with me tonight. *Je connais bien Nice,* and I have the perfect place for us—very quiet, very select."

"I'm sorry," Lindsay apologized briefly, "I—"

"Miss Tabor is having dinner with me," Carey inserted smoothly, his eyes bland as they met the other man's, his manner assertive. An unspoken message passed between them, and finally the Frenchman bowed fluidly in Lindsay's direction.

"Then perhaps at a later time?"

"I'll see you down here at eight," Carey said brusquely, his American accent distinctively curt, cutting through the other man's liquid notes. Before Lindsay had time to protest, he was striding toward the elevators.

"He is your lover?" Louis Perrault followed her to the desk, where she requested a safety box along with her key. Turning as she waited for the clerk to return with it, she gave the sprightly Frenchman a withering look.

"No, he is not," she snapped irritably. "I come along on these tours to do a job, Monsieur Perrault, not make myself available for sexual encounters. Now if you'll excuse me...." Furiously she stuffed the Eurospan envelopes into the box, locked it and handed it back to the slyly smiling clerk, who obviously understood English, or Louis Perrault's version of it.

Up in her room, she toyed with the idea of calling Carey and canceling the dinner date she hadn't actually accepted, then shrugged and decided to go along with it. The alternative was dinner in the hotel, where most of the passengers would be eating, and after a long day of travel in their company she was sated with it.

"Damn!" she exclaimed when, unpacking the supplies from her shoulder bag, she came across Philip's envelope addressed to Hilda Keller in Vienna. She had been so furious with Louis Perrault that she had neglected to put it in the safety box along with the other things. She would have to go down early and deposit it before leaving her room for the evening.

CAREY TOOK HER to a restaurant within walking distance of the hotel, a small place that was, he assured her, well-known for the excellence of its seafood. A postage-stamp dance floor hinted at an intimacy Lindsay hesitated to encourage, but unless she wanted to make a scene, she had no choice but to accept when Carey rose between courses and put his hands on the chair back.

Maybe she should have refused, she thought tremulously moments later. The beat was slow and decidedly French in its romantic overtones, and she felt herself slipping into a treacherously dreamy state of mind. Her body responded pliantly to the firm message of Carey's as he guided her slowly between the other couples, his breath stirring the loose flow of hair against her temple.

Between times, the excellently cooked food slid unnoticed down her throat, and she only partially heard the conversation Carey conducted single-handedly. Part of her acknowledged that his witty anecdotes could keep the most sophisticated woman amused, but she was more occupied with his reasons for suggesting this evening to talk. Talk about what? Surely not the light subject matter he'd tossed at her so far! She started, realizing he'd asked a question that required an answer.

"Wh-what?"

"What would you like for dessert? They do a very good—"

"Nothing, thanks," she refused hurriedly.

"You won't mind if I have their pièce de résistance?"

She shook her head, content to watch while he devoured what would have been called deep-dish apple pie in the States.

"Oh, man—" he finally wiped his mouth with the snowy napkin "—if I could find a woman who cooked like that, I'd marry her."

"I'll see what I can come up with on my future tours," Lindsay said dryly, her hand straightening the dessert fork in front of her as she went on, "Carey, you said you wanted to talk to me about... several things, I think you mentioned?"

He grimaced as he glanced around at their fellow diners, who were raucously enjoying their evening out. "This place has got a lot noisier since I was last here. What do you say we leave our serious talk till we get back to the hotel?"

"Why don't we have our coffee back there?" she countered, her eyes meeting his levelly across the table.

"All right," he said immediately, signaling for the check. Within minutes they were strolling back to the hotel across a paved park where raised beds still gleamed with autumn flowers. Intoxicated by the wine she'd had and the moon that hung like a shimmering white bowl in the sky, casting a glow almost as bright as daylight, Lindsay made no objection when Carey linked his fingers casually with hers. Her senses were alert to the soft balmy air on her skin, the exotic sound of French voices from others walking through the park.

"So who is—or was—Geoff?" he asked, so off-handedly that it took several seconds before the question got through to her. Her hand tightened convulsively in his.

"I...er—"

"Oh, come on, Lindsay, you can tell me," he said with a hint of impatience. "I hadn't expected that a woman of your age would be a virgin, but I have to admit it shook me a little to know that you let me go that far while you're still hung up on some other man."

"I'm not hung up on Geoff!" she denied hotly, trying vainly to disengage her hand from his. "He—he's just someone I used to know, and I—I guess I've never been that close to anyone else until...until now."

"How long ago did you know him?"

She shrugged. "Three years."

"And you're still—" Carey stopped abruptly, then said in a softer tone, "He must be some kind of guy if you still think of him when somebody else is making love to you."

Anger flared deep inside her, partly from his probing, but mostly from a resurgence of old hurts. "He's not," she said fiercely. "He wasn't . . . honest with me."

"Oh," he said thoughtfully, his long legs slowing their pace until they stopped moving altogether under the gnarled branches of an ancient olive tree. With a curiously gentle movement, he drew her into the undemanding shelter of his arms.

"Was he married?"

She nodded wordlessly.

"And he wanted that relationship as well as the one with you?"

Again she nodded, but this time she lifted her head and her eyes sought the outlines of his face in the dark shadows under the tree. "It wasn't the way it sounds," she said earnestly, as if she felt it mattered to him. And suddenly, whitewashing the affair for him mattered so much more than it ever had to her. "He wanted to marry me, but there were children."

He raised his brows without comment, but he said nothing until he had lifted his hand to her cheek, his fingers lightly, almost impersonally caressing the area beside her eye before trailing down her cheekbone to the soft vulnerability of her mouth.

"You really are a romantic, aren't you?" he said

somberly then, his eyes glinting fitfully in the light that filtered down through the branches. "And far too trusting."

"No, I'm not," she insisted, though she was incapable of drawing away from the deceptively casual line of his body that radiated a sweetly familiar warmth into hers. "If you mean that I was about to repeat the same mistake with you, you're wrong. I know about you." She changed to a lighter tack. "No commitments, no deep relationships, no—" she shrugged "—ties that bind. See how well I know you?"

He released a long-drawn-out sigh. "I doubt if you know me at all, sweet Lindsay. And now, unless I'm very much mistaken—" he raised a wrist close to his eyes to read the dial of his watch "—it's time for you to get to bed. Don't you have an early start tomorrow?"

The words had the effect of a pail of cold water thrown into her face, and Lindsay stepped back defensively, her expression and voice hardening as she said, "Yes, I do. The Cannes trip starts at nine."

Her arm was stiff under his guiding fingers as they crossed the road and went into the hotel. The foyer was deserted as she turned to thank him for dinner, the bright lights throwing the planes and hollows of his lean handsome features into relief.

"My pleasure," he said enigmatically, and his smile held a remoteness that followed her all the way to her room. Damn him! Telling him about Geoff, his wife and his children had turned Carey into a virtual stranger. Perhaps he thought she'd tried to entice Geoff to leave them! But how could she have done that, when she hadn't known for the longest time about his Janey and the two sons who awaited him in the States? What did it matter, anyway, she thought savagely, flicking on the closet light before opening the doors to hang her dress, pausing with it clasped under her chin as she stared down at her travel bag positioned just inside the entrance.

It did matter, she suddenly realized. It mattered a lot what Carey Hudson thought of her.

Her foot stubbed against the travel bag, drawing her attention to it. Had she left it there? No, she was sure she hadn't. She'd tucked it farther back, behind a sturdy pair of walking shoes. She lifted her eyes to the twin bed that had been turned down for the night. The maid? Surely not. Not one of them had ever rifled through her things in all her tours. They all knew she worked for her living like themselves and shrewdly decided she had nothing worth stealing.

Nothing worth stealing.... A prickle ran up the small hairs at her nape as she bent again over the bag. Perhaps if the zippered compartments had been opened, but she had no way of knowing that. On a hunch, she hung up her dress and went to the dresser drawers, opening them one by one, the cold hand of fear twisting in her midriff when she saw that hose, slips, underwear had been disturbed and replaced slightly askew from her normal careful arrangement.

Her heart had seemed to stop for an instant, but now it began to beat in trip-hammer fashion, making her feel nauseous. Someone had broken into her room and searched through her things, looking for something. It wasn't hard to guess what the something was. Thank God she had taken the buff envelope down to the safety-deposit box before going to dinner with Carey.

Carey! Drawing in a deep calming breath, she went to the phone at the bedside, sinking down on the folded-back coverlet when her knees began to tremble uncontrollably. This was one time when she needed the strong calm assurance of his arms. She was completely lost in a strange bewildering world. By contrast, Carey was wholesomely normal.

She dialed the first two digits of his room number, then replaced the receiver. Dear Lord, how could she confide in him, a senior member of the company she worked for? It was as good as signing her own death warrant in the travel industry. And she loved her job—or had until this tour.

Damn Philip! He had professed to care for her in the same way she cared for him. But if he really loved her as the sister who had been too distant for too long, would he have exposed her to his kind of harassment? Maybe she should have taken his advice and ditched the envelope. It would have served him right.

Then she sobered, visualizing the elderly couple, Elena's parents, in their joy at being reunited with their daughter and the grandchildren they had never seen. And knew she would do no such thing.

She would just have to be more careful, on her guard.... It shouldn't be too difficult to pinpoint the passenger Philip had indicated was interested in what she was carrying. Her mind went first to Louis Perrault—was Carey right about him? He *had* been there when she'd stuffed the Eurospan documents into the safety box. But no, the vapid Frenchman was the last person a foreign power would use to advance their purpose. He just wasn't the type to be trusted with cloak-and-dagger stuff.

Her mind swiftly tabulated the other members of the tour—the pipe-smoking Brad Dakers, the prim irascible Frank Harben, either one of the Strangeways, Joel Carter, the— Yes, there was a possibility in Carl Timms. He seemed the kind to revolt against a democratic society while enjoying its advantages. She would watch him, take great care to know where he was at any given moment.

God, she seemed to be acting out the scenes in a spy film, and the thought sickened her.

SHE WAS GLAD in a way that Carey didn't make an appearance for the morning visit to Cannes or the afternoon tour of the perfume factory at Grasse. She even relaxed a little as she ate lunch with Pierre at an outdoor restaurant in Cannes, where a warm sun still permitted that luxury. London right now would be suffering the first cold dreary snaps of winter, and once more Lindsay appreciated one of the many advantages of being a tour director as she let the sun's warmth permeate her skin and touch on the glossy darkness of her hair, which was drawn loosely back today and was caught at her nape by a broad tortoiseshell clasp. On the surface, she was a feline wallowing in unaccustomed leisure; not far underneath was a woman beset by conflicting emotions.

She hated the suspicions that now filled her mind. Her eyes had gone speculatively from one member of the tour to another as they had passed into the bus, sizing up her charges, questioning whether or not any were capable of treason.

Vying for her attention was her confusion about her feelings for Carey. There was no question that he attracted her physically. The night in Lucerne would never have taken place if that hadn't been so. Sighing, she conceded that he could be right. She was a romantic with long-range dreams of, if not that rose-covered cottage, then its modern equivalent—a helpmate who shared not only his bed but his life in all its aspects. She suspected that this was too encompassing a role for any woman Carey took into his life.

She opened her eyes to slits, and her gaze fell on Pierre opposite, seeing the flash of his eyes as he flirted outrageously with a young woman seated two tables away. Did the wife he had married so young know about and accept his constant infidelities, secure in the knowledge that he would always come back to her?

"Oh, Lindsay, I'm so glad you're here." Lila's quivering indignant voice brought her back to reality. "Could you come and talk to this waiter? I know he's charging me for things I'd never eat in a million years."

Stifling another sigh, Lindsay stood up, following the older woman to a distant table where a waiter wore the frustrated look that was rapidly becoming familiar to her where Lila was concerned. His angry gestures approximated those of the woman at the highway lunch stop, but this time it took considerably longer to persuade him that Lila had not really intended to order fish *and* omelet *and* tender breast of chicken.

All she had wanted, Lindsay translated, was soup and a chicken-salad sandwich, secretly sympathizing with the waiter's obvious disparagement at the American woman's choice of meal when the glories of French culinary art were hers for the asking.

Resignedly she stayed close to the excited Lila that afternoon and all through their conducted tour of the Fragonard factory, still finding it interesting to see the immense vats used in the various processes of distilling flowers into pure essence. Lindsay remained by her side, too, in the upstairs salesroom, where chic saleswomen with a rather superior air offered a bewildering selection of flowery and exotic perfumes to test. Lila sampled so many that it was impossible to distinguish one perfume from another on her hands, her wrists, her arms.

"Definitely the freesia scent," Lindsay recommended firmly when the older woman began her usual dithering, causing the slightly bored saleswoman attending them to raise her elegant brows.

"Oh, dear, do you think so?" Lila fretted, her hand hovering over another expensive flacon. "I thought I might try something more...adventurous, you know."

She finally settled for the light flower perfume when Lindsay pointed out, tongue in cheek, that the scent she hankered after was favored by Parisian

ladies of the night. At last they moved over to where
Irene Harben was delightedly picking up boxes of
soap realistically shaped and colored as fruit and
vegetables.

"They'll make lovely gifts for our grandchildren,"
she confided happily, her arms full. "I'm sure Frank
will love them, too, although he had to leave as he
was beginning to feel quite ill. He doesn't care for
perfume at the best of times, and the air in here was a
little thick for him. He wouldn't even let me test the
perfume on my wrists," she ended wistfully.

Lindsay was inclined to agree with Frank and the
other men who sat queasily beside their wives when
the bus loaded up once more. The air was filled with
the scent of heavy perfumes that vied with one
another for supremacy in the enclosed space. Feeling
squeamish herself, she switched on the air condition-
ing to full blast as Pierre pulled out of the Fragonard
courtyard. By the time they reached the hill town of
St-Paul-de-Vence, most of the heaviness had disappeared, leaving only an acceptably light flower perfume in the air.

The ancient town was one of her favorite tour
stops, and Lindsay left the passengers to discover its
delights for themselves while she toiled alone up a
narrow cobbled street to a walled area overlooking a
verdant valley below. Even more breathtaking was
the carpet of russet-and-gold ivy that clung tenuously
to the crumbling stonework of the old buildings
poised fortresslike above the valley.

Would Carey appreciate St-Paul-de-Vence—its
steep cobbled streets lined with tiny stores in which

local artisans displayed their hand-wrought goods with simple pride—as much as he had the Swiss mountains, the glory of the sunset in Nice? Perhaps. But he would never agree with her view that, out of all France, this was the one place to live. His style would lean more toward the artificial brilliance of the Riviera or the smart sophistication of Paris, not the gentle peacefulness of this place, where history slumbered under a benevolent sun. . . .

She moved away when the familiar voices of her tour group reached her, and she made her escape down lesser alleyways that brought her once again within sight of the waiting bus. A group of men and one woman were playing a form of bowls with a small silver ball in a sandy courtyard. From the vantage point of a veranda overlooking the playing area, the three-way intersection of country roads and the bus parked opposite, Lindsay watched the game while she sipped on thick sweet coffee. A few members of her group were discernible behind the steamy windows of the hotel bar, and she marveled anew at their apparent indifference to their unique surroundings. After all, a bar was a bar, be it in St-Paul-de-Vence or Main Street, U.S.A. Still, everyone to his own taste. It didn't really surprise her that Carl Timms would absorb local color in a bistro.

"Come back here!" She heard a local shepherd's peremptory injunction to a massive flock of sheep streaming over the crossing and watched, amused, as the flock turned obediently on an upward path. A sooty-black maverick veered off independently toward the town drinking fountain. Lifting delicately

tapered front hooves, the animal immersed them in
the lower basin while its black velvet lips fastened on
the spout above, which dripped pure mountain water.
Anxious sheepdogs seemed discomfited by this flagrant disregard of their authority, and they rushed to
nip at the ewe's heels until, her thirst quenched, she
withdrew with dignity from the fountain and leaped
away to rejoin her more orderly sisters uphill.

"Mind if I join you?" A hesitant voice came from
her left, and the smile was still on her lips when she
turned her head and saw Joel Carter standing awkwardly beside her table, a half-finished beer in his
hand.

"No, of course not, Joel." She broadened her
smile. "But it's almost time for us to leave." She
gave him a quizzical look as he pulled out the chair
across from her and sat down. "I'd have thought
you'd be taking in the atmosphere of St-Paul-de-
Vence instead of...." She waved a hand at the glass
beer mug.

"Oh, I've been here before," he explained earnestly. "My father financed a trip to Europe for me when
I convinced him that I wanted to be an artist."

"So what happened to your career as an artist?"
she prodded gently when he paused.

"Oh, I have no talent in that direction," he admitted candidly. "I soon found that out when I looked
at all the true masterpieces in Europe. Now I'm over
here to find worthwhile paintings by modern artists
to sell in the gallery I'm opening in New York."

"Your father must be a very understanding man,"
she commented.

"It wasn't that way at first. He wanted me to follow him into his brokerage business, but it didn't take him long to realize that I just wasn't interested in the rise and fall of the stock market. But I know I can make a go of the picture gallery," he rushed on, no longer tongue-tied as he warmed to his subject. "I'm a fairly good judge of what's worthwhile."

Lindsay felt a mild pang of sympathy for the man whose son had opted out of a no doubt lucrative business for the ephemeral rewards of the art world. "Do you have other brothers who might be more interested in the business world?"

"No." He grinned unexpectedly, looking like a mischievous twelve-year-old. "But I have a sister who's a whiz with figures, and dad's finally caught up to the late twentieth century. Sandra's a lot more suited to the dog-eat-dog world than I ever could be."

"Good for her."

The problems of the Carter family slid to the back of her mind as the first of her brood began sauntering back to the bus, although she made a mental note to cross Joel off her list of possible suspects out to steal Philip's letter. A man who shied away from everyday commerce was hardly likely to engage in the cut and thrust of espionage.

IGNORING THE BED that seemed to beckon to her when she returned to her room after dinner, Lindsay took time only to prepare for the evening tour of Monte Carlo, which loomed next on her horizon.

The plain brown high-necked wool dress she

changed into contrasted drably with the finery the other women had chosen for their fleeting visit to the tiny municipality, she realized when her eyes ran comprehensively over the group assembled in the foyer. Irene Harben sparkled in sequin-studded satin, and Lila's tiara strove valiantly to outshine any that Princess Grace might have possessed.

How could she possibly explain tactfully that the evening tour included only a view of Monaco's nightlights and a section of the fabled casino not usually frequented by big-money gamblers? As always, she would have to rely on the general glamour surrounding nightlife in Monte Carlo and hope that a glimpse of a famous figure entering the casino would suffice. On the way from Nice to Monte Carlo, she attempted to cushion future disillusionment by offering the standard Eurospan prize.

"There's a special prize for the one who tries his luck and comes up with the highest winnings of the evening," she encouraged gaily as they entered the casino. She saw with relief that the Ferruccis were enthusiastically leading the way to the hungry machines that swallowed francs as if they were American quarters—in spite of the fact that banks of Las Vegas-style "one-armed bandits" were clearly not what they'd expected to find.

Everyone seemed to have a reasonably good time, either people-watching or gambling cautiously at the lower-stake tables. At the end of it all, Lindsay made a small ceremony of presenting an enameled replica of their tour bus to the grand winners, Paul and Mary Strangeways, and the male half of the duo made a quick speech of appreciative acceptance. The group then reassembled and emerged outside the casino just as Pierre, with perfect timing, drove the bus up with a flamboyant squeal of wheels.

"When are we going to meet the Rainiers?" a disappointed Lila wondered plaintively as the interior lights of the bus dimmed and were replaced by the yellowish glow of buildings and street lamps. "I did want to ask the prince if he ever intends to take his younger daughter to America for a visit."

"He may," Lindsay soothed, grateful for the solitary voice from somewhere in back that began to sing *The Star-Spangled Banner*, going it alone until first one and then finally the whole group took up the strains. Lindsay herself forgot the dual heritage that was hers—English mother, American father—and joined in.

"I'm sorry." She regretfully cut short a further bid to extend the evening's singsong, switching on the microphone. "We're just arriving back at the hotel. I also hate to remind you that at seven-thirty tomorrow morning, we'll be on our way again. It's a long day's travel, but we'll take time out to have lunch at Rapallo in Italy, and then pay a visit to the famous Tower of Pisa before going on to our next big stop in Florence. So have a good night, sleep well, and I'll see you bright and early in the morning."

A tremor coursed through her as she went into her room, but she dismissed it as an overreaction to the break-in of the night before. Whoever had rifled through her room must be aware by now that whatever he or she was seeking wasn't there. So far so good.

AFTER A DECENT NIGHT'S REST, Lindsay wore a smile that was completely genuine the next morning as she welcomed passengers aboard. Exhausted from yesterday's hectic itinerary, her mind set at ease about her room being ransacked further, she had slept like a baby.

"Would you like us to stow some of those in the luggage compartment?" she asked helpfully when Charlene Warner struggled to her seat laden with a multitude of packages and bags.

"And have them disappear forevermore?" the blond woman screeched unattractively, drawing the curious eyes of the other passengers as she arranged her luggage in the vacant place beside her window seat, squeezing past the pile to settle herself huffily for the long day's drive. Lindsay shrugged faintly and turned away, knowing that precious time would be wasted trying to persuade the woman that her luggage would be far safer tucked away in the locked compartment under the bus than being hauled in and out of hotels.

Lindsay nodded to Pierre, and as the bus pulled away from the white-pillared hotel, she picked up her microphone. "Good morning, everybody," she began in a cheerful tone. "I hope you enjoyed your stay in Nice. It's one of my favorite places, and I'm always a little sad when we leave it behind. But then I console myself with what's coming next." She paused. "For most of the day, we'll be following the

Mediterranean coastline, which, on a day like this, is really beautiful. We'll stop for lunch at Rapallo, just past Genoa, and go on from there to Pisa...."

Once across the border into Italy, where customs inspection was cursory, the bus faithfully followed the road to San Remo, the resort town where they stopped for coffee, before pressing on to the lunch break at another of Lindsay's favorite spots, Rapallo.

She wasn't the only one who regretted the shortness of their stay there. The Italian Riviera's capital of flowers, where carnations and roses and mimosa bloomed in profusion during the spring, was still gorgeous now with the blossoms of autumn and the scent of lemon and eucalyptus in the air.

"We're only stopping here for *lunch*?" Debora Dakers asked regretfully as she stepped from the bus and drew in a lungful of the perfumed air wafting from a nearby park. Her eyes fell on the sunlit calm of the Mediterranean just beyond the gardens. "This is heaven."

"You'll have to set a book here," Lindsay teased her, "and spend a few months researching it."

Debora shuddered. "A book? I've never written a book in my life, and I'm sure I'd never want to. Fiction is not my forte. I write articles, mainly for magazines." She twisted her head to look up at her husband, who stood poised on the step above her. "You're the novelist in the family, honey. Why don't you set one here?"

"You also wanted me to set one in Paris, another in Nice," he reminded her dryly, though all the love in the world was in the quick squeeze of his hand at her waist, in the arm he left there as they sauntered off together toward the seafront cafés, some of which were closed for several weeks at this time of the year. Lindsay watched them go, a wistful look in her dark eyes. Now that was a marriage, she reflected, where love transcended even career rivalry. How would Carey react to a wife with career ambitions of her own?

The question disappeared like vapor when he descended from the bus, giving her only a tight smile and a nod before going, surprisingly, to join Louis Perrault, who was studiedly pretending interest in the tiny lemons forming on the closest of the trees.

"How about joining me for lunch?" Carey suggested in a tone that seemed to take for granted the other man's agreement, and Lindsay saw the Frenchman's eyes swivel around to her as she waited for Pierre to lock the bus. Had he expected her own company at the meal break? If so, she was grateful to Carey for relieving her of that particular burden. But she was thoughtful as her steps fell in with Pierre's for the walk from the seafront lined with hotels and restaurants to the bistro at the far end that tourists seldom found.

Why had he deliberately sought out the other man's company? Was he still suspicious of Perrault's presence on the tour, or.... No. It certainly wasn't that he wanted to keep her apart from the flashing-eyed admiration of the dapper Frenchman!

At Pisa, she spent most of her time taking pictures for those passengers who had elected to scale the leaning tower. It was no hardship for her to remain on terra firma. Vertigo always assailed her even when she walked into the entrance staircase—a psychological disability that affected her only here—so she was content to take charge of various cameras and click their shutters for the more intrepid, who daringly traversed the sloping balconies circling the tower.

It was time to go when the last of her charges had come down from the slanting heights, but she didn't really regret missing espresso coffee in the café across the street. Lunch at Rapallo had more than satisfied her.

"My family comes from around here," Tony Ferrucci divulged when they were on their way to Florence, where they would spend the next three days. "Lucca. Do you know it?"

Lindsay smiled and looked at Pierre, who gave his Gallic shrug and turned off on the road to Lucca. "We don't have time to stop over, Mr. Ferrucci, but Pierre is going to drive you through Lucca so you can see the place where your ancestors came from."

"Jeez, that's great! Did you hear that, Gina?"

His plump, solid-looking wife displayed less excitement, at first, than he did, but her dark eyes obediently took in the ancient, sun-drenched buildings Tony pointed out as the bus traversed Lucca's narrow streets. Gina's own family, Lindsay had gathered, came from much farther south, where poverty walked hand in hand with hunger. The two whose origins were firmly rooted in Italian soil seemed overcome as the bus sped on toward Florence and the art treasures that would mean far less to them than that fleeting glimpse of Lucca.

"Why don't you take an overnight trip from Florence?" she suggested later, bending over their plush-covered seats located toward the back of the bus. Her smile encompassed the placid Gina, but her attention was mainly on Tony when she joked, "Who knows? Maybe you'll find a long-lost relative there."

"Yeah, that's true." Tony turned excitedly to his wife. "What do you say, Gina? Should we do that?"

"Accommodation in Lucca is very low-priced right now," she coaxed when Gina hesitated, "and I might be able to get you a refund on your night's accommodation at our hotel in Florence."

The possibility of that was as remote as finding a hen with teeth, she knew, but Lindsay wanted Tony to see the town of his forefathers, even if it meant that the money would come from her own pocket. It was unlikely that the Ferruccis would pass this way again, so it was a golden opportunity.

Gina nodded into Tony's excited face, and he beamed up at Lindsay. "We'll take the offer. Thanks a lot, Lindsay."

"I'd appreciate it if you didn't mention the hotel arrangements to the other passengers," she put in hastily, envisioning a deluge of requests to transfer hotel accommodations from one point to another, which was why the company had such a stringent rule about it, she supposed. "This is just between you and me, okay?"

And the man sitting in the seat behind, she realized

belatedly as she straightened and met Carey's hard stare. Her eyes took on a defiant glint. He must have heard her offer to the Ferruccis, knowing that the company would never permit such a swap in accommodation for fear of setting a precedent. Well, she didn't give a damn! She would take care of it herself, and that way the company spy would have no cause for concern.

Their hotel in Florence, overlooking the Arno and within sight of the Ponte Vecchio, took in her charges like a mother hen ushering her chicks to warmth and safety. Her own room overlooked the lamp-lit river, too, and Lindsay had no qualms about the suites she directed her passengers to. Florence the beautiful awaited them.

# CHAPTER EIGHT

"YOU WILL PLEASE COME and stand here with me," the guide intoned, his tall sturdy frame overshadowed by the ornately decorated cathedral that Lindsay loved for its very embellishments. Many people thought the cathedral's eye-catching grandeur was too much, but she had always loved it, been enslaved by its beautifully molded perfection since her first visit there as a novice tour director. She stepped back when her tour gravitated toward the well-versed guide.

"Aren't you coming in?" Joel stopped to ask, and she shook her head. For one thing, whenever she accompanied a tour, passengers tended to turn toward her more familiar figure with their comments and questions, annoying the specially hired guide. For another, she preferred to soak up the warmth of the sun as well as the church's outer beauty.

Regretting now that she'd chosen a warm, short-jacketed rust tweed suit to wear, Lindsay wandered to the other side of the massive duomo with its breathtaking decorative white-and-greenish-black marble facade, wondering as she often did about the Florentines of old and their superb craftsmanship. In the days when there were no power tools to work with, had they resented the fact that a building such as this one would never be completed in their life-time? Or had they regarded adding their small contri-bution as a privilege? What would they have thought if they'd known about the thousands of people who came every year from all parts of the world to drink in the beauty they'd helped to create?

"I guess the men who built this had no idea that people of the twentieth century would still be coming to marvel at it." A male American voice echoed her thoughts from behind. She swung around, unable to hide the welcoming sparkle in her near-black eyes.

"I—didn't expect you here," she said stiltedly, her eyes dropping to the casual elegance of Carey's black blazer and high-necked white cotton shirt. White again! Did he use the pristine color so much because he knew how attractively it contrasted with the light tan of his lean face? No, he wouldn't do that. Carey was anything but studied and vain in his dressing. "You weren't on my list for the city tour."

"Conducted tours aren't my favorite thing." He grimaced. "I like to go where the mood takes me." His eyes seemed to take on a more yellowish tint from the sun, making him look like a lion basking under the shelter of an African tree, keeping an alert watch on the females in his harem. "For instance, my mood this morning dictates a leisurely drive into the hills and a picnic lunch in some secluded spot with a black-haired lady I've discovered is free this after-noon. How about it?"

Her eyes veered away from his again in sudden panic and fastened on the emblem emblazoned on the pocket above his heart. The intensity of her own desire to drop everything and go with him overwhelmed her.

"I really shouldn't do that," she murmured, drawing a ragged breath as she forced herself to look up at him. "I should be available if I'm needed—"

"What—by people who have all the wonders of Florence at their fingertips?" he asked incredulously. "Believe me, what with the Uffizi Gallery for the artistically inclined and the abundant leather goods for the less discerning, you won't even be missed. Besides, I'll get you back in time for predinner complaints, if that's what bothers you."

"Well, then, yes," she agreed, knowing that she hadn't really hesitated because of her duty to the passengers. She was far more concerned about the responses an afternoon in the hills around Florence would evoke. . . .

LINDSAY WOULDN'T HAVE BEEN HUMAN if the powerful growl of the open-topped sports car, drawing envious glances from male Italian bystanders, hadn't sent a thrill of exhilaration through her. Nor was she oblivious to the slanting glances from chic Florentine women and well-heeled tourists, who stopped to stare openly at the man behind the wheel, his dark hair whipping attractively over his tanned brow, his arms sinewy brown.

She was glad that she'd changed into a simple butter-yellow cotton dress with a low neckline. Reveling in the breeze whipped up by the car's motion, Lindsay settled farther back into the soft leather of her bucket seat as they left Florence and began the

long wind up into the green-shaded hills surrounding
the city. Her eyes flicked to Carey's muscular physique, contoured to the seat beside her. He, too, had
changed into more suitable apparel for a warm afternoon: a casual short-sleeved shirt and cream-colored
pants in smooth cotton, white socks and comfortable
brown leather moccasin-type shoes.

Standard garb for a well-to-do tourist, but there
was nothing standard about her flaring awareness of
his attractiveness. The long lean lines of his body
sparked a yearning that started in the pit of her
stomach and rose to her throat, leaving her breathless
and rather resentful. Why was she so vulnerable
where Carey Hudson was concerned? Why had she
consented to come on this stolen afternoon outing,
anyway, with a man who had treated her with only
token politeness since that evening in Nice?

"I thought we'd have lunch while enjoying a view
of Florence—" Carey glanced sideways at her
"—and then go on to Prato. Do you know it?
There's evidently a wealth of art in the Palazzo
Pretorio as well as—"

"In the church of San Domenico," she finished
for him, quoting from one of her brochures. "'a
gothic church boasting the priceless works of—'"

"Do you know that the most difficult person to
impress with one's smattering of knowledge is a tour
guide?" Carey complained in pretended frustration,
and Lindsay laughed ruefully, expelling the tension
that had been mounting. His own smile was self-
mocking, and Lindsay suddenly felt the need to
reassure him.

"Don't worry about it. I've never been to Prato. I'm just quoting blind from a travel brochure I picked up somewhere along the way in case someone ever asked me about Prato and its marvels." She paused. "No one has so far."

His grin was wide and free and provided a glimpse of what he must have been like when he was younger. "Good. So you're as much in the dark as I am."

Moments later he drew the car into a natural indentation in the road and switched off the engine. The sudden silence was punctuated by the sound of running water, of birds twittering their alarm at being invaded by the human creatures who detached themselves from the alien noisemaker and fumbled around in the back of it.

"How's this?" Carey indicated a cushiony grassed area sloping down to the reduced but still active stream that bubbled and gurgled over stones made smooth by centuries of erosion.

"Fine." Lindsay helped him spread the lunch provided by the hotel. Every detail had been taken care of, even to the red-and-white checked cloth that stood out brightly against the landscape. There was food enough for a party of six, she noted when the picnic hamper was unloaded: tomatoes in aspic, tender moist chicken, succulent spears of asparagus, crisp rolls spread thickly with butter. The hotel—and Carey—had excelled in thoughtfulness, concocting a palate-tingling lunch accompanied by a light white wine.

Lindsay could have drooled over the feast spread before her, her stomach reminding her that she had eaten only a meager breakfast consisting of rolls and coffee. Carey watched her, amused, as she reached for a succulent chicken thigh and sank her white teeth into it.

"You're like a starving refugee," he remarked in an inoffensively indulgent tone, his own lean fingers curling around a dark-meated drumstick.

"I feel like one," she admitted in a muffled tone, all embarrassment gone in her efforts to satiate her hunger. "Perhaps it's the air out here."

"Could be," he agreed noncommittally, spooning another helping of the jellied tomato onto her plate. "More wine?"

"Please."

She held out her glass for him to fill from the bottle, amazed at the way she was suddenly able to relax and enjoy herself. Whether this was due to the balminess of the air, the prospect of Florence's tiled roofs or the fact of Carey's undeniably exciting presence, she wasn't prepared to say. After she'd taken the edge off her appetite, she refused the cheese and crackers Carey offered, lying back with a contented sigh on the short springy turf that formed a fragrant cradle for her body.

She was vaguely aware of Carey looming over her, his voice sounding detached when he asked, "How about coffee? Would you like some?"

"Later," she murmured, willing the continuance of the strange lethargy that invaded her limbs. How wise the Italians were to insist on a siesta after a filling midday meal! A meal accompanied by wine....

She slept dreamlessly, more restfully than she had

since the tour began. When her eyes finally opened, they went to the source of a persistent buzzing in her ears.... Flies were feasting noisily on the remains of their lunch, the odd one taking time out to investigate the smooth swell of her thigh under her skirt, which had hiked up to display an embarrassing length of leg. She shifted and grew still again when a dark-haired arm tightened around her middle in a possessive gesture that snapped her eyes open. She was wide awake now and turned her head to see Carey asleep by her side. Not just asleep, but with his head on her outstretched arm, cushioning him from the spiny undergrowth of dried grass.

"Carey," she murmured, moving her hand lethargically to the hard line of his jaw, which appeared only a little less forceful in sleep than it did when he was conscious. Without knowing what prompted the action, she let her fingertips move over the harsh lines that ran from nose to mouth, wondering at the reason for their deep-bitten quality. He wasn't a man who laughed a lot. Even his smiles came so unexpectedly that they changed his features entirely. Her forefinger touched lightly on the shape of his lips, relaxed and somehow vulnerable, and she remembered the feel of them, not just at her mouth, but over every inch of her skin, kissing her in places that became new erotic points because of his touch. Even Geoff....

She bit down on her soft lower lip. Had she ever really loved Geoff? Or had it just been the aura of glamour that surrounded him and his job, the romance of Rome in a carefree summer, the newness of passion? Could she have responded to Carey so totally that night in Lucerne if Geoff's imprint was still on her?

Her eyes lifted, and shock riveted them to the open, faintly amused tawny brown of Carey's, embarrassment staining her skin a deep pink.

She hurriedly gathered her wits. "I—I was trying to wake you up."

"You certainly succeeded in that," he said, his voice unusually soft.

"I think we should...get going if we want to see the Prato today." She moved to get up but found Carey's arm still held her casually around the waist. He drew her back to the hard dryness of the sunbaked grass.

"Why? It's not going anywhere, is it?"

At another time, a vision of the centuries-old village arising and departing might have struck her as funny, but now she could only lie numb under his shadow as he raised himself onto one elbow and looked lazily down at her.

"What were you thinking about just now?" His voice was still thick with sleep, but there was an animallike watchfulness in his narrowed eyes.

Lindsay blinked, cursing the lethargy that pinned her to the hard unyielding ground. "Just that it was time we made a move."

"Liar. You were thinking about your precious Geoff, weren't you, and wondering if you could bring yourself to forget him long enough to have sex with me."

Gasping, she flailed her legs and struck with her

fist at the sinewy forearm barring her escape. "You arrogant...bastard!" she flung back wildly. "You think every woman you meet can't wait to fall into bed with you!"

"They usually do," he retorted mildly, "except for the odd one who puts up a token resistance."

"This is not token," she gritted through painfully clenched teeth. "Let me up right now or I'll—"

"You'll what?" He actually chuckled as he caught the arm she raised again to strike him, pinioning her wrist to the arid grass beside her head, half-leaning over her.

"I'll have you thrown off the tour!"

"An executive of the company?" His brows lifted maddeningly; his mocking question needed no reply. In a showdown, his word would be believed in preference to her own. She couldn't believe he would take that kind of advantage, but it seemed he was prepared to. The time was surely at hand for her to hit him as far below the belt as he was threatening to strike her.

"Go ahead, then." She stopped struggling. "Rape me if you must, but you'll never be half the man Geoff is!"

The sharp hiss of his indrawn breath told her that she'd struck home, but when he spoke moments later his voice was cool and controlled. "Maybe that's something we should put to the test. And it won't be rape—I can promise you that."

There was no gentle wooing in the way his head swooped down, his lips capturing hers in an abrasive kiss that robbed her of the breath needed for protest.

The pressure of his mouth against hers, the weight of his body as it half lay over hers stifled any thoughts of rejecting him. In order to disarm him she had to be quiescent...*had* to be....

The feel of his hand at the buttons of her sun dress brought a low moan of protest from deep in her throat. But as if she had urged him on, he triumphantly parted the bodice of her dress and fastened on the creamy mound of her breast, his fingers teasing the dark red of her nipple to quivering awareness.

His mouth left hers, and she drew a ragged breath of relief...a premature relief that gave way to agonized pleasure at the feel of his lips, his tongue, nuzzling the roused peak of her breast. The sensation felt like fire, like molten honey that warmed and spread all over her and bathed the starved centers of her being. Helpless against the raw primitive need that surged through her, Lindsay closed her eyes and moaned softly in her throat when he pushed away the other side of her unfastened bodice, the sun warm on her bared flesh for a moment until his dark head moved and his mouth repeated the movements that sent her reeling into a limbo of pure feeling.

He seemed to sense that moment of capitulation, reinforced by the blind seeking of her hands under the tight fit of the shirt that spanned his chest. He paused to throw it off, then pressed back down on the soft mounds of her breasts.

A soft whimper escaped from her throat. "Carey...love me, Carey."

As if the words had opened a Pandora's box of caring, Carey suddenly became a tender wooer, a pursuer. The hard muscles of his thighs slid between the eager spreading of hers, his hands slowly, sensuously inching the confining lace panties down over her hips, bunching the patterned cotton of her dress up to her waist. "Oh, God, Lindsay, I want you so much!"

It didn't matter to her how many women he had mesmerized with those words. All Lindsay knew was that her own body ached with a new longing, a hunger that wouldn't be satisfied until they knew each other completely, until they became one. She unbuckled his belt, tugged down on the zipper of his slacks, hungry for a greater closeness. Pushing down the thin cotton of his briefs she caressed him, and a harsh cry broke from her throat when his hips pressed into her. Pleasure invaded every atom of her being. Her whole life seemed to have been lived for this moment, when the man she loved made love to her so intensely, even if it wasn't love he felt.... Her fingers plowed wildly into the thickness of his dark hair, her nostrils filled with the warm male scent of him and the musky perfume that rose from the sundried soil around them.

The moist sheen on his muscled chest tasted warm and salty to her boldly exploring tongue, his pleasure hers when he groaned and sought the tender hollow of her throat, reaching hotly with his lips for the erratic beat of the pulse just under her jaw. Borne on a cresting wave of almost unbearable sensation, Lindsay curved the long line of her legs around the irresistible undulation of his hips, crying out hoarsely as she awaited the moment when they would merge, when the mounting tension inside her would explode into a bursting series of ever widening spasms of delight.

His abrupt cessation of movement left her gasping, her fingers tearing uselessly at the sparse clumps of grass within their reach. *Damn him,* she sobbed inwardly, every sense clamorously craving the final fulfillment. He had proved his point and saw no reason to—

The sound of soft bells penetrated her consciousness, and she turned her head to see a flock of sheep meandering heavily, following the lone figure of a shepherd to the valley below.

Lindsay expelled her breath on a deep-drawn sigh, shifting her gaze to the man who had drawn away from her and now sat watching the progress of the sheep as they stumbled happily after their mentor. He had heard what her bemused senses hadn't. And now his profile was hard, closed against the question in her eyes. Humiliation swept over her as her fingers fumbled in their closing of the bodice over her swollen breasts, as, in a return to modesty, her hands smoothed the creased lines of her skirt to knee length.

She must have been crazy to respond so easily to his lovemaking, she thought bleakly. What had possessed her—to want to give herself to a man who obviously cared nothing for her?

"Let's go," he suggested distantly, rising and cinching the belt around the trousers he'd half abandoned in the throes of making love to her. "Do you want to see the wonders of Prato?" he asked abruptly.

She shook her head. How could she concentrate on the wonders of an ancient world while the realities of her own world impinged so harshly on her battered senses?

THE PIAZZALE MICHELANGELO was filled, as usual, with tourists from almost every country under the sun. Nonetheless, the photographer managed to reserve a corner of the square for the placement of his photographic subjects.

"The tall lady there—" he waved an imperious hand in Betty Timms's direction "—will you please go to the back row? That's it. Yes...." His eyes fell thoughtfully on Lindsay. "Miss Tabor, if you can take your place at the far end of the middle row?"

The sputtering sound of a sports car drew every eye to the low-slung Ferrari that purred to a halt just short of the assembled group.

"It's Carey Hudson," Charlene announced, her eyes bearing a distinctly predatory gleam as they lit on the lean tall figure that leaped agilely from the car. "Come and stand here with me, Carey," she called out as his eyes swept coolly over the group.

"It will be better if you take a place beside the tour manager," the photographer overrode her frostily, refocusing his protuberant lens on the reformed group as Carey went to stand at Lindsay's side.

"Thank you," he said after several clicks of the shutter. "The photographs will be available for your inspection later today. But it would perhaps be better if you placed your orders now, since you will be leaving Florence tomorrow."

There was a general surge toward the vanlike vehicle he'd driven up in, and Lindsay detached herself briskly from Carey's side.

"Oh, Lindsay—" Lila rushed up breathlessly "—is this the only picture of the tour we'll have? I was hoping we'd have a background of Rome. You know—all those ruins."

While she persuaded Lila that Florence provided the best all-round background, Lindsay was aware of Carey striding decisively toward the parked Ferrari, of the slide of his long body behind the wheel. The leathery scent of the sports car's interior lingered nostalgically in her memory, and she watched openly as Carey gunned the powerful motor and backed away from the curb, a pang of envy shooting through her. How wonderful it must be to shuck off the cares of the workaday world and take off wherever fancy dictated!

LATER IN THE AFTERNOON, as she lay relaxing on her bed, she was still wondering just why Carey had turned up for the photography session. Group activities of any kind weren't his thing—he had said as much—so she hadn't really been surprised at his nonappearance for the communal tour dinner the night before. Nor had Charlene's absence registered unduly, not until the after-dinner group erupted noisily into the foyer and Lindsay caught a glimpse of Carey's arm around Charlene's waist as he ushered her into the elevator. They were both dressed formally, he in a dinner jacket, she in a long black evening gown.

The same nauseous feeling gripped her now as she recalled the hot rush of blood that had made her smiling responses to the joking remarks of her tour group purely automatic. She didn't need the wisdom of Solomon to surmise why Carey had sought out the overblown charms of the man-hungry Charlene. She was more easily available for the consummation he had been denied up there in the hills surrounding Florence. He needed that ultimate release—or so he would probably argue.

But what about her? She needed it, too; last night's sleepless hours had told her that. Every part of her had ached with her need of him. Maybe that was the difference between them.... He could find solace in another woman's, any woman's arms, whereas her tortured mind had been filled with a fantasylike reliving of those passionate moments on the hillside.

A tentative knock at her bedroom door brought her hurriedly to her feet. A young delivery boy handed a thick package to her, and his olive-skinned face broke into a delighted grin when she abstractedly handed him a too generous tip.

"*Gràzie, signorína,*" he thanked her quickly, making his escape before she had time to realize her mistake.

Lindsay forgot him immediately as she wandered back into the room, her fingers loosening the gummed seal and drawing out the ordered copies of the photograph taken that afternoon.

It was similar to every other group tour—smiles beaming out at her from Brad and Debora Dakers, Paul and Mary Strangeways, a hesitant smile from

Betty, flanked by a surly Carl. Joel, Lila—even Frank Harben sported an attempt at a smile, a grim stretch of his narrow mouth.

But what drew her astonished attention was the woman molded to Carey's side as if she grew from it. The smile she had expected to appear frozen looked, instead, like the tremulous offering of a woman in love for the first time. Even more remarkable was Carey's side-and-downward glance, which the camera had caught in clear detail. It was almost as if—no. It truly was the look of a man intensely interested in the woman at his side.

It must have been a trick of the lens—

The telephone rang beside her bed, and she transferred the picture to her left hand while she reached for the receiver.

*"Prónto."*

"You can forget the Italian if we're to have any kind of conversation at all," Carey said dryly in her ear. "It's not one of my languages, I'm afraid."

Her errant pulse began to beat in an unsteady rhythm, but she managed a cool "Do you have many?"

"I have to admit that English is my best," he confessed, seeming in a light mood. "With French as a runner-up and Spanish a very poor third."

"Oh." She was inexplicably tongue-tied, and her eyes fell on the picture still clutched in her hand. Trick photography or not, a disturbing shiver of pleasure rippled through her as she looked again at their pose. Stupidly, as she realized immediately, she said, "Do you need me for something?"

Silence stretched for so long between them that she was sure they'd been disconnected. Then Carey said in a strange voice, "I'm beginning to think I do, in more ways than one. But for the immediate future, namely tonight, I'd like to take you to a hotel not far from here where we can have dinner and dance—"

"No!" Lindsay's voice came out even more sharply than she'd intended. Last night's tossing and turning had taught her one thing; casual affairs of two or three or four weeks' duration could never be for her. Nothing in her experience had prepared her for a purely sexual relationship such as a man like Carey Hudson would offer. She had been programmed to think in terms of lifelong relationships like her parents' marriage, like Philip's and Elena's marriage. She had pictured a future with children and two loving parents to rear them, not hurried gropings in hotel rooms and olive-scented hillsides. "I... can't," she said with less force than she would have liked, and blinked when Carey's voice came back at her completely changed.

"I'm not asking you for a date, as such," he said in a chilling tone. "This is business. The hotel I have in mind might very well fit into one of our less exclusive tours, and I'd like your opinion on how it stacks up. I'll pick you up in the hotel lobby at eight—and don't wear anything too fancy. It's not that kind of place."

He left her no time to protest further, replacing his receiver with a firmness that shot through her eardrum. Slowly she hung up and stared at the green-patterned carpet at her feet. His high-handed attitude

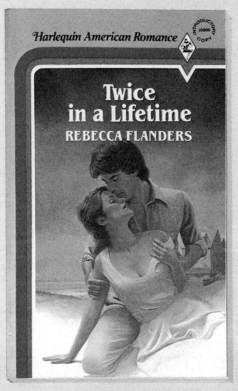

# Enter a uniquely American world of romance with

## *Harlequin American Romance.*™

*Harlequin American Romances* are the first romances to explore today's new love relationships. These compelling romance novels reach into the hearts and minds of women across America…probing into the most intimate moments of romance, love and desire.

You'll follow romantic heroines and irresistible men as they boldy face confusing choices. Career first, love later? Love without marriage? Long-distance relationships? All the experiences that make love real are captured in the tender, loving pages of *Harlequin American Romance*.

What makes American women so different when it comes to love? Find out with *Harlequin American Romance!* Send for your introductory FREE book now.

# GET THIS BOOK FREE!

**MAIL TO:**
Harlequin Reader Service
2504 W. Southern Avenue,
Tempe, AZ 85282

## YES! I want to discover *Harlequin American Romance*.

Send me FREE and without obligation, "Twice in a Lifetime."
If you do not hear from me after I have examined my FREE
book, please send me the 4 new *Harlequin American Romance*
novels each month as soon as they come off the presses. I
understand that I will be billed only $2.25 per book (total
$9.00). There are no shipping or handling charges. There
is no minimum number of books that I have to purchase.
In fact, I may cancel this arrangement at any time. "Twice
in a Lifetime" is mine to keep as a FREE gift, even if I do
not buy any additional books.

154-CIA-NAD2

| | |
|---|---|
| Name | (please print) |

| | |
|---|---|
| Address | Apt. No. |

| | | |
|---|---|---|
| City | State/Prov. | Zip/Postal Code |

Signature (If under 18, parent or guardian must sign.)

This offer is limited to one order per household and not valid to current
Harlequin American Romance subscribers. We reserve the right to
exercise discretion in granting membership. If price changes are
necessary, you will be notified. Offer expires January 31, 1984.

PRINTED IN CANADA

# Experience *Harlequin American Romance*™...

with this special introductory FREE book offer.

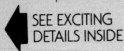 SEE EXCITING
DETAILS INSIDE

Send no money. Mail this card
and receive this new, full-length
*Harlequin American Romance*
novel absolutely FREE.

sent prickles of resentment to the short hairs at her nape, but on the other hand. . . . On the other hand, he was an executive of the company and so was free to order her to be present on company business. Which, according to him, this was. But could he really be that cavalier about what had happened between them yesterday? Her mouth tightened. Obviously he could, and she wasn't going to be the one to make emotional waves over an incident that was run-of-the-mill for him.

ALTHOUGH HE HAD TOLD HER not to wear anything fancy, she reached into the closet that evening and settled her fur stole around her shoulders, which were bare. The style of her cunningly cut black cocktail dress was figure defining yet understated, and the blue fox looked too chic to be the fake fur it was, although she was certain it would have cost very little more for the real thing. So why had she dressed this way, when Carey had specified otherwise? A gesture of defiance to prove her independence? A need for the confidence that wearing the fur inspired?

She pressed the elevator button for the lobby and leaned back against the padded arm rail as she descended, alone, to the ground floor. She compressed her mouth into a taut line. She needed no gestures to prove her independence or to give her confidence. Carey Hudson was a man like any other, happy to sweeten his European trip with a passionate affair.

The doors opened, and her breath drew in on an audible hiss, seeing him. She had been mistaken about one thing. He wasn't the least bit like any other man, not in any way. The sexual aura around him hadn't just come to the fore during that half-hour on the hillside yesterday. She had felt it, known of it, since that first day in London when he had strode confidently into the Eurospan departure hall.

His eyes approved the elegant simplicity of her dress as she forced herself to walk toward him, pausing when another couple passed between them, pulling in another deep breath that enabled her to meet the glint of admiration flickering in his tawny eyes.

"Every color I see you in seems just the right one for you, so much so that I'll forgive you for disregarding my advice," he complimented her huskily, his fingers brushing the thick pile of her stole as he took her arm to escort her to the door. "A gift from an admirer?"

"Yes, as a matter of fact," she retorted coolly, aware of interested glances in their direction. She supposed they did make a striking couple to a stranger's eyes, but she was careful to keep her smoothly made-up face expressionless at the thought. Thinking of her father's furrowed brow and bent shoulders, she guessed he was probably her greatest admirer so far in her life. It seemed childish, suddenly, to deny him as the donor of the stole. "He also used to take me to the zoo, and to Disneyland, and—"

"Your father?"

Was it her imagination, or did Carey seem relieved to know that it wasn't some well-heeled boyfriend who had bestowed the fur on her? There was no time for speculation on that point, for he was ushering her into the taxi then and they were being smoothly borne away from the hotel steps.

"I expected the Ferrari," she remarked, settling back at his side and feeling around in her small black purse, finally extracting a folded square of silk. Deciding to play it light, she held it up for his inspection. "See, I was all prepared."

She saw him grimace in the taxi's dim light. "I had to return it this afternoon. There wouldn't have been time before the early start tomorrow. Anyway—" his head turned, and she felt his eyes on her "—the Ferrari would have been murder on that hairdo, and I'd have hated to spoil the hairdresser's work."

Lindsay put an unconscious hand up to the smooth backswept style it had taken her over an hour to arrange, reassuring herself with her fingertips that the teased tendrils still curled loosely around her cheeks.

"I don't have the patience to sit in a salon chair," she stated calmly, inwardly marveling at the cozy intimate turn of the conversation. Even her stomach muscles had relaxed, but they contracted once more when Carey casually rested his hand on hers in her lap.

"Clever woman to know what suits you so well, although—" his shoulder touched hers as he turned his head to look more fully at her profile "—it makes you look...I don't know...elegant but unapproachable."

"Isn't that the way a tour guide's supposed to look?" she dodged shakily, relieved when they arrived at their destination and Carey became preoccupied with paying off the driver and escorting her into the garishly modern decor of the huge hotel. A small frown settled between her eyes as they took in the loud conviviality of the place, repartee being bandied around by a group of what looked like American college students traveling together.

"You don't like it?" Carey asked unexpectedly, and a flush rose to her cheeks.

"I guess being with Eurospan for so long has spoiled me," she said apologetically. "The other companies I worked for before used places like this, and there were very few complaints from the passengers, so it must be me."

He was urging her toward the back of the lobby, and she felt surprise that he had obviously investigated the lay of the land beforehand. Opening one half of the massive double doors leading into the vast dining room, he ushered her inside with a touch on her lower spine. Lindsay knew at once why he had advised her to dress simply. Every one of the hotel's patrons was casually attired, from the black high-necked sweaters and hip-hugging cords of Florence's youth to the open-necked shirts and simple dresses of the men and women of the tourist brigade.

She was acutely aware of being vastly overdressed when brows lifted and eyes stared as she followed a waiter to a table in the far corner of the room. Carey, following closely behind, fared no better as the patrons took in his tailored black blazer and charcoal slacks with their knife-edge pleats. The one small consolation was that, seated with their backs to the wall, no eyes burned into their shoulder blades.

Looking back on it later, Lindsay reflected that the evening had been a disaster from that point on. Conversation was impossible because of the thrumming

beat of a four-piece band not far from them, a din
that was augmented by the raucous voice of an overblown woman singer, whose eyes returned again and
again to Carey with a meaningful soulfulness that he
ignored completely.

"Let's get out of here," he mouthed, frowning
ferociously, leaving her no choice when he rose and
plucked her stole from the chair back, carrying it
over his arm as he pressed her back through the, by
now, even more curious stares.

Muttering a choice oath, he escorted Lindsay
through the heavy doors to the comparative quiet of
the lobby, running an irritated hand through his hair
before draping the stole around her shoulders. His
hands dropped to the cool thickness of the fur, pressing into it.

"I'm sorry about that, Lindsay," he said in a
strained voice. "I had no idea it would be quite that
bad. Look, why don't we go back and have something in the hotel?"

"That sounds fine," she agreed with a warm smile
that seemed to surprise him as much as it did her. Her
first impulse had been to smooth over his embarrassment, but on a deeper level, she knew she couldn't
have borne it if the evening had ended right there,
finished before it had begun.

Their own hotel lobby was an oasis of reverently
hushed peace when they returned to it. Lindsay was
already walking toward the main dining room when
Carey caught her arm. Turning around in surprise,
she saw that his face was drawn taut in anger.

"I've just seen Perrault heading toward the dining

room," he said tersely, his fingers still curled loosely around her waist. "I'm not in the mood to suffer his company gladly tonight. Why don't we go up to my suite and have something sent up?"

Lindsay's eyes grew wide, staring into his. "I . . . don't think that's wise, is it?"

"Wise? Who cares about wise? Oh, for God's sake, don't look at me as if you're thinking I can't get you up there fast enough to ravish your—" he paused significantly, and a hot flush burned Lindsay's cheeks "—your chastity! You must be able to take care of that pretty well by now, considering your experience."

Lindsay gasped as if he had struck her, and for a moment he looked nonplussed. "Look, I wasn't referring to your past love life. I meant your job. You must have had to cold-shoulder any number of footloose male passengers." When her expression remained frozen, he added exasperatedly, "Lindsay, I am tired, I am hungry, and I just want some peace and quiet to eat my meal. I feel badly because I asked you to have dinner with me and you haven't eaten yet. I'd also enjoy your company with the meal."

Put like that, it would have seemed churlish to stamp off to her room in high dudgeon. But Lindsay was far from sure of the rightness of her decision to accompany him to his suite as the elevator bore them quietly upward. Was she more afraid of his forceful masculinity or of her own overwhelming awareness, her vulnerability whenever she was near him?

WHILE CAREY, loosening his tie with one hand, ordered supper on the phone, Lindsay took a seat in one corner of the capacious living-room sofa and glanced at her surroundings. The suites provided by Eurospan—the Endor Corporation now, she supposed without happiness—were in luxurious keeping with the high price tag on the deluxe tour.

Adjoining the spacious living area was the bedroom, dominated by a king-size bed. Antique furnishings decorated both rooms, chests and dressers of carved polished walnut complementing the deep-down comfort of chairs and sofas, a comfort that was missing from many modern furnishings. Not an envious person, nonetheless Lindsay had sometimes wondered what it would be like to travel in this kind of luxurious style. There would be clothes to match, of course—silk peignoirs, chic Balmain one-of-a-kind dresses, the fine leather of Italian shoes—

Catching herself up, she glanced around at Carey's turned back, noting reluctantly the way his shirt clung opaquely to the muscles of his shoulders and faithfully followed the tapering lines of his body to the loose cinch of his slacks. A strangling feeling of claustrophobia seemed to close her throat, and she swallowed quickly. It had been a mistake to come up here to his suite, she told herself bleakly, averting her eyes. She should have—

"Wh-what?"

"I said I've ordered what I think you'll like." Carey looked at her quizzically as he sauntered over to her, tossing his freed tie on the back of an armchair before seating himself on the other end of the sofa. "You're not one of those female militants who cries 'foul' if a man makes a simple decision for her, are you?"

"I don't ever recall using the word 'foul' except in its accepted sense," she conceded, "but I do like to make the decisions that concern me."

He expelled a gusty breath. With a weary gesture toward the phone, he said, "Be my guest. Cancel the coq au vin and order whatever you like."

Lindsay hesitated, her taste buds stimulated by the thought of a dish she would probably have chosen for herself on this occasion. Substantial enough to be filling, light enough not to sit heavily on her stomach, which often happened when she ate this late.

"The coq au vin will be fine," she seceded honestly, and saw a glint of humorous triumph appear in his eyes. "But I *will* use the phone to check on my messages, if you don't mind."

Anything to detach herself from his overweening presence, she thought wildly as she rose in answer to his shrug of acquiescence. About to dial the desk, she turned when he spoke from the small bar in one corner of the room.

"What would you like to drink? There's Scotch, gin, vodka—you name it."

"I. . .I'll have Scotch and soda, thanks." She had a feeling she was going to need something strong to get her through the rest of this unexpected evening. Swiftly her finger dialed. Her voice was briskly efficient when she asked if there were any messages for her. On being told there were none, she continued,

"I'm in suite three-six-five if you need to get in touch with me." It was only as she replaced the receiver in its cradle that she realized the conclusion the clerk might draw from her statement. Shrugging slightly, she walked back to the sofa and resumed her seat, nodding her thanks when Carey handed her a glass, ice tinkling gently against the sides.

He had made the drink strong, but she welcomed its bracing properties and, conversely, the subsequent relaxed feeling that had her leaning back against the deep cushions, enjoying a conversation she would never have thought possible with Carey. The stiff Scotch in his hand seemed to untie the knots of tension within him, too, and he opened up about himself in a way he never had before. He had questioned her before this, drawn her out about her family, her background, but had kept his own counsel about his own life.

He owned an apartment in New York, he said in answer to her query, and a lodge in the Catskills that had been left to him by his mother. Smiling a little, he elaborated, "I'd like to spend more time there, but it hasn't been possible. I travel around a lot for the company."

"You must have found it lonely sometimes," Lindsay probed hesitantly, "growing up without a mother." With the family closeness she had taken for granted in her early life, it was hard to imagine the devastating loneliness a six-year-old boy must have felt on the premature death of his mother.

"Lonely? I don't think that's quite the word for it." Carey stared at the drink held loosely in his hand. "Desolate, maybe, or feeling completely abandoned by the one person who cared for me because I was me—not like the moronic calculating machines my father later married. It got to be a routine I recognized: first the fawning over me, thinking it would please him—which it did—and then the not so subtle hints, when they'd hooked the old man, that my education would be far more beneficial if it took place as far as possible from New York."

Lindsay wanted to ask him if that was why he had never committed himself to a permanent relationship with a woman, but that seemed too personal a question, even given their newfound ease with each other.

She asked instead, "What about your father? He must have cared for you a lot, you being his only son."

Carey shrugged, his eyes narrowing as he glanced in her direction. "He didn't care as long as his... creature comforts were cared for. Most of his time was—still is—taken up with forming new branches to his business empire. And home, when he could spare the time to be there, was a place where he wanted to relax and gather his forces for the next acquisition." The bitter echo of his voice left a void between them.

"Well, er—" Lindsay sought to fill the silence "—is that why you've never settled in one place? I mean, because you have no ties at home?"

He glanced at her quizzically. "I could say the same about you," he retorted logically, draining his glass and setting it down on the low table beside the sofa.

"Well, yes...I suppose that's true, but—but I

have part of my family in England, which is my home base with Eurospan.''

"Ah, yes, your brother.'' He stood up abruptly, indicating her glass. "Let me freshen that for you.''

Her eyes went involuntarily to the open neckline of his shirt as he bent across the table and picked up her glass. The wiry curls of his chest hair, erupting darkly from the pristine whiteness of his shirt, affected her sensuously and filled her mind with the images that had tormented her the night before. Only a slight leap of the imagination was needed to feel the harsh bristles of those body hairs against the yielding softness of her own flesh. As if he were again kissing the jutting rise of her breasts, her nipples hardened and pressed against the smooth line of her bodice, her eyes reflecting her total recall of her body's reaction to his lovemaking.

Poised in his half-bending position above her, Carey, too, seemed caught up in the tableau of remembrance, his eyes seeming to grow progressively, elusively darker as they bored into hers.

Neither of them moved position when the first discreet buzz came from the suite's door bell. But on the second more peremptory ring, Carey straightened unhurriedly and walked with his easy rhythm to admit the room-service waiter, who wheeled in a red-covered folded table and proceeded to extend it before reaching into the heated compartment below to extract covered plates and set them at opposite sides of the table. After swiftly laying cutlery at each place, he bustled around the suite, bringing two high-backed chairs over to complete the intimate dining area.

"The wine, *signóre?*" He indicated the bottle reposing on a bed of ice in a silver bucket.

"I'll see to that." Carey signed the check with a quick scrawl, and the waiter bowed obsequiously from the room. To evoke such satisfaction, Lindsay surmised, his tip had probably approximated a month's wages.

"Shall we?" Carey invited, holding her chair and sliding it under her when she took her place. His gestures had an air of romanticism that appealed to the dreamy aspect of her personality. Yet there was something missing in that regard as they ate the expertly prepared meal. For a moment, when he had been telling her about his father and the endless line of stepmothers seemingly plucked from the tales of Grimm, there had been a vulnerable openness to him, a desire to reach out for the comfort of another human's compassion. But as if he regretted that openness, Carey talked more objectively now about his first trip to Paris.

"There was so much that I'd expected—like the grandeur of the Louvre, the horrible connotations of the Conciergerie, where Marie Antoinette was imprisoned, the old Paris that existed side by side with the new. What I wasn't prepared for was the shrewd, go-ahead attitude of the business community. I learned a lot from that Paris experience."

Lindsay couldn't pretend to empathize on that point. Her life in Europe had followed a more artistic route. As a student at the Sorbonne, she'd lived on the fringes of a society that still protested as a matter of course against the type of multinational corporation Carey represented. His world would have been incomprehensible to her student friends.

And what would they think of the lavishness of her surroundings now? Her eyes went around the elegantly appointed suite, registering the antique furnishings, the ambience of a gilded bygone age. Her eyes were faintly mutinous when they returned to meet Carey's.

"Did you really learn so much?" she queried softly. "Did you find out that all of Paris doesn't consist of high-powered businessmen—that there are whole families that subsist for a month on what you would spend for a day in a hotel like this?"

She hadn't meant to sound so socialistic, but Carey interpreted her remarks in that way.

"Your student friends did their work well, instilling their socialist values in you," he remarked dryly, his eyes like gold marbles through his narrowed lids.

Lindsay met his gaze boldly. "You don't have to be a socialist per se to see that there are vast injustices in the world." Her voice had taken on an irritated tone, partly because she had never swallowed whole the views of Michel, Jean-Paul or the superbly feminine Catherine, her intimates during her year in Paris. Mostly, however, she wanted to prove herself a caring person in Carey's eyes, and she despised herself for that weakness.

They had reached the coffee stage, and she swallowed the remainder of it before standing up and saying firmly, "Thank you for the dinner. It was delicious. If you'll excuse me now, I have an early rise in the morning."

Carey got up, too, his voice sardonic as he came around the table to look down at her quizzically, his broad chest on a level with her eyes. "You're a curious mixture, Lindsay Tabor," he said softly. "One part of you represents the perfect tour hostess, cool and calm and efficient, yet you fight a losing battle against the other half, against your natural instincts.

"You don't need me to tell you that you're beautiful, Lindsay," he added huskily, his hands reaching out to circle the pliant warmth of her waist and draw her to him. "But I'll say it anyway. You're soft and warm and beautiful, and I'd like it if you'd consider spending the night with me. We do have some unfinished business between us, I believe?" he ended, a tawny gleam in his eyes, his palms running with easy familiarity over her form-fitting dress, arousing a mass of conflicting emotions even as her hips swayed with dangerous intimacy toward his.

His thighs were firm bastions against the tautly held muscles of her limbs.... *Damn him,* she thought furiously, her body seeming to melt of its own volition into his. Yet she averted her mouth when his sought to claim it, so that his fingers curled around her chin, urging her to meet the downward thrust of his lips. She felt their warmth, their moistness, the deliberate sensuality as his tongue sought to part her own resisting mouth.

And then suddenly it was as if another being invaded her body, one free to accept and glory in the fiery glow claiming her lips, her skin, her flesh. She responded to his forceful demands, her hands seeking the cool virile thickness of his hair as she molded herself even more intimately to his muscular length. The impatient stroking of his hand against the prim arrangement of her hair sent pins flying and caused the downward tumble of her hair across her shoulders, its thick dark tresses covering the rise of her breasts like a blanket of soft black velvet.

But still his fingers found the sensitive peaks that thrilled to his touch, sending almost painful surges of longing to every part of her straining body. His fingers dipped lower, pushing down the draped neckline concealing her breasts, drawing low guttural moans from her throat when his lips found and teased the tips to hardness.

She was so lost to the sensations overtaking her body that the discreet buzz of the telephone failed to impinge on her senses until the second or third ring. By then, Carey had dropped his arms from around her and reached for the black receiver on the side table behind them. A violent tremor shook Lindsay as she raised her hands to smooth back her tumbled hair. She pressed her hands over her ears to still them, closing her eyes as if to shut out the lingering clamor of her senses.

God, what a fool she was to let her convictions drift away like mountain mist whenever he touched her. Her premonition had been right. She shouldn't have come up here to his suite after what had happened yesterday. She didn't even have the consolation of knowing he had forced her cooperation. Her mouth had parted willingly for his kiss; her flesh hadn't shrunk from his. The tour was only one-third

of the way through. How was she going to cope for
the rest of it—by giving in to the sexual cravings he
aroused in her, or by suffering endless repetitions of
last night's tormented sleep?

She flinched when Carey put down the phone and
came to touch her arm. Her hands unglued themselves from her ears, so that his voice was no longer a
muffled undertone when he spoke. Concern replaced
the nervous anxiety in her eyes when she saw the
deeply gouged lines on either side of his compressed
mouth, the grim coldness in eyes that were no longer
a lazy tawny color but a hard mid-brown.

"Wh-what is it?" she whispered through dry lips.
"Have you. . . had bad news?"

His brows lifted fractionally. "Me? No, but I
think you have. The desk clerk just called to tell you
that the Eurospan safety-deposit box has been
broken into and its contents stolen."

Lindsay stared at him in blind incomprehension.

# CHAPTER NINE

FEELING AND LOGICAL THOUGHT returned only as Lindsay waited for the elevator at Carey's side, he grimly silent. Then her brain raced to absorb the situation.

All her cash for running expenses had been in that box, and there would be the nightmare job of obtaining fresh currency for the countries remaining on the tour. The hotel was, of course, responsible for replacing the value of articles deposited in their safety boxes, but processing a claim would take a lot longer than the time at her disposal. Early tomorrow morning—it was almost that now—the bus would be leaving for Rome and points south.

It was only as they neared the ground floor and the reception area that she gasped aloud, remembering Philip's envelope, which had been deposited along with the Eurospan cash and records.

"What is it?" Carey rapped out, startling her with the rough timbre of his voice.

She gave him a quick nervous glance, glad when the elevator came to a halt and the doors glided open. "I—nothing. I'm just wondering how I'm going to—to replace the money in a hurry."

The clerk, his black hair polished to a jetlike

gleam, burst into a spate of Italian when he saw them approach.

"Speak English," Carey commanded tersely.

*"Sí, sí, signóre."* The thin young man deferred to the male of the twosome, but Lindsay didn't care. Her thoughts were too engrossed with the implications of losing the buff envelope that represented freedom for two old people in Warsaw.

"Nothing like this has ever happened before in the hotel," the clerk said defensively, obviously wishing he were anywhere but behind the solid barrier of the front-desk counter. Fright had made him lose much of the English fluency he prided himself on. "It happened at the time of the change from day to night staff. For only a moment or two the desk was not inhabited, no?"

"You mean you were late coming on duty," Carey stated flatly. "How late?"

The young man strove for a dignified poise. "No more than a few minutes, *signóre.*"

"How many minutes?" Carey pursued relentlessly. "Five—ten—what?"

"Perhaps ten—no more than fifteen minutes," the clerk confessed weakly.

"How many boxes were rifled? Oh, God," Carey said with steely exasperation when the clerk's face registered incomprehension. "How many boxes were opened and robbed?"

"Only the one, *signóre.* There would not have been time for more, you see, because—"

"All right, all right," Carey put in impatiently. He glanced at Lindsay. "Miss Tabor will let you know the amount she needs to have replaced to carry on with her tour.''

The clerk's face registered dismay. ''But, *signóre,* I have not the—the authority to do this thing. The manager, he will have to give his permission.''

''And where is he?''

''He will be at the hotel at nine tomorrow morning, *signóre.*'' His tone reflected reluctant relief at the prospect of a greater authority relieving him of the necessity of confronting the hard-eyed American, although Lindsay privately thought his tardiness in arriving for duty would probably earn him instant dismissal.

''Get in touch with him right now, and tell him to get his tail over here immediately,'' Carey ordered flatly, ignoring the clerk's sharply indrawn breath at this disrespect for the hotel chief.

Nevertheless he spoke hurriedly, obsequiously, into the telephone, saying shakily as he replaced the receiver, ''*Il*—the manager will be with us very soon.''

''Ask him to come up to my suite when he arrives.'' Carey took Lindsay's arm, and she dazedly drew her attention back from the entrance doors she had been fixedly staring at for the past few minutes. She could have sworn that the jaunty man who had gone confidently through the swinging doors, a camel coat slung negligently around his shoulders, was Louis Perrault. But why had he been leaving the hotel at this late hour?

''Let's wait for the manager in my suite,'' Carey was suggesting in a voice that brooked no objection, and she went with him to the elevator, frustratingly aware that she and not he should be the one taking command in a situation like this. Her effort to resume control was met with a cursory put-down.

"I can deal with this," she began.

"I doubt that." He jabbed a forceful finger at one of the buttons on the elevator wall, his hand still loosely holding her elbow as if he suspected she would make a dash for the lobby before the doors closed. "It's high time we had a talk, you and I."

Lindsay pulled her arm away and clasped her hands tightly together in front of her, her eyes sparkling frostily as she watched the floor indicator light up. "It's hardly the time for a tête-à-tête," she said with unveiled sarcasm. "I should be down at the desk filling out claim forms or talking to the police or somebody." She shrugged, then threw him a sharp glance. "I presume the police have been sent for?" She redirected part of her anger to herself for neglecting to ask that very thing of the desk clerk.

Reaching his floor, Carey guided her out of the elevator with a light hand at her waist before answering. As they faced each other in the hall, he said quietly, "I've asked them to hold off on that for the time being."

"*You've* asked them?" Lindsay almost choked. "What gives you the right—"

"I have every right, and you know it," he snapped, looking irritably around when the second elevator gave a pneumatic hiss and stopped to disgorge passengers. "We can't discuss it here. Let's go to my suite."

Lindsay had perforce to follow him along the carpeted passage, her resolve hardening to clear the air once and for all between them. The remainder of the tour would be impossible if he continued to usurp her position of authority. Why did he always send her emotions into such chaos that they teetered first one way, then another? Earlier in the evening he had shown himself to be a good companion, almost a friend. Twenty minutes earlier she'd been like putty in his hands, willing him to go farther in his lovemaking. And now his arrogant high-handedness made her despise him and all he stood for. When he unlocked the door she brushed past him into the living room, marching to the center and turning to face him, two pink circles of anger highlighting her cheekbones.

"Look, we have to get this straight," she said directly, irritated when he walked past her to the drinks cabinet and began to pour Scotch into two glasses, as if what she had to say was unimportant. Her voice trembled with suppressed rage as she went on. "Either you're in charge of this tour, or I am. I'd prefer not to contact head office for a decision on the point, but I will if I have to." She stared at his turned back and decided to appeal to his sense of executive reasoning. "How would you like it if someone higher than you in the company was constantly stepping in and taking over your responsibilities? Wouldn't you feel just a little unnecessary in the company scheme of things?"

He was actually smiling as he came toward her and handed her one of the glasses. "Maybe that's why I chose a branch of the business nobody else wanted.

I'm my own boss, and I don't even have to attend executive meetings.''

Lindsay's fingers closed automatically around the cool stubbiness of the glass as she stared blankly at him. "I don't understand.... What exactly do you do?"

The smile disappeared, a closed expression taking its place. "That's not important," he dismissed coolly, his gaze assessing as it ran over her. "What is vital is that you tell me exactly what it was you had stashed away in that safety-deposit box."

Her brows came down in a puzzled frown. "You know what was in it—the cash flow in various currencies, refunds on canceled side tours, expenses over and above the regular—"

"Don't play with me, Lindsay," he interrupted her harshly, exasperation edging his voice. "You don't imagine somebody robbed the Eurospan safety box for the sake of a paltry few hundred dollars, do you? They'd have gone for one loaded with jewelry, which many of them are in a hotel like this."

"But...there wasn't time," she protested faintly, a premonition accelerating her heartbeat to a jerky rhythm. "You—you heard the clerk."

"There was plenty of time to get what they set out to take," he stated flatly, his gaze seeming to anchor hers like a pin piercing a butterfly's wings. "And they knew what they were after, didn't they, Lindsay?"

Her mouth suddenly felt sawdust dry, and she moistened her lips with her tongue. The back of her neck was stiff with tension, though her brain seemed to snap elastically with the snatches of thought pouring into it.

"I—how should I know?" she asked shakily, wishing she could sink into the comfortable depths of the sofa she had used earlier.

As if he had read the thought, Carey gestured to the sofa with an imperative hand, remaining in a standing position himself when she tottered numbly to it and collapsed on the enfolding cushions.

"You've never carried material like this from your brother before, have you?" he asked in a voice so sympathetic and gentle that she shook her head dazedly.

"No, I—" She stopped abruptly, her fingers flexing on the glass she still held as she looked up swiftly into his enigmatic eyes. Damn him, he had made her betray Philip—and more important, the elderly couple who were no doubt counting the hours until their reunion with their daughter. "What are you going to do?" she asked dully.

"First I'm going to hear why you agreed to act as your brother's agent in the transmission of secret documents," he said grimly, drawing up the tub chair juxtaposed to the sofa and dropping into it, "and then I'm going to— But never mind that for now. The hotel manager's going to be here within minutes, and I want to hear your story before he does. So go ahead. What reason did your brother give for turning you into a traitor to your country?"

"Philip wouldn't do that!" Lindsay gasped. "He—he asked me to deliver a package to—to a certain person in Vienna. That doesn't mean he's a—a spy! Or that he tried to make me one. All he wants is for Elena's parents to get out of Poland. Is that so bad?'' Her eyes glittered scornfully into the calculated blandness of his. "But you wouldn't understand the value some people place on family relationships, would you?" she said with bitter certainty. "You've never known family love in your own life, so you can't recognize it in others!"

Ignoring the flinch that momentarily altered his expression, she raged on. "Somewhere in Warsaw there's an elderly couple waiting for whatever it is Philip gave me to deliver in Vienna. They're waiting—" she drew an unsteady breath "—to join Elena, their daughter, and the grandchildren they've never seen. Are you going to deny them that pleasure in their old age?" She glared defiantly across at him, aware that a few words in the right ear would destroy her career with Eurospan, with the tourist industry.

Carey said nothing for a long time, shifting his gaze from her passionately animated expression to the calmer depths of the drink still clasped in his hand. Finally he drew a ragged sigh and said resignedly, "No, I'm not the ogre you seem to think I am, but I'm also not as gullible as you." His head had dropped slightly, but now he raised it to look at her with harsh directness. "Maybe your brother is only interested in pulling his in-laws out of a sticky situation in Poland. On the other hand, he could be one of the revolutionary hotheads places like Oxford seem to spawn."

"Philip isn't like that!" Lindsay cast around in her mind for a convincing argument, finally fastening on the manner of his upbringing. "He's the most English Englishman you could ever meet," she cried desperately, too overwrought to recognize the significance of the brief smile that played across his lips. "He's played polo with Prince Philip, had tea with the Queen Mother! The club he belongs to in London is as truly British as it can get!"

"Probably it is," he agreed wryly. "But many of Britain's top spies belonged to that same club and no doubt had tea with members of the royal family."

"Oh, God," she gritted through clenched teeth, "how can I convince you that Philip isn't a spy, that he's just a man who—who wants to make his wife happy?"

"That may be true. But what about his country's welfare?" Carey retorted grimly, rising with a lithe movement when the buzzer sounded at the outer door. Turning back, he cautioned her seriously, "Let me deal with this. Don't say anything."

The admonition was unnecessary. Signor Carelli, the hotel manager, adhered closely to the Latin presumption that women were not suited to the complexities of business and addressed his remarks solely to Carey, with an occasional side-glance of apology to Lindsay, as if the crudity of the situation were unfit for her ears.

As it happened, she heard little of the exchange between the two men. Too many devastating thoughts were circling wildly in her brain. Uppermost was the searing knowledge that Carey was frighteningly knowledgeable about Philip, Elena, the whole mixup with Elena's family—too knowledgeable for a

company-oriented executive of the Endor Corporation. Yet he was part of that conglomerate—wasn't
he? What had he said? "I chose a branch of the
business nobody else wanted. I'm my own boss...."
His own boss. But she dismissed the likelihood of his
actually owning the Endor Corporation, with its far-
flung business enterprises. The head of such a conglomerate would be as firmly tied to his executive
desk as the humblest secretary was to hers. So what
was he?

The hotel manager was bowing deferentially over
her hand, murmuring his apologies for the inconvenience and assuring her that the hotel would reimburse
the Eurospan coffers to the full.

"I appreciate, *signorína,*" he murmured in the
fulsome tones that complemented perfectly his indulgently rounded figure, "that you do not wish to
involve the police in this matter. You will understand
that the hotel has no desire to attract unpleasant attention. The currency taken from your strongbox will
be replaced immediately, if you will kindly inform
the desk of your requirements."

"*Gràzie.*" She spoke with automatic politeness,
her eyes searching for Carey's. From the schooled
blandness of his expression, she knew that he had
divulged nothing of the underlying reasons for the
theft. "I have a separate list of the monies deposited
in the box, and I will inform the desk of the
amounts." For once she blessed the foresight of
Eurospan in insisting on twin copies of every expen-
diture, every deposit.

The manager bowed his way from the room. She

felt drained by the time Carey came back to stand silently before her, his eyes coolly noncommittal when they met hers.

"With any luck, none of the passengers will fly into a panic about losing their valuables to light-fingered *banditos*," he commented without emotion. "Meanwhile, I think I should pay a call on Monsieur Perrault. Something tells me that he's not the simple tourist he pretends to be."

Remembrance struck Lindsay like a bolt of lightning, the casual drape of a camel coat over plump assertive shoulders too vivid to forget.

"What did you think of?" Carey asked perceptively, and she shrugged self-deprecatingly.

"I could be wrong, but I thought I saw him leave the hotel when we were down in the lobby."

He swung back to face her, the fervent curse he emitted startling her into attention. "Why in hell didn't you tell me about this before?" he said explosively. "He could be miles from here by now."

"I—I wasn't that sure...."

His eyes narrowed to a sarcastic gleam. "Are you really as stupidly naive as you seem?" he lashed out furiously. "What did you think your brother was sending so secretively to this woman in Vienna—a greeting card?"

Lindsay flushed but stood her ground. "No," she said quietly, in contrast to his harsh tones. "I thought it might be money or—or some kind of documentation to secure the release of Elena's parents. I still think that's what it was. Whoever's stolen it obviously thinks the same as you. But you don't know Philip the way I do. He'd never expose me to danger, not knowingly. He even—'' remembering, she tilted her head at a higher angle ''—called me in Lucerne and said in so many words that I should ditch the package if too much interest was shown in it. So he must have suspected that the contents would be misinterpreted because of his job. Just as you did.''

He stared thoughtfully at her, his mouth compressed in a thin line. ''He could also have discovered that someone who knew about the top-secret documents was on the tour and likely to do anything to get them.'' His brows lifted as he added sarcastically, ''Such as knocking you unconscious when he was halfway through searching your room because you got back earlier than he expected. Or do you still believe touching the light switch gave you an electric shock?''

''No, I— There was another night,'' she confessed haltingly, knowing it was too late for concern about her career now. ''Someone had been in my room, moved my things.''

''Why in hell didn't you tell me this?''

''Why should I? You're a representative of the company, and I wanted to keep my job.''

''So you did suspect there was more than just a bundle of money or false-identity documents in the package?''

''No, I.... I don't know what I thought.'' She swung away from him and paced nervously to the undraped windows, looking at but not seeing the lights of the Arno strung along each bank. ''I'll call

Philip,'' she suddenly decided, already on her way to the telephone when Carey's peremptory voice stopped her in mid-stride.

"No!"

"What do you mean?" Her head tilted to one side, questioningly. Other queries began to tap at her brain for recognition. "Who are you?" she asked as if she had never seen him before. "You don't work for Eurospan or the Endor Corporation at all, do you?"

"No to the first. Yes to the second," he said grimly, his hand indicating the sofa again. "Sit down and I'll tell you about it—but it has to be short, because I have to track down Perrault or whoever he's handed the documents to."

"THIS IS JUST a mini introduction to Rome," Lindsay said into the speaker as Pierre pulled the darkened bus away from the luxury-class hotel. "A moonlight miscellany, if you like, of some of Rome's ancient monuments. Mostly we'll stay on the bus, but we'll get out to walk up to the Campidoglio, which dates back to the earliest days of Rome, since it was designed as a fortress to defend the city."

Later, leading the diminished group up the wide ramp of shallow steps, she enlarged on her previous statement. "This site was chosen by the Romans as a fortress because of its strategic position close to the Tiber River. Anyone who wanted to get into the city had to come upriver, so the Romans could pretty well control entry into their domain. Here in the square—" she indicated the deserted area flanked by imposing buildings on three sides "—a statue of the emperor

Marcus Aurelius used to stand. The statue was brought here comparatively recently, in 1538. But as this is one of the few surviving monuments of an emperor on horseback, we shouldn't mind that this wasn't the original site. The statue was recently relocated to protect it from the effects of air pollution. The building right ahead of us was the Temple of Jupiter...."

Normally she loved this part of the Rome segment, this quiet lamp-lit time when it was especially easy to conjure up those long-past days of senators in their sweeping togas conversing reasonably together as they went from one place to another about their business. But tonight she was abstracted, and her spiel purely automatic.

Brad Dakers, enjoying a pipe, moved over to join her where she stood apart from the others. "Where did it all go?" he mused softly. "All that power, all that strength, wealth—all of it. What happened to it?"

Lindsay involuntarily recalled Carey's statement about the ancient Romans and how they had squandered the power and strength that had been theirs. She shivered a little, wondering aloud, "Are we doing the same thing—whatever they did—with our civilization?"

"It's a scary thought, isn't it?" he acknowledged quietly. "Are we so caught up with money and possessions and bigger and better ways of making war that two thousand years from now people will come to look at New York, London, Paris, and wonder what happened to make them all fall down around our ears?"

"Oh—" she laughed shakily "—I'm sure we must have learned some lessons along the way!" Recalling that Pierre would now be awaiting them in an illegal-parking spot, she ushered her charges down the steps again, resuming the tour by pointing out the remains of the once mighty Roman Forum, its defaced pillars having miraculously withstood complete eradication with the passage of time; the Column of Trajan; even the much younger Trevi Fountain. This last was an instant hit with the women passengers, at least, and they insisted on making the pilgrimage down the steps crowded with tourists and locals alike to throw wishing coins into the fountain.

"What nonsense," Frank Harben commented disparagingly as he watched his wife go with springing steps to the flood-lit fountain.

"Don't you want to come back to Rome, too?" Lindsay teased carefully, still not sure how far she could go with the self-oriented businessman. "That's what it means, you know, when you throw a coin in the fountain—that one day you'll come back to Rome."

"I'm not at all sure I'll want to," he said disagreeably, his brows rising in skeptical embarrassment as his wife obviously made a silent wish and lifted her arm high to throw her coin.

"Three days isn't possibly enough time to see even a particle of Rome," Lindsay staunchly defended the city. "I lived here for a year, and I just barely scratched the surface."

Harben looked almost human as he glanced curiously at her animated face. "What were you doing here for a year—working?"

"Not in the sense you mean. I was studying the language."

"So you could get a job as a tour guide?" The question was thrown out with acid distaste, and Lindsay's smile became forced.

"I enjoy my job. It's interesting, and I get to visit the places I love most of all in Europe—Rome, for instance." Her smile faded, a pensive frown replacing it on her expressive face. Rome had always been her most favorite city of all, because of Geoff. With every return to it, she'd had to struggle to forget how romantic the city had once been for her, forget the intoxication of wandering hand in hand through its narrow side streets, its parks and piazzas, with the man she loved. Only this time it was different. She hadn't spared one thought for Geoff or for the way her life had been shattered by him.

"I'm sorry." She realized with amazement that Frank Harben was apologizing, albeit stiffly, as if bending his arrogant spirit in deference to a female was unfamiliar to him. "I shouldn't put you down because of what you do. You see, I have two daughters. One is married and has three children and is miserably unhappy. The other is still wandering around trying to find herself, whatever that may mean. I wish," he said heavily, "that even one of them could be as happy in what she's doing as you are." His eyes moved quickly to his wife, who was returning up the steps. "Well, are we coming back to Rome?"

Irene stared at him in astonishment. "How did you know that was what I wished for?" Her tone conveyed not only surprise but a wary pleasure.

Smiling, Lindsay moved away and a few minutes later shepherded her group onto the bus again, electing to stay there while they spent half an hour in the Piazza Navona, which had once been a sports stadium seating twenty thousand Roman spectators but was now a mediocre marketplace for displays of made-for-tourists paintings and cheap souvenirs. The three fountains, particularly the central Bernini masterpiece with its lovingly sculpted figures, were the only redeeming features of the Piazza Navona, in Lindsay's opinion, but passengers generally enjoyed the charged atmosphere of the night-lit market.

"You would like me to stay with you?" Pierre asked from the door, and she shook her head.

"No, you go ahead. I just want a little quiet time."

His bright dark eyes regarded her quizzically. "You have much to think about, no?"

Lindsay smiled wryly. "Yes, I have a few things I have to get straight in my mind."

"Does it concern Monsieur Hudson and his sudden departure from the tour?" he quizzed gently.

She pretended to be puzzled. "Mr. Hudson had to leave to attend to business. I told you that. He'll be rejoining the tour later."

"*Certainement*. And Monsieur Perrault? He, too, will be returning?"

Her frown deepened. "I don't know. He. . .left the hotel the night before we left Florence, and although his luggage was still in his room, he obviously hadn't returned overnight. He knew the tour conditions—that if a passenger doesn't turn up for departure, the bus leaves without him." She shrugged, a gesture that Pierre duplicated before going off to the café he frequented at the entrance to the piazza.

A sick churning began once again in her stomach, prompted by unfamiliar waves of fear. Not fear for Perrault's fate. If he was what Carey suspected, he deserved everything that came his way. It was Carey she was concerned about....

Sighing, she leaned her head back against the plush seat back in the darkened bus and closed her eyes against the distraction of a hand-holding couple, so obviously in love, sauntering past outside. Once that might have been her and Geoff, oblivious to what went on around them. She impatiently dismissed that memory and concentrated on what Carey had told her that night before he'd left Florence in pursuit of Louis Perrault.

It hadn't really surprised her too much to know that he wasn't entirely what he'd seemed. Some inner sense had told her all along that however anxious the Endor Corporation might be to school its executives in every phase of its far-flung operations, it would hardly waste the time and talents of one of its top-paid employees on such a trivial task that almost anyone else could—and did—perform. Usually the sleepers were so-called average housewives, retired teachers or ex-businessmen grateful for a free luxury tour of Europe in exchange for a comprehensive report at the end of it.

Was it the naiveté Carey had criticized her for that had kept her suspicions at bay, the same naiveté that had made her blindly believe in the supposed simplicity of the task Philip had entrusted to her?

Her eyes opened and focused on the blurred white face of the clock centered on the entrance wall. Why hadn't Philip explained the true nature of her mission—given her a real choice to accept or reject it? If what Carey had told her was true—and he seemingly had the full force of the United States government behind him—then for some time her brother had been passing information gained from his job to a foreign power.

Her teeth dug painfully into her lower lip. Even if the lives of Elena's parents were being threatened, did that give him the right to sell out his country? What would she have done had the circumstances been reversed? If she were married to—to Carey, say, and his elderly parents were being victimized, parents he loved as deeply as Elena did hers?

She released her breath on a long-drawn sigh. That wasn't a fair comparison. Philip was madly in love with Elena, and she had sacrificed so much for him. That situation didn't exist between her and Carey, except that— Oh, God, she had wanted to call him back that night in Florence when he had hurriedly packed a bag and left her in his suite with the request that she pack the remainder of his things and take them on ahead to Rome.

"I'll catch up with the tour when I've finished this business with Perrault," he had said, stopping in the middle of the living room, his hair mussed from raking his hand through it as he made it brutally clear that Philip's seemingly innocuous package was loaded with information that could be disastrous if it fell into the wrong hands. His face seemed ravaged, haggard, by the enormity of the task the government had imposed on him.

Lindsay had still been in shock as she tried to grasp the possibility that the brother she adored was involved in the totally alien and frightening world of espionage. But the probability of danger to Carey rose like a miasma to constrict her throat and make her whisper almost inaudible.

"Take care. He's...dangerous."

Carey dropped the travel bag he was carrying and came swiftly toward her, a slight smile only seeming to highlight the grim lines around his mouth.

"I'm very aware of that," he said softly, his forefinger coming up to brush tentatively over her quivering mouth, his eyes betraying a depth of emotion his stiffly held lips denied. "I'm sorry I had to be the one to disillusion you about your brother, but I do have to do...what I have to do."

Lindsay nodded, awkward tears springing to her eyes, their sparkling wetness studding her lashes like brilliant gems. "I—I know. I want you to do what's right." She was beyond knowing what right and wrong were by that time, teetering between her loyalty to Philip and the overwhelming sureness of Carey.

As if they were lovers parting temporarily, Carey bent and kissed her hard, his mouth dry against hers. "And you won't call him?" he questioned huskily, going on before she had time to consent or deny. "I know it's not easy for you to think of your brother as a—as an agent for another country, but you can't help him now by warning him that we're on to him. He might genuinely believe, as he told you, that they'd let his wife's parents go if he supplied enough information, but that's not the way they work.

"If the old people are still alive, they'll never give them up in exchange for the information you've been carrying. They'll milk their source dry, and then...." He shrugged significantly. His hands settled on Lindsay's shoulders, his fingers bony hard against her skin. "If you call Philip," he said tersely, "it's possible he'll do something foolish, like coming out here, and they'll know he'd be useless to them for further secret information. They won't have any second thoughts about disposing of Elena's parents, too—if they're still alive."

Recalling those words now made Lindsay shiver uncontrollably for a moment. It was like a nightmare from which she would never awaken until all the participants in the drama had been neatly disposed of: the old couple frozen in their anticipation of an early reunion with their daughter and her children, Philip desperately anxious to effect that reunion, Carey endangering his own life to intercept the vital knowledge that Philip had misguidedly thought to use to procure the parents' safe conduct to the States.

Her agony over the break with Geoff had come to seem unimportant in the face of so many emotional drawstrings. When she spared thought for him at all, Geoff came off as immature, seeking to develop confidence in his masculinity through affairs with other women. Yet what normal woman would be content to stay with a husband who had been found thousands of miles from home with another woman? Lindsay suspected he made a habit of this, and

Geoff's wife apparently sanctioned these amorous attachments, however fleeting—if, in fact, she knew about them.

That wasn't the way a relationship should be, could be, Lindsay realized starkly. If she were in love with a man like Carey, she would never— But who was she fooling? She *was* in love with Carey, in a way she had never dreamed possible. She had known that from her inner tension when he left the suite that night, left so quickly that she sensed tremulously an equal depth of feeling in the rigid set of his shoulders, in the forceful erectness of his head, his tightly knotted neck muscles, the very obvious effort he had made not to turn around again. In love with a man whose sole purpose right now was to destroy the life of the half brother she adored.

The murmurs of the returning group made her straighten up and finally get to her feet. Pierre gave her a searching look when he unlocked the door and stepped up into the bus, but he said nothing as their passengers trooped, chattering, after him.

The voices quieted as the group made its way back to the hotel through almost deserted streets. Rome could be a cultural shock the first evening, even for those who knew the city well. Each one of Lindsay's passengers looked drawn and faintly bemused when she turned to face them in the hotel foyer.

"For those of you taking the city tour, including the Vatican tomorrow morning and the Villa d'Este in the afternoon, I'll be here to see you off from the hotel. For most of the day you'll be in the good hands of our Rome guides, who will be pleased to answer any questions you may have. Our guides are chosen from among the most knowledgeable people in each place we visit, so I'm sure you'll enjoy what they have to show and tell you about.''

"You mean you won't be with us at all tomorrow?'' Lila asked, obviously distressed at the thought.

"The guides are far more familiar with what you'll be seeing than I am," Lindsay answered calmly, camouflaging the exhaustion that had overtaken her. "You'll be well served by them, I know."

Carl Timms put in impudently from the back of the group, "What are you going to be doing while we're hotfooting it around the Vatican and these gardens?"

Her first instinct was to say that she would be sitting with her feet up in the garden park at the rear of the hotel, but she substituted, "I'll be setting up arrangements for the next leg of our trip—and of course I'll be available on your return for anything you might need."

"*Anything?*" Carl Timms queried snidely, his eyes running boldly over the lines of her figure. "I'll certainly think up a service or two you can perform for me when we get back." He ignored the dark flush that swept up over Betty's cheeks and the shocked glances from the rest of the group.

Lindsay, her eyes as sharp as needles, said briskly, "I'll be interested to hear what you and your wife think of the Villa d'Este as a subject for your artwork, Mr. Timms!"

Joel Carter stopped beside her as the others fanned

out toward the desk. "You handled that very well, Lindsay," he said pompously. "Can you imagine the gall of that man? I don't know why his wife puts up with him. She's such a nice person."

"Yes, she is," Lindsay agreed, a speculative look coming into her eyes as she watched Joel go to claim his key, his entire body seeming to bristle with indignation. Had Betty found herself a champion, she wondered. Joel was nothing at all like the burly Carl in stature, but mere physique wasn't something that mattered to a lot of women. Sometimes gentleness and understanding rated far higher than muscles and brawn. Carl, in his way, was good-looking and, she supposed, sexually attractive to some women. But why, indeed, had Betty chosen a man who seemed so ill suited to her sensitive nature?

*"Gràzie,"* she murmured to the clerk who handed out her key, ignoring his boldly appraising assessment of her. The last thing she needed tonight was to cope with the amorous advances of a front-desk Lothario.

*"Signorína,"* he called out, turning to the pigeonhole bearing her room number. "There is a telephone message for you." His brows rose above the slip of paper he unfolded, and he looked at her curiously. *"L'ufficio di polizía,"* he said, more as question than statement. "You are to telephone this number. Will you call from here, or ...?"

Lindsay disappointed him. "I'll call from my room." Her heart was thumping in her chest as she walked with forced calm to the elevator. Something had happened to Carey, she knew it, or why would the police department want to speak to her? She should never have let him go after Louis Perrault like that! They should have called the police in Florence—let them take care of it. Carey was no spy hunter. Tracking down disloyal characters who sought to betray the firm that employed them was no preparation for dealing with the deadly seriousness of the spy game.

Expelling her breath in an explosive sigh, she stepped off the elevator, knowing that nothing she could have said or done would have prevented Carey from doing what he had set out to do. *Dear Lord,* she prayed as she let herself into her room, *don't let Carey be the first death in my tour career.* The very thought made her finger tremble in the dial holes of the telephone beside the bed.

"*Prónto.*" The voice was impatient, gruff.

"I—there's a message at my hotel to call the police department," she said, automatically forsaking Italian for her mother tongue. "This is Lindsay Tabor of Eurospan Coach Tours.... Somebody there wanted to speak to me."

"*Un moménto, signorína.*" The receiver was laid noisily on the desk top, then immediately snatched up again and the message repeated in heavily accented English. "One moment, miss." This time the person evidently covered the receiver, muffling the ensuing conversation. Finally, a brisker voice sounded clearly in her ear.

"Signorína Tabor? This is Capitano Scorsi. I regret to trouble you, but we have a problem that our Florence department thinks you can help us with."

"F-Florence?"

"Yes. There was an unfortunate incident there last night—your party was there until this morning?" he interrupted himself to ask impatiently, going on when she confirmed the fact. "It is understood that two members of your tour did not proceed to Rome as planned. Is this information correct?"

Lindsay cleared her throat, her fingers tensely entwined in the white spiral of the telephone cord. "I—yes, that's right. Mr.—"

"I have their names," he cut her off. "Signor Perrault and Signor Hudson. We have investigated and we believe that one of these passengers is the man whose body was taken from the Arno early today. The hotel staff in Florence has made an identity, but we would like you to confirm it. If I send a car for you, will you come down to identify the pictures we have just now received from Florence?"

"Wh-which one do—do they think it is?" she asked through suddenly parched lips, sitting down abruptly on the bed that had been turned down by the maid for the night.

"We would prefer that you make the identity without—what do you say—without prejudice," he said smoothly. "The car will pick you up in fifteen minutes."

# CHAPTER TEN

THE SMOKE-FILLED CAPTAIN'S OFFICE seemed a fitting site for the conclusion to the past twenty-four-hour nightmare sequence of events. Lindsay was scarcely aware of the open surprise and admiration reflected in the expressions of the policemen lounging around the station house as she was ushered into Captain Scorsi's inner domain.

It was numbness of the senses that made her exchange preliminary pleasantries with the tall, heavily built police chief, accept the proffered wooden chair placed across the desk from his own comfortably padded one. Frozen into her brain was the one thought that had circled tirelessly there all the way across the city: Carey was dead, and she had never told him she loved him. That the realization of that love hadn't come until he was marching out of his suite the night before made no dent in her icy regret.

The amenities dispensed with, the police captain withdrew a sheaf of enlarged glossies from the folder in front of him, holding them at an angle out of her view as he looked across the desk, a hint of compassion in his dark eyes. "These pictures, *signorína,* they are not very pleasant. Violent death never is."

Lindsay's eyes, even blacker than his, stared fixedly back. "V-violent...?"

He shrugged his muscular shoulders. "This man was shot at very close range before being dropped into the river. The only piece of evidence as to his identity was a ticket stub his killer or killers overlooked. It was that ticket stub that led us to the hotel and your tour."

Lindsay's senses suddenly thawed, and she wanted to scream hysterically as he still held the pictures out of her view. Ticket stub, she thought wildly.... Either one of them could have had such a thing on his person. She drew a deep tortured breath.

"Show me the pictures, captain."

His hand seemed to move in slow motion as it selected the top photograph and slid it across the desk.

Lindsay forced her eyes to the top edge, which showed the parapet bordering the Arno River and an early-dawn mistiness over the water.

"Can you identify the man, *signorína?*" the police captain prodded gently.

Her gaze dropped to the gray-suited man lying as if asleep on his back, only the small black hole drilled into his temple an indication that this was no ordinary sleep.

Lindsay drew a shuddering sigh. "Yes, I can identify him," she said shakily. "It's... Louis Perrault."

LINDSAY PAUSED as she came out onto the portico of the hotel, settling her sunglasses on her nose as the unseasonal warmth of the Rome sunshine hit her.

The resplendently adorned doorman turned from seeing off two of the hotel's guests in a taxi, and his eyes took in with appreciation the young woman's copper-colored blazer and beige slacks that seemed made to blend with the round urns of yellow-and-bronze chrysanthemums flanking the imposing entrance. Climbing up the broad shallow steps to the portico, he offered politely to obtain a taxi for her.

"No, thanks," she said in his own language. "I'll walk."

He watched as she went down the steps with a free-swinging stride. She paused at the lower level, then turned toward the street that would lead her into the tourist heart of Rome, the Via Veneto.

Lindsay's choice had been purely automatic. Mingling with other tourists might stop the incessant thoughts that had destroyed sleep for her the night before. Only toward dawn had the police chief's grilling voice been obliterated in the exhaustion of sleep.

His interrogation had overpowered her guilt feelings at knowing it was Louis Perrault and not Carey who lay dead somewhere in Florence. Relief had flooded her at that initial realization, an incredible lightening of her mood, until the chief's subsequent questioning got through to her.

"Did Signor Hudson have any reason to feel animosity for the victim?" he had asked in a pointed line of questioning.

Buoyed by her relief, Lindsay had answered with a vehement "No, of course not. They hardly knew each other."

His hard eyes had appraised her directly over the

desk. "There was no competition between them, as there might be between two men for the favors of a certain woman? Someone like yourself, for instance?"

"Certainly not. I take my job very seriously, captain," she said with outraged dignity. "I make it a point never to become involved with passengers on a personal level. You can check that with my home office, if you like."

"I already have, Miss Tabor," he had retorted smoothly, surprisingly, "and they have confirmed what you say. You understand, we have to pursue every lead we can in a murder case."

Murder case.... The two words seemed to circle in her brain as if they were stuck in the worn groove of a record. Despite her denials to the police chief, she had to face the possibility that Carey had been responsible for the death of the seemingly innocuous Frenchman. He had set out from the hotel with the express purpose of tracking down Perrault and retrieving the documents Philip had entrusted to her. Was she wrong in concealing that information from the Italian authorities?

"Lindy! Lindy, is it you?"

She turned blindly toward the source of the voice that had penetrated her consciousness as she walked obliviously by a sidewalk café on the Via Veneto. Her brain quickly tabulated the fact that no one but Geoff had ever abbreviated her name in that familiar way. Through the dark lenses of her glasses, she scanned the milling throng enjoying the unusual warmth of the Rome sunshine.

Then Geoff materialized in front of her, his cheeks seeming sunk beneath the vivid blue of his eyes, his beard more bushy than she remembered, straggling across the lean hungry-looking thinness of his face. His rangy figure was the same, and the faded jeans that hung from his hipbones had the washed-out appearance of many years of wear.

"Geoff?"

"The same." He grinned widely, displaying his strong teeth in the smile she knew so well. "I've been back in Rome for a year or more now—guess the agency couldn't get along without me!"

She looked with a clinical appraisal at the man who had filled her romantic dreams for so long. Yes, the agency had lost a top newsman in Geoff Boler when domestic reasons had called him back to his home territory...just as she had always believed she had lost the one man she could love.

"Say, why don't you join Luisa and me?" Geoff invited expansively, and Lindsay's gaze went to the sulky dark beauty eyeing them from a back table in the café.

"I— No, thanks, Geoff. I'm with a tour company and I have to get back to the hotel."

"What kind of touring company?" he queried, frowning with all too familiar impatience. "Theater?"

"No. I work for a company that conducts tours to Europe, by bus."

"You're kidding!" His brows lifted disbelievingly in a bushy blond arc. "I'd never have believed you'd settle for the bourgeois traveler in Europe. But then, you always were filled with romantic notions from an idyllic past, weren't you, Lindy?''

"I'm earning an honest living," she said coolly, surprised by her own rejection of those counter-culture values Geoff espoused, values he had once made attractive to her schoolgirl mentality. At the time she had rebelled against the morals of her parents, not through any conviction of her own but largely, she now knew, because they were horrifically out of step with the world Geoff inhabited.

"Oh, honey," Geoff said with a studiedly rueful grin, "I wish you luck—but are you really having as much fun now as we had when you were in Rome?"

"No," she admitted, surprising herself only a little less than him. So many things that had been obscured before were now, with her newfound insight, star-tlingly clear to her. "But I don't need what someone like you has to offer anymore, Geoff," she said half-regretfully. "Sure, it was fun for a while, but I've found the real thing now, and it's more than fun. It's wonderful. You should try it sometime."

His baffled expression followed her as she walked away from him, past the curious gazes of the café's patrons. She raised a hand to summon a cruising taxi.

After giving the hotel's location, she leaned back on the cushioned seat. It seemed incredible that she had confronted the Geoff of her dreams and emerged victorious and free. The girl, inexperienced and im-mature, that she had once been no longer existed. For so long she had wanted the permanence of undivided love, the same kind of love that united her parents, her brother and his wife, even Geoff and his wife, however tenuous their relationship was. But those silken ties no longer mattered to her. She was now in love with a man who seemed to make a profession of loving and leaving women. For the first time in her life she wasn't bothered about the hereafter in a love relationship. Carey was now, and now was forever.

Lila's accusing voice beset her in the hotel foyer. "Oh, Lindsay, where have you been?" she cried plaintively. "I've been looking all over for you. You wouldn't believe how *rude* the guide was at the Villa d'Este!" The older woman trotted puppylike at her heels as Lindsay strode to the desk and requested her key. "I mean, those fountains and water displays at the villa were quite marvelous, but when I asked the guide about the necessity for those lewd statues where water was flowing from—well, the bosoms of naked women," she elaborated shyly, "he was quite offhand. I hope I'm not a prude—" she pursed her lips into severely prudish lines "—but I do draw the line at obscenity."

"Surely obscenity is in the eye of the beholder, Mrs.—er, Lila," Lindsay remarked, only partially interested in the older woman's vaporous remarks. "Most people take statues at face value and are more interested in the sculptor's art than in the conventional point of view."

Lila followed her to the elevator. "But I don't think it's right, do you, that even statues should display their female parts for every lustful male who happens along?"

"A woman's breasts had a different significance

then than they do now. The female form was revered, in works of art, at least,'' Lindsay explained, pressing her finger to the elevator button and smiling to an astonished Italian couple who obviously understood English. ''This is your floor, isn't it?'' she asked pointedly when the arrow indicated the number three.

''Yes—but, Lindsay, I wanted to ask you about dinner—'' Lila's voice was swallowed up in the vacuum created by the closing of the doors. The small sensation of guilt Lindsay felt at ignoring the beseeching tones of a paying passenger was swallowed in the thought that had haunted her all day.

Where was Carey, and how much did he have to do with the death of Louis Perrault?

''Look what I bought, Lindsay.''

Mary Strangeways delved into a bag bearing the logo of the cameo factory they had just visited, bringing out a box that she opened proudly to display an exquisitely carved necklace.

''It's beautiful.'' Lindsay smiled dutifully, handing back the delicately wrought jewelry. ''You have a very indulgent husband.''

''A very broke one,'' Paul inserted dryly, coming up the steps of the bus behind his wife. ''Let's hope Capri has less expensive souvenirs.''

''At this time of year, it usually does have reduced prices,'' Lindsay consoled him, making an automatic count of the heads present before nodding to Pierre, who immediately put the bus into motion. ''How did you enjoy the cameo factory?'' she asked without benefit of microphone, and a jaded-looking Charlene favored her with a frosty stare.

"I didn't buy any of that overpriced jewelry," she snapped viciously, "so I'm afraid your commission won't be as high as it might have been."

Lindsay's eyes lost their friendly sparkle as they honed in on the irascible woman, whose purchases so far had made it difficult for her to slide into her seat.

"Are you implying that I receive a percentage of sales made to my passengers?" she asked with deadly calm as Pierre pulled the bus onto the undulating highway that would take them to Sorrento.

Charlene snorted audibly, her eyes seeking approval from her fellow passengers. "Don't sound so self-righteous," she said caustically. "Everybody knows that you get a cut from all these places you lead your passengers to like lambs to the slaughter." She waved her hand derogatorily. "Restaurants, souvenir shops, factories."

"Is that how you make a profit from your dress shop in Chicago?" Brad Dakers questioned her sarcastically, earning a flaring look from Charlene as she twisted in her seat to stare at him.

"Of course not. We do things differently in the States, thank God!"

"You mean you don't give a cut to the tour companies who direct business your way?" he persisted, earning himself a venomous look.

"It's not the same thing at all," she blustered.

"I'd like to bet," he retorted incorrigibly, "that more than half of your business is done with tourists to Chicago."

"However that may be," Lindsay inserted firmly, "I've never yet received a commission such as you mention. But if you have a legitimate complaint about my conducting of the tour, you'll be given the opportunity to air it on the summation sheet you'll be receiving toward the end of the trip." She summoned a smile for the remainder of her passengers. "Now before going over to Capri, we're going to take a run down to Pompeii, which as you all know...."

Relegating Charlene's unjustified accusation to the back of her mind, she proceeded to recap the history of Pompeii, the city engulfed centuries ago by the outpouring of lava from the nearby mountain, Vesuvius. "The crater has been dormant for many years, so there's no possibility of our being caught in a new eruption. Usually the mountain is shrouded in mist, so we're lucky to have such clear weather."

By the time the bus dropped its passengers at the site, the remote brooding mountain had been photographed from every visible angle. "You'll have time after the conducted tour to have a cup of coffee here before getting back on the bus." With those words Lindsay sped the tourists on their way, her smile fading as she watched them go up the first grassy track between two rows of crumbling stonework that had once been houses for the ill-fated townspeople. Normally she welcomed the hour's break and spent it sunning herself at one of the nearby café's outdoor tables, but today she would have welcomed any distraction from her thoughts. Even Pierre had wandered off to one of the many souvenir stalls clustered around the entrance, his lack of fluency in Italian no

drawback in his attempts to charm one of the pretty
female vendors.

Sighing, she resigned herself to solitude, carrying
her coffee to a sunny spot on the patio, opening the
paperback novel she always carried for moments like
these. But the print could have been in Chinese for all
she understood of it.

Where was Carey? Why hadn't he been in touch
with her? Had he been responsible for Louis Perrault's horrible death, and was he now hiding out
from the police? The possibility that he could cold-
bloodedly kill another human being—even if his victim had been an unsavory character like Perrault,
who wasn't averse to violence himself—sent cold
shivers down her spine. Yet wasn't it because of her,
because of Philip's involvement in intrigue and espionage, that he'd been forced into it?

The incessant questions that had buzzed around in
her brain all night long returned. Why had Philip involved himself, her and now Carey in a dangerous
situation he knew nothing about? He wasn't a stupid
man—far from it—

Her eyes snapped open. A horrifying suspicion had
come to her, Carey's words echoed in her mind:
"Maybe your brother is only interested in pulling his
in-laws out of a sticky situation in Poland. On the
other hand, he could be one of the revolutionary
hotheads places like Oxford seem to spawn."

Dear God, wouldn't she have known if he was a
Polish agent? Surely he would have dropped some
hint without even meaning to. The idea was completely impossible. She knew him too well to—

She drew her breath in sharply. What did she actually know about him, apart from what had been revealed in the course of a few nights here and there, spent with his family in their pleasant country house? He had never told her and she had never asked about his work, except in general terms. Starkly she realized that he might have been the world's master spy and she would never have considered the possibility, happy as she was at finding a new family far from the old.

The Philip she thought she knew would never have exposed her to the violent nature of espionage. But if he was what Carey suspected, then his fanaticism would overrule any affection he felt for her. True, he had made a tentative effort to avert danger by calling her in Lucerne and telling her to ditch the papers. But he knew her well enough to realize that the plight of Elena's elderly parents would blot out any fear of possible harm to herself.

The sound of familiar voices alerted her to the fact that her charges were returning in what seemed like a surprisingly short time from their tour of Pompeii. There was no time to escape the inevitable onslaught, and within minutes she found herself surrounded by the members of the tour group, all of them trying to talk at once, most of them seeming to assume she had never visited the ruins herself.

"It's hard to imagine just how it was before the lava poured down...."

"The guide told us most of the people had left because they'd been warned...."

"Yes, but those two slaves...." Debora Dakers

shuddered, explaining to Lindsay, "They couldn't get away because they were chained, and nobody thought to release them in their hurry to get out...."

"But the lava preserved them in some way. They almost look alive inside those glass cases. One of them, especially, made the tragedy very real for me," Brad Dakers said solemnly. "His arm was held up in front of him as if he were warding off the certain death coming to him. And God, what a death!"

"Hell, those molds weren't real," Carl Timms jeered, his skepticism belied by the pale underlay to his tanned cheeks. "It's all a gimmick to impress the tourists."

Lindsay rose with her empty cup. "No, it isn't," she corrected quietly. "You'll find that out for yourself if you ever get the time to visit Naples and the museum there." She smiled briefly around, then glanced at her watch. "See you back at the bus in fifteen minutes."

THE ENCHANTED PILE OF ROCK that was Capri brought to mind the image of an animal basking contentedly in the fiery gold and red of sunset. Lindsay gazed distractedly over the boat rail and watched the white spume frothing by, bursts of laughter reaching her ears from farther forward on the open deck, the voices growing louder with each round of drinks the attentive stewards delivered. Her hair whipped in black strands around her face when the sea breeze caught it, but she felt too lethargic to even bother brushing it back.

Capri! The tiny island that spelled romance with its

feudal atmosphere and central square that looked like the setting for a comic opera. A setting made for a love affair.

But how did you have a love affair without a lover? God alone knew where Carey was, and even if he were here, it was highly unlikely that he would succumb to the idyllic magic of the island. The soft breezes blowing from it now brought the scent of lemon trees, the heavy fruitiness of persimmons, the sharper tang of fishnets from the boats anchored under the shadow of the looming rocks. A love affair consummated on Capri could never be shrugged off with a cynical nod to amorous experience. It would be an event that would be remembered for a lifetime, she suspected. But Carey just wasn't that kind of man. Sentimentality, the trappings of romance weren't for him—especially not with the sister of a traitorous spy!

She was almost glad when the hustle of arrival and dividing the passengers between the two minibuses awaiting them at dockside scattered her thoughts. She reassembled them in a more efficient pattern, reviewing the itinerary. Pierre and the larger vehicle had been left behind in Sorrento, as usual. Capri's narrow winding roads were impassable for a bus of that size. They wouldn't see their driver again until the day after tomorrow, when they docked at Naples.

Up and up the small buses climbed, drawing anxious squeals from the female contingent and harrumphs from the men as the driver negotiated hairpin bends with calculated daring. There was a momentary stop in Capri itself before tackling the even steeper rises to Anacapri at the island's summit.

Lindsay had grown to expect the murmured sounds of delight when the buses pulled into the street-side courtyard of the imposing hotel, set craggily upon cliffs commanding a view in every direction. She particularly loved the hotel itself, with its peaceful gardens of terraced greenery reaching down to a swimming pool at the very edge of the cliff. The interior, too, was relaxing yet grand with its floors and pillars of marble, a glassed-in dining room providing spectacular views by day and night.

*"Buona sera, signorína,"* the beaming hotel manager greeted her. "Everything is ready for your party. And for you—" his plump olive-skinned face creased into a deeper smile "—we have your favorite room."

*"Gràzie,* Signor Bonelli," Lindsay replied to the kindly manager, who was usually devastated when she arrived in mid-season and her ocean-view room was not available. "As I told you on the telephone, we aren't a large group this time, but I think most of my passengers will want to eat in the hotel, for tonight at least."

The manager spread his hands in a fulsome gesture. "That will be no problem at all. We still have most of our kitchen staff." The hotel, she knew, would be closing for the winter in two more weeks.

Quickly scanning the suite listings he handed her, she saw with a plummeting feeling that he had assigned the two-room suite adjoining her own room to Carey. "I'm...not sure if Mr. Hudson will be rejoining the tour here," she said apologetically, "but the suite will, of course, be paid for."

"Ah, I know these American businessmen and their mad rush from one place to another." Signor Bonelli shrugged genially, though Lindsay wondered if this shrewd businessman would countenance a no-show. Her next words tested the theory.

"Unfortunately, the passenger who joined the tour in Lucerne, Monsieur Perrault of Paris, will not be with us for the rest of the tour."

A sharp frown creased the heavy flesh between the manager's brows. "You said nothing about this when you telephoned last night, *signorína*."

"I didn't know then," she explained awkwardly. "You see, Signor Bonelli, Monsieur Perrault met with a-an accident in Florence. He—he's dead."

The manager quickly crossed himself and said with pious concern, "What happened? A heart attack?"

"You could say that." The stoppage of the heart for whatever reason could be considered a heart attack, she supposed.

"There will, of course, be no charge for the suite the unfortunate *signóre* would have occupied," the manager said with dignity, and Lindsay thanked him gravely before going out to her waiting charges in the bus. She had said nothing to them about Perrault's sudden demise, only informing them that Carey Hudson had been called away temporarily on business.

"Oh, dear," Lila Beaumont fretted, grabbing at Lindsay's arm as the other members of the group clustered around the reception desk. "What suite number did you say for me?"

"Two-ten. It's a lovely suite, with balconies where you can enjoy breakfast with the greatest view in the world at your feet."

"Isn't it a little chilly for breakfast outside?" Lila commented doubtfully, her lower lip quivering uncertainly.

"Not in Capri. Anything's possible at any time of the year."

"Really? Well, I hope it is for you." Lila patted her arm vaguely after that cryptic statement and took a few steps toward the desk before turning back in confusion.

"Two-ten," Lindsay reminded her gently, smiling as the older woman trotted off to obtain her key. If ever anyone needed someone to lean on, it was Lila Beaumont! Still, one had to admire her fortitude in setting out alone to tour Europe. It couldn't have been an easy decision, considering her seeming incapacity to make up her mind about the most trivial aspects of her daily affairs.

Lindsay blessed Signor Bonelli's thoughtfulness as she opened the shutters onto her tiny balcony and stepped out to grip the rail. The Amalfi coastline was outlined by a string of yellow lights, and tomorrow she would look out on the incredibly blue waters surrounding Capri. What more could a person want?

*Love,* her traitorous heart demanded instantly, painfully. The love of a man for the woman in her, a totally enveloping experience that would blot out the past. *Oh, God, please let Carey come and share this magical island with me!*

"THE WRITER-SCIENTIST, Axel Munthe, made the Villa San Michele his home for many years," she began next morning as she led the group up a narrow staircase. "This was his bedroom." She indicated the somberly lit low-ceilinged room that must, she thought privately, have once provided a more livable environment than it now did with its sparsely arranged furniture. The kitchen, with its archaic hanging pots and other cooking utensils, drew interested exclamations from her charges, but it was the spicy scent of the well-laid gardens and the viewpoints of the Caesars with their panoramic spreads of lemon groves and blue sea beyond that inspired the greatest admiration.

"Can't you just see Tiberius standing here?" Irene Harben breathed, her eyes trained mistily on the vista of cliff and sea.

"It was more likely to be Caesar Augustus," Lindsay inserted. "He seems to have left evidence of his occupation all over Anacapri. Long before Axel Munthe built his home over these ruins, this was the favorite residence of Caesar Augustus."

And who could blame him for that? Lindsay retraced her steps to the meticulous gardens branching away from the villa, leaving her tour to appreciate the views that had changed little since the time of Augustus, let alone Munthe. The physician-scientist had been a humanitarian, which wouldn't have been difficult in surroundings like these, she thought whimsically.

Fifteen minutes later she rejoined the group outside the villa, expecting any question but the one

Tony Ferrucci posed. "Where's the nightlife around here?" he demanded, Gina one step behind him. "That get-together in the hotel last night was fine, but it could have been a little livelier. Isn't there a disco or something like that in Capri?"

Lindsay bit back the irritable comment that sprang to her lips. "I don't believe so, but there are a few sidewalk cafés that might interest you if you'd like to take in some local color. At this time of year the patrons are mostly residents, and with your Italian background you'd probably enjoy mixing in."

In the tiny square, she counted heads before going into her detailing of the next destination. "We're going to take a trip to the Blue Grotto now, another famous spot that needs no introduction. Hopefully we'll be able to enter the grotto if the seas aren't too restless, but if they are— Well, we'll at least have seen something of Capri's most famous attraction." Walking to the head of the first of the waiting minibuses, she supervised the loading before taking her own place beside the driver of the second bus.

Despite the calm appearance of the sea, boat rides into the grotto itself were prohibited that day. "I'm sorry, but we have to take the boatmen's word for it. They know when it's safe and when it isn't. But you can go down these steps and take a look at the entrance to the grotto, if you wish."

Lindsay waited under a gnarled tree beside the flight of steps as her tour load ventured down the steep cliff face to glimpse what they might have seen more fully if conditions had been favorable. Then they would have sat in boats that rose on the tide to bear them under the cliff and into the azure blue of the cavern. As it was, the tide would have forced the small boats too close to the arched entrance.

Joel was the first to return, his breath coming in deep gasps as he crossed to where she leaned against the tree. "Why didn't you come down with us?"

"I've walked those steps too often to find them fascinating anymore." She smiled, pleased about the easy friendliness that had sprung up between them in the past few days. Although. . . .

She frowned slightly as she turned back to the spread of cerulean water. It might have been better if his attention was still centered on her. She could handle his admiration, but could Betty Timms? More to the point, could Carl? His macho disregard for his wife's feelings obviously wouldn't extend to accepting another man's interest in her. These days Carl's heavy scowls would deepen perceptibly whenever he noticed Betty's and Joel's heads close together, their conversation so engrossing that neither appeared to remember his existence. Much as she hated to interfere on the marital front, Lindsay decided that now was a good time to set a warning bee buzzing in Joel's ear.

"You get along very well with most of your fellow passengers," she complimented him adroitly, and Joel flushed with pleasure.

"Do you really think so? I try to be friendly, but a lot of the time people don't respond, you know? Like Frank Harben, though his wife's really nice. . . and that fellow who dropped out of the tour, Carey Hudson? He was kind of remote, and I always felt he was treating me like a, I don't know, a temporary fact of his life.''

*Join the club,* Lindsay was tempted to say, but this opportunity to warn Joel was too good to miss. "People sometimes misunderstand others who want to be just friendly,'' she said aloud. "Carl Timms, for instance.''

"God, he's a real boor, isn't he?'' Joel agreed innocently. "I can't imagine what Betty sees in him. She's so *sensitive*. And talented. Have you seen any of her paintings? She's terrific! It took some doing,'' he asserted with modest pride, "but I think I've persuaded her to let me show her work in my new gallery. She has a—an immediacy, an ability to make a scene come alive. I mean, anyone who's been to Europe and seen the Louvre, Versailles, the sun setting in Nice, will be immediately transported back to those places by the brilliant simplicity of her paintings. She's a superb artist, although she's modest about it—''

"And Carl—what does he think about his wife being exhibited in New York?'' Lindsay interrupted his effusive flow. Joel's animated expression was replaced by one of irritation at her question.

"Carl? I don't know if Betty's even told him that I want to exhibit her work—I doubt if he'd be interested. I gathered from Betty that he—and she, until now—regarded him as the artist in the family. But as far as I know, he hasn't lifted a drawing pencil on this trip.''

Lindsay assessed him sagely, her eyes going over the drawn features, the warm glint of the sun on the soft brown hair falling over his forehead. Could he really be this naive?

"Didn't it occur to you that Carl could be jealous of the professional attention you've been paying his wife?" she suggested gently. "He's been the artist in the family, as you've just said. Until now Betty's just dabbled at it. From what I know of artists, they have very fragile egos, and I doubt if Carl is an exception."

Joel stared at her blankly, his eyes narrowed against the sun. "But I'd be more than willing to look at his stuff, too." He sounded amazed, and Lindsay breathed a sigh of relief. His interest in Betty really was more professional than personal. "If he's any good, I'd be glad to exhibit his work. The more sales I can negotiate, the better pleased my father will be. But—" he shrugged despairingly "—Carl's not very forthcoming with friendliness *or* his work."

"Maybe he thinks you're interested in Betty for more personal reasons?"

His stare was even more uncomprehending. "I don't under— Oh, my God, you don't think he...? But she's—she's married!"

The horrified expression on his face almost made her chuckle. Was it possible that a man in this day and age could look upon a married woman as sacrosanct? For someone like Joel this evidently was so, although she sensed that he was flattered by—even a little proud of—the assumption Lindsay had made.

"Why don't you talk to him about his work, too?" she advised. "I've never met an artist who would turn down an offer of exposure to the buying public."

Lila emerged, gasping, from the labyrinthine depths of the plunging staircase. "Lindsay," she enthused, "you missed a wonderful sight. You should have come down with us."

"I've seen it many times before, and I don't like to crowd the viewing area for those who haven't," she said, tongue in cheek.

"Good for you." Lila gathered breath for her next spate, which was mostly directed at Joel, who was obviously absorbed in his own thoughts. "Dedication to duty is a dirty phrase these days, it seems. It's so refreshing to know that at least some young people have absorbed some of their parents' values."

Had she, too, noted the blossoming closeness between Joel and Betty? Reflecting on Lila's words, Lindsay somehow knew that her own mother, anxious as she was to see her daughter happily involved in a permanent relationship, would understand her inarticulate longings, although she might not approve of Lindsay's assuaging those longings without being married.

The knowledge that Philip, Deirdre's beloved first child, was selling top-secret documents to agents in Poland—was in fact committing treason—would affect Deirdre much more drastically than her daughter's more contemporary attitude toward sexuality.

# CHAPTER ELEVEN

LINDSAY SMILED and wished her charges a pleasant lunch and free time, which would last until the celebratory dinner that night. The next day they would take the early boat to Naples, where Pierre would meet them, and then on to Assisi, midway between Naples and Venice, their last big stop before Vienna.

Signor Bonelli insisted that she join him at his secluded corner table for lunch. Consequently, the service was even more attentive than usual. Sipping on the semisweet wine that accompanied the main dish of assorted Mediterranean seafood, Lindsay laughingly answered the manager's question about how she intended to spend the rest of the afternoon.

"With a book and bed," she said lightly.

He shook his head disapprovingly, then switched to English, which he was wont to practice on Lindsay. "You are like an old lady," he reprimanded sadly, "catching the winks where she can."

"The winks?" Lindsay's brow furrowed. She wished he would stick to Italian. "Oh, you mean 'forty winks,' as in an elderly lady who catnaps?"

"Catnaps? What is this?"

"It means...oh, it means older people who drop

off to sleep for a few minutes whenever they can. And not only the elderly. Younger ones like me feel the strain of a month's tour of Europe. I'm learning to pace myself on these long trips.''

But this time her Mediterranean-style bedroom failed to entice her. Ten minutes after lying back on her bed, she rose and padded barefoot to the balcony, feeling the warmth of the sun as her eyes adjusted to the light cast from it. A blue glint caught her eye. The swimming pool. Possibly it would be a little chilly for her, but this might be her last chance to swim in the open air on this trip.

Animated at the prospect of enjoying an hour or two of her free time alone, she hurriedly donned a white bikini and matching terry cover-up, relieved to find that the pool, reached by rough-cut steps into the rock descending sharply from the hotel's upper terraces, was deserted.

The air was actually hot, so that, diving, she gasped in shocked reaction to the coolness of the water. But gradually her body adjusted to the temperature, and she struck out for the far side of the pool, feeling the tension in her muscles yield to the growing warmth of her body, generated by her flailing arms. Once, twice, three times she pushed away from the smooth side. Swimming back underwater to her entry point, she glided up to break the surface, her hands coming up as she stood up to slick back her dripping hair and clear her eyes. Opening them, she smothered a scream.

A fully dressed man, the legs of his lightweight coffee-colored trousers only six inches from her startled gaze, stood looking down at her speculatively from narrowed eyes.

"*Scúsi, signorína.* You are Miss Lindsay Tabor?"

"I—yes, I am. Who are you?" Her eyes held an apprehensive gleam as she stared up into the man's hatchet-thin face. He had pale olive skin and an aquiline nose, his eyes deeply set under heavy black brows.

"I will introduce myself in one moment, but perhaps you would prefer that we talk over there?" He indicated an alcoved area where loungers and small tables were set out for swimmers. His words made her conscious of being at a disadvantage, here in the pool, her chest still rising and falling rapidly from her swim. But she still hesitated, and he said somewhat impatiently, "You have no need to fear me, Miss Tabor. I am an agent of the police, yes?"

"*Agènte di polizía?*" she translated half-aloud, and he gave her a brief smile as he stepped back.

"You have a better grasp of my language than I of yours, Miss Tabor, so we will perhaps conduct our interview in *italiàno.*"

Her mind racing, Lindsay used the steps to leave the pool and followed him to the seating area, wringing out her hair as she went, more confident once she'd snatched up her robe and fastened it around her. Visions of Carey floating, like Perrault, in the Arno made a cold lump of fear form in her chest. Why else would the police have sent a man to interview her here? On the other hand, they could have reached her by telephone....

"My name is Roberto Marsini," the man introduced himself when they were seated at opposite sides of an umbrella table. "I am an investigator for an international organization you may have heard of—Interpol, no?" Her frozen stare told him that she had indeed heard of the organization. "Captain Scorsi in Rome has been assigned to the case of the unfortunate Signor Perrault, who was found in Florence—"

"I know," Lindsay inserted hastily. So far he had said nothing about Carey being similarly "unfortunate."

Marsini leaned forward in his chair, and she sensed that he must be very good at his investigative job. Those fiercely penetrating eyes would intimidate anyone. "On the same night that Signor Perrault was brutally murdered, Miss Tabor, another of your passengers also left the tour—a Signor Hudson."

Lindsay nodded, moistening the dryness of her lips with a quick sweep of her tongue. "I told the captain that Mr. Hudson had to leave on business but that he will be rejoining the tour when he can. In fact, I was expecting him to return for the Capri segment."

"And he has not, of course?" Marsini settled back, but his air of relaxation was obviously a pose. His eyes were still pinning hers with their intensity. "The fact is, Miss Tabor, that Mr. Hudson has vanished." He spread his long thin hands wide. "Gone. There is no trace of him in France, in Switzerland or in Italy. You knew, of course, that he is employed by the same company as yourself?"

Not knowing what else to do, Lindsay nodded. Had she told the Rome police captain that? She was confused. She couldn't remember.

"But none of the Endor Corporation's offices have seen him since he left Paris with the tour, and he made no appearance at the Rome office. You can understand—" he shrugged "—why the police department wishes to interview him. A client of yours is found murdered, and another disappears from that time on. A man who has nothing to hide does not make himself invisible, Miss Tabor. What connection was there between the two men?" His voice hardened as he rapped out the question, taking her by surprise.

"Why, I—none, as far as I know. Mr. Hudson didn't care for Monsieur Perrault, but very few of the passengers did. You can ask them if you like."

He smiled thinly. "That won't be necessary. Our intention is not to alarm your passengers. What you have told them about Signor Perrault is acceptable to them and to us." He was silent for long moments, seemingly lost in his thoughts. Then he threw out in a voice of steel, "Where is Signor Hudson, Miss Tabor?"

Lindsay's eyes widened in shock. "I—I have no idea where he is," she answered truthfully. "He said he had to attend to business and would rejoin the tour later. That's all I know."

"So?" His deep-set eyes probed hers disbelievingly. Then he went on softly, "You were...more intimate with the Hudson man than you usually are with your passengers, were you not, Miss Tabor?"

Lindsay swallowed convulsively as apprehension seemed to shiver down her spine. How did he know all this? It was like a nightmare vision of the police state, where every movement was followed by harsh appraising eyes. It was terror more than anything that made her voice convincingly sincere.

"For a while, perhaps, but...." She shook her head and gave him a steady look. "I've been hurt before by a man similar to Mr. Hudson in outlook, and I have no wish to repeat the experience."

The recessed gaze was thoughtful. Then he shrugged. "However that may be, I believe he will try to contact you again. When he does so, you must get in touch with me immediately." A sardonic smile twisted his narrow mouth when the obvious question was reflected in her eyes. "Don't worry, Miss Tabor. I will be close at your side until Signor Hudson makes his reappearance. I will not be so obvious as to join your tour at this late date, but be assured that I will be following your movements closely."

He stood up, a menacing figure—tall, tough as whipcord—and looked down at her. He was still smiling slightly. "We do not regard murder lightly in Italy, *signorína,* regardless of what you may have heard, and I assure you that Signor Perrault's killer will be found."

As if they had just had a normal conversation, he bowed from the waist and swiveled on his heel. A moment later he was swallowed up in the verdant greenery surrounding the cliff path leading to the hotel. Lindsay stared after him, aware of the diminishing heat of the sun as it dropped toward the horizon.

But it wasn't only the loss of the sun's warmth that chilled her to the marrow. She had been exposed to the unknown dangers of international espionage by her own brother, and now the man she had finally let herself love was being hunted by an international police organization dedicated to avenging Louis Perrault's death.

Could Carey have murdered the Frenchman, after all?

SIGNOR BONELLI GREETED HER as she entered the dining room, his smile paternally proud as he led her to the long side table reserved for the Eurospan group and settled her at the head of it. In heavily accented English, he said, "This is your special evening, the last of our tours for the season. We have for your pleasure the brothers Lambertini, who will make music for dancing while you enjoy your dinner."

The group, in frilled white shirts and tight black trousers, was already ensconced and tuning up on the dais at the far end of the small dance floor, and Lindsay forced a smile of appreciation for the rotund manager.

"*Gràzie, signóre,*" she thanked him sincerely, continuing in fluent Italian, "I am sure my patrons will enjoy the evening you have provided."

The manager bowed himself away, and she ventured a smile in the direction of the Harbens, the Strangeways, the Dakers and Ferruccis and for Joel Carter, seated, surprisingly, between the two Timms. Charlene, at the opposite end of the table, ignored her arrival, but Lila beamed shortsightedly and waved her fingers in Lindsay's direction.

"I'd like to make a toast," Tony Ferrucci proposed, holding his glass high as he looked around the table and finally fastened on Lindsay sitting rather uneasily in her chair. "To the best little tour guide in the business."

"I'll certainly second that," Brad Dakers, at her right, agreed, and the rest of the table raised their glasses with him in tribute to Lindsay.

She waited until the glasses were lowered again before proposing her own toast. "To the best tour I've ever conducted."

"I bet you say that to all the groups you've guided," Brad teased, and Lindsay smiled easily.

"I do, but I'm not being dishonest. Each one of my tours is very special to me. I get to know the passengers so well, their likes and dislikes, what makes them tick."

"Oh, come now," Frank Harben said portentously from her left. "A few weeks is hardly long enough to get to know what makes someone 'tick,' as you put it. No one displays normal personality streaks on a tour such as this."

"I'd like to bet Lindsay doesn't agree with you," Brad challenged. "For instance...suppose there'd been a murder on this tour, and every member of it was a suspect. Which of us would you choose, Lindsay, as the killer of, say...oh...Louis Perrault?"

Lindsay started and felt the warm rush of color to her cheeks. Did he know—did he suspect—that...?

"I know Perrault died of natural causes," he said, waving his hand casually, "but suppose someone had killed him? Put a bullet through his head and tossed him into the river?"

He *did* know! Lindsay's head whirled, and she felt the color ebb from her face. Oh, God. Was the pleasant easygoing Brad involved in this, too? But—

"I think my husband is plotting the course of his next book," Debora inserted dryly, turning to give him a curious look. "Are you thinking of branching out into detective fiction?"

He grinned. "Depends on how long it takes Lindsay to figure out who's the culprit in this case. Go ahead, Lindsay, take a stab at it."

"I'm not very good at guessing games," she confessed, wishing someone would direct the conversation into less meaningful channels. A movement at the entrance caught her eye, and she saw the Marsini man, in a dark suit and white shirt that emphasized his swarthy looks, being led to a table at the far side of the room. He took the chair that afforded him a clear view of the Eurospan table—and her! Confused, she turned back and pretended animated interest in the problem Brad had posed.

"Oh, well, let's see." Her eyes went feverishly to Frank Harben, who had swiveled in his chair to glare balefully at the musicians, as if he resented their enthusiastic noisy performance. Only Debora and Brad were close enough to hear her over the din. "Mr. Harben?" she suggested quickly, and Brad shook his head.

"Too obvious. Guess again."

Her eyes went farther around the table. "Not Carl Timms, for the same reason. Perhaps—" her gaze rested on the person next to Carl "—it could be Joel Carter. He's just the type—quiet and even tempered on the surface but with all kinds of vengeful emotions seething underneath.'' She couldn't prevent a quick glance in Marsini's direction, shivering when she saw his deep-set eyes trained on her above the large white menu he was supposedly studying.

"No." Brad deflated her again, smiling as he turned to Debora. "You know, I really might do something with this, since Lindsay's finding it pretty hard to pinpoint the guilty one."

"She's hardly started yet," his wife retorted, but her glance was fond as it met his.

In likely order of descent, Lindsay distractedly named everyone apart from Lila, who was chattering in her incessant way to Charlene, who pointedly ignored her. It couldn't be Lila, so that meant.... "Oh, you disappoint me," she told Brad, caught up despite herself in the mystery he had set up. "You must mean Pierre, and he's pretty obvious, too, isn't he? I mean, it's as if the butler did it."

"You didn't choose him until now," the writer pointed out, obviously enjoying the exercise. "Anyway, I'm playing fair and only using someone who is at the table now—which excludes Pierre and, incidentally, Carey Hudson. You haven't mentioned him yet, but I'll kindly give you a bonus and tell you that it isn't him, either."

"But there's no one left, except—" Her eyes swept around the table again and lit on Lila's plump figure. "You can't be serious," she protested. "It can't be Lila."

"Why not?" Brad laughed delightedly. "She's the last one you suspected."

"But she's so...uncomplicated."

"That's how all the best murderers in fiction appear, isn't it?"

Frank Harben rejoined the conversation, having caught the last part of it as the music became more subdued. "I will never understand people who read that trashy kind of fiction," he stated sourly, picking at the antipasto the waiter had placed in front of him. "They'd be far better off improving their minds with real literature—like...." He waved his hand vaguely.

"*War and Peace*?" Brad postulated quietly. "Or Churchill's *History of the English-Speaking Peoples*?"

"Exactly!"

"But doesn't a steady diet of any one thing make a man narrow in his outlook?" Brad persisted. Their argument raged on, and Lindsay was relieved when she could escape to the pocket-sized dance floor with bouncy Tony Ferrucci. Too many intense emotions were battling for supremacy inside her, not the least of which was the question of what had happened to Carey.

The conjecture followed her to her room when she finally detached herself from the others, who were intent on making the night a memorable one in the annals of their European trip. She had been conscious—too conscious—of the Interpol agent's hooded watchfulness as she made her way from the dining room. Would he follow her?

In her room she stared unblinkingly at the telephone on the night table, willing it to ring and bring

Carey's distinctive voice to soothe the fears that trembled through her. *Where was he?* She sat down on the bed beside the telephone. Guilt mingled with her concern as she clasped her hands so tightly together that the knuckles showed white. Carey wasn't a trained agent as Marsini obviously was—trained and prepared to hunt down and even kill those who broke his country's laws. Yet he might well have killed Perrault with a courage she would have lacked herself.

And all this had come about because Philip wanted to please his wife. How far did love have to go to prove its worth? Would Elena herself countenance the danger to life and limb in this effort to rescue her aging parents from Poland?

The telephone rang, its strident note slicing through her like a knife.

"H-hello?" Her Italian forsook her.

As if he spoke from a million watery miles away, Carey's voice carried, disembodied, to her ear. "Lindsay?"

"Wh-where are you?" she asked dazedly, her fingers clasping the white receiver as if glued to it.

"Never mind that. Are you all right?"

"Y-yes, I'm okay. But, Carey—"

"Okay, listen to me," his voice went hurriedly on. "I've got what our friend was looking for. Do you understand?"

The envelope—he had found it! What had he forced himself to do to get it? "I—yes, I understand," she said in a rush. "But, Carey—"

"I don't have long to talk," his remote tones cut

in. "Your next stop's Assisi, isn't it? I'll join you there if—"

"No, don't do that!" she cried involuntarily, glancing over her shoulder as if expecting Marsini to materialize through the locked door. Lowering her voice, she went on, "There's...someone here waiting for you. He—he wants to talk to you about Florence."

"Florence? Who is it?" His voice sounded neutral over the crackling on the line.

"His name's Marsini. He—he's from Interpol."

"*What?*" He sounded startled to say the least, but when Lindsay began to repeat herself he cut her off brusquely. "All right, I heard what you said. Has he threatened you in any way?"

"No, not really.... He's just such a—a cold person," she stammered. "It's you he wants to speak to, about—"

"I know what he wants," he interrupted grimly. "Look, can you handle stalling him until I make new plans? Carry on with the tour as normal, and I'll be in touch. And, Lindsay...."

"What?" she whispered.

His voice was suddenly husky, full of meaning. "Take good care of yourself for me, will you?"

He hung up before she could form a sound past the thickness in her throat. It was several seconds more before she replaced her own receiver.

THE TRUTH WAS TOO NIGHTMARISH to contemplate, especially when the sun sparkled so warmly on the smooth blue waters as the ferry left Capri behind.

She sat alone on a rear bench on the open deck, glad for the first time to see the last of the romantic isle. After this episode, would she ever enjoy it again with the same carefree happiness?

She had relived her telephone conversation with Carey as she lay staring at the darkened ceiling. He hadn't denied any part in Perrault's death—just seemed a little surprised to know that Interpol was on his trail. And by warning him about that, she realized she had committed herself even more deeply to the whole ghastly business her brother had involved her in. Involved Carey in, too....

Rage still seethed within her at Philip's casual acceptance of danger on her behalf—well, perhaps not casual. In her mind's eye she could still picture the evident strain around his eyes and mouth when he had handed her the package. He'd known what was involved, yet he'd used her regardless of the inevitable danger. She had even come to the conclusion that Elena's parents might be a smoke screen to cloud Philip's real intentions. They had probably been dead for years or, if not, were too old to go through the traumatic experience of escaping a regime they must have become reconciled to over the years.

Carey was right; she was too naive for her own good. She had trusted Philip for all the wrong reasons. Her own longing for a family beyond the one she had grown up with had dictated her total acceptance of Philip, his job, his life. Had he cynically planned to use her obvious adoration at some later date?

Yet how could she be that wrong about a person?

She had never doubted for a minute that Philip was just as he appeared—a loving husband and father, a devoted brother, content with his lot in life. The chill thought returned to her that Elena herself might be involved in all this. What could be more perfect than two spies, one from each side, teaming up for some unknown political motive?

Several times during the night she had sat up and switched on the bedside light, her finger hovering over the telephone dial. Why hadn't she called Philip, she wondered now as the breeze created from the boat's motion riffled through her hair. Why hadn't she disturbed his sleep the way he had disturbed hers, confronted him with her newfound knowledge? But she had promised Carey she wouldn't do that, so she didn't.

She rolled over restlessly. It was all so confusing. Couldn't she trust anyone anymore? She had let herself fall in love with Carey, but was he any better than Philip if he could bring himself to murder a man in cold blood? Maybe he wasn't what he said he was, either. With the naiveté he had accused her of, she had believed he was connected with the Endor Corporation. What if he wasn't? What if he was just as embroiled in the world of espionage as Philip was?

She had fallen into a restless sleep on that thought, but only minutes later, it seemed, it was morning and she had to get up, bright and alert, to organize the departure from Capri. Her senses had been so numb that even the sight of Roberto Marsini entering the dining room ahead of her had had no power to stir her. He had been on the boat, too, but had made no overt attempt to approach her huddled figure on the bench, contenting himself with a searching glance from under his hooded eyes as he settled himself on the far side of the boat.

She didn't need or welcome Pierre's ribald comments about her washed-out appearance when he met them with the bus at dockside in Naples. She knew she was paler than usual and that her eyes had circles under them, proclaiming to all and sundry that she had spent a sleepless night. Or, as Pierre obviously relished suspecting, a night filled with every shade of debauchery his mind could conceive. How she wished that was the reason for her pallor!

THE ANCIENT HILL TOWN of Assisi, with its magnificent basilica named for St. Francis, was eerily impressive under the gray mist of rain that greeted them as they approached. Lindsay picked up the microphone and schooled her voice to impersonal efficiency.

"I'm sure Saint Francis of Assisi is a familiar name to you. He was born here in Assisi in 1182 and lived in a very worldly way until he received his divine calling around 1206. He is known mainly for his care of birds and animals, but his concern was for all of God's creatures.

The Basilica of St. Francis was erected for the purpose of entombing the saint's remains, and for those of you who wish to attend, masses are held at regular times in the Lower Basilica. Meantime—" she changed course "—on our right is another church, called St. Mary of the Angels, which was built much more recently. We'll pay a quick visit here in the morning, which I'm afraid won't give you much time to study the magnificent works of art, but we do have to press on to Venice.''

Not long after that, they began the winding ascent through narrow streets to the hotel situated close to the basilica. So emotionally numb was she that it didn't surprise her at all to see Masini's tall figure stalking into the hotel in Assisi just behind her as she went to ascertain room numbers for the party. By now Lindsay had also come to expect the complaints of passengers whose rooms faced the jumble of weathered tile roofs rising up the hill. This sight was a far cry from the panoramic view from the rear of the hotel, which overlooked the pastoral Spoleto Valley. She was not surprised by her group's reaction.

''I refuse to accept this—this poky room I've been given!'' Charlene stormed back down the curving staircase to the small reception area, where Lindsay still stood. ''I paid for first-class accommodation, and this is so far from it that it's laughable!''

Laughing certainly wasn't what the irate woman was doing, and Lindsay sighed inwardly. There was always a problem here, the Eurospan travelers being used to the more luxurious facilities provided in the larger centers.

''I'm sorry, Mrs. Warner,'' she quietly apologized. ''One of the drawbacks in visiting a small place like Assisi is that it can't quite offer the standards of the rest of the tour. But it's only for one night. Don't you think it's worth a little discomfort to visit a wonderful shrine like the basilica? Not many tours—''

"I don't give a damn about shrines and basilicas," Charlene shrilled wildly. "Did I ask to come to this godforsaken place?"

The criticism was hardly apt, Lindsay reflected sourly, but she let it pass. Charlene was already raving on.

"And don't tell me there aren't better rooms," she accused the tour director venomously. "The Dakers and the Harbens have beautiful rooms with balconies and a view. Why can't I have the same?"

"I don't assign the rooms, Mrs. Warner," Lindsay returned coolly, conscious of the reception clerk's distress. His knowledge of English was, fortunately, almost nonexistent. "The hotel has already done that by the time we arrive. In this case, the larger rooms are at the rear, so they've naturally selected those for the couples on the tour. All I can suggest—"

"Suggest?" Charlene screeched, beside herself with fury. "I'll tell you what *I'm* going to suggest! I'm going to pick up my bags and take the best room they have in the best hotel in Assisi and charge it to Eurospan!"

A flurry of scarves on the staircase behind Charlene drew Lindsay's attention and a quickly stifled groan. Lila Beaumont was the last person she needed to see at this moment.

"Is something wrong, Lindsay?" She blinked owlishly, looking from Charlene's puce-colored face to Lindsay's tautly controlled features.

"No, it's just that—"

"What do you mean, 'no'?" Charlene demanded indignantly, whirling on the bewildered Lila. "I've been given a room unfit for habitation,'' she spat.

"Oh...well, I'm sure Lindsay can fix that for you, honey." Lila gave Lindsay a meaningful look. "What sort of room did Carey have assigned?"

"Carey?" Lindsay looked at the room list, clipped to the top of her board. "He has...room twelve."

"That's at the rear, isn't it?" Lila cooed happily. "Well, then, why can't Mrs. Warner have that? It doesn't seem likely that he'll be rejoining us here, does it?"

Surprised by the older woman's resourcefulness and annoyed that she hadn't thought of the solution herself, Lindsay nodded briskly. "That's true. If you'll wait here, Mrs. Warner, I'll make the necessary arrangements."

As she walked toward the desk, she heard Charlene's triumphant sneer. "It certainly pays to keep these people in line. If I'd said nothing, I'd have to put up with that tiny room overlooking those dreary rooftops."

"I quite like that view myself," Lila murmured, and Lindsay felt warm gratitude sweep through her. The view Charlene had denigrated was the one Lila had been offered and had accepted without demur.

Her own room was in the less favored part of the hotel, but she breathed a sigh of relief when she reached it, having soothed Charlene's ruffled feathers by personally escorting her to the room Carey would have occupied. The other woman was too involved in her own triumph at having procured a balcony view of the spreading valley to notice the stiffness of Lindsay's smile.

By this time her luggage had been delivered to her own room, but Lindsay unpacked only the necessities for this overnight stop, too distracted to summon any interest in the task. She wandered to the window, easing past the narrow twin beds filling most of the room, and looked out on the rain-splattered roof tiles opposite. Over the years, so many people with problems must have looked out on those same tiles—but surely none with a problem like hers! Whether it was caused by the smallness of the room or by the menacing closeness of Roberto Marsini, she felt a claustrophobic urge to flee.

Shrugging on her raincoat, she snatched up a silk scarf, tying it under her chin as she hurried down the staircase and out of the hotel. She paused on the narrow sidewalk that edged the steep hill leading to the basilica. The old city, its houses tumbling down the hillside, was filled with the atmosphere of another time, another century. There was an almost palpable air of reverence, as if the saints who had once lived here still spiritually pervaded the streets and buildings. Charlene, she reflected dryly, wouldn't spend five minutes drinking in that reverent air; champagne was more her line. Turning to her left, she took a few paces, stopping when a voice accosted her from the rear.

"Hey, Lindsay, where are you going?"

Turning, she saw Paul and Mary Strangeways and the Dakers coming up from the shopping area farther down the steep incline. "I'm just going into the basilica for a while."

"Haven't you seen enough of churches on all your

tours?'' Paul joked heavily, his raincoat buttoned to the neck.

"This one's special." She smiled back, forcing sternness as she added, "You've all visited the basilica, haven't you?"

They looked sheepish, like children caught in some act of mischief.

"Well, no," Brad spoke up. "We thought we'd take it in tomorrow morning."

"There won't be time then; we leave early again. Why don't you come along with me now? It's really very beautiful, and I'd hate you to miss it."

"All right, teach, lead on." Brad was the spokesman again, the others following his lead as he went to join Lindsay.

Leaving the tunneled entrance to the rectangular square, they avoided the rain by utilizing one of the covered arcades at either side of it. All were suitably awed when they finally arrived at the imposing main entrance.

"I'll let you wander around on your own," Lindsay said as they entered the high-ceilinged upper level. She walked with a soft tread to the stairs that led below to the many chapels dedicated to various saints and to the tomb of Saint Francis himself. She wasn't Catholic, but it always calmed her spirit to spend a few moments here. The sound of chanted responses came to her even before she reached the tiny chapel where Mass was being celebrated. Standing in the vestibule reserved for nonparticipants, she noticed Gina and Tony Ferrucci inside the chapel, heads reverently bent.

Her eyes lifted and went to the simple but colorful altar, to the priest and altar boys performing the Mass. An indescribable sense of peace enveloped her, miraculously easing the fears that had haunted her for so many days now. Instead of raging against Philip's perfidy, she felt a strong flow of thankfulness bathing her. Her eyes grew wide and luminous.

She had waited so long for love to touch her life—a real love to negate the false coin of Geoff Boler's, a love balanced between the physical, mental and spiritual. Like a divine revelation, the knowledge came to her that if Carey survived this crisis in their lives, they would become one in that special way. Her lids closed. *Please, God, let it be.*

"You are a religious person?" a voice said in Italian close to her ear, and her eyes flew open as she jerked her head sideways to look at the man who had spoken so quietly. Marsini!

She drew a deep breath and stepped back from the grilled rail enclosing the chapel. "Not especially, *signóre*. I just find it peaceful here."

The hooded gaze lifted from hers and roamed around the thick stone walls, the tableau being reenacted before them. "Yes," he agreed softly, "it is very peaceful here. I hope Signor Perrault has found a similar tranquillity."

The horrible reality descended on Lindsay again, erasing the calm certainty of moments before. "I certainly hope so," she said firmly, retreating a few steps and gasping when Marsini's hand closed like a vise on her wrist, forcing her closer to the glittering steel of his eyes.

"He would rest more peacefully if his killer were brought to justice, no?"

Lindsay stared at him, hypnotized by the shiny brown eyes that seemed to leap out from under his recessed brows, every one of her senses alerting her to the fact that he would have no qualms about destroying Carey to prove his point.

"I say again, Miss Tabor," Marsini said in English, "that you must let me know immediately Mr. Hudson contacts you. If he is not connected with Perrault's death, he has nothing to fear from us."

Lindsay checked a relieved sigh. Obviously he knew nothing about Carey's call last night. She had wondered if Marsini had the power to have her telephone tapped.

"Why should he contact me?" she prevaricated, surprised when her slight tug at her wrist released it from his hold. "If he killed Louis Perrault, it's hardly likely he'd hang around Europe waiting to be accused." She summoned a scornful tone. "To be frank, Signor Marsini, I think you're wasting your time and that of your department. Now if you'll excuse me, I have to get back to the hotel."

Expecting a sharp command to halt, she walked rapidly along the corridor and up the steps to the upper level without incident. In case Marsini had followed her, she schooled her steps to a steady gait, past the priest talking earnestly to a tourist anxious to light candles for his Italian ancestors. She drew a deep relieved breath when she stepped out into the drizzle.

Oh, Lord, she couldn't wait for this tour to end.

Maybe she would never conduct another.... Maybe? It was almost a certainty. One way or another, whatever happened to the participants in this present drama, her connection with Philip would come to the attention of the Endor Corporation, and her tour career would be finished. Damn Philip! She loved her job, the people she met and Europe, which was almost home to her now.

Her steps slowed as she neared the hotel. She was also in love with Carey, but gone was her faith in divine intervention. Even with the danger surrounding him now, Carey had given her no reason to believe that he wanted more than a casual affair. What she felt for him could never be compressed into a few days, a few weeks. A whole lifetime wouldn't be enough to—

Forcing the painful thought away, she pushed one half of the double doors aside and stepped into the hotel foyer, untying the scarf from under her chin.

## CHAPTER TWELVE

THE SUN BLESSEDLY SHONE on Venice, bringing out
the misty golden glow that Canaletto had captured so
well on canvas. The light, so important in Venice,
was just right when Lindsay checked her group into
the internationally famous hotel fronting on the
Grand Canal.

Not even Charlene could complain about the hotel
appointments, where tasteful luxury greeted her on
every side. But then she was only one member of a
more appreciative group. Gratifying gasps of awe
came from several of the passengers as they peeped at
the elaborately scrolled furniture in the salon; the
majestic sweep of the central marble stairs, covered
in a burgundy carpet, leading to the upper floors; the
pillared magnificence of the discreetly lit lounge bar.

Lindsay's own room, though it looked out on to a
lesser narrower canal, was spacious and comfortable.
An enormous bathroom contrasted markedly with
the confined space and erratic plumbing in the Assisi
hotel the night before, and she promised herself a
long soak in the wide marble tub before slipping out
to find a quiet restaurant.

The phone rang before she had taken three steps
toward the bathroom for her promised soak, and she

erased all trace of irritation from her voice when she picked up the gilt receiver and said, *"Prónto."*

"I told you never to use that strange language to me," Carey's voice chided humorously, and her heart did a double flip before settling into a quickened beat.

"Carey?" she breathed. "Where are you?"

"Close enough to share dinner with you," he returned quietly.

"Oh, Carey! Really? Oh—well, the hotel dining room is quite good, or...."

"I think we'd better take the 'or' for this time. Why don't you order a single dinner that's enough for two, and I'll join you as soon as I can?"

"Yes, all right."

How stupid could she be? Of course he couldn't make his presence in Venice obvious. Roberto Marsini's presence must hang as menacingly over the hotel for Carey as it did for her. A single meal from room service that would be sufficient for two.... What could she order? Spaghetti? Too obvious. No. She would order cannelloni with a hearty meat sauce.

The order placed, she next turned her attention to what she should wear for this momentous meeting. Smiling, faintly humming, she sifted through the dresses she had unpacked such a short time before. Surely a private assignation called for something less formal than the expert cut of the white brocade or the sophistication of the black silk? Her hand hovered over and withdrew an oyster satin caftan she always brought along but seldom used. It would do for this occasion.

Rosy from a speedy shower, she had just slid into the cool fabric when the room bell chimed melodiously. Wafting scent from every pore, she walked to the door and opened it, half-expecting Carey but not surprised to see a sleek-haired waiter with a prepared room-service table.

"Oh. Just bring it in, will you?" She followed him to the center of the room, where he busily unloaded his cargo of spicy-sauced cannelloni and a multitude of accompanying dishes. *"Gràzie,"* she murmured, conscious of his bold stare of admiration as she signed the room-service check. There was also a curious glint in his eyes when he looked back from the door.

"You are traveling alone, *signorína?*"

"No," she returned shortly, "I'm with fourteen other people, and I like to eat in peace occasionally."

Shrugging off her pointed reference, he left the room, and Lindsay paced nervously around it. The numbness that had filled her for days had suddenly disappeared, leaving an almost painful sensation in her stomach. She paused in front of the three-way mirrors over the gilt-and-white dressing table, wondering if she had imagined that husky note in Carey's voice at the end of that phone call in Capri. Had she overdone the emphasis on her good points tonight—the shining black hair left loose to frame her face, the light but telling eye shadow and pencil to draw attention to the glittering near black of her eyes, the careful outlining of her mouth with pale but noticeable color?

Dear Lord, she realized suddenly, she was all set

for a torrid night of romance instead of the deadly serious meeting Carey probably had in mind!

Snatching up a tissue from the white box to her right, she was aiming it for her lips when a scratching sound came at the door. She froze, her eyes wide as they stared at the door's reflection in the mirror. Was it Carey, or had someone brushed against the panel with his room key as he passed by?

The sound was repeated, and doubt fled as she rushed to the door and threw it wide. "Carey!" she cried delightedly, and he put a quieting finger to his lips, slipping into the room and leaning back on the door once he'd closed it. His eyes went with almost impersonal interest over her, and her heart thudded sickeningly in the certainty that she had been right about the inappropriateness of her appearance. A man being hunted across Europe by Interpol would hold romance as last on his list of priorities!

Then his eyes lifted to meet hers, and what she saw there made her give a strangled cry and reach out her arms to meet his quick step forward. She was holding him and his arms were clutching her to the taut line of his body, his mouth seeking blindly for hers and finding it, a groan coming from deep in his throat as he kissed her like a starving man unexpectedly finding himself in a land of plenty. His hands ran jerkily across her spine from nape to hips, drawing her to the fierce arousal of his body. She sagged against him, his passion instantly putting a flame to her own, until her mouth opened to give him access and the pointed tips of her breasts pressed eagerly to the unyielding hardness of his chest.

She was totally lost in the sensual world they shared, so that she moaned disappointedly when he pushed her from him, sliding his hands over the oyster satin covering her shoulders and arms and finally holding her loosely by the wrists. His eyes were heavy lidded, an echo of the passion that still coursed recklessly through her.

"I wish there was time for this." His voice was a thick murmur, his eyes slumberous and molten as they met hers in a gaze that seemed to go on forever. "But there isn't."

Common sense told her he was right, but sense had nothing to do with the fire that leaped from pulse to pulse within her, a fire he had torched and now wanted to douse. "No one knows you're here," she pleaded huskily, freeing her wrists, unable to keep from stretching out her hands to touch him again. He couldn't mean to walk out as if nothing had happened between them. Her fingers found the short silky hairs at his nape, and she pressed the length of her body to his. "Carey, please...."

He sucked his breath in sharply, and for a moment, as his hands grasped her waist, she thought he would kiss her again. Instead he thrust her decisively away and let his arms fall to his sides, his shoulders rigid under the dark jacket he wore.

"For God's sake, Lindsay!" His voice softened a little when she flinched and bit down on her lip. "Don't make it more difficult for me than it already is. These people are deadly serious, and they wouldn't hesitate to kill either one of us, just as—"

"Just as you killed Louis Perrault?" The accusa-

tion was out before she could stop it. This was no
time for hurled insults, particularly when Carey had
become involved in the first place because of her,
ultimately because of Philip.

"That's what you believe?" he asked quietly.
"That I killed a man?"

Lindsay moistened her dry lips. "I'm sorry. I
shouldn't have said it like that."

"Is there a polite way to accuse somebody of
murder?"

"I guess not." His jaw had tensed to a rigid line,
and she turned away from the stony hardness in his
eyes, walking unsteadily over to the table, where the
food lay, congealing unappetizingly. Keeping her
back to him, she said in defeat, "Maybe I do seem
naive and too trusting to you, but the things that
have been happening on this trip haven't made it
your usual 'highlights of Europe' tour! I've been
knocked out, according to you, in my hotel room,
had my room searched and my safety-deposit box
robbed, been questioned about you by the police
because one of my passengers was dredged up out of
the Arno, murdered. And now an Interpol agent is
shadowing my every move." Her voice trembled
precariously. "And I don't understand any of it,
most of all why my b-brother got himself and me into
this."

Her noisy gulp obscured the sound of his footfall
on the thick carpet. Then Carey was turning her
around, pulling her into the incredible gentleness of
his arms, stroking her hair as he pressed her cheek to
where his heart was beating in quickened rhythm.

"I'm sorry, Lindsay," he murmured soothingly, "I shouldn't have blamed you for thinking I might have killed Perrault. It's a wonder you're still sane after all that's happened—" he released a ragged sigh "—and, I'm afraid, all that's still to happen." His arms tightened around her when she trembled. "Oh, darling, don't you think I want to protect you from all of it? It's hell for me knowing you're in constant danger, and the only thing I can do is keep away from you. As long as they think I still have that envelope, you're safe, because they wouldn't gain anything by hurting you."

Lindsay raised her head and stared up at him with luminous puzzled eyes that appeared darker because of the pallor of her skin. Later she would remember the sound of his voice as he said, "Darling," but for now there was too much to ask in too little time. "As long as they *think* you have it?" She frowned. "Don't you?"

"It's in a safe place," he answered evasively, his eyes somber when they met hers. "You won't see it again until you get to Vienna. That's the only way you'll stay safe."

"Oh, God." She shuddered. "It's like a nightmare that I'll never wake up from. Can't you explain it all so I can understand?" she pleaded desperately. "If I could see some reason why Philip's doing this...."

She felt bereft when Carey took his arms away, and she watched, puzzled, as he went to the small radio on the night table between the beds and tuned it to a forumlike program. Obeying when he beckoned for her to join him on the side of her bed, she gave him a questioning look as she sat down. He put an arm around her to pull her closer.

When he said, nodding at the door, "Just in case there's anyone outside," a sense of unreality descended on her. This kind of situation happened only in spy movies—but wasn't that the kind of drama they were involved in? Despite the warmth of the arm Carey held loosely around her, she shivered.

"I'll have to make this as fast as possible," he said hurriedly, his voice only just audible above the animated discussion of early Florentine art that was going on in a studio not far from where they were sitting. "For a long time now, there's been a leak of vital information from the British nuclear-development field. The so-called iron-curtain countries were creaming off the top of the nuclear-warfare operation, and nobody knew where they were getting their information from. To cut the story short, the leakage was eventually traced to the establishment in Surrey, where your brother works."

Lindsay winced and looked down at her hands, twisted tightly together in her lap. "There are lots of people working there," she pointed out stubbornly. "Philip was part of a team, I believe. . . ."

"A team that consisted of two people," Carey said grimly. "Your brother and one other man, who died a year ago. The point is the information went on flowing after his death, so that pretty well eliminates him as the source."

That left Philip, she thought dully, staring at the tips of her sandals peeking out from under the rich oyster satin of her robe. Somehow it had never seemed real before, but now she couldn't ignore the deadly seriousness in Carey's voice. He believed it, his tone impersonally sure. But why? Why? Philip had everything a man could want—a job he enjoyed, a wife who adored him, two beautiful children. He was suddenly a stranger to her, his brotherly affection a mockery of what it should have been.

"If... Philip did this," she said carefully, "it must only have been because he wanted to obtain freedom for Elena's parents." She turned her eyes on him with haunting appeal. "They're old. They've never seen their grandchildren...."

"Lindsay—" Carey grasped her hand in his strong one "—we have to face up to the possibility that Elena's parents may no longer be alive. If they are—" he shrugged "—the other side may have been using them as bait to force your brother into releasing confidential information." His tone made it obvious that he didn't really consider that a possibility.

"Philip," she whispered, uncaring if the words reached Carey or not. "He's made me an accomplice. No one will believe I—" She jumped to her feet and stared wildly around her, trapped in a snare of Philip's making. He had used her without regard for her safety, and she was entitled to fight for her own survival. The man Carey was at such pains to avoid, Roberto Marsini, leaped into her mind. "I'll call Marsini," she said desperately, her hand on the telephone when Carey jerked it speedily away, his eyes showing pinpoints of anger.

"Don't be ridiculous!" he rapped out. "Marsini's no more an agent of Interpol than you or I. He's a local operative for the people who badly want that information you've been carrying!''

Lindsay sagged against him, too shocked to panic. Had the world always been like this, and she alone blithely ignorant of it? She thought unexpectedly of Lila Beaumont and stifled an hysterical giggle. What would the older woman think of all these intrigues within intrigues? Lila's mind was disoriented enough at the best of times!

Lindsay realized then that Carey was lightly shaking her, and she stared dazedly into his suddenly concerned eyes. Had she been so out of it for a moment or two that he was worried that she'd lost control completely?

"Smarten up, Lindsay," he was whispering hoarsely, his fingers gouging the soft flesh of her upper arms in his anxiety. The glazed expression abruptly disappeared from her eyes when a loud rap, evidently not the first, came from the bedroom's outer door. She watched dazedly as Carey looked searchingly around and then disappeared into the closet, his dark-trousered legs clearly visible under her knee-length wardrobe. As if she were standing off watching herself, she moved like an automaton to close the louvered doors before going to the main door and calling out, "Who is it?"

"Roberto Marsini," the muffled reply came. "May I see you for a moment, Miss Tabor?" he added in English.

Lindsay feigned a fumble with the door fastenings, which had been unlocked since Carey's precipitate entry. Her hands fumbled with the chain lock as if she had indeed been sequestered securely in her room.

"Signor Marsini?" she said to the dinner-suited man filling the doorway, his face twisted into a semblance of an apologetic smile.

"I was concerned about you, Miss Tabor." He stepped boldly into the room, his wary eyes sweeping all four corners before coming back to light on the untouched meal at the center table. "It worried me that you had not come down to take dinner in the hotel, but I see now that you decided to dine in the privacy of your room." His gaze went to the bedside radio, still pouring forth its chatter of voices. "It is unusual to find an American lady so absorbed in an Italian program of art criticism that she forgets her dinner until it has gone cold." He smiled sparely.

"Is it?" Lindsay's indifference was sheer pretense as she walked to the table and looked down distastefully at the once beautifully prepared meal. Her heart was a painful thud in her breast, Carey's words echoing hollowly in her mind: "Marsini's no more an agent of Interpol than you or I." The tall thin Italian seemed more menacing than ever now. Even Carey's silent presence inside the closet did little to ease the fear she felt. Nonetheless, she turned calmly to face Marsini. "It's important for my job that I'm aware of current thinking about art in any of its forms in Italy. Though the average tourist just wants to see Michelangelo and the Sistine Chapel," she acknowledged, "some of my passengers are a little more discerning. They're interested in the more obscure painters, like—"

"Yes, of course, Miss Tabor," Marsini interrupted her, moving smoothly to the door and looking back at her enigmatically from there. "You have heard nothing from Signor Hudson?"

"Carey? No, I haven't—and I very much doubt I will," she lied with an ease that surprised her as she went to join him like a hostess bidding a guest farewell. "It's hardly likely he'd show up on the tour again now, is it?"

"Why do you say that?"

Suppressing the shiver his steel-cold voice sent through her, Lindsay shrugged. "Isn't it obvious? If I'd killed a man, the first thing I'd do would be to get out of Italy pronto. Signor Hudson is probably safely back in the United States by now."

Marsini eyed her thoughtfully from his dark eyes. "Perhaps so, Miss Tabor, but in the unlikely circumstance that he has not done so, you will notify me the moment he contacts you?"

She forced a laugh. "I've told you there's absolutely no reason why he should choose me to get in touch with. But yes, if it makes you happy, I'll notify you immediately."

Had she been too eager to deny a connection with Carey? A frown was etched between her eyes as she noisily replaced the chain lock and slid the regular door lock into position. She had been so conscious of Carey's presence in the closet that she was sure Marsini must have sensed it. But then he wouldn't have left so easily—would he? She jumped when Carey slipped up behind her and put his hands on her shoulders.

"Shh," he cautioned as she swung around to face him with a half-strangled cry. Whispering, he went on, "Obviously he's watching your room, so I have to get out of here some other way than through that door. Does the window to the balcony open?"

Lindsay shook her head in bewilderment. "I—I don't know, but what good would that do? I'm on the third floor, and there's nothing connecting the balconies to the ground."

"I always knew that course I took in alpine climbing would come in handy." He smiled without humor, then turned to the lattice-paned window, which slid upward to his touch. Rain gusted in, dampening the ocher-colored carpeting.

"There's nothing but the canal down there," Lindsay whispered fiercely. "You'll drown!"

He turned his head and smiled again, this time a glint of humor lightening the gravity of his features. "I was also the champion swimmer in my final year of college," he said huskily.

"Carey, this is ridiculous—foolish." The nightmare that had begun in Philip's quiet study in Surrey had broadened and lengthened to frightening proportions. "I won't let you."

"You don't have a choice, lady." He touched her cheek gently with his fingers, the fingers she loved so much—long, tapering and capable. "We have to play this game out to the end, whatever that may be. I'll be in touch with you again when you reach Vienna."

"But, Carey, I—" It was useless. Her words fell on empty air as he vaulted lightly over the knee-high sill and disappeared into the darkness. Like a child pressing her nose against the forbidden treats in a candy-shop window, Lindsay searched desperately for some sign of him. But all she saw was a swift dark shadow sliding over the wrought-iron rails enclosing the small balcony. A thousand conflicting emotions raced through her and crystallized into one predominant thought: he hadn't kissed her goodbye. Anything could happen to him out there, and she would never know again the swift hard warmth of his lips against hers, the rush of passion that made her bones turn to water, her heart melt.

*Dear God,* she prayed, *let him be safe....*

THE TELEPHONE JANGLED, and Lindsay, still immersed in sleep, groped for the pseudo-antique receiver and thrust it under her tousled hair. The night had been far gone before she had dropped off into an uneasy sleep, punctuated by dreams of Carey's body being dragged from the Arno, a neatly drilled hole at his temple intriguing her with its symmetrical neatness.

*"Prónto,"* she said muzzily.

"Is that...? Oh, don't tell me they've given me another Italian," a distracted wail came through, and Lindsay snapped to attention.

"No, this is Lindsay, Mrs. Harben. Can I help you?"

"Thank God it's you at last." Irene Harben almost sobbed her relief, alerting Lindsay to the likelihood of an emergency. "It's Frank, he—he's dreadfully ill, Lindsay. Can you come? I tried to get a doctor, but no one seems to understand."

Every other consideration slid from her mind as Lindsay groped for her slippers beside the bed. "I'll see to it," she said crisply. "Try not to worry, Mrs. Harben. I'll be there in five minutes."

Two of the precious minutes were used up in rousing the hotel doctor, who had evidently not been given the message that he was needed. Then Lindsay leaped into slacks and sweater, not even taking time to brush order into her unruly hair before speeding along the corridor and up to the next floor.

She found Irene Harben composed but pale when she was let into the suite. "Frank thinks it's the water in Venice," she explained quickly as she led the way to the adjoining room, where her husband lay helpless under the covers of the wide bed. Lindsay's heart sank when she looked closely at him. His face had the pasty pallor of sickness, and beads of sweat stood out on his brow.

"The doctor's on the way, Mr. Harben," she soothed. "Please don't worry. You'll be in very good hands. He's an excellent doctor."

The man reached out his hand from under the covers and clasped hers in a deathlike hold, his eyes humbly pleading as they looked up into hers.

"You'll stay here?" he muttered feverishly. "I can't...speak this damn lingo."

"But I speak yours," the doctor inserted dryly from the doorway, and Lindsay relinquished her place by the bedside to his unruffled presence, obediently leaving the room when he gestured briefly with his hand.

Irene Harben was pacing distractedly back and

forth between the sofa and picture window overlooking the grayish green waters, where steamships came and went constantly. "What am I going to do, Lindsay?" she fretted. "If Frank has to be hospitalized here, you'll have to go on with the tour and leave us in Venice—and neither of us speaks the language!"

"There are excellent English-speaking doctors in hospitals here if he should need one," Lindsay said with matter-of-fact calm. "As for the tour—well, Eurospan will see that you get safely back to the States."

"But—" Irene's lip quivered "—it's going to spoil everything, isn't it? We've met such nice people on this tour, people we're comfortable with, and if Frank has to go on with a totally new group of people, I don't know what he'll do!"

"You don't have to join up with another tour," Lindsay assured in her gentlest voice. "We only have a few more days of this one, and arrangements can be made for you to fly home from Venice instead of Vienna. You can always take another tour later if you wish."

Irene shook her graying head despairingly. "Frank will never agree to come back again. You see, his—his company has retired him against his will, and although I know it isn't true, he'll insist we can never afford a trip like this again."

Irene's pacing stopped abruptly, and Lindsay turned her head as the doctor opened the connecting door from the bedroom. He addressed Irene in perfectly accented English.

"Your husband is suffering from no more than an

overdose of food unfamiliar to him as well as water his system is unused to. I will send some medication for him, and you must be sure that it is taken as I prescribe. He must rest in bed for at least forty-eight hours.''

"Two days?'' Irene looked doubtfully at Lindsay, relief mingling with a new concern. "We leave tomorrow, don't we?''

The doctor intervened before Lindsay had a chance to speak. "You may leave Venice tomorrow, provided your husband submits to the treatment and rests while he is traveling. I leave him in your hands, *signóra*.'' He bowed, acknowledging Lindsay with a murmured *"Signorína,''* then bustled from the room.

"I didn't thank him,'' Irene said regretfully. "I didn't even ask what his charge would be.''

"You'll find it on your bill at the end of your stay,'' Lindsay assured her. "Now that I know he's going to be okay, I'll go and get properly prepared for the rest of the day.''

"Oh, my dear,'' Irene said contritely, "I got you up so early, and you must get little enough sleep as it is.''

Little enough, Lindsay admitted wryly to herself, Carey's stealthy visit of last night leaping back into her mind. But she forced a smile for Irene Harben's worried eyes and said, "No problem. I'm just glad everything's going to be all right.''

Despite the earliness of the hour, Mary Strangeways was standing in the open doorway of the suite opposite the Harbens, her blue flannel robe incongruously homey amid the hotel corridor's plush decor.

"Is something wrong?" she asked, round eyed.

"Mr. Harben was taken ill," Lindsay explained briefly, "but the doctor says he'll be just fine with a little medication and rest. If you'll excuse me, I have to go get ready for the lagoon trip."

Mary's brows lifted in astonishment. "Haven't you seen the weather?" she asked disbelievingly. "There's a solid sheet of rain coming down, and we certainly won't be interested in any boat trips on the lagoon. I doubt if anyone else will be, either."

"Oh." Lindsay's mind flew back to the other occasions when rain had made the lagoon a miserable gray waste as the tour boat battled the waves to reach the lace-making island of Burano and the glass-blowing center at Murano. "I'll get in touch with the others and tell them the trip's off for today. But there's still lots to see in Venice itself," she added brightly, "and sometimes it's more fun wandering around on your own."

"Sure, we'll enjoy it," Mary agreed amenably, but Lindsay wondered about the others moments later when she wandered to the window of her room and looked out morosely at the rain streaming down. The passengers would be fortunate to find a street in central Venice that wasn't awash with the rain that had fallen during the night. Board planking, she knew, would be erected across the main thoroughfares, allowing a precarious crossing from one point to another. But not all Americans were equipped to deal with that kind of watery hazard. Sighing, she turned back to the telephone in order to pass on the change of plans to the other passengers. She called Lila Beaumont first.

"Oh, don't worry about me, honey," Lila assured her liltingly over the phone. "I wasn't going to be there, anyway. I met the most wonderful man last night just as I was going into the dining room," she confided girlishly. "His name is Cesare Romaro. Don't you think that's such a romantic name? He insisted that I go out to dinner with him, and today he's taking me home to his palazzo—can you believe that he actually has his own palace here in Venice?" she gurgled ecstatically, and a protective instinct arose in Lindsay. How many American widows had already been taken in by this dark-eyed Latin, who probably needed an infusion of healthy dollars to shore up his crumbling family home?

"Lila, be careful," she cautioned. "There are a lot of impoverished gentry in Venice who'd just love to refurbish their mansions with someone else's money."

"Oh, you're a sweet child," Lila patronized her indulgently, "but you really don't have to worry about me. Cesare doesn't need my money. He's into all kinds of things on his own account. He owns a large chunk of several resorts around Italy and even into Switzerland, so he certainly doesn't need my widow's mite," she ended facetiously.

"Yes, but—"

"Honey, I have to go, because Cesare is going to pick me up in his own boat. Can you imagine? Of course, it's just like having a car back home, because the waterways are their highways here, but it sounds so impressive, don't you think?''

''Yes, it certainly does,'' Lindsay said, resigned. She was responsible for her passengers only insofar as the logistics of the tour affected them. Apart from that, they were on their own.

But still Lila's infatuation with the apparently suave Cesare Romaro bothered her long after she'd canceled the day's outing with the other members of the tour. The older woman was so naively trusting where men were concerned—who wouldn't want to trust a seemingly genuine made-for-movies Italian prince when he appeared in a woman's life? Lindsay was as worried as she would have been had a pseudo lover approached her mother. Poor Lila, so desperate for a man to care for her that she would fall for a gigolo type, which this Cesare Romaro sounded like! There must be some way to circumvent the romance—and, of course, the solution was ready-made. Tomorrow the tour would be pressing on toward Vienna, staying overnight at the frontier town of Villach.

The romance of Venice would be a wistful sigh in Lila's case. . . .

''GOOD MORNING. I hope you enjoyed your visit to Venice, in spite of the weather.''

''I'd like to come back and see it when the streets aren't running with water,'' Brad Dakers spoke up wryly. ''It must be great in summer.''

''Is is, apart from the smells,'' Joel Carter volunteered, embarrassed when a battery of curious eyes centered on him. "I mean," he explained diffidently, "with that much water everywhere, and people dumping all kinds of garbage into the canal system, it starts to smell."

Surprisingly, Carl Timms supported him. "That's true. I spent a summer there once, and it has to be smelled to be believed. I guess it has something to do with the tides or something like that."

"Anyway—" Lindsay stepped adroitly into the thoughtful silence "—Venice can be and is a wonderful city that conjures up the grandeur of times past. In a romantic sense, it's the most evocative of all Italian cities." Was she saying that because of the connection it now had with Carey? But she couldn't let her thoughts dwell on his danger-fraught visit to her room, as she had yesterday until she drove herself distractedly from the hotel and sloshed despondently through the flooded streets. Instead she went on, "Venice is reputedly sinking back into the sea, although whether that's an established fact or a devious plan to drum up funds to keep the floating city going is anybody's guess. Whatever, none of us would like to see the beautiful buildings that hold so much history, so much splendor, sink below the waves."

"Relax, Lindsay," Brad called above the engine's roar. "We gave already."

Lindsay joined in the ripple of laughter before continuing, "Our next overnight stop will be at Villach, on the Austrian-Italian border. It's a small town, so don't expect the luxury provided by the larger centers on our tour." This last was aimed at Charlene

Warner, who stared gloomily through the window and appeared not to hear. "And the day after that, as you know, we reach Vienna, the end of our tour. Yes, I know—" she smiled sympathetically when several of the passengers groaned "—it's a sad thought, but there's a lot to see in Vienna before you set foot on your plane back to the States. We'll take you for a drive through the Vienna Woods, made famous by Strauss, and we'll also visit the seat of Austrian royalty in times past, Schönbrunn Palace. The Empress Maria Theresa was the mother of Marie Antoinette, who was brought up in Austria."

A light and brief description of Austria's history helped pass the reasonably short journey to Villach, and there was still time to shop for cowbells and postcards, leather goods and Christmas novelties when they pulled into the central square and were assigned their rooms in the adjacent hotel. Suites were nonexistent, and Lindsay was prepared when Charlene made her dissatisfaction known.

She cornered Lindsay in the narrow entrance hall. "I've paid for a suite and I insist on having one."

"You've paid for the best accommodation available in each city the tour visits," Lindsay corrected evenly, "and this hotel doesn't happen to run to suites." Her attention was caught then by Frank Harben, who had propped himself against the reception desk and looked deathly pale. "Excuse me."

"No, I will not excuse you until I'm satisfied that I have the type of accommodation I've paid for," Charlene insisted, threatening a repeat of the scene at

Assisi. Lindsay gritted her teeth and glanced down her list of room assignments.

"You have the Maria Theresa room," she said shortly, "and I'm sure you'll find everything to your satisfaction there."

"I'd better," the other woman promised darkly, "or Eurospan will have one hell of a bill to pay for the first-class accommodations it promised and didn't deliver!"

She flounced off, encumbered by the various boxes and packages she had purchased on the trip, and Lindsay stared stonily after her. The squeaky wheel, as Sally in London had reminded her, definitely got a generous portion of lubricating oil. Not that it improved Charlene's temperament; she was easily the most unpopular member of the tour. Why? For a woman who seemed to have set out with high hopes of sharing her holiday with a man, she had shown her most unattractive side. Sighing, Lindsay dismissed Charlene from her mind and hurried over to where Irene Harben was picking up her room key.

"How do you feel, Mr. Harben?" she addressed the older man in a tone that hid her concern. He looked about ready to collapse, but he waved a feeble hand.

"I'll feel a lot better with a bed under me," he said with a surprising hint of humor, "and bathroom facilities close by. I'm sorry I had to interrupt the trip so often today."

"No problem at all. It happens on nearly every tour. In fact, it's more surprising when someone doesn't pick up some kind of bug on our travels than when they do.'' Lindsay's smile encompassed both of them. ''Why don't you let me escort you to your room, and then I'll arrange for you to have dinner up there so you'll have a nice long rest before we set out again in the morning. I'm afraid it's an early start and a long day.''

''Oh, I'm sure Frank will feel up to it after a good night's rest.'' Irene smiled with relief, earning an irritable shrug from her husband as she put a hand under his elbow.

''For heaven's sake, Irene, I can manage to walk to the elevator!''

Forewarned, Lindsay contented herself with assisting with their hand baggage. After seeing them settled into their small but comfortable room, she left them after promising to send up a dinner menu shortly. People never ceased to amaze her, she reflected while walking back to the elevator. Frank Harben was as irascible as any passenger she'd ever had, but he was coping magnificently with an illness that would have felled many a younger man. Some of his crustier edges had fallen away, too, after his open show of dependence on Lindsay before the doctor had arrived in his room. Had time permitted, they might have become friends of a sort.

Not so Charlene Warner. The dinner menu, exclusively Austrian, satisfied every taste but hers.

''I want a steak,'' she demanded loudly from the obligingly hovering waiter, her thumb and forefinger separating to indicate thickness, ''broiled and with a garnish of mushrooms and green peppers.''

*"Ja?"* the young waiter replied, anxious to please but completely at a loss.

Lindsay stepped in and explained in German what was requested, and he nodded comprehendingly before replying regretfully that green peppers were impossible but green beans could be substituted. The lady, he elaborated, would have to wait some time before her meal was ready.

"You'll have to wait a little longer," Lindsay translated as he hurried off toward the kitchens, "but your steak will arrive in due course—without," she added with unworthy satisfaction, "the green peppers. They'll bring you green beans instead."

"Even that will be better than sausage and sauerkraut," Charlene sneered, condemning the majority of the group who had chosen just that.

"You'd have been served more quickly," Lindsay retorted. "Every country has its own specialty, and Austria is no exception. The Wiener schnitzel here can't be compared to anything the States has to offer in that line."

"I'd never dream of eating such revolting food at home," the other woman snapped haughtily. "So spare me the accolades about sausage and sauerkraut. American food has been good enough for me all my life, and it's good enough for me now."

"Oh, go can the patriotic act!" Brad broke in disgustedly. "It beats me why you came to Europe if you're not willing to live a little differently than you do in the States."

Charlene threw him a venomous look. "I came to

Europe on business, to buy fashions for my salon in Chicago.''

''Then you admit America isn't number one in everything,'' Brad shot back triumphantly, making a great show of forking sauerkraut from his plate.

Lindsay withdrew mentally from the backbiting. This often happened toward the end of the tour when people were becoming jaded with the wonders of Europe, too aware of the foibles of their fellow passengers. Instead, she let herself dwell on Carey—not the aura of danger he had come to represent, but the more personal aspects that danger had obscured lately. It was so easy to imagine him here, eating with the group as he had so many times on the tour. He ate with neatness and without fuss, enjoying food without making a fetish of it. His hands had the length and shape of an architect's, she mused—strong, competent hands that suggested they could take care of any problems that might arise. His smooth firm jaw, pugnacious on occasion, gave the same impression: strength and the ability to stand alone against all odds. He didn't need anyone, she realized unhappily, man or woman, to go through life with.

''I doubt if Carey Hudson will be joining us again, don't you?'' Brad uncannily penetrated her thoughts, and Lindsay's hand jerked on her almost full glass of red wine. It slipped from her fingers, spreading a bloody stain on the white purity of the cloth. Her face echoed that whiteness in the resulting hiatus, when people on either side were jumping up and dabbing at the wine pool with their napkins.

''Lindsay, honey, are you all right?'' Lila appeared at her side and gathered up the sodden napkins to hand to the waiter, who had materialized at her elbow. "You've been so quiet all through dinner. Is something bothering you?"

Lindsay wished the older woman's voice could have been pitched a little lower. As it was, every eye was upon her strained face, now flushed with embarrassment.

"I'm all right, thanks," she managed, forcing a tremulous smile for the concerned faces around her. "I just have a slight headache, so if you'll excuse me I'll go on up to my room."

Despite her protests, Lila insisted on accompanying her. "You really don't look well, honey," she said in a worried tone as they waited for the elevator. "Why don't I call the hotel doctor for you? He'll fix you up in no time. You could be coming down with whatever bug hit Frank Harben."

"No, really, it's just a headache. I'd feel foolish having the doctor come and prescribe aspirin when I have some in my room." She produced a confident smile, her headache more real than imagined by now. "It's good of you to bother, Lila, but I'm truly all right. A good night's sleep is all I need—honestly."

Lila ignored her protests and rode up with her in the elevator, trotting breathlessly at her side as she tried to keep up with Lindsay's usual brisk pace to her room.

"I wasn't going to have dessert, anyway. Cesare says he likes a well-padded woman, but I've noticed he eyes the tall thin ones a lot more than the well-set women we've seen in passing." She followed Lindsay into the narrow bathroom passage that opened out into the small square bedroom. "Now," she ordered, "get yourself into bed, and I'll phone and get them to bring you some hot milk. The aspirin will take effect a lot faster that way."

Lindsay succumbed and let the older woman indulge her maternal instincts to the full. In a way, she thought as she changed into her nightdress in the bathroom, it was comforting to be treated like a sickly child, and Lila would leave her that much more quickly if she went along with her fussing. After rinsing her face and cleaning her teeth, she came out to find the covers of one of the twin beds turned down invitingly.

"I feel such a fraud," she confessed, half-ashamed of the pleasure that warmed her when Lila tucked the bedclothes around her.

"I really don't know why, honey lamb," Lila soothed her indulgently, sitting down on the edge of the bed and giving Lindsay a surprisingly shrewd look from her pale blue eyes. "You know what I think? I think you need a man of your own to fuss over, instead of babying the geriatric set on these tours. You're a woman who has a lot to offer a man, honey, and it bothers me to see you waste your youth and beauty on ungrateful people. I thought for a while that you and Carey had something going between you, but then he up and left the tour."

Lindsay was relieved to hear a knock at the door, and an affectionate smile tilted her mouth as she watched Lila bustle over to retrieve the hot milk she must have ordered while Lindsay was in the bathroom. What a sweetheart she had turned out to be! Her conscience pricked her at the memory of her initial reaction to the clinging Southerner. She had expected the older woman to be her biggest problem on the tour—which in some ways she had been, but she was more than proving her worth now. Another pang of guilt shot through her when she remembered that although Lila had mentioned his name several times as if inviting comment, Lindsay had completely ignored the topic of Cesare Romaro. She made an effort to remedy the oversight when Lila hurried back into the room, the glass of milk centered on a round tray.

Struggling free from the covers to sit up and swallow the aspirins Lila had laid ready on the night table, Lindsay looked questioningly at the older woman as she again settled herself on the bed. "Lila, are you very unhappy about leaving Venice and . . . Cesare?"

She was surprised by Lila's cheerfulness. "It's only for a little while, honey. Knowing it's not for long helps considerably."

Lindsay's eyes widened above the rim of the glass. "Not for long?"

"Only as long as it takes me to close up the house in the States. In the meantime, Cesare's going to look for a nice apartment for me in Venice, one I can lease for a year or so. He wants us to get to know each other better." She smiled indulgently. "He's very proper, you know, and he doesn't want us to rush into something we might regret later. Of course, I knew right off that he's the man I want to spend the rest of my life with, but—" she sighed "—I guess he's not as impetuous as I am."

That, Lindsay thought, was just as well. She looked searchingly at the other woman. "You're absolutely sure, so quickly?"

Lila extended one plump beringed hand to pat Lindsay's forearm. "When you get to my age, honey, and you've buried three husbands, you get to know about these things." Her voice dropped to a throatier level. "I know you were worried that Cesare was one of those Italian gigolos you hear about, but he really isn't like that at all."

"Oh, Lila—" Lindsay opened her arms and the other woman came into them, hugging her "—I'm so happy for you. I just didn't want you to be hurt."

"I know that, honey, and I appreciate it." Lila sat up briskly, tears sparkling in her eyes as she said, "Now you get some sleep and don't worry about a thing. I have a feeling that Carey's the man for you, and he'll turn up again sooner or later."

"Oh, Lila, I hope so," Lindsay whispered. "I really do love him."

# CHAPTER THIRTEEN

"THERE'S A LEGEND attached to that crumbling old castle coming up on our right," Lindsay said over the speaker next morning as Pierre maneuvered the bus through the Austrian mountains towering at either side. "Would you like to hear it?"

The response was guarded, but she launched into the tale anyway. It was a story of unrequited love that brought heartbreaking retribution on the heads of the luckless participants. There were so many of these legends centered in Austrian and German mythology that should, and perhaps would, be set down comprehensively on paper one day by someone far more talented than she.

"Did you enjoy that?" she asked, smiling tentatively as she looked from one face to the other. "Yes?" she prompted into the silence.

"It was fascinating." Surprisingly, it was Betty Timms who spoke up. "But why didn't the princess do something to get herself out of a fix like that? If she had bribed one of the castle guards, for instance, to hand her the key to the keep, she could have been home free and rejoined her lover."

"Ah, yes," Lindsay conceded lightly, "but she had nothing to bribe him with apart from her virtue, and she couldn't give that away, because she wanted to marry the prince. In those days, remember, men weren't as liberated as they are today." She let the wave of knowing laughter subside before altering her tone to briskness. "Now we're going to stop here for lunch before pressing on for Vienna, which we should reach just in time for a shower and change of clothes before hitting the high spots. I'll hand you a list of those high spots as you leave the bus, and of course—" her gaze clashed meaningfully with Charlene Warner's "—you're free to choose from that list or not, as you please."

She waited at the door beside Pierre until all the passengers had disembarked for the lunch stop. About to step back on board to collect her purse, she looked curiously around at Pierre when he put a detaining hand on her arm.

"You are feeling better today?" he asked searchingly.

"I'm fine." Her brows drew down in a puzzled frown. "How did you know I wasn't feeling well last night?" As usual, he had eaten dinner separately from the group at a secluded table near the kitchen, where his slightest whim was catered to by a strong handsome Austrian woman who welcomed his infrequent stopovers during his trips.

He shrugged. "I get to hear of things," he said casually, his eyes growing sharper as he continued to look at her. "You know that I am here to help you at any time you need me, Lindsay."

Surprised by his intensity, Lindsay covered it by laughing ruefully. "As long as I don't need help when you're romancing your amours scattered around Europe," she teased.

"No, I mean it, Lindsay. If you ever need help, don't forget I am here."

Touched, Lindsay nevertheless assumed the light tone that she usually used to address Pierre. "Now you offer, when the tour's almost ended! Come to think of it, there *is* something you could do right now."

He looked at her eagerly. "Yes?"

"Yes." She grinned, her eyes twin sparkles as she looked up at him. "You can rush ahead and grab us a table before that other tour lets off its passengers." She nodded at the sleek gold-and-blue bus angling into the parking area. "We only have forty minutes here, remember." ·

Giving her a disgusted look, Pierre checked that the vehicle was securely locked before striding away toward the restaurant, his shoulders hunched against the freezing breeze flowing down from the surrounding mountains. Lindsay followed more slowly, shrugging into the blue lightweight jacket filled with goose down that she always kept handy for this leg of the late autumn tour. How she wished that she could confide in Pierre—in anyone! It was maybe the worst thing about this whole nightmare that she had no one reliable to talk it out with. She was closer to Lila than to anyone else on the tour, but the older woman would probably have a fit if she knew of the intrigue surrounding them. As for Pierre—he was an excellent driver and an amiable companion on the whole, but not someone she'd trust with a secret.

Pierre had thoughtfully ordered her lunch with his own, hefty Austrian fare that didn't appeal to her at all in her present state of mind. Nevertheless, she made a show of enjoying the heavy dumplings in veal stew. Fortunately, Pierre ate stoically through his own meal without attempting any polite conversation.

Her mind seemed to be sinking in unison with her stomach from the heavy weight of her thoughts. Soon, very soon, this tour would be over, and with it the horrific tension and uncertainty that Philip had set in motion. She speared a square of veal onto her fork, then lowered it to her plate again.

What had happened to Philip? Was he already in prison awaiting a spy trial? Carey must have reported to Washington about the papers her brother had attempted to pass into foreign hands through his seemingly innocuous half sister. And Elena? Would she believe that the ends justified the means—that this treacherous act was acceptable because Philip had been motivated to perform it because of her elderly parents? Lindsay steered her thoughts quickly away from the children. How would they ever deal with having their father branded a spy?

The remainder of that day's journey passed in a haze. It seemed as if all her muscles were permanently tensed, and she couldn't shake her dull feverish headache. There was also the heartbreaking knowledge that this would be the last tour she would conduct. It wasn't even remotely conceivable that the Endor Corporation would continue to employ her after her involvement in such an infamous spy case that would probably attract considerable attention, at least temporarily.

Her fingers tightened on the microphone, a wave of nostalgia washing through her as she identified the various districts they passed through. Later she distributed the tour-summation sheets to the passengers, telling them there was no need to return them until the last evening in Vienna. Charlene's look was triumphantly venomous as she snatched the envelope from Lindsay's hand.

"I certainly will give them my opinion in no uncertain terms," she snapped, her eyes raking over Lindsay's figure in her buttercup-fresh yellow blouse and straight skirt that outlined her shapely hips. "For one thing, I'm going to suggest that they choose their female tour guides more carefully. It doesn't make for efficiency when the guide is more interested in attracting well-heeled male passengers than in ensuring the comfort of the rest of us." Ignoring Lindsay's gasp, which was echoed by several passengers in the adjoining seats, she went on smugly, "I'm saying this now in front of everyone, because I've no doubt you'll thoroughly inspect these forms before they reach your superiors—*if* they reach the higher-ups at all!"

Lindsay was too stunned to do more than gape at the other woman's twisted face, but she felt suddenly removed from the situation as an unexpected champion replaced her.

"Listen, you—" Tony Ferrucci leaned across to the startled Charlene "—Lindsay's the best tour guide this company ever had! She's good-hearted and she knows more about Europe than you or I ever will! On top of that, she's clever enough to speak I don't know how many languages—and, oh, yes, she's beautiful, too. That's what gets to you, isn't it?'' He straightened and looked at her contemptuously. "You know you can't compete."

"Please sit down, Mr. Ferrucci," Lindsay begged, horrified at the turn of events. "I'm sure Mrs. Warner didn't mean—"

"She'd better not have," Tony warned darkly, but he turned in his seat beside Gina and contented himself with glowering occasionally at Charlene.

Lindsay glanced down uncertainly at the blond woman, who had averted her gaze to stare stiffly through the window. "Mrs. Warner, I—I'm sorry about this. You're entitled to give your personal opinion of the tour and if that's how you see it, then—"

"He's right, you know." Charlene turned back, revealing the torrent of tears that ran down her powdered cheeks. She laughed awkwardly as Lindsay slipped into the seat beside her and looked at her anxiously. "I *am* jealous of you. You have everything I've always wanted and never had—beauty, poise and a nice personality."

"That's not true," Lindsay breathed, her ire disappearing in the face of the other woman's obvious distress. "You have so many things and qualities that I don't! You're a successful businesswoman, which I could never be. You—"

"That's not your style, anyway—and I was beginning to think it wasn't mine, either," Charlene countered wearily, brushing a hand over her cheeks to wipe away the tears. "That's why I came on this tour, you know. I wanted to find a man rich enough to make my dress shop unnecessary for my survival. The only possible one on this tour was Carey Hudson—" she smiled defeatedly "—but he only had eyes for you until he left so suddenly. I should have remembered that like attracts like—youth attracts youth, beauty attracts beauty. Harry told me that, and I didn't believe him."

"Harry?"

Charlene smiled and leaned her blond head back against the seat rest. "He's been a friend for years and he keeps asking me to marry him. He's...he's nice, but he's so ordinary," she elaborated. "He has a men's-clothing store, but he barely scrapes a living out of it. I'd have to keep up my own business."

"Would you be happy staying home even if you lived in a mansion?" Lindsay asked gently. "You seem to me to be the kind of woman who needs her own outlet for her talents."

"You could be right. My ex-husband wanted nothing more of me than to run his tract house and give him as many kids as we could produce, and I resented it." Charlene stirred and looked at Lindsay appraisingly. "I can't say I don't still resent you, too, but I won't be turning in a bad report on you." Her eyes flickered ahead. "Your driver seems to be trying to attract your attention, so you'd better go."

Lindsay got up, wanting to say more but unable to think of anything that would consolidate the tenuous rapport she had established with Charlene. She smiled instead and looked questioningly at Pierre as she slid into her seat beside him.

"Are you not going to say something about Vienna?" he asked with raised brows, and her eyes darted to the environs of the city flashing by on either side. Her hand fumbled for the speaker as she drew a tranquilizing breath.

"As you can see," she said calmly, "we're now approaching the imperial city of Vienna. It's all you've ever imagined, and probably more. You may be disappointed to find that the Danube is not blue, as Strauss portrayed it in his music, but a muddy yellow. Perhaps he can be forgiven for that poetic license, because he put the Danube on the international map." She paused. "In certain places you will see buildings painted in what has become known as Habsburg Yellow. Some think it's a rather garish color, but personally I love it. It gives light and life to a landscape that's sometimes quite drab...."

Her talk continued almost automatically until Pierre drew the bus up to the magnificent hotel that was to be their home base for this last part of the tour. Then she gathered up her clipboard, feeling another pang of nostalgia as she said, for what might be the last time ever, "If you'll stay in your seats until I come back, I'll give you your suite numbers and tell you what's happening tomorrow."

There were no complaints, not even from Charlene, about the accommodation Eurospan provided for this, the final stop on the itinerary. Lindsay watched and waited while her charges collected their keys from the long reception desk inside the main doors and made inquiries there about the opera and other nightlife. Even Frank Harben seemed rejuvenated enough to hold a lengthy conversation with the reception clerk about a box at the opera for him and Irene.

While she waited, Lindsay cast apprehensive glances at the plush red velvet curtains festooning the lobby. But it was stupid, she told herself, to expect Carey to materialize from behind the thick draperies, Philip's envelope in hand. He would choose his time to visit her in her room.... Her breath drew in quickly just then when the revolving doors ejected a familiar sinister figure into the deep-carpeted foyer. Roberto Marsini glanced around and honed in on her suddenly wary stance. His blue black head dipped in a deep salute, and Lindsay gave him a jerky nod.

*Please don't let Carey make his appearance now,* she prayed, her eyes feverishly circling the foyer as she moved closer to the reception desk. But of course he wouldn't, she chided herself silently, smiling as she took her key from the suave clerk, whose eyes ran appreciatively over her.

"*Danke,*" she murmured, arranging her shoulder bag more securely as she strode toward the elevators. Her finger pressed uselessly at the Up button, since all three elevators were busily delivering her own passengers to their respective floors. Marsini glided up behind her while she waited.

"This is a beautiful hotel," he remarked without looking at her. "I am not too familiar with Vienna, but it would seem that the Imperial is centrally situated."

"Yes, it is."

Ignoring her frigid response, he stepped into the newly arrived elevator behind her and pressed the button for the eighth floor, two above hers. The doors whispered to a close, and they began to move upward.

"I would be honored if you would have dinner with me, *signorína,*" he said with surprising diffidence, looking at her for the first time. "As a stranger in Vienna, I would appreciate your guidance in the best places to eat."

"The hotel dining room is renowned for its international appeal," she said coolly, forcing a smile as the elevator slowed for the sixth floor. "I'm sorry, but I have several things to arrange for the tour's stay in Vienna, so I won't be dining out. Good evening, *signóre.*"

She stepped out into the hall, feeling relieved when the elevator hummed busily as it bore Roberto Marsini to a higher floor. He was still suspicious, still sniffing at Carey's trail. *Dear God,* she prayed as she walked the plush-carpeted passage to her room, *don't let Carey underestimate Marsini's determination.* Unlocking her door, she pondered the real reason for his dinner invitation. Had it been extended so that he could keep a closer eye on her and the man he thought might contact her? Why, if he suspected her of carrying Philip's papers, hadn't he searched her room, as Perrault had? Or was it that he was simply more skilled at his trade? She couldn't imagine Marsini, as efficient as he was, inventing a ploy as obvious and clumsy as the Frenchman's rifling of the safety-deposit box in Florence.

Sighing, she threw her shoulder bag on the striped Regency coverlet of one of the twin beds and turned to cross to the bathroom, which opened off the far left corner of the room. She was too weary to do more than wash and refresh her makeup. She'd find a quiet restaurant where a woman dining alone would excite no comment—

She froze as the door she was heading toward began to swing silently open. The scream that began to form was suspended as her eyes widened on a man whose muscular legs were encased in blue jeans, his chest covered by a thick white fisherman-knit sweater.

"Carey?" she breathed disbelievingly. Then, as anger overcame relief, she exhaled indignantly. "You scared me half to death!"

"Sorry about that," he apologized softly, apparently unable to prevent a smile from tugging at his mouth. His eyes, lit with warm eagerness, swept hungrily over her neatly fitting brown tweed suit and lemon-fresh blouse before rising again to her face. "I thought it was best that I get here before you and your shadow put in an appearance."

"But how did you get in?" She was still stunned from the shock of seeing him, but her pulses were slowly responding to his presence, quickening at her temples, her wrists.

"As our friend Perrault found, a plastic credit card goes a long way. You should always be sure to put the chain lock on your door when you're in your room."

"I will."

A silence stretched between them, a gap that seemed to be filled with her doubts and fears. The man she loved was standing a few paces from her, and all she could do was to stare at him blankly, paralyzed when her every impulse was to run to him and feel his arms close protectively, lovingly around her.

"Carey?" she whispered into the void, her eyes clinging to the changing expressions in his.

"Oh, my darling," he said in a voice choked with emotion, finally opening his arms in mute invitation. "I've missed you so damn much. I've been crazy with worry about you." The last words he muttered against the lightly scented warmth of her neck as he avidly kissed the soft skin...before trailing up to each eye in turn and pressing his lips lightly there... before hurriedly covering the lips she raised eagerly, parting them as his kiss grew more demanding. For long moments Lindsay was unaware of anything but the need to press close to him, to express physically the love she felt for all of him. Her hands ran with sensuous awareness over the thick wool of his sweater, warmed by the muscular flesh she felt beneath....

Her luminous eyes registered shock when he put her from him and said hoarsely, "No other woman has ever affected me this way, and wouldn't you know I can't follow through? Things are happening so fast, my darling, that we can't afford the time for this."

Bemused, she missed the warmth of his body close to hers, the excitement his arousal sparked deep within her. But as Carey gradually gained control of his emotions, a sickening sense of impending chaos and doom returned to her.

"What's going to happen, Carey?" She whispered the question, more scared than she had ever been in her life. Uncertainty tore at her, because she didn't think she could face the evening that lay ahead, the danger to herself, to Carey. His answer did nothing to ease her anxiety.

"I'm not sure myself, except that you'll be well protected when you deliver the papers to the Keller woman. They've promised me that." His own frustration at leaving her safety in the hands of others showed in the drawn lines around his eyes and mouth. He walked around her and crossed to the window, though he made no attempt to pull back the creamy lace curtains that obscured his view of the street. His back to her, he asked abruptly, "What instructions did Philip give you for delivering the envelope?"

Lindsay moistened her lips, feeling foolish as she stammered, "I—he didn't say. I just presumed that I'd take it as soon as possible after getting here."

"Good God!" He swung around and furiously stared at her. "Doesn't he care at all about you—or if not you, then his precious damn papers he's almost had you killed to deliver?"

She opened her mouth to defend Philip, more from habit than conviction, but no words would come. The searing truth was that Carey was right, and it hurt. It was anticlimactic when the telephone between the beds rang with a muted tone. She stared at it, trancelike.

"Answer it, Lindsay!" Carey's sharp voice broke the spell, and she went woodenly to pick up the receiver.

"Miss Tabor?" A woman's throaty voice, heavily accented, greeted her.

"Yes."

"Come tonight at seven." The line went dead in her hand, and Lindsay stared dazedly at the receiver before replacing it on its cradle and turning to give Carey a haunted look.

"I . . . guess that was Hilda Keller. She w-wants me to come tonight at seven," she parroted tightly. The woman's call, with its stark overtones of secrecy and intrigue, brought home all too vividly to Lindsay that the nightmare would end, one way or another, that night. Violent tremors seized her, and she wasn't aware of Carey moving swiftly toward her until he took her in his arms and hugged her fiercely.

"It's going to be all right, darling—I promise you that. Now at least we know the time and place. It's possible she might have set up another meeting place with another contact. It's obvious she's not aware of Perrault's and Marsini's activities." He was really speaking to himself now, affronting Lindsay with the note of satisfaction that crept into his voice. Pulling away, she stared at him, her eyes dark pools fringed with the blue black of her curving lashes.

"You're enjoying this, aren't you?" she said slowly. "All the excitement, the danger. . . ."

His attention abruptly focused on her again. "*Enjoying* it?" he echoed savagely. "For God's sake, Lindsay, I haven't had a whole night's sleep since this whole thing began! The only thing I'm relieved about is that now I know you're going to be okay. All the security measures can be set in place before you even leave the hotel. You won't be in danger for a minute.''

Lindsay wished she could feel as sure as he did that the evening wouldn't end in catastrophe, but there was no way the cold ball of terror gathering in her stomach would be dispersed by words, no matter how confident.

Turning away, she said dully, "And how am I going to get out of the hotel without Marsini's knowing? He could be watching my room right now, waiting for me to make a move.''

"What did you tell him when he asked you to have dinner with him?''

She shrugged. "That I had things to arrange for the tour's stay in Vienna and I'd be eating in my room.''

"Okay." He paced thoughtfully back and forth while she watched him from the bed; her legs had threatened to give way under her. He swung back. "Here's what you'll do. Call him up and say that your work load isn't as heavy as you thought and that you'd like to change your mind about dinner. Arrange to meet him at seven in the lobby.... By that time you'll be long gone, according to my plan.''

"You think he's going to believe I've had a sudden change of heart?'' she queried sarcastically. "I haven't exactly welcomed his company with open arms before.''

"He'll come," Carey dismissed her objection confidently, "if only to satisfy his male ego. No man can resist an overture from a woman who once turned him down."

Roberto Marsini was probably the exception that proved the rule, Lindsay thought bitterly. Ice water, not blood, must flow through his veins.

"Call him now," Carey urged impatiently, stilling her misgivings. "I have to leave and get things set up." He came to the bed and pulled her up, his strong hands under her elbows, until she stood close to him. The storm in her eyes abated when he slid a hand under the thick roll of hair at her nape and tilted her face up to his. "In a few hours it's all going to be over," he said huskily, "and we can start thinking of more important things—like a honeymoon in Capri and whether it's wise to bring up kids in a New York apartment. Things like that."

Lindsay swallowed, blinking as she looked into the yellowish glow of his eyes. Unsteadily she said, "Is that your way of proposing?"

"It will have to do until all this is cleared up." He bent and firmly kissed her trembling mouth, imbuing her with a fledgling belief that when the night was over the nightmare would be over, too, promising a chance for them to make a viable future...together. Her mouth was pliably soft under his, more tender than passionate.

"You'd better go," she said in a jerky whisper, but her hands clung to the warm wool of his sweater when he straightened. "I—I'll call him now."

Carey's hands covered hers as he looked gravely at her. "Everything's going to be fine—it has to be. For the first time in my life I'm really in love, and I have to watch the woman I'm in love with go through something like this. I'll make it up to you...." He bent swiftly again to kiss her lips, briefly, tensely. And then he was gone, moving into the dusky shadows of the entrance passage.

Lindsay felt petrified yet euphoric as she reached for the phone, asking for Herr Marsini's room. The intermittent buzzing went on in her ear for what seemed like an eternity, but at last the receiver was picked up and she recognized Marsini's voice.

"Signor Marsini? This is Lindsay Tabor."

"Miss Tabor?" He sounded puzzled but interested. "What can I do for you?"

Lindsay breathed a sigh of relief when she heard the click of the door closing behind Carey. He had paused to listen to the opening of their conversation, but at least he was safe for the time being. She returned her attention to the man on the other end of the line and summoned all her acting ability to strike the right note of apology and eagerness.

"I've been thinking over your invitation to dinner," she ad-libbed in what she hoped was an appropriately contrite tone. "I'd like to take you up on it, if I may. There isn't as much to arrange as I thought, and eating a meal alone in my room doesn't appeal very much right now. Of course, I'll understand if you've made other arrangements."

There was a silence, then smooth assurance. "No, I have made no other arrangements, Miss Tabor. I would be honored to have you join me for dinner. My only embarrassment—" he gave a facsimile of a chuckle "—is that I am at a loss to know the best restaurants in Vienna. Perhaps you can recommend a favorite place?"

"The hotel dining room is excellent," she repeated her previous advice, "but if you'd prefer somewhere more ethnic, there's the Rathauskeller on—"

"I will find it," he interrupted smoothly. "At what time should I make reservations?"

"I should be free by seven. Why don't we meet in the lobby then?"

"I look forward to it, Miss Tabor," he came back gravely. "Until seven, then."

A feeling of elation gripped Lindsay as she replaced the receiver. It had been almost too easy. Carey had been right. Even Roberto Marsini, the machine-made agent, was vulnerable to women.

An agent of whom? The thought pursued her as she placed her call to the Eurospan office in London. It was obvious that he wasn't connected with Hilda Keller. If he were, there would be no need for him to trail across Europe in the wake of the tour. Ominous initials flashed before her eyes—the letters K.G.B., denoting the Soviet intelligence service, taking precedence. But why would two Eastern-bloc countries vie with each other for secret information? Surely Poland and the Soviet Union shared many of the same goals.

Her thoughts were interrupted by Sally's crisp "Eurospan Tours, may I help you?"

"It's Lindsay," she answered Sally's bright greeting.

"Oh, hello, Lindsay. How are things going? Any problems?"

*Yes,* she wanted to scream at the voice that sounded so normal, so tranquil. *Tonight I might be killed.* "Are there ever in Vienna?" she countered instead.

"Good. Look, there's no need for you to call in for the rest of your stay there unless something drastic happens, and I don't expect that. You're catching the usual flight back two days from now?"

"I hope so."

"Is something wrong?" Sally asked sharply, unusually irritated. Perhaps something had, in fact, gone wrong with Sally's latest love affair.

"No," Lindsay replied, suddenly deflated. "I'll see you on Thursday."

Her despondent mood stayed with her as she changed into warm slacks and a lamb's-wool sweater in a golden shade that blended with the sharp lemon of her blouse, the collar of which she spread over the V neck of the sweater. Pacing restlessly around the room, waiting for the minutes to pass until the appointed time for her to leave the hotel, she froze in sudden panic. *Where was Philip's envelope?* Carey had presumably been in charge of it while he'd been on the run, but he had made no mention of it tonight. Did he expect her to face espionage agents without the prize that made the operation viable?

Evidently he did. A feverish search of her room revealed nothing more than a street map of Vienna, casually marked by the pen of a previous occupant obviously unfamiliar with the gridiron of streets surrounding the hotel. A blue ball-point line started out from the side entrance and meandered three blocks before tapering off ineffectually.

Lindsay felt equally ineffectual as she bit down on her lower lip and tried to control the panic rising within her. Without the envelope her mission was an abortive one—or was Carey so confident about the success of the mission that he didn't think she'd need it? Was she just a pawn in his clever game of espionage on a grand scale? He didn't give a damn about her, she silently raged, crumpling the pen-marked map angrily between her hands. She wasn't even sure how to reach Hilda Keller, although the woman's address was seared indelibly in her mind: Friedrich Schmidt Platz, 216. It could be anywhere in the city, though the name was imposing.

About to toss the hotel map into the wastebasket, she focused again on the wavy line that tapered off after the part word "—rikstrasse." Quickly she smoothed the map flat and saw with a tingle of excitement that the missing letters provided the full street name—Frederikstrasse. For long moments she stared at the map, knowing that Carey had provided, like the voice of a ghost, directions to the woman she sought.

IT WAS RIDICULOUSLY EASY to make her escape from the hotel, and Lindsay chided herself afterward for her caution in using the deserted side entrance. She slipped into the anonymity of the general gloom that enveloped Vienna. A misty drizzle dampened everything in sight. Most hotel patrons would be dressing for dinner at this hour, far from the chill that penetrated to her very bones as she walked quickly to the corner, where taxis hummed busily by. Pedestrians, huddled into their turned-up coat collars, hurried to fire-warmed homes or the homey ambience of steam-heated restaurants.

Lindsay plunged her hands into the deep pockets of her goose-down jacket and quickened her steps past the solidity of apartment houses set back from the sidewalk behind low stone walls. Now and then she glanced over her shoulder, a prickling sensation at her nape warning her of potential danger lurking in the shadows cast by the tall lamps, which dropped light intermittently along the boulevard. She was being paranoid, she told herself. Battling her shrinking spirit, she tried to press on without betraying the deep misgivings besetting her.

By withholding the envelope Philip had entrusted to her, she felt, Carey had left her like a duck without feathers to brave the unknown alone. Had he set her up to draw the spies out in the open, where he could pounce on them?

Of course he wouldn't have.... Carey loved her, had asked her to marry him in a roundabout way. Had he known how frightening this walk to Hilda Keller's would be? Her thoughts veered off as she approached the final intersection, where a dimly impersonal light shone above the inscription: ''Frederikstrasse.'' She had a sensation of déjà vu as she turned into a narrower side street, a replica of hundreds she had passed obliviously on previous tours. A movement farther down the cloistered street, lit sporadically by orange-shaded lamps whose fitful illumination merged into shadowed areas, filled her with panic.

It could be one of the agents Carey had so confidently told her would be watching over her. Now, faced with the eerie silence of Hilda Keller's side street, Lindsay wondered about the Louis Perraults, the Marsinis, who might be lurking in the fraught silence surrounding her.

Her breath caught in a strangled gasp when a black shadow detached itself from the square base of the third lamp. She released it in a sigh of relief when a twitching tail and sensuously rubbing body against the painted iron identified the shadow as a cat.

The animal seemed endearingly familiar and alive, and Lindsay smiled as she walked with renewed confidence into the street, chiding herself for her own overworked imagination. Superstitiously, she took the black cat's appearance as a warning that the agents Carey had mentioned were in position close by. She began to scan the dimly lit numbers of the apartment buildings she passed. She paused a third of the way down the cloistered street. This was it.

Tentatively she climbed up the steps leading to the gray stone building, peering at the numbers and names. Three names from the top she discovered "H. Keller—216." The solid wood door clicked open seconds after she pressed the button beside Hilda Keller's name, and she stepped into a square hall covered in large black-and-white squares. There was no elevator—only a wide staircase at the rear of the hall, its steps carpeted in dull red.

Still holding the main door open with a restraining

hand, Lindsay jumped when something soft rubbed against the thick fabric of her slacks. Looking down, she saw the black cat swish his erect tail and lower his ears as he reversed course and brushed sensuously across her shins. She bent down and flattened the alert ears in a caress.

"You shouldn't be here," she whispered. "You should be home in the warm."

Ignoring the admonition, the feline emitted a vibrant purr as he stalked past her, his eyes narrowed to yellow slits of appreciation as her hand fondled the soft silk of his fur.

Poised over the purring cat, Lindsay had no time to register more than the sound of running feet that grew louder as she began to straighten up. The hand she pressed against the solid wood of the outer door slackened and fell as a forceful blow struck her head from behind. The last thing she saw was the widening of the cat's yellow eyes as she pitched forward to the floor.

# CHAPTER FOURTEEN

"LINDSAY? LINDSAY!"

The voice that repeatedly called her name drew her out of a relaxed dream world to the reality of a gigantic hammer pounding in her brain and to the discomfort of the hard pallet on which she lay. Opening her eyes was too momentous an operation even to attempt. The sound of her own voice reverberated loudly in her head, screaming about the pain there. Anger mingled with anguish as the other voice seemingly ignored her plea for help and went steadily on, repeating her name. Incensed, she forced her lids open as another protest formed. Hazily she focused on Carey's face bent close to hers. Strange, she could hear now that what emerged from her parched throat was no more than an incoherent whisper.

"Head hurts."

"I know, darling, but you're going to be all right." His voice sounded different somehow, strained. "We're taking you back to the hotel, and a doctor will give you something for it there. No. don't close your eyes again. Try to stay awake."

Hotel? Back to the hotel.... Where was she now? It seemed too much trouble to wrack her throbbing brain. She let her lids droop again and tried to hear what the other voices behind her were saying. But all she caught was a snatch here and there.

"Get one here. No state to. . . ."

"Car outside."

She felt herself being lifted, a jacket being settled around her shoulders, strong arms that she knew were Carey's carrying her gently, though his voice rumbled angrily against her ear when he addressed someone. She slid off into darkness again and knew nothing of the car ride or being carried into the hotel and up to the bedroom. Once she opened her eyes and saw a strange man leaning over her. He was frowning at a more familiar face behind him. Why was Pierre here in her bedroom?

DAYLIGHT WAS FILTERING from behind the heavy draperies when she awakened, and she panicked. The quality of the light was such that she knew it was late—so late that she had for the first time missed a scheduled tour, the one to Schönbrunn?

Raising herself on one elbow, she quickly snapped on the bedside lamp to check the time, wincing as a dull ache spread forward across her head. Her eyes focused incredulously on her watch dial, which read eight-twenty. She had never slept this late on any of her tours, but she could make the trip to Schönbrunn if she went without breakfast.

She threw the covers back—and froze with her feet on the floor, staring at the soundly sleeping man in the next bed. Carey! She looked dazedly down at her revealing peach nylon nightdress. Had they. . .? But no, they couldn't have. He was fully dressed in the blue jeans and white sweater he'd worn last night when he'd visited her in this room. Then why...?

Memory balked, then deluged her with a sea of impressions—the damp dark streets of Vienna, the fear as she walked along, the black cat that had momentarily scared her out of her wits, the same black cat whose yellow eyes had widened in fright in the hallway of Hilda Keller's apartment. Hilda Keller! *What had happened last night?*

"Carey!" Leaning across, she shook his shoulder and he started, the heaviness of sleep still in his eyes as he stared owlishly at her. "Carey, wake up! What's going on? What happened last night?"

Awareness replaced the sluggishness, and he swung himself in one neat movement to the edge of the bed. "You okay?" he asked.

She nodded, then grimaced when the movement brought dull pain. "Apart from the biggest headache I've ever known. Carey," she repeated tensely, "what happened last night?"

Giving her a contemplative look, he ran a hand over his darkly shadowed jaw. "A lot happened, but I'm not about to start in on explanations without having a shower and a shave and some good strong coffee inside me." He stood up, stretched, then reexamined her. "Sure you're all right? That was some clunk you took on the head."

"I'm fine," she dismissed his concern impatiently, "but I have to know what happened, and I have no intention of waiting until you've completed your toilet and taken breakfast!"

"Afraid you'll have to, sweetheart." He bent and

kissed her mouth, adding in a whisper, "You're a lot sexier than I am in the morning."

Her mind was too filled with questions to respond in kind, but her cheeks took on a pink glow as she drew the sheet up around her, covering the salient points her nightdress inadequately obscured. "At least tell me one thing," she demanded hotly. "Who hit me?"

Straightening up from sliding into his casual shoes, he gave her a level look and said briefly, "Marsini."

Lindsay's breath caught audibly in her throat. So he hadn't believed in her change of mind about having dinner with him! "But how did he...?"

"I'm not saying another word." Carey moved off to the door, turning there to add quietly, "There's someone else who wants to see you, so why don't you come to my suite when you're dressed? I'll order up coffee and breakfast there."

"But I can't!" she wailed in frustration, not knowing if she loved or hated him at that moment. "I'm going to be late for the Schönbrunn tour as it is."

"No, you're not. Pierre says he's listened to you do your thing often enough that he can give them the highlights of Vienna on the way and hand them over to the palace guide when they get there." He opened the door. "Half an hour?" Without waiting for her answer, he was gone.

LINDSAY ARRIVED AT CAREY'S SUITE at the same time as the room-service waiter, who wheeled in a table laden with covered dishes that gave off a tantalizing aroma, reminding her of how ravenous she was. She had eaten nothing since the previous day's lunch stop, and even then she had simply toyed with her meal.

Carey, dressed casually in gray flannel slacks and a navy knit shirt that clung to the contours of his hard-muscled chest, had the waiter wheel the table to the bay window of his sitting room. He indicated a chair opposite his own for Lindsay when the waiter retreated, pleased with his tip. Carey poured coffee from the large carafe and set her cup before her as he sat down himself and started to uncover the dishes that were driving Lindsay's digestive juices mad.

In silence she watched as fluffy, pale yellow scrambled eggs were revealed, followed by crisp slices of bacon, tiny sausages, grilled tomatoes, piping hot toast protectively covered with starched white napkins. Too hungry to stand on ceremony, Lindsay liberally helped herself and saw Carey do the same. They munched in companionable silence until Lindsay finally put down her knife and fork and somewhat guiltily held out her coffee cup for a refill.

"I was hungry," she confessed.

"So was I."

She looked at him, belatedly contrite. "I guess you didn't eat dinner last night, either."

"No, nor lunch, so you're lucky I didn't start on your delectable curves this morning." He smiled, but the gesture made little impression on his eyes, and Lindsay knew that their comfortable sense of oneness was over temporarily. Strangely, the questions that had spilled so demandingly from her mind earlier now lay dormant, because she longed for this intimate rapport to go on and on. His somber expression told her this wasn't possible.

"Before anyone else gets here," he said quietly, "there are a few things I want to say. I can clear up some of the questions in your mind, but I have to leave it to...others to explain the rest."

"Why can't you tell me?"

A shutter seemed to fall over his eyes. "Because I think you should hear all sides impartially. I'm not exactly unprejudiced."

She shook her head, puzzled. "I don't understand. If you're talking about Hilda Keller and Marsini and their ilk, I don't need to look on them impartially. As far as I'm concerned, they're the lowest form of life on the planet. To resort to murder and violence to gain superiority in an arms race that could destroy the world is callous and inhuman—at least, I presume that's what this intrigue is all about." She stopped there and bit her lip, lowering her gaze to the cooling coffee in front of her. Was Philip any better than they were, betraying his country to make that superiority possible?

"I agree with you," Carey said levelly, "but who's to know what motivates people like Hilda Keller, Marsini and the rest? Last night she raved on like a madwoman about her husband being interned in Germany during the Second World War, about how she hates everybody and everything that comes out of the Western world—apart, of course, from the information she fed to her bosses in Warsaw. She was Polish originally. Then she married Heinrich Keller, an Austrian and a Communist sympathizer."

"What about Marsini?" Lindsay reminded him.

"Ah, yes, Marsini. He's an agent, sent to replace Louis Perrault. It seems they are both members of a radical right-wing faction that got wind of the data your brother was filtering through to the Soviets via Poland. They intended to intercept the document you were carrying and use it to plunge into the arms race themselves—talk about delusions of grandeur!"

His jaw hardened when Lindsay pressed her lips together to still their sudden quivering. "But you have to make your own judgment about Philip's actions, Lindsay. I admit to prejudice where he's concerned. Whatever his reasons, he had no right to expose you to a situation you knew nothing about."

"It hurts so much to know that he—that he...." She could barely control her tears.

The sharp ring of the suite's door bell made her jump nervously and look across at Carey, who cursed softly and got up, muttering, "I told him to wait for my call."

Lindsay drew several deep breaths as she watched him stride to the hall and disappear from view. Perhaps the caller was a member of the Austrian security service, or whatever it was called. No doubt they wanted to question her about her part in this whole affair. For the first time she considered the possibility that her innocence might not be believed, and a chill trickled down her spine. They *had* to believe her, she thought desperately as subdued voices came from the hall. Her motives in accepting the envelope from Philip had been humane, if naive. She had wanted to save the old people, Elena's parents.

"I haven't told her you're here yet." She heard Carey's voice raised in anger, but the man with him came in anyway and stood looking at her from the arched hallway.

"Lindsay!" he said with gruff emotion, and her senses reeled. Philip? How could it be Philip standing there so suavely normal in a dark pinstripe suit and a mutely colored club tie? Her heart froze inside her chest, then lurched sickeningly. She felt faint.

"I told you she's not well enough for this kind of shock," Carey said savagely, striding toward her and drawing her up protectively into his arms. From that shelter, she stared numbly at her half brother.

"I'm sorry, Lindsay, but I just had to see you. I know it's a surprise for you, but I can't let you go on thinking that—"

"Her thinking just about equals mine," Carey interrupted him with deadly calm, turning to face the other man but keeping his arm around Lindsay's shoulders. "And in my opinion you should be sharing a cell with Hilda Keller and Roberto Marsini right now! In my country, Mr. Raines, turning over top-secret information to alien powers is regarded as a treasonous act."

"In mine, too, Mr. Hudson," Philip retorted coolly, superbly controlled as he walked toward them, pausing a foot or two away. "And that's one of the reasons why I contacted our security people the moment I was approached by those 'alien powers' you mention." He turned his blue black head to look at the inviting arrangement of sofas and armchairs to his left. "May I suggest that we seat ourselves comfortably for this letting down of our collective hair?''

Setting the example, he moved to the armchair flanking one of the sofas and waited politely until at last Lindsay detached herself from Carey and followed him, a delirious hope forming. Surely Philip couldn't be this blasé if he were guilty of such a serious crime. Or, she thought deflatedly, was he just a master of steely diplomacy? She glanced up, troubled, when Carey came to join her.

''I'm not a skilled espionage agent.'' Philip uncannily read her thoughts. ''Simply a man confronted some eighteen months ago by a tricky situation. I was offered, in exchange for information available to me because of my work, the nonharassment of my wife's parents. They were then living in a small town close to Warsaw, and as you know—'' he addressed Lindsay directly ''—Elena has been afraid of reprisals from the Polish government since her defection to the West to marry me.

''I said nothing to her and mulled it over myself, finally coming to the conclusion that the security fellows knew much more about the whole thing than I did. I contacted them, and a week later the wheels were set in motion for the pattern I followed for the next eighteen months. I supplied formulae for the experiments I was working on, and they left my in-laws alone, providing photographs to ensure my continued cooperation. I had no way of knowing whether the government would ever have harmed them. From all reports, they've been fine up until recently. But once more was discovered about my work, I knew I couldn't take any chances.''

"So you did give them secret information?" Lindsay interjected in a disappointed tone, drawing a smile from Philip.

"Up to a point, yes. But the information they were fed was very carefully selected, by me, to provide only sufficient data to keep them convinced of my reliability. In most cases—" he paused "—the information was made available to international scientists shortly thereafter, so the damage to our security was minimal. And we managed to keep quiet the fact that much of this data was later released in the West."

Lindsay saw his hand go down to flick an imaginary speck from the knee of his trousers, the gesture telling her that he was not as collected as he appeared. She hadn't realized she'd been holding her breath as he spoke, until an explosive sigh escaped her. The ache in her head was forgotten. Philip was still the brother she knew and loved, and guilt followed at her own readiness to believe the worst of him. Carey must be feeling that, too. She glanced at him as he sat forward on the sofa, her eyes reflecting the heady relief Philip's statements had brought. But Carey's expression was stony as he narrowed his eyes on Philip. Her hand reached out to his arm in a tentative appeal.

"Carey...."

As if she hadn't moved or spoken, he addressed Philip. "What you say might just possibly be true—" his tone indicated he doubted the fact "—but even if it is, it doesn't explain why you used your sister to get this so-called innocuous information across. *You* had a choice of whether or not to go along with it; you gave her none."

Philip nodded, turning toward Lindsay, who saw beyond his controlled expression to his deep pain. "It wasn't an easy decision for me to make for her. In fact, I turned the suggestion down several times before I was convinced that she would be in no danger, that she would be well protected at all—"

"Well protected!" Carey snorted his disgust. "She's had at least two attempts made on her life, not to mention having her room searched at regular intervals during the tour. And you say she was well protected?"

Philip's control slipped for a moment as he lashed back at the other man. "That was my understanding. As soon as I became aware that Louis Perrault, an agent unknown to us, had been put on the tour, I telephoned Lindsay at Lucerne and advised her to get rid of the papers." He drew a calming breath and went on more evenly, "I only agreed to use Lindsay when our normal method of getting the information to the Keller woman failed, for involved reasons I won't go into now. Lindsay and I don't share the same surname, so it was thought she would be safe from interference."

"Safe from interference?" Carey stared at him in disbelief. "How in God's name could you have believed that the Soviets—or this other group, for that matter—didn't know every last thing about you, including the color of the socks you wore last Monday? These people are obviously ruthless."

"I know that now," Philip acknowledged tightly.

"Our security people knew it, too, but they used me in their turn—used my concern for my wife's parents. Call it naive, if you will, but I believed they would be released from Poland with the delivery of this last piece of information." He turned to Lindsay. "You must believe me. I really thought that would happen and that there would be no danger to you. Otherwise I would never have consented to drawing you into the whole sad mess."

Her throat felt dry and aching. "And it was all for nothing?" she whispered, her eyes wide on his. "Elena's parents are still in Poland?"

For the first time a vestige of a smile was reflected in his eyes. "No, they're not. For some reason, perhaps to convince me that they were sincere in their guarantee of safety, the Polish people had the old couple moved to the border, ready to hand them over when the final papers were received. They allowed one of our agents to verify this, though, as I understand it now, there was never any intention to release the couple then or in the future."

"So they're...still there?" she asked thickly.

"No." He smiled more fully. "That agent worked fast to get them out. As a matter of fact, they're in a room one floor down from this, enjoying their first breakfast in the West. They want to see you. They don't speak English, but they've mastered 'Thank you.'"

"Oh, Philip," she breathed, "that's marvelous! So it was worthwhile, after all." She turned shining eyes on Carey, whose expression was still stubbornly set.

"So you're to be congratulated on a mission accomplished," he put in caustically, and Lindsay's elation turned to hurt. "But was the protection of two old people whose lives are pretty much behind them worth the risk of a young woman with everything before her?"

Philip flinched. "No, it wasn't," he said quietly. "Knowing what I do now, I wouldn't expose her to that kind of danger. I'm an average kind of man who feels basically that this kind of thing only takes place in highly dramatic films and literature. I don't expect you, as an agent of your own country's security service, to see the average man's point of view, but—"

"I'm not an agent," Carey broke in curtly. "I was asked to take on the assignment because I was employed as a troubleshooter for my father's business interests—" he seemed not to hear Lindsay's gasp "—which happened to include the acquisition of Eurospan Tours. I had a ready-made cover. Like you, Mr. Raines, my government used me for its own ends. I was to determine who was leaking this information. My government didn't give a damn, either, that nothing in my background had prepared me for all this."

"Your government?" Philip looked sharply at him as Carey rose and thrust his hands into his pockets, straining the gray slacks across his flat hips. "I wasn't aware that the Americans had been brought into the picture at all."

Shock had riveted Lindsay's eyes on Carey's face, but now sickening waves of revulsion came and went inside her, forcing her to her feet. She rushed headlong toward the door, the two men's startled expressions scarcely impinging on her senses. All she knew was that she had to get out of there, away from their acrimony and away from the knowledge that Carey had lied to her.

She slipped into the mercifully waiting elevator and hurriedly pressed the button for her floor, ignoring the pounding of feet along the corridor and Carey's "Lindsay! Lindsay, listen to me!"

In her room, the door locked securely behind her, she went slowly to the window, staring out unseeingly, dry eyed as Carey pounded on the door.

He had lied to her, at least by omission of the truth. How could she gave guessed that he was an agent for the U.S. government—even temporarily— that he'd been spying on her in more ways than one? And on top of that, his father owned the company she worked for. Why hadn't he told her all this? Every other aspect of the nightmare tour dissolved into unimportance beside this. She loved him, but how could there be real trust in a relationship that started out with dishonesty?

Carey was growing more and more incensed at her silence. "Lindsay, open this door right now, or so help me I'll break it down!"

She looked woodenly around at the door. The sour thought came to her that the expense of replacing it would mean nothing to the son of a man who could doubtless buy the hotel itself many times over.

It was her long-imbued training as a responsible tour director that finally impelled her to the door to unfasten the locks. Carey glared at her, his hair disheveled as if he had been running his hands through it in frustration.

"How dare you run out on me like that?" he demanded in a furious undertone, striding past her into the room and slamming the door behind him. She felt strangely dead, even when his hands shot out to grasp her shoulders and haul her around to face him. Every line on his face was etched starkly into his skin as he glowered at her. He drew a deep breath. "Never do that again! If there's something on your mind, stay and tell me about it. What kind of future do we have if you don't stay and talk about problems that come up? I warn you now, Lindsay, that this is the first and last time I'll ever come after you."

Her mouth firmed to an ungiving line before she glared back and said acidly, "What kind of future do we have if you base it on a lie?"

"All right," he acknowledged grimly. "I didn't tell you the whole truth about who I am. There wasn't time to tell you a lot of other things, either—about women who made themselves available to me because of who I am, not what I am. You were the only one who put up any resistance at all—because you didn't know I was the son of the chairman of the Endor Corporation! I thought that finally I'd found a woman I could believe loved me for myself, not for the wealth my family represented. Oh, hell." He dropped his arms and swung away from her, his tone moody and hopeless as he went on. "Why would I expect you to understand any more than the rest of them did? I wanted a woman who saw *me*, with all my faults, and still loved me in spite of them."

Tears that had been checked within her now cascaded down Lindsay's face. She was powerless to stop them, just as she was powerless to take that vital step toward him and put her arms around him and tell him she loved him in just that way. She was realizing too many things, too fast, too late. It wouldn't have made any difference to how she felt about him had she known who he was. But, she admitted honestly, it would have made her draw back, deny her feelings—as she had been doing since he had uttered those words a few moments earlier in his suite.

"Carey, I—I see only that one fault, and I . . . guess I can forgive that."

He stared at her with eyes that seemed to reach deep into the soul of her before he spanned the distance between them and pulled her urgently into his arms.

## CHAPTER FIFTEEN

ALTHOUGH IT WAS STILL early March, the sun's warmth penetrated the creamy folds of her peignoir as Lindsay stepped out onto the tiled terrace. Leaning on the yellowed stone parapet wall, she gazed with delight at the view spread before her. The Amalfi coastline on the distant mainland was a jumble of weathered rock and spacious hotels, of homes perched on impossibly steep outcroppings that swept sheerly down to the blue tranquillity of the Mediterranean.

Closer, the breathtaking shoreline of Capri reminded her that this island had been chosen by some of Rome's most world-weary emperors for their summer retreat. The vine-covered slopes falling away from the point where she stood also grew a variety of citrus fruits, and the mingled sharp and sweet odors of lemon and orange blossoms filled her nostrils as she inhaled deeply. A smile touched her mouth and lingered.

Even after three days in this enchanted spot, she was still slightly bemused by Carey's intuitive knowledge of what would please her. From their wedding at her parents' home in Philadelphia to this idyllic honeymoon villa set high on Anacapri, he had second-guessed her most cherished romantic fantasies.

Neither of them had wanted to wait this long for their marriage, but circumstances had dictated the timing. Despite the sun's warmth, Lindsay shivered and drew her robe more closely together. Only a small part of the decision to wait had been hers....

The last two days of her last Eurospan tour still seemed like a dream from someone else's memory. Even now, when she had finally come to terms with the accumulated shock effect of that tour, only snatches of scenes, faces, came into focus with any kind of clarity. She remembered insisting on accompanying her passengers on their last bus ride to the airport, their faces vague blurs as they thanked her and said goodbye: the Dakers, the Harbens, the Strangeways...Charlene Warner, oddly emotional as she bent to brush Lindsay's cheek with her lips. Clearest of all was Lila's plump face looking up anxiously into hers.

"You're sure you don't hold it against me, honey?" she had asked for the umpteenth time since confessing the secret she had so skillfully harbored all through the tour.

Lindsay had shaken her head, giving Lila a reassuring smile that was by then automatic. In fact, the shock of discovering that the older woman was the sleeper the company had sent along to evaluate the tour had made little impression on her. It was just one more twisted facet of this fateful trip. Later, she would recall in greater detail Lila's superb acting ability. She was neither vapid nor helpless in reality.

Her own reality had seemed suspended for the next few weeks. She had flown back to England, this time accompanied by Carey and her brother, as well as the trembling excited elderly couple, who thrilled to their first flight. Lindsay relived, too, Elena's overwhelming joy at seeing her parents again, her gratitude to Lindsay, tempered by her unspoken question later when her eyes met Philip's. . . .

It was the same question that Carey had been less subtle about concealing: had it been worth risking Lindsay's life for? His had been the only dry eye in the comfortable sitting room of the Surrey house as the old people chatted animatedly with their daughter and met their grandchildren. Elena was the only one present who understood their language.

For Lindsay, it was enough that the ends justified the means. Yes, Philip had made a calculated decision to use her, based on the assurances he'd been given that she would be well protected. Pierre! Who would have guessed that the philandering bus driver would have the finesse and fortitude to undertake the task of protecting her? A wry smile twisted her lips when she thought of Brad Dakers's game of "choose the killer" in Capri. Pierre and Lila had been her last choices, rejected because they were too obvious!

She sat sideways on the sun-warmed stone parapet, staring at without really seeing the workmanlike outline of a fishing boat that was making its way into the harbor with its early-morning catch. The only flaw in her newfound happiness was the animosity that existed between her husband and her brother. She cared a great deal for Philip, but Carey was so much more a part of her life, her future now. Her first loyalty would always be to him. If only he could accept, as she did, that Philip had had to make that vital decision under stress and that speculating about what might have happened had it ended differently was futile.

Besides Carey's own thinking under stress hadn't been brilliant at times. Sending her to Hilda Keller's apartment without the vital papers was an instance of this. Marsini and his cohorts hadn't spared her because she wasn't carrying the documents. It had been a rare moment of tunnel vision for Carey.

Actually, no one had emerged blameless from the whole affair. The world of espionage, she had discovered to her amazement, was far from the well-knit network she'd imagined. Apart from the bumbling, cutthroat activities of this radical European faction, Western powers had proved to be just as disorganized. British Intelligence had confined the operation to its own security forces; the Americans, when they got wind of the leakage, had set about exposing it, using their own resources—and amateurs, at that! Still, if they hadn't, she mused, she and Carey would never have met....

A pair of smooth-muscled arms slid around her from behind and lifted her, drawing her back against the hard length of a now intimately familiar figure in a loosely tied robe. Her hair was swept aside, and her nape tingled at the lingering pressure of Carey's firm lips.

"What are you trying to do?" he murmured. "Drive the local fishermen berserk as well as me?"

"I might try," she threatened huskily, "if their sight's that good!"

"Why do you think I rented a villa surrounded by a ten-foot wall? Not for privacy, as you thought, but to keep out the hordes wanting to replace me." His arms tightened around her, pressing her back against him. She could feel the rasp of his crisp dark chest hair through her gossamer-thin peignoir. His cheek rested on the silky blue black gloss of her hair. "What were you thinking about so seriously?" he asked abruptly.

Her laugh was a little forced. "I was wondering how Lila's getting along with her Cesare. Do you think they'll make something of it?"

His chuckle rumbled in his chest and vibrated between her shoulder blades. "The guy has my respect for trying."

Lindsay twisted around indignantly to face him. "She's not really like the person she—"

"I don't give a damn in hell what she's like," he growled. "All I'm concerned about right now is that my bed was distinctly lacking when I woke up a few minutes ago—lacking you. And that," he pronounced with mock grimness, bending to scoop her into his arms and stride to the opened terrace doors leading into the bedroom, "is something I mean to remedy immediately."

Her body responded with a ready ardor when he stood beside the bed and deposited her on her feet, unhurriedly drawing the silken folds of her robe from her, allowing it to drop with a whisper around her as his fingers eased the narrow straps of her nightdress over her creamy shoulders, his head bending to the aroused tips of her breasts that showed mistily through the transparent nylon.

She had learned how to please him in these past days—nights—as he pleasured her. Her hands groped, felt for the tie of his robe and slid inside to stroke his heated flesh until he groaned and crushed her to him, his mouth seeking the answering warmth of hers. Like a well-orchestrated symphony of movement, they fell together to the cushioned softness of the bed and began the age-old but ever new ritual that expressed the love between them....

Passion spent, they slept, but Lindsay awakened before Carey and lay watching him sleep on the adjoining pillow. His firm jaw was relaxed, as was his well-shaped mouth, the lines erased from around it. His dark brown hair, usually meticulously groomed, lay in half-curled strands on his broad tanned forehead, which was damp from the sultry air filtering through the net curtains at the open terrace doors.

She smiled. He would hate to know that he looked, in sleep, like a sixteen-year-old innocent. But of course he wasn't that. Sobered, she let her gaze drift to the slow hypnotic flutter of the draperies. She was too clear-eyed to think there would be no thorns in their future relationship. Each of them was a strong individual with firmly held opinions, goals and values. But if, as Carey had suggested that day in Vienna, they faced up to their problems together, as they arose....

She had been surprised to discover the strong romantic streak in her husband, a sensitivity to her own feelings that had resulted in the fulfillment of her long-held fantasy—to be married at home, in Philadelphia.

His surprise had been greater than hers when his own father, notified briefly of his son's marriage, descended on her parents' roomy two-story home and installed himself in the largest of their guest rooms until the ceremonies were over. After several late-night talks, Carey had told her that his father had changed considerably since the last of his young wives had flown away on the wings of alimony. Puzzled, he had said that the old man seemed more interested in the grandchildren not yet born than in taking another excursion into recapturing his lost youth. Lindsay felt compassion for the older Hudson, who had everything material but very little in an emotional sense.

She liked him, perhaps because he bore the same impressive stamp and features of the man she loved, but more probably because he'd persuaded Carey to give up his scalp-hunting job with the conglomerate to take the place long prepared for him as the future head of the enterprise.

"Dammit," he had exploded half-sheepishly one evening when they had been left tactfully alone, "he had me feeling guilty about the inheritance of my kids, who aren't even born yet!"

Lindsay didn't care what position he held in the company as long as it was far removed from the game of cheat and counter-cheat. One brush with the espionage business had soured her on it forever. "You can do a lot more good for a lot more people from the executive offices," she pointed out reasonably.

"It could mean more travel," he warned darkly. "Can you handle that?"

"I guess so, because I mean to travel with you, for a while at least, and make myself useful as an interpreter. I've had enough of the tourist trade, but I'd like to put my education and experience to work in another area. For quite some time I've been seriously considering setting up my own bureau of translation, perhaps in New York."

His frown had dissolved into a smile, his eyes taking on their tigerish yellow gleam. "That sounds like a solid idea—and just think how proficient our kids will be in languages."

"We can discuss that again when the kids start to put in their appearance," she insisted stubbornly. "Agreed?"

"Agreed."

She smiled again now when Carey sighed contentedly and reached sleepily for her. She had learned that nothing in the world remained static. She also knew that life, like love, was lived for this moment—now...and now was forever.

# A Harlequin
# ROBERTA LEIGH
## Collector's Edition

A specially designed collection of six exciting love stories by one of the world's favorite romance writers—Roberta Leigh, author of more than 60 bestselling novels!

1 **Love in Store**     4 **The Savage Aristocrat**
2 **Night of Love**     5 **The Facts of Love**
3 **Flower of the Desert**  6 **Too Young to Love**

Available in August wherever paperback books are sold, or available through Harlequin Reader Service. Simply complete and mail the coupon below.

---

**Harlequin Reader Service**

In the U.S.
P.O. Box 52040
Phoenix, AZ 85072-9988

In Canada
649 Ontario Street
Stratford, Ontario N5A 6W2

Please send me the following editions of the Harlequin Roberta Leigh Collector's Editions. I am enclosing my check or money order for $1.95 for each copy ordered, plus 75¢ to cover postage and handling.

☐ 1     ☐ 2     ☐ 3     ☐ 4     ☐ 5     ☐ 6

Number of books checked_____ @ $1.95 each = $_____

N.Y. state and Ariz. residents add appropriate sales tax   $_____

Postage and handling                                       $_____.75_____

                                              TOTAL   $_____

I enclose_____

(Please send check or money order. We cannot be responsible for cash sent through the mail.) Price subject to change without notice.

NAME_____

(Please Print)

ADDRESS_____ APT. NO._____

CITY_____

STATE/PROV._____ ZIP/POSTAL CODE_____

Offer expires 29 February 1984.                    30856000000

RL-A